Vlain and the Last Wild

"The world breaks everyone and afterward some
are strong at the broken places."

Ernest Hemingway

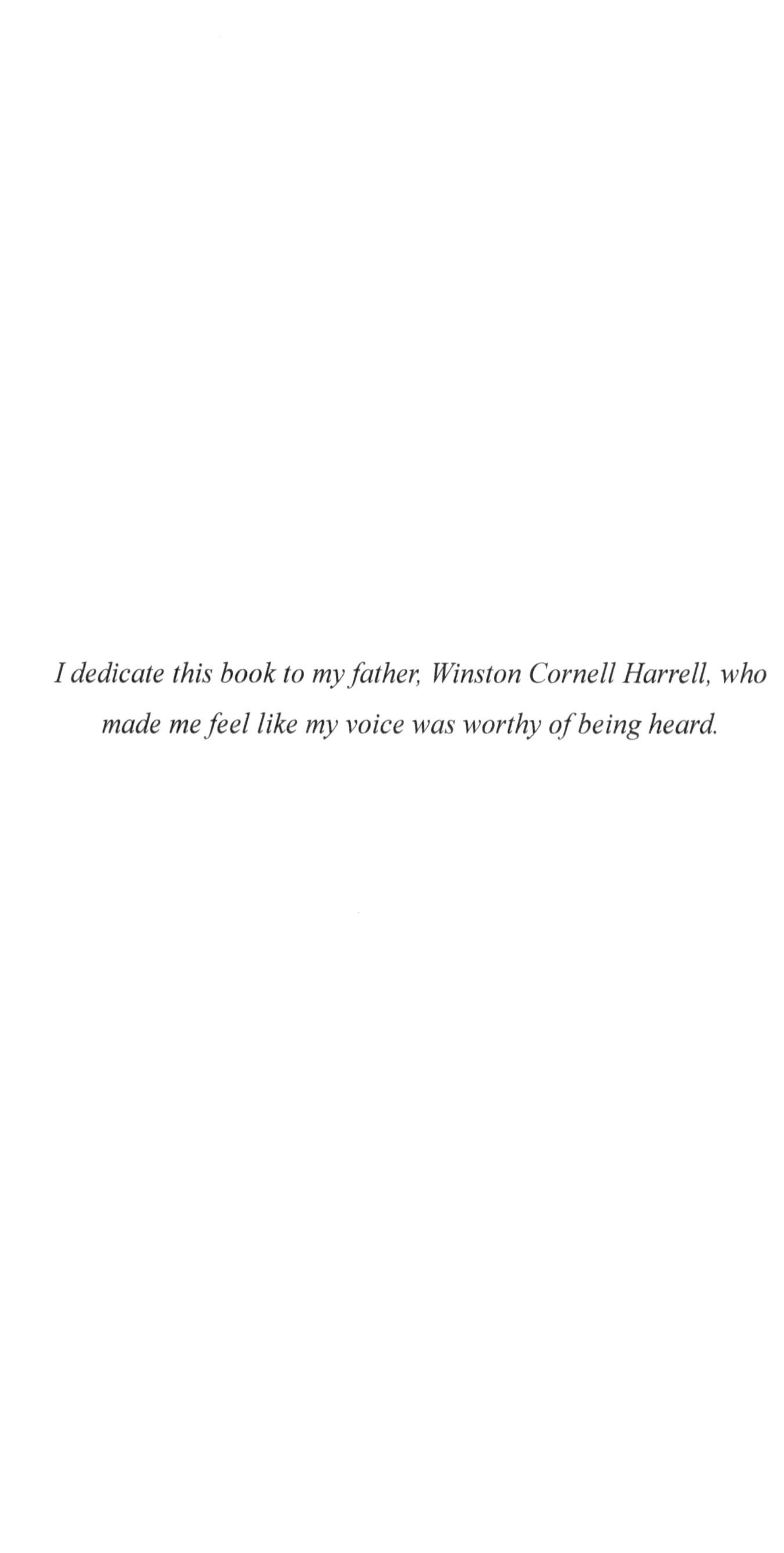

I dedicate this book to my father, Winston Cornell Harrell, who made me feel like my voice was worthy of being heard.

Contents

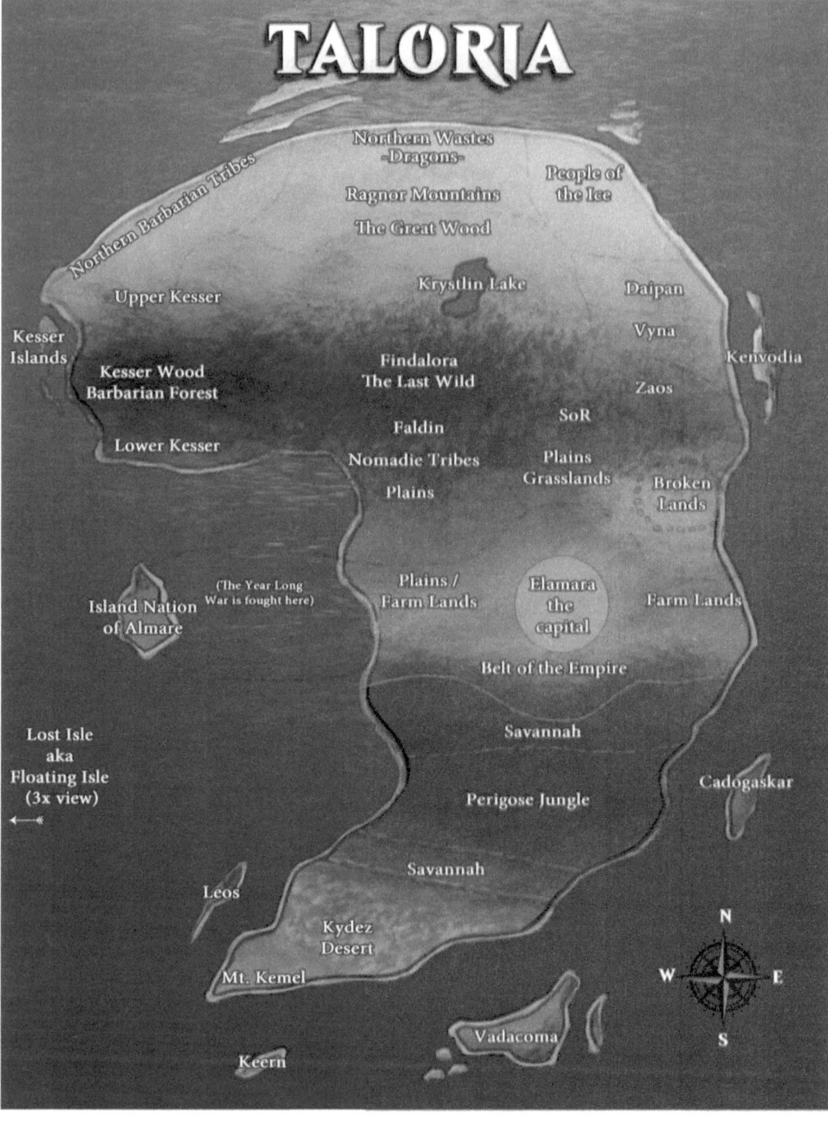

TALORIA
Northern Wastes
-Dragons-
People of
the Ice
Ragnor Mountains
Northern Barbarian Tribes
The Great Wood
Upper Kesser
Krystlin Lake
Daipan
Vyna
Kesser
Islands
Kenvodia
Kesser Wood
Barbarian Forest
Findalora
The Last Wild
Zaos
SoR
Faldin
Lower Kesser
Plains
Grasslands
Nomadie Tribes
Plains
Broken
Lands
(The Year Long
War is fought here)
Plains /
Farm Lands
Elamara
the
capital
Farm Lands
Island Nation
of Almare
Belt of the Empire
Lost Isle
aka
Floating Isle
(3x view)
Savannah
Cadogaskar
Perigose Jungle
Savannah
Leos
Kydez
Desert
Mt. Kemel
N
W   E
S
Vadacoma
Keern

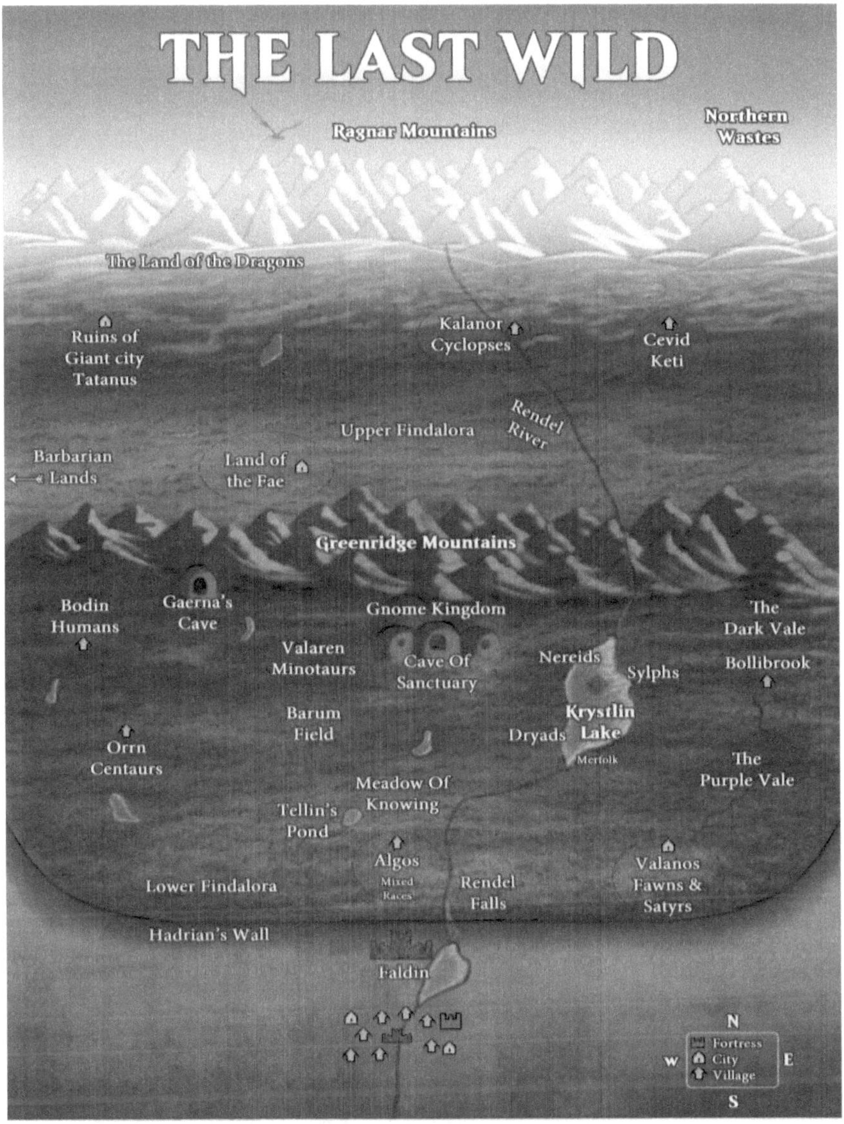
THE LAST WILD
Ragnar Mountains
Northern Wastes
The Land of the Dragons
Ruins of Giant city Tatanus
Kalanor Cyclopses
Cevid Keti
Rendel River
Upper Findalora
Barbarian Lands
Land of the Fae
Greenridge Mountains
Bodin Humans
Gaerna's Cave
Gnome Kingdom
The Dark Vale
Valaren Minotaurs
Cave Of Sanctuary
Nereids
Sylphs
Bollibrook
Barum Field
Krystlin Lake
Dryads
Merfolk
Orrn Centaurs
The Purple Vale
Meadow Of Knowing
Tellin's Pond
Algos
Mixed Races
Rendel Falls
Valanos Fawns & Satyrs
Lower Findalora
Hadrian's Wall
Faldin
N
W
E
S
Fortress
City
Village

PROLOGUE

Over one hundred people had arranged themselves in a semicircle around a massive wooden wagon. A cleverly constructed stage had been lowered down from the side of the wagon to face the crowd, and a curved iron rod extended out from the wagon, from which hung a thick, red velvet curtain. The people sat on the lush grass of the meadow as they eagerly stared at the curtain before them. Suddenly, it parted in the middle to emit a short, slim man dressed in a green tunic. His long hair had been dyed a deep green, and his dark green eyes sparkled with mirth and mischief. He bowed low as he stepped onto the stage. Excited shouts and screams erupted from the crowd. The people closest to the stage threw flowers and coins at his feet.

"Gailin! Gailin! Gailin!" the crowd chanted in one thunderous voice as the little man comically danced a jig all about the stage. His expression remained both comical and earnest throughout the bizarre dance routine. Eventually, he stopped in the center of the stage and held up his hands, appealing to the crowd to quiet down.

"Thank you, good people of Elamara!" he shouted happily. His broad smile revealed gleaming white teeth and was utterly infectious. "Are you ready to laugh, cry, and watch in disbelief as we transport you to the Last Wild?" he asked. The crowd roared a resounding "yes," accompanied by much screaming. "I can't hear you," Gailin said teasingly while holding his hand up to his ear. This time, the screams were deafening, and his eardrums buzzed as they were overloaded by the din. "I'll take that as a yes," he said. Perhaps it was a bit of stagecraft, but his emerald eyes seemed to glow with an eerie inner light. "In this play, you'll witness the beastly denizens that populate the mightiest forest in all of Taloria! You know these fell beasts as the woodlanders!" The crowd roared in excitement. "And, of course, you'll witness Vlain the Vanquisher as he battles them!" This last pronouncement sent the spectators into a frenzy. Gailin proceeded anew after they finally quieted down. "Now gather round while my troupe and I reenact the tale of the lost 9th Legion! No doubt, many have told you they simply vanished into the forest mists, never to be seen nor heard from again, but that's not so. On this day, you'll witness the true fate of the Legio IX Elamara!" The crowd went wild one final time, and then, after their voices died down, the curtains parted.

THE MARCH NORTH
Chapter 1

Emperor Justus frowned as he looked out across the banquet table at the august personages he had assembled for the night's feast. There, seated before him, were senators, military officers, various lords, ladies of high station, and several locals from the distant trading outpost known as Faldin. Vlain and Gailin, however, were conspicuously absent. It was considered a high honor to be invited to the royal palace for a feast, and yet the men had so far failed to appear. Emperor Justus lifted a goblet filled with wine to his mouth and drank deeply to quell his rising irritation. He knew both of his would-be guests were busy men, so he doubted their lateness should be taken as a snub. Vlain, the sword-wielding champion, was constantly going from one adventure to the next across the entire length and breadth of the Talorian continent. Gailin, the famous actor and comedian, was usually acting at the Orpheum or touring with his crew. Sometimes, he'd accompany Vlain on a journey.

Both men had recently returned to the capital after one such adventure. Word had it that they had sailed aboard a ship named the Phoenix into unknown waters to find a lost, floating island laden with treasures. Unsurprisingly, Vlain and the crew had vanquished the threats they had encountered during the dangerous, months-long voyage. In fact, part of the reason the emperor had invited them to the feast was to hear of this adventure firsthand, but right now, he simply wanted to know where they were. The young man smoothed out his paludamentum, a purple cloak designed to show his imperial station, then adjusted the golden laurel wreath on his head. He impatiently tapped his fingers against the tabletop. He was about to send a servant to search for them in the city when they finally sauntered into the courtyard.

The servant at the entrance to the courtyard blew his silver trumpet twice, then loudly proclaimed, "Your Excellence, Vlain Verous the Last and Gailin Emerus the Green have arrived!" The proclamation prompted all at the table to arise. Of course, Emperor Justus could have remained seated since he held the highest station in Taloria. Still, he chose to stand to show his respect for both men, even though they were over an hour late.

"Please forgive our tardiness, your excellency," Vlain said as he bowed to the emperor.

"It's all my fart, my lord," Gailin said after he rose from bowing. "I meant to say fault. You see, *hiccup*, I insisted we try Higorian mead during lunch, and...well...it's far stronger than the ballads proclaim." Gailin belched, then clamped his hand over his mouth in embarrassment. His ruddy cheeks and garish green hair made him look both ridiculous and endearing.

Emperor Justus held up his hand to stop a sentry who moved forward to smack Gailin for his impertinence and apparent intoxication. The man resumed his post beside the ruler. The emperor smiled in amusement as he studied the famous thespian. The comical little man always had that effect on everyone he encountered. All gloom and sadness fled from a place whenever Gailin the Green arrived. The comedian's presence saturated the air with mirth and laughter.

Vlain's bearing, on the other hand, was somewhere between that of a conquering general and a lion in repose. He was a commanding figure as he stood there dressed in an immaculate white tunic and brand-new brown leather sandals. However, it was his sword belt that caught the emperor's eye, for it held the fighter's fabled twin orichalcum long swords. It was said that Phaelos, the greatest philosopher and inventor to ever live, had forged the weapons for Vlain to aid him during the One Year War. Each sword was sheathed and attached to a leather belt on both sides of his hips.

As a boy, the emperor had witnessed Vlain put the bright copper-colored blades to work when he had single-handedly killed a terrifying chimera in the gladiator arena. He shuddered at the bloody memory as he resumed studying the fighter. Vlain had the build of a wrestler, but his movements were quick and fluid despite his heavy muscles. He was tall but not unusually so; his skin was light brown, and his curly, auburn hair fell neatly to his shoulders. His clean-shaven face was plain and would have been forgettable if not for the few scars that lined it or for his amber eyes, which shimmered with a reckless light. They reminded the emperor of embers in a fire, and he found it difficult to hold the man's gaze for more than a few seconds. Despite these impressive attributes, however, Vlain had obviously been drinking. Usually, this would have offended the emperor. It was, however, consistent with the man's rowdy reputation, and he needed Vlain's help after all, so he made light of it.

"I would offer you both a libation, but if anything, we must catch up to you." His comment prompted rolling laughter from the numerous guests seated at the long banquet table. Vlain and Gailin laughed good-naturedly as they sat down before the food-laden table.

"Trust me, your magnificence, we always save room for another round," Gailin said with a wink and a nod.

"Tell me, Vlain the Last, did you earn that title because you arrived late to dinner?" The question came from a man with long blond hair and crystalline blue eyes. He was handsome with an athletic build and appeared to be in his mid to late twenties. The symbol of a large eagle had been painted in white on his black chest plate, signifying the 9th Legion to which he belonged. His broad, circular, metal belt buckle was a cingulum militare, which was only worn by officers who commanded a legion or occasionally by the emperor himself.

"Hardly," Vlain exclaimed. "It's because I'm the last to fall in a fight."

Gailin smiled in amusement at his friend because his statement, although true, wasn't why he was referred to as the last. Gailin also knew, better than anyone, that Vlain couldn't tell him the truth without revealing too much about himself.

"And who might you be, young one?" Vlain inquired.

The golden-haired man bristled at the adjective. His eyes narrowed with injured pride as he glared at Vlain from across the table. "I'm Commander Prydus Orilius of the 9th Legion and son of Lucius Orilius, the senator and advisor to the emperor."

Vlain took an immediate dislike to the man. He seemed too proud and arrogant, especially for one so young. He nodded in understanding as he broke a leg off a huge roasted bird and then took a bite out of it. Of course, the fighter recognized Prydus's father, Senator Lucius. His wise counsel had guided the young Emperor through many difficult times. The bearded, gray-haired senator smiled and nodded at Vlain in a conciliatory manner. Vlain returned the nod, then reached for a cup of wine with which to wash the meat down. Lucius cleared his throat and opened his mouth to speak, but the emperor's voice suddenly rang out, thereby silencing him.

"Allow me to introduce my guests to you, Vlain," the young leader said for all to hear. "You've already met Commander Orilius and his father, Senator Orilius. To the commander's left, we have Captain Caladin, then Captain Snill, and Captain Oudeteros."

The emperor waved at the men. Vlain studied each of them in turn. Captain Caladin was a giant of a man who probably stood over seven feet tall and must have weighed nearly four hundred pounds. Although there was some fat on his broad frame, most of him appeared to be muscle. Though, he didn't look very bright. Captain

Snill wasn't much bigger than Gailin, but there was a shrewd cunning in his small, dark eyes. His long, pointy face reminded Vlain of a shrew. Captain Oudeteros had ebony skin native to the people who lived in the tropics. He sat with the rigid bearing of a military man as he gazed at Vlain. His square-jawed, impassive, bearded face gave nothing away, making it impossible to read his thoughts.

"On the other side of the table, we have the entourage from the northern outpost known as Faldin. Governor Worrington sits to your left, Lord Bevel to Gailin's right, and lastly Vorsord the Hunter."

Each of the men nodded politely at Vlain as the Emperor called out his name. The governor was a portly, middle-aged man with a rumpled, disheveled look even though he was dressed in expensive silken robes. Lord Bevel had a long, lean face that looked forlorn regardless of his expression. Vorsord had a shock of spiky red hair on his head and sported a thick, bristly mustache. The hunter gazed suspiciously at everyone gathered around the table.

The emperor then called out the names and titles of various lords and ladies of the court, but if Vlain heard any of them, he gave no indication. He simply gnawed on the thick bird leg while staring stoically into his cup of wine.

After Emperor Justus had introduced everyone, he clapped his hands, prompting several servants to refill the guests' cups and carry away empty plates and platters. They soon returned bearing trays laden with bowls of fruit and an assortment of sweets and desserts. The emperor resumed speaking after the guests started eating and drinking again.

"I called you all here to discuss the dire circumstances facing Fort Faldin. Unfortunately, the attacks from the beast-men of the northern wood, known as the woodlanders, have recently intensified. The trade route from Elamara to Faldin has been decimated due to the woodlanders' constant raids on our caravans. This cannot be tolerated!"

"Here, here!" Lord Worrington shouted after swallowing a bite of cake. Lord Bevel and Vorsord clapped enthusiastically while Commander Orilius and the other military officers coolly regarded them. Vlain watched all of this with impassive eyes.

"So, if it's war the woodlanders want, then it's war they shall have," Emperor Justus resumed. "Commander Orilius will lead the 9th Legion, a force of over four thousand men, to Faldin. Once there, he'll oversee the repair and expansion of the existing fort. After that, he and his brave men will protect the caravans whenever they approach or leave Faldin and take the fight to the woodlanders if need be. Thus shall peace be restored to our northern neighbors!"

"And how do I fit into all of this, my liege?" Vlain's deep voice cut in.

"Come with me, and I'll tell you," the emperor said as he stood up and beckoned to the fighter to join him. "We'll walk through my gardens while these good people enjoy the culinary delights of the royal kitchen."

Vlain and Gailin exchanged a curious look. Vlain pushed himself back from the table and walked over to the emperor. Prydus watched intently as they walked past a gushing fountain and out into the surrounding gardens. Vlain marveled at the beauty of the curated landscape. There were musicians perched on boulders and benches as they deftly played harps and flutes. They also passed a painter who stood in front of an easel as he labored to capture the rich beauty of the gardens on the canvas. Vlain was impressed by the man's creative use of colors.

"To answer your question," the emperor began, "I want you to join the 9th Legion and ride with Commander Orilius to Ft. Faldin. Although he's a capable officer, he's still young and somewhat inexperienced. He could use a seasoned veteran like you to help him stay the course."

"Forgive me for asking, your excellence, but if he's so inexperienced, then why place him in charge of the legion? I would make a better commander..."

"Of that, I have no doubt," the emperor conceded. Both men paused for a moment as a brightly plumed peacock meandered across their path. "But Prydus's father, Senator Orilius, has proven invaluable to me after the untimely death of my father. To put it mildly, I owe him a favor. I asked him how I could repay him for all of the wise counsel he's given me over the years. He replied by asking me to put his son in charge of the 9th so that Prydus could test his mettle in combat and prove himself a worthy leader. His goal is to become a general by the time he's thirty. He has grand ambitions, that one."

"He lacks manners and humility," Vlain countered.

"Then help him acquire them," the emperor replied with a grin.

Vlain grunted in displeasure and kicked at a rock in his path. "If I can't be the commander of the 9th, then what will be my rank if I accept your offer?"

"The highest rank I can offer you is colonel." Before Vlain could object, the emperor held up his hands to silence him. "But you would be the lead officer, second only to Prydus in the chain of command. Also, your salary will be six times greater than that of the captains. Of course, that's a confidential matter that must stay between us."

"I'm good at keeping secrets," Vlain said.

"So I've heard."

Both men grew silent as they passed a beautiful young woman

who sat in a tree as she sang sweetly and strummed her fingers across the strings of a lyre. She was dressed in a white toga and wore a wreath of wildflowers. Her voice was both soothing and inspiring. A small waterfall gurgled merrily as it fed a narrow creek that meandered past the tree in which she was perched.

"As tempting as your offer is, you should know I'm wealthy, at least for the moment," Vlain confided. "My recent ocean adventure was profitable, to say the least."

"Ah, yes!" The emperor exclaimed. "I heard about your voyage aboard the Phoenix with Captain Aera and her hardy crew. Rumor has it you endured the mother of all tempests and battled pirates, sirens, trolls, and a giant sea serpent during your travels!"

"It's all true," Vlain said with a weary sigh. "But trust me, the deadliest challenge awaited us on the Lost Isle." The emperor watched as a pained expression quickly formed and then vanished on Vlain's tanned, weathered face.

"I would love to hear all about it tonight, but right now, I need to know if you'll accept the officer commission in the legion," the emperor replied. "You indicated the pay, although generous, wasn't enough to sway you, so let me further sweeten the pot. I'll also grant you an estate near Faldin and the title of earl should you accept."

"All right," Vlain said with a gruff laugh. "But not because of the pay or the promise of land or title. My heart longs once again for the open road and the adventures it brings. Although I've enjoyed my stay in your fair city, I need to feel the wind on my face and to look on unknown lands."

"I should have known your restless soul would seal the deal," Emperor Justus replied as he patted Vlain's shoulder. "Then we have an accord?"

"Yes," Vlain said as he shook the emperor's hand. "If you honor one last request."

"And that is?"

"Introduce me to the fair maiden we saw playing the lyre. I think she'd make fine company."

"You never change," the emperor said with a smile.

***

The following day, Commander Orilius readied the 9th Legion for the march to Ft. Faldin. They departed for the northern outpost in the afternoon, but Vlain didn't accompany them. Emperor Justus gave him leave to gather loyal men who had fought with him in the uprising against his late father, Emperor Hadrian, and in the Year-Long War, which had prompted the Great Rebellion. It took a few days, but over fifty men eventually responded to Vlain's call.

Emperor Justus smiled as he watched Vlain and his followers leave the capital the next day. He knew what Vlain was doing. The wily fighter was amassing as many men as he could get to help the 9th Legion win the upcoming war against the woodlanders. However, he was also surrounding himself with a loyal fighting force if he and Commander Orilius clashed. The emperor admired Vlain's subtle tactics. The adventurer was apparently as skilled in political battles as he was in those involving the sword. Despite his admiration for the man, however, he was glad to see Vlain go; he tended to cause trouble whenever he stayed in one place for too long.

Gailin waved goodbye to his long-time friend as he led the newly minted legionnaires out of the gates of Elamara. Even though the famous actor often chronicled and later reenacted Vlain's adventures on stage, he had declined his invitation to accompany him this time because he had just signed a one-year contract with Theater Row. Gailin would spend the next year touring the capital with his troupe of actors as they reenacted events that had occurred during Vlain and Gailin's recent maritime voyage. Gailin was sad to see his friend go, but he was secretly glad to sit this adventure out because of what he had heard about the vast, northern forest called the Last Wild. Men said it was inhabited by carnivorous beast-men and other monstrous creatures. If even half the rumors he had heard about it were true, then he was happy to remain behind in the comfortable confines of civilization. In Elamara, he was guaranteed endless food, strong drinks, potent weed, and all the admiring fans he could fit into his bed each night. Such was the life of a celebrity.

Vlain and his men made good time as they traveled north along the caravan route. Since they were a smaller force and they were all mounted cavalry, they caught up with Commander Orilius and the main force within a few days. Everything went smoothly for a while. Then the weather took a turn for the worse. Unseasonal monsoons unleashed torrential downpours onto the 9th Legion day after a muddy day. One evening, just before they were about to make camp, Vlain watched as a spear of lightning shot down from the roiling, gray clouds to immolate several men. The concussion and searing heat threw Vlain from his horse and caused his eardrums to bleed. Thankfully, his sense of hearing returned shortly afterward.

The relentless rain soon made a mess of the road they traveled on. Time and again, the supply wagons got stuck in the mud, and many teams of horses were required to pull them out. They were beset by mudslides after that, which often made the road impassable. Vlain and his fellow legionnaires were often forced to dismount, grab shovels, and spend hours digging a path through mounds of mud. One time, Vlain saw a group of men and horses get pushed off a mountain road by a massive mudslide, only to plunge into a swollen, turbulent river in the valley far below. None of them were ever seen again.

However, the worst incident was when a giant redwood tree,

whose root system had been exposed to the heavy rain suddenly fell onto a marching column of men. Vlain had heard the roots snap as the enormous tree started falling and thus had time to grab a couple of men by their chest plates and hurl them out of harm's way. Even so, a dozen legionnaires were flattened by the tree as it slammed into the earth with bone-crushing force. Caladin, Vlain, and several others had grabbed axes and spent hours chopping the tree into small enough pieces for the horses to haul away. They eventually removed enough of the trunk to free up the road for travel again. After that, it didn't take long for some legionnaires to start whispering that the mission was cursed and that they should return to Elamara or risk further angering the gods. In fact, many men began praying to Jaina, the Goddess of Life and Light, for safe passage.

Vlain and the other officers carefully watched their men for signs of mutiny. Although it never occurred, several legionnaires deserted in the dead of night. Commander Orilius and Captain Snill led a horse-mounted search and returned with the men the next day. In the gray morning twilight, Vlain and the other officers watched with grim faces as the deserters were hurled from a bridge with nooses tied around their necks. He watched as the broken men swung wildly about before finally coming to a stop beneath the bridge. It was a sight that would haunt him forever.

As bad as the rain and mudslides were, they paled in comparison to the writhing clouds of mosquitoes and biting flies that assaulted the legionnaires after each rainstorm. Malaria soon began to spread throughout the legion. Over a hundred men fell to the dreaded disease before it ran its course. A few days later, scores of legionnaires fell ill after drinking from a contaminated well they had found beside the road. Vlain would never forget the sounds of their retching or their cries for help from the haggard clerics who tended to them in their final hours. As rugged as Vlain was and no stranger to the hardships of the road, he began to wonder if the 9th

Legion was indeed cursed.

Eventually, the weather improved, which prompted Commander Orilius to celebrate Bellin, the god of alcohol, feasting, and merry-making. The suggestion had actually come from Vlain and his men, but he had presented it in such a way as to make Prydus feel like it was his idea. After the hellish march north, the 9th Legion desperately needed something to lift their spirits and take their minds off those they had lost on the trail. It worked beautifully. Vlain smiled as he watched his legionnaires unload barrels of ale from the wagons and pass flagon after flagon to the thirsty soldiers. He and his crew had just finished raising pavilions and tents so that the men could take shelter from the elements while they celebrated. Captain Oudeteros and a platoon of his best archers and spearmen soon returned from the prairie with dozens of freshly killed deer and elk draped across the backs of their steeds. The legionnaires drank, feasted, and partied deep into the night. The only thing missing were women, but there was nothing to be done about that. Still, Vlain was glad to see the soldiers' morale rise back to where it should be.

Vlain was just starting to think their bad luck was behind them when a group of bandits attacked the legionnaires' eastern flank in the early hours. Due to the darkness and since the legion was spread out across the plain, the bandits had underestimated the size of their force. Before they could realize their mistake, Vlain and over fifty of his men were in hot pursuit of the fleeing highwaymen. They overtook them at sunrise, and although the bandits outnumbered Vlain's crew and fought with desperate ferocity, they were eventually cut down by the legionnaires. Most of the bandits wore little to no armor, and only a few had decent shields or bucklers with which to block the tips of the legionnaire's sarissas. Vlain ordered his men to form a wedge formation and then drove it into the center of the bandits. He watched with grim pride as his well-trained soldiers slew the bandits almost to a man. A handful of survivors broke for the open plains when they realized they had lost. Vlain's men turned to him for orders.

"Let them go so they can tell all whom they encounter that these lands are under our protection now." He turned his white charger around and gestured for them to follow him back to the main force.

Commander Orilius impatiently awaited Vlain's return. He paced back and forth in the field where the tribute to Bellin had occurred last night and cursed under his breath at Vlain's uncanny luck. He was always in the right place at the right time, and circumstances clearly favored him whenever the unforeseen occurred. Vlain had rescued two men right before a giant tree had fallen onto the road, and now they ceaselessly praised him. Vlain and his men seemed immune to the ravenous mosquitoes and devilish flies that had beset the legion after every storm. Vlain's platoon was now the first to taste combat since the 9th had left the Belt of the Empire, the swathe of farmland surrounding the capital city, Elamara. How lucky could one man get? It sickened Prydus, so he hoped something terrible had befallen the charismatic fighter so the focus would shift back to him where it belonged. His face fell when he saw Vlain and his crew proudly march their horses into the field.

"We caught up to the bandits and slew most of them," he said with a salute.

"Most of them?" Prydus asked. His heart soared at the opportunity to criticize the actions of his obnoxious rival finally. "You let some of them live?!"

"Of course," Vlain replied. "They'll spread the word that we're here, making the bandits think twice before they attack us again or the trading caravans."

"We spare no enemy! You should have pursued them and slain them or brought them back here for a hanging," Prydus shouted. "In the future, you'll eradicate the enemy. Am I clear, colonel?"

Vlain glowered at him while fantasizing about drawing one of his swords and removing his head from his shoulders. It took all of his resolve to resist the powerful impulse. In the end, he simply turned his mount around and motioned to his men to follow him back to their campsite.

"Do I make myself CLEAR, Colonel Verous?!" Prydus snarled.

Vlain stopped, turned his horse back around, fixing him with a withering stare. "You're more than welcome to pursue and kill the few remaining bandits yourself, commander."

"I wanted YOU to do it," Prydus bellowed.

"As I said before, a greater message will be delivered by sparing their lives."

Both men glared at each other. Vlain was ready to pull both swords from their sheathes if he saw Prydus or anyone else make a hostile move. He knew he and his platoon could cut a bloody path through the surrounding legionnaires, then hit the prairie and hopefully reach the great forest before Prydus's larger force could overtake them.

Prydus was wondering if he had the skill to defeat Vlain in combat. As a boy, he had heard unbelievable tales about Vlain's fighting prowess but had yet to see him in action. Secretly, he doubted any man could be that good. Furthermore, he was at least ten years younger than Vlain. There was also another reason for his confidence that he wasn't ready to reveal. Prydus scowled as Vlain led his men back to their bivouac site.

"I haven't given you permission to leave!" The commander shouted.

"We're done here," Vlain replied. "Unless you'd like to work this out in private."

I'll take you up on that soon enough, Prydus thought, but he said nothing.

***

Vlain was mounted on Viscol, his white stallion, as he watched his legionnaires perform combat drills in the meadow below. He was proud of how organized, disciplined, and precise his men were as they shifted from one formation to another while engaging another unit in mock combat.

Captain Oudeteros slowly rode his horse up the small hill until it stood beside Vlain's. The fighter gave no indication that he was aware of his presence. He seemed utterly absorbed with the activities of his men below. Oudeteros studied the battle-scarred veteran at his side. The sun highlighted the white eagle painted with wings spread wide on his chest plate and made the red plume on his helmet glow like fire. He wore steel gauntlets and greaves, which he had painted black to match his helmet and chest plate. Oudeteros felt like he was looking at a living legend, some larger-than-life character that had emerged from a fairy tale to walk Taloria. Had he known of a fraction of the quests, wars, and adventures Vlain had survived, he would have realized the man was indeed legendary. However, word of Vlain's exploits hadn't yet traveled as far south as the tropics, which was where the dark-skinned man had been born and raised.

"I'm about to join the commander and the other captains for a game of Six," Captain Oudeteros said after he cleared his throat. "You should come along. It'll keep your mind sharp."

"I'd rather eat a bucket of scorpions covered in dung," Vlain replied.

A deep, guttural laugh exploded from Oudeteros. "Come now," he said after his laughter had died down. "I know he can be a pain in the ass, but here's a chance to trounce him at something he's good

15

at.”

Vlain's eyes lit up. Although he hadn't played Six in years, he knew he could beat Prydus. Still, he wasn't fond of spending any more time with him than he had to.

“That spoiled brat is only good at demonstrating what a lousy leader he is,” he said.

“The pot's at one thousand copper marks, and we're drinking Higorian absinth.”

Vlain arched an eyebrow. He wasn't one to pass up alcohol, especially spirits that had been fermented by the legendary Higorian monks.

“Very well, but I'm leaving as soon as I win.” He waved at Lieutenant Meris, his second in command, indicating he should take over as drillmaster, then turned and left with Oudeteros.

The two men rode their horses in silence. Vlain had to admit the Southerner was growing on him. Although Oudeteros strove to remain neutral in the brooding feud between Vlain and Prydus, he consistently demonstrated unwavering professionalism. On top of that, he took excellent care of his men. Vlain also respected him because he was the only other high-ranking officer who didn't have his nose firmly lodged up Prydus' ass.

“I've been wondering, why didn't the mosquitoes and flies bother you and your men during our journey north?” the captain asked.

A wry smile formed on Vlain's scarred face. “On my last adventure, Captain Aera told me lavender can be crushed to form oil that repels insects when you rub it on yourself. I bought a bottle in Elamara and shared it with my men to test it out. Turns out, she was right. I should have known an imm...that someone as old as her would know what she was talking about.”

"Lavender of all things?!" Oudeteros exclaimed while shaking his head in disbelief. "So that's why you all smelled like women! Why didn't you share it with the rest of us?"

"I didn't know if it would work, and the stuff costs a blaeting fortune."

A scowl replaced Vlain's smile the moment Prydus' opulent tent came into view. It had been set up in a clearing far apart from the other smaller tents. As they drew closer, Vlain saw Prydus and the other captains sitting beside a crackling fire. The young commander took a swig from a clay jug and then passed it to Caladin. Oudeteros cleared his throat when they were a stone's throw away from them. Prydus looked up at him, then locked eyes with Vlain.

"Captain Verous, how good of you to join us," Prydus said mockingly.

"Don't get too excited," came Vlain's sarcastic response. "I'm only here to relieve you of your booze and coppermarks."

"Is that so?" Prydus replied with a derisive laugh, which was echoed by Caladin and Snill. "Such confidence, I almost admire that."

"Almost?" Vlain asked as he dismounted his white charger.

"You should know I haven't lost a game in years."

"Then you weren't properly challenged, but I'll soon remedy that," Vlain said as he sat down on an upright log that had been placed next to the fire.

Captain Oudeteros rolled his eyes as he looked at both men. "Someone pass me the absinthe before this manly exchange gets out of hand."

He took a long swig from the jug and then passed it to Vlain while Prydus pulled a square-shaped, wooden, checkered board from a cloth bag at his side and set it on top of a tree stump in their center. He then pulled a jar from the pack, which contained thirty small, smooth stones. He unscrewed the lid and poured the stones onto the board. The rocks had been painted five different colors, and there were six stones in each color set.

"I'll be white," Prydus said as he pulled those stones to himself.

Vlain chose black, Oudeteros took blue, Caladin red, and Snill chose green.

Prydus pulled a pair of thirty-two-sided dice from his pocket and tossed them onto the board. The dice gave him a combined score of thirty. Vlain rolled a combined score of forty-two. All of the other men scored lower than them. Vlain chuckled as he felt the power awaken within him. It felt like the flush of a fever mixed with a drug high and the adrenaline rush he always got right before combat all rolled into one. It was both delicious and vertiginous at the same time.

"I go first," Vlain said. He rolled a ten, then placed one of his black stones on the tenth square.

Prydus rolled a ten as well. He nudged Vlain's black stone off the square with his white one, then plucked it off the board and set it to the side.

"First kill," he said with a cocky smile.

A maximum of six people could play the game at a time. The objective was to replace every opponent's stones with yours. You rolled the dice to see what square you'd land on with each of your six stones. White stones could only move forward to take another player's square. Black could only move backward, blue could only go right, red only to the left, green could only move diagonally left, and grey diagonally right. Players could only move one square per turn. Whoever lost all of their stones first lost the game. If a player amassed twenty-one stones or more, then they also won. A player could forfeit the game at any time, but they had to remove all of their stones from the board. Of course, the removal of those stones opened up new strategic possibilities for the remaining players. Six was the perfect combination of luck and strategy. The roll of the dice to determine where your stones first landed on the board was luck. The strategy came in choosing whether to move or not when it was your turn and capitalizing on a player's sudden exit. It was a game of ever-shifting possibilities combined with random chance. Elamara, the empire's capital city, held tournaments for the top players and paid the final winner handsomely in gold and prestige.

Vlain hadn't played Six in a few years but had been good at it before the Change. After that, everything was assured. Even once daunting challenges had become so easy that the uncertainty of life ebbed further away with each victory. Making the right choices hadn't gotten any easier, though. Neither had his relationships with ordinary people. The Unchanged, as he and Gailin called them, were still just as challenging to deal with as ever.

Vlain's plan was to give ground to Prydus for a while to lure him into becoming overconfident. Then, he'd slowly turn the tables on him. The afternoon wore on into the evening. The firelight cast warped shadows of the men out into the darkening meadow. An occasional firefly floated past them now and then. Prydus angrily swiped at the glowing insects, but Vlain let one land on his finger so he could study it up close.

Caladin was the first to lose all of his stones to other players. He grumbled in frustration, then took a long swig from the clay jar. The huge man crossed his arms over his barreled chest and frowned as he watched the game unfold. Snill was second to lose. Prydus had acquired most of his stones. The evening darkened into night. Suddenly, Oudeteros announced he was leaving the game. He removed all of his pieces from the board, then tried to look bored as he watched Vlain and Prydus play.

The commander was only a few stones away from collecting a winning twenty-one. Prydus chuckled in glee as he removed Vlain's black stone from the board. He only needed two more to win. Everything fell apart for Prydus after that. Vlain couldn't help but smile as he moved a stone backward and took one of Prydus's stones off the board. Prydus cursed his luck and glared at Vlain as he took all but one of his stones off the board. Eventually, Vlain collected twenty-one of his stones and declared himself the winner.

"Looks like you finally met your match," Vlain said.

"You got lucky, was all," Prydus shot back. "Two out of three?"

"Sure," Vlain casually replied. "Everyone else staying in?"

The men all shook their heads "Yes." The second game went similarly to the first. Prydus maintained a healthy lead until the last few minutes of the game, and then Vlain suddenly overcame him by collecting the winning twenty-one stones. The third game, however, was a different affair. Snill lost all of his stones, then Caladin withdrew all of his pieces. Vlain started out strong, but his winning streak fizzled out after he took most of Prydus's stones off the board. Oudeteros then collected the required twenty-one stones, thereby beating Vlain. Vlain had outlasted Prydus, though, and had won two out of three games, making him the night's winner.

"So you can lose after all?" Prydus asked as he studied Vlain distrustfully.

"Of course. Did you expect me to win every time?" Vlain asked.

"I did, actually."

"Why's that?"

"Because I know a cheat when I see one," Prydus said right before he spat at Vlain's feet.

Vlain leaped backward while simultaneously pulling both swords from their sheaths. Oudeteros blinked in amazement. The fighter had moved so fast; his eyes had only seen a blurry, warped image of the man. Prydus gained his feet a few seconds later and drew his sword as well. Both warriors glared coldly at each other.

"You're such a poor loser that you must accuse me of cheating to retain your pride!" Vlain shouted.

"Nonsense. I sensed magic afoot while we played," Prydus replied. "I think you have a charmed item on your person that threw the game."

"I have no such item," Vlain shot back, which was true. "You grasp feebly at twigs."

"I won the last game, commander, so his luck has limits," Oudeteros reminded him.

"Not if he intentionally lost," Prydus countered. "It makes his victories less suspicious that way but still allows him to win the night's tournament."

"You just can't stand to lose, can you?" Vlain asked.

"I'm fine with losing fair and square..."

"Gentleman! Please! Let's work this out like officers," Oudeteros shouted while placing himself between both men.

"A splendid idea!" Vlain exclaimed. "I exert my officer privilege to challenge Commander Orilius to a duel so that I may defend my honor. If he wins, I'll forfeit my victories to him, but if I win, he must publicly apologize for calling me a cheat."

Silence reigned as all eyes turned to Prydus. The commander was honor-bound to accept Vlain's duel, or he'd lose face. In times of war, duels were fought hand to hand to minimize the severity of the injuries. Each duelist could strike and or wrestle until a winner was determined. A duelist could win if he beat his opponent into submission if his opponent tapped out or if the required two witnesses agreed upon a winner. Since they had three ready witnesses, the duel could commence. Vlain warily eyed Prydus as the young man glared at him.

"Since I'm the commander and thus integral to the success of the legion, I can't risk injury this close to war," Prydus craftily answered.

"Of all the cowardly..." Vlain interjected.

"So, I substitute Captain Caladin in my place," Prydus finished. "That is if you accept my request to fight in my stead?" he asked the huge man.

"I accept," Caladin's deep voice rumbled.

Prydus smiled in satisfaction. He had manipulated Vlain into a tough spot. Prydus had lost some face by substituting Caladin in his place, but his position as commander afforded him that opportunity. Now, if Vlain backed out, due to Caladin's imposing stature and ridiculous strength, he'd look like a coward, and his honor would remain questionable.

"I accept the substitution," Vlain eagerly replied.

***

"Are you sure you want to do this?" Oudeteros asked as he gazed at the enormous man who stood at the other side of the field. "It's rumored he's a descendant of giants, and it may be true. Look at him; he's the size of a house!"

"An outhouse, maybe," Vlain replied with a smirk.

Vlain and Caladin stood in the center of a circle roughly twenty feet in circumference. Several legionnaires had hurriedly painted it white and placed tiki torches every ten feet or so along the perimeter. The duelists weren't required to stay inside of it, however. It was meant to be a point of reference so they wouldn't wander all over the field while they fought. Vlain watched as several lieutenants approached the circle to stand beside Oudeteros. It hadn't taken them long to flock here after they had learned about the duel.

Vlain shrugged his shoulders and rolled his neck to limber up. He noticed a few men had started placing bets as to who the victor would be. He smiled in amusement when he realized they were mostly betting against him.

"If you're smart, you'll wager your marks on me," Vlain casually told Oudeteros as he jogged in place. "Come to think of it, grab a hundred coppers from the satchel on my mount. Why shouldn't I profit from this as well?"

"Awful certain of yourself, aren't you?"

Vlain was about to ask him if he knew who he was, but then he remembered Oudeteros hadn't been in the emperor's service long enough to have heard all the stories about him. He then wanted to give the southerner a list of his victories in which he had overcome ridiculous odds, remarkable warriors, powerful villains, and nightmarish monsters. But all he said was...

"I've fought bigger and won."

Since Prydus was the highest-ranking officer present, the duel wouldn't begin until he dropped his gauntleted fist. Vlain and Caladin watched him like hawks. As soon as his fist fell, both men surged toward each other. Caladin lumbered forward like a ponderous behemoth, but Vlain ran lightly and nimbly across the grass. Just as both men were about to collide, Vlain leaped to the side and ducked beneath Caladin's fist while punching him in the stomach. The big man grunted in pain, then whirled around to face him. He swung at Vlain's face, but the fighter blocked with his forearm. Caladin cocked his arm back while swinging at him with his other arm. Vlain blocked it as well, then kicked him solidly in the groin. Caladin wheezed in agony as Vlain's kick lifted him several inches up off the ground, causing him to hunch over in pain. Before he could recover, Vlain grabbed the back of his head with both hands and jammed his knee into his unguarded face. Caladin's nose broke, and his blood sprayed the ground. To his credit, he didn't fall. Vlain snarled in irritation, then delivered a roundhouse kick to his chest. Caladin staggered back, then Vlain slipped behind him and planted his foot behind his opponent's ankle. He grabbed the huge man's jawline with both hands. Then, with a twist of his hips, flipped him over his shoulder. Caladin drove his knee deep into the black soil as he struggled to stand back up. Vlain, however, had anticipated his reaction and clamped an arm around his bull-like neck, thereby cutting off his air supply. It didn't take long before the great shoulders slumped, and Caladin lay gasping on the ground in defeat.

"Yield, proxy of Orilius!" Vlain shouted.

Caladin struggled for a few more seconds, then finally shuddered to a stop. "I… yield," he said.

"Louder, for all to hear!"

"I yield!" Caladin coughed more, then spoke.

Vlain released his thick neck, stood up, and rested his boot on Caladin's broad back. He placed both hands on his hips, then stared defiantly at Prydus.

"Your champion has spoken, as has Fortuna," he said with a smirk. Vlain was alluding to the goddess of luck, who had apparently sided with him. The fighter smiled, knowing the pot had grown to a hefty sum since most of those present had bet against him. Oudeteros smiled along with Vlain as he envisioned all the coppermarks that would soon be his.

Vlain strode toward Prydus as he struggled to choke down his rage. His long fingers twitched as they inched toward his sheathed sword. He so desperately wanted to draw down on this insubordinate cur, but his hands were tied. As far as everyone could tell, Vlain had won the duel fairly. In fact, he had done so with such speed and efficiency that he had humiliated Caladin and, thus, by extension, Prydus.

"I'm waiting, commander," Vlain said as he drew near.

Prydus grimaced, then took a deep breath. His face grew beet red. "I apologize for calling you a cheat. My assessment of your character was flawed," he finished through clenched teeth.

"Apology accepted," Vlain loudly replied, then he whispered into Prydus's ear. "That should be you lying on the ground. A real leader never uses another man to fight his own battles."

Prydus glared at him as he walked away, then angrily waved his arms about while he shouted at the gathering of legionnaires to disassemble. Soon, everyone had left the clearing except the commander and Caladin, who still lay face down in the mud.

"Get up, you lout!" Prydus hissed.

Caladin groggily raised his head, then unsuccessfully attempted to push himself up from the ground. Prydus got down on a knee and then used both arms to pull the huge man up from the muck. Blood oozed freely from Caladin's smashed nose as he strove to find his footing.

"You embarrassed me today," Prydus said as he draped one of the legionnaire's massive arms over his shoulders and staggered forward.

"Sorry, my liege...he was too fast and I..."

"No need for a report. I was there," Prydus snapped as they

slowly made their way back to Caladin's tent, where a Jainan cleric was waiting to treat his injuries.

Prydus spoke no ill of Vlain after that. Still, he never invited him to another game of Six nor included him in any event. As far as the commander was concerned, Vlain and the legionnaires under his command didn't exist until there was some loathsome or exhausting job that needed to be done. Then and only then would he call Colonel Verous and his cohorts for aid, which usually involved digging latrines or some other form of heavy labor.

Vlain and Oudeteros, however, remained in high spirits because they had both earned a small fortune from the proceeds of the duel. Their happiness was reinforced by the knowledge that they were drawing close to Fort Faldin. The terrain had slowly changed from a rolling prairie to a sparse forest of pine trees. Their long, brutal journey northward was finally drawing to an end.

And what then? Vlain thought. *What devilry will we face in the Last Wild? What monstrous forms will nature send against us?*

FORT FALDIN

Chapter 2

The 9th Legion streamed into the village of Faldin at noon the following day. Commander Orilius rode at the head of the procession, followed by his four senior officers, who in turn were followed by his lieutenants, then came the horse-mounted cavalry, and lastly, the weary infantry. Prydus smiled with all the charm he could muster and waved like a politician at the startled peasants whenever he encountered them. At first, the people stared at him in bewilderment. After they realized reinforcements had arrived to defend their beleaguered outpost, however, they smiled back and threw flowers at the hooves of the legionnaires' horses.

"Welcome, legionnaires! Deliver us from the cruel devils of the forest!" a group of old men shouted as the procession passed what looked like a sprawling combination of a pub and restaurant.

"We shall do our utmost!" Prydus shouted in reply.

Vlain absorbed every detail about the town. Most of the buildings were made of wood, but now and then, a stone structure came into view, which meant Faldin was highly susceptible to fire. The village wasn't small, but neither was it big enough to be considered a city. Judging from the layout, he figured it had a population of a few thousand people. Now and then, he saw what looked like the village guardsmen clad in fish mail armor and armed with sabers and pikes. Their angular steel helmets reminded him of those worn by the conquistadors he had fought in the One Year War on the Isle of Almare. Memories of their snarling faces, as well as the pain and rage they had ignited in him as he slew them by the score, suddenly threatened to overcome him. He shook his head from side to side in a vain attempt to dislodge the visions from his mind.

One of the guardsmen suddenly waved at him, causing Vlain to automatically reach for his sword grip. He stopped in mid-movement, then smiled uneasily and waved as he passed the man.

The last thing the 9th needed was an incident brought on by his war-rattled mind while it tried to bring peace and stability to a region long marred by conflict. Not to mention, Prydus would relish the opportunity to discipline him for assaulting a harmless civilian.

"You aren't alone. I, too, remember the carnage those mercenaries caused in Almare all those years ago," Meris said.

Vlain nodded in acknowledgment but said nothing. For a moment, he felt embarrassed that he had forgotten Meris was at his side. Faithful, fearless, and courageous, Meris always came to Vlain's call when he needed dependable men to fight at his side. Not to mention, the man was a superb swordsman. How many wars, sieges, and battles had the two of them fought together? They had known each other since they had both served in the 7th Legion when they had been young men. Vlain trusted Meris with his life, and he knew Meris trusted him with his. Unfortunately, it was easy to forget the man was present whenever he fell into one of his quiet spells.

"We've witnessed too much bloodshed in our time," Vlain finally responded.

"No doubt there," Meris replied. Governor Worrington, Lord Bevel, and Vorsord the Hunter had chosen to journey from Elamara back to Faldin in the protective company of the 9th Legion. A wise choice, considering how often the trading caravans were beset by bandits and other calamities. Vlain and Meris watched as the three delegates from Faldin detached from the legion to ride off into the village. Their job was done now that they had successfully pleaded their case to the emperor and been granted the military might required to hopefully defeat the woodlanders. They could now resume their old lives.

Vlain had spoken to the three men on several occasions during the long trip north. Governor Worrington was a typical politician to the point of being a living cliche. He was careful to always say and do the right things for fear of offending someone. The governor was good-natured and well-informed, though, and his smooth voice was pleasant to listen to. He was also a crafty debater and long-winded when it came to discussing the history of Faldin. Vlain's eyes had glazed over many times when he had done just that. In fact, Vlain had offended the governor when he had fallen asleep in the saddle while the man had waxed on about his lineage and how pivotal his ancestors had been in creating Faldin.

Vlain suspected that Bevel's desire to see the woodlanders defeated wasn't just motivated by a desire for safety. Lord Bevel, it turns out, was a successful timber baron. He had cornered the market on shipping wood from Faldin to Elamara and other cities within the Belt of the Empire. The businessman stood to gain even greater profits if he could acquire new kinds of trees with strange colors and exotic properties, which he said were only available in the woodlanders' domain. Despite his success in life, Lord Bevel consistently looked depressed. Vlain and Meris often imitated his sorrowful expression whenever the man wasn't looking at them. They'd continue this game until one of them either cracked a smile or was forced to look away to prevent themselves from laughing.

Vorsord the Hunter, was a wealthy man who owned several large-scale farms just outside of Faldin. When Vorsord wasn't supervising the workers on his plantation, he led hunting parties into the forest to bring down game such as deer, elk, and boar. The fearless hunter and his men had encountered the woodlanders on several occasions during these forays, and had emerged victorious so far. He was one of the few men in Faldin who wasn't afraid to set foot in the great forest. In fact, he had invited Vlain and Meris to accompany him on his next hunting trip. Vlain could tell that

Vorsord loved fighting the woodlanders whenever the opportunity arose. He seemed to hate them even more than the governor or Bevel did. Rumor had it that the beastmen of the wood had kidnapped his eldest daughter years ago in retribution for killing one of their own during a skirmish. If that was true, then Vlain could see why Vorsord harbored such enmity for them.

The legion soon left the sprawling village behind. As they continued on, they saw an occasional homestead or farm here and there, but the land north of Faldin was mostly uninhabited. Vlain soon saw why. Several of the homes in the area had been put to the torch, and by the looks of things, it had happened recently. Vorsord had told him that the woodlanders sometimes left the safety of the forest to burn houses down in the dark hours. They were clearly displeased that humans were venturing so close to their domain and were trying to encourage them to leave.

At last, Fort Faldin come into view. It was less impressive than Vlain had imagined it since it had fallen into an advanced state of disrepair. The Fort was made of mammoth, white stone blocks and looked like it could only house a few hundred men. Vlain could see numerous cracks in the ramparts even from a great distance. One of the walls was so badly damaged that several men could have walked shoulder-to-shoulder through the gaping hole in the center. Burnt smudges surrounded the hole in the wall, indicating some burning projectile had been launched into it at a horrific speed. Vlain's heart sank when he realized how much work the Fort would require to become an effective base of operations.

As bad as the Fort looked, the surrounding wall made of upright timber beams was in an even sorrier state. Many of the sharpened tips of the beams had been broken off or ground down. Wide sections of the wall were missing or had collapsed, leaving gaps so large that over ten men could have marched through them side-by-side. Parts of the dilapidated wall had been severely burned, and other sections had been reduced to splinters. Vlain could only imagine the brutal assault required to reduce the wall to such a pitiful state.

A moat filled with brown, brackish water surrounded the circular, wooden wall. Pikes, spears, and other sharp objects had been planted into the muddy shore closest to the wall to make fording the barrier more difficult.

As the column of men drew closer to the Fort, Vlain's eyes were pulled northward to Hadrian's Wall. The tall stone barrier had also been badly damaged, and whole sections were missing. Huge holes had been punched through it by boulders that now lay in shattered fragments on the side opposite of the forest. The elements had also taken a toll on the man-made barrier. Moss and lichen grew on the sides of the wall, and weeds sprouted on top of the walkway. Vlain had heard about the construction of the Great Wall when he was a boy, and it sounded like an impressive feat. Unfortunately, it hadn't been an effective barrier. The woodlanders had assailed it until they had created numerous holes and wide cracks, which granted them entry into the lands of man. The wall was one of Emperor Hadrian's major failures, and he had had many during his embattled reign.

Then Vlain finally saw it, lurking behind the ruined wall like a colossal, emerald beast: The Last Wild. Its vast, green body, formed from countless giant trees, filled the entire horizon and receded into the misty distance as far as his eyes could see. Its size and grandeur boggled his mind. Vlain had seen many forests in his time but never on such an enormous scale. Each tree was nearly as big as a redwood, and some were even larger. It was a sprawling expanse that extended for thousands of leagues, which was undoubtedly the case if Vorsord's description of it was to be believed. Vlain felt ridiculously small and insignificant as he took it all in.

"Jaina's light!" Meris cursed in awe. "Have you ever seen such a thing?"

Vlain shook his head from side to side. "The mother of all forests! It must rival the Belt of the Empire in size," he answered.

Prydus held up his gauntleted fist, giving the signal for the legion to stop marching. The entire formation halted as if they were one being. Prydus then flashed a hand signal for Vlain and his three captains to approach him. The young commander started speaking when they were all gathered before him.

"Have your men set up camp in this field. I want at least ten legionnaires from each cohort patrolling our perimeter throughout the night. Come to my tent at first light, and we'll tour the fortress to learn the full extent of the damage. You have your orders," he finished.

Vlain walked back to his legionnaires to relay the orders. After all the tents and pavilions had been set up, the smoke from thousands of cooking fires filled the still evening air. Vlain stepped outside of his tent and sat next to a campfire to have dinner with his lieutenants. He had hand-selected them in Elamara. Vlain had fought alongside them in many battles and wars over the years, so he trusted them implicitly. There was Belor the Brave, who could shoot the eye out of a sparrow from one hundred yards. Vlain had never met a better archer in his life. Next, there was Hildin, who could track anyone or anything across all types of terrain. Then there was Paetro, his twin, who always knew when trouble was coming or when they were being watched. In all the years Vlain had known him, the man's instincts had never been wrong. Lastly, there was Bollis, who was a fearless soldier and an incredible cook. His father was a chef at a popular restaurant in the capital. He had shared all of his culinary secrets with Bollis during his childhood. Vlain and the others often joked that Bollis could make a delicious stew from nothing more than muddy water, twigs, and stones.

Vlain had given Bollis leave to go back to Faldin to buy fresh food for his officers for the next few days. They were all dreadfully tired of the hard, dry biscuits and bland beef jerky that had sustained them while they traveled north. Bollis had bought a dozen rabbits, several chickens, various spices, and an assortment of vegetables. He had used the rabbits, vegetables, and herbs to make a mouth-watering stew for dinner.

"Jaina's light, Bollis! If your wife ever kicks you out of the house for good, then you're welcome to be my full-time cook," Vlain said between spoonfuls of hot stew.

"I'll let her know. Maybe she'll treat me better if she knows she has competition," Bollis replied in a world-weary tone.

"She'd treat you better if you stopped screwing every barmaid you can find," Meris said with a wry smile. Bollis chucked a biscuit at Meris's head, but he ducked right before it could find its mark.

"Careful! Those things are hard as bricks. You could have taken an eye out."

"Maybe that would improve your looks," Bollis shot back. Meris stuck his tongue out at him.

"I'm amazed Shaila hasn't left you with all the shenanigans you've pulled over the years," Belor interjected.

"She would have long ago if it weren't for my cooking," Bollis answered with a wink. "How about you? Have you found a woman foolish enough to marry you yet?"

"I did, but it turns out she was already married," Belor replied with a dry laugh. "Her husband even came to my villa. We clashed swords over her. I won, but I told her to leave with him. She was one of Lilith's Brood, if you know what I mean."

"He got the raw end of the deal," Vlain said with an ominous chuckle.

"Indeed," Belor replied. "And what of you, Vlain? Working on wife number four yet?"

"Number five, you mean," Vlain corrected. "I'm quite content to never marry again. I'm on the road too blaeting much. All that traveling kills a marriage." The fighter used the ladle in the cooking pot to pour more stew into his wooden bowl.

"It's done wonders for mine," Meris said.

"That's because you two grow closer the more time you spend apart," Vlain replied. "A perfect marriage, if you ask me."

"Here, here!" Belor exclaimed in approval. He moved forward to knock his cup of wine against Vlain's. "I wish I could find a marriage like that, but all I ever get are one-night stands."

"What's wrong with that?" Vlain asked.

"Some of us want to put down roots and start a family."

"Well, I've definitely started a family," Vlain replied.

"And then some!" Meris said. He then gave a low whistle to emphasize his point. Vlain threw a pebble at him. Meris caught it then tossed it away. "What of you, Paetro? Found a lass to settle down with yet?"

"Nah. I'm on the road too much like Vlain. Maybe after I retire."

"Who will want your old, wrinkly ass then?" Belor asked.

"That's where we're different. You'll get fat and wrinkly with time, but I age like fine wine," he said in a haughty, superior tone. The men laughed at his antics.

After the laughter died down, Meris fixed Vlain with a stare. "What do you think of our situation, boss?" he asked.

Vlain took a deep breath and set his empty bowl down.

"Commander Orilius is young and inexperienced. He and I don't get along, as you've all probably learned by now. Be that as it may, he's still our leader, and I'll respect his rank as long as I serve in the 9th. He's not a lost cause, though. I've often seen him reading scrolls about military tactics and strategy written by the empire's war masters, which shows his desire to learn. So, let's help him do that. Whenever you have a suggestion, bring it to my attention, and I'll share it with the commander. Hopefully, he'll be receptive."

"And the woodlanders?" Meris asked.

"You can see how formidable they are from the damage they've inflicted on Hadrian's Wall and on the fort, so we shouldn't underestimate them. Also, they know the lay of the land better than we do since they're fighting on home ground. We must quickly catch up to them in that regard."

"The men in town said they look like an unholy mixture of man and beast and that they act like wild animals," Bollis said.

"We should assume they're as intelligent as we are until they give us a reason not to," Vlain countered. "Let's treat them like we would any other standing army, study their tactics, and counteract them accordingly."

"How many of them are there?" Belor asked.

"Estimates vary," Vlain said after taking a drink of wine. "Some say they number in the hundreds, others in the high thousands. Some reports made by the city guard describe woodlander raids as frenzied and disorganized. Yet, other reports describe them as efficient and disciplined. Once again, I advise against underestimating the enemy. Let's assume they have many thousands of warriors and can effectively coordinate their assaults."

"Are we here to eradicate them or to simply discourage them from attacking human settlements?" Paetro asked.

"Based on what the emperor and commander shared with me, I think most of the people in Faldin just want to be left alone. Whether or not the beastmen comply remains to be seen. For example, we could repel them, but an incident in the forest between human hunters and woodlanders could reignite the conflict. Ultimately, we may have to press them into signing a peace treaty."

"Assuming they have a concept of such a thing and assuming they'll honor it," Hildin said.

"The 9th will remain here until peace is established one way or another," Vlain replied.

"Are other legions on the way, or are we on our own?" Meris asked.

"There's no backup coming," Vlain answered.

"Then let's hope we're enough," Belor said.

After that, the topic turned to old wars the men had fought long ago in various parts of Taloria. Some of these wars had been fought beneath the standard of the 7th Legion, while others had been fought with nothing more than a shared ideology to unite them, as had been the case with the Great Rebellion. Vlain, with an army of just a few hundred men, had successfully led a series of bloody revolts against the late Emperor Hadrian. The Rebellion had instigated the One Year War, and most of the men there had participated in it. The small island nation of Almare had fought for its independence against the mighty Elamaran Empire. Vlain and his men had helped the Almarens gain their freedom.

The war, fought mainly on the ocean, had lasted for exactly one year, thus its name. Of course, Vlain and his men hadn't been the only ones who had contributed to the Almaren victory, but from the way they embellished their roles, you'd never have guessed it.

At one point, Meris made eye contact with Vlain, and the men excused themselves. They had both been busy supervising the placement of tents and pavilions earlier and thus hadn't had an opportunity to bathe in a nearby river before dinner. Now, it was their turn to wash the grime of the road off their travel-stained bodies. Fortunately, the swift Rendel River flowed out of the Last Wild, or Great Wild as some locals called it, and passed over the plain for a few miles before bisecting the city of Faldin. Vlain and Meris cast off their soiled clothes and waded into the river. They emerged from the water a minute later to lather up with soap, then slipped back into the water to rinse off.

"It's colder than I thought it'd be," Meris said after pushing his wet bangs out of his eyes.

"But it's a warm night, so we'll dry off in no time," Vlain commented. A short silence gripped them while they trod water and watched as the dark blanket of night was drawn over the glowing pink and purple hues of twilight.

"How's it been for you?" Meris finally asked.

An ironic smile formed on Vlain's scarred face. "You mean as one of the *Blessed*?"

"I was going to say, as an Eldur, but yes."

"It's all the same, regardless of what you call us."

"I can only imagine what it's like," Meris said with a trace of awe. "To have the unfailing confidence that comes with such a gift..."

"Or is it a curse that pushes the uncertainty out of my life till I grow numb with each passing victory?" Vlain asked.

"Don't give me that," Meris said as he splashed water on Vlain's face. "Your victory against Caladin clearly made you happy. Jaina, that was a beat down!"

Vlain held up his hands to block the jet of water. "I only liked it because I was envisioning Prydus when I pummeled the big man. I should have been fighting him."

"I know," Meris agreed. "But the fight made you feel alive. That was my point. There's still plenty of life in you. Don't make it sound so dreary."

"I enjoyed it," Vlain admitted.

"I knew it."

"But that satisfaction is getting shorter and shorter-lived. Sometimes, I don't even feel it, so I do more and more..."

"Extreme things, hoping you will," Meris finished for him. "I know. I've watched your struggle. It must be a huge relief and yet maddening at the same time. Jaina! I'm envious of you! The certainty of surviving every conflict, of knowing you'll get to go home at the start of every war..."

"But that certainty soon becomes a prison. True challenges disappear when you know how every fight will end."

"So you regret asking for it?" Meris asked.

"Of course not," Vlain said. "I wouldn't have been able to save you or countless others if I hadn't. Did you know some folks are saying I'm Jaina's champion now?! Can you believe that? They say she's using me to erase Thania's evil creations one by bloody one. Maybe she is. Anyway, there's another side to it you haven't considered. It came at a cost."

"And you'll never be done paying it," Meris finished. "But why shouldn't it cost you something? Everything else in this blaeting world does."

"True enough," Vlain solemnly replied.

They soon emerged from the water, dried off with some blankets, donned their dirty clothes, and began walking back to camp. In the morning, Vlain would have Bollis gather up all of their soiled garments then take them into town for proper cleaning. Now that they were finally back in civilization, why not take advantage of its benefits like laundry services? In the meantime, they'd have to make do with their smelly clothes.

"If it's any consolation, I think you asked for the right thing," Meris suddenly said.

"Glad to hear it," Vlain replied.

"Sure, it was selfish in a way, but you also used it to help others. So, I agree with those people."

"Which ones?"

"Those who say you're the Divine Lady's champion."

Vlain smiled in gratitude, then clasped his friend firmly by the shoulder. "I couldn't find a better friend if I tried."

"No, you couldn't," Meris agreed as he walked away.

"See you bright and early," Vlain said right before he knelt down and crawled into his tent.

***

The dream began as it always did. The children crowded around him on the dusty, narrow street of his hometown, Vaya. They pushed and jostled him about while shouting in his face, "Plain Vlain! Plain Vlain! Plain Vlain!"

He tried to shove them away, but he lacked the strength to do so. He was seven years old again. Most of the kids were bigger and older than him, and he was outnumbered five to one. Vlain tried to run past one of the boys, but he rammed him with his shoulder,

39

thereby knocking him back. Little Vlain retreated until his back encountered a wall. Dead end. The children closed in on him like a rabid pack of wolves.

"You're so plain and boring!" one boy shouted in his face.

"You're so ordinary and common," a girl piped in.

"You're average at best," said another boy.

"Your face is sooooo forgettable; it's laughable!" another girl giggled.

"I bet you wish you were special, don't you? I bet you wish you weren't so plain?!" The two girls chimed in perfect unison. "Plain Vlain! Plain Vlain! Plain Vlain!" The ceaseless, torturous litany went on and on.

Suddenly, Vlain screamed in defiance, then charged the boy in front of him. He fought hard and almost pushed free of the knot of children, but they dragged him back into their midst, then shoved him to the ground and kicked him. Vlain curled up into a ball and was just about to give up when he saw a stick lying on the ground. He grabbed it and shoved it into the feet and legs of the children until they parted, allowing him to run free.

Vlain ran and ran, not stopping until he knew he had lost them. Then and only then did he slow down. He knew he would be safe at home, but he didn't want to see his father's disapproving look or for his mother to fuss over something she couldn't do anything about. His brother and sister would both sigh in disappointment, then pretend he wasn't there. All the things the neighborhood children had said were true, which is why their words stung him so profoundly. He had been born plain and achingly average in looks, abilities, mind, and even temperament, but there wasn't a Jaina damned thing he could do about it. Vlain knew it was alright to be ordinary, especially since most people were, but the way the children had said it made his heartache. He didn't want to be forgettable anymore! He wanted so badly to matter, to stand out, to demand attention, and even lead...

"What is your heart's desire?" A voice with a strange, alien accent hissed into his ear.

Suddenly, Vlain was twenty-four years old and dressed like a legionnaire. He leaped back to look at the figure that had appeared behind him. He couldn't tell if it was male or female. It was deathly pale, had pitch-black eyes, and was spectrally thin. Vlain wondered if it was a demon, but it had elfen ears and was undaunted by sunlight, which made that unlikely. The androgynous face possessed a fierce, otherworldly beauty. Its eyes, however, were black wells filled with anger and bitterness. He also saw madness lurking there, born from millennia of unending isolation and boredom.

Just like its gender, its age was impossible to determine. One moment, it looked tenderly young, and the next, witheringly ancient. It all depended on how the light and shadow hit its face and from which angle Vlain saw it. The strange being was dressed in a tattered, billowing black cloak. Its head was wrapped tightly in the same material, so he couldn't see its hair. Only its pale face and hands were visible. Vlain watched in fascination as the moth-eaten fabric swirled and writhed as if it were suspended underwater. The being's expression was sardonic and mocking, yet he somehow sensed it was compelled to obey him.

"You have only to ask," it said, taking a step forward.

"You know what I want," he found the courage to say.

"Of course, but you *must* say it. That's how it works."

Vlain was just about to answer Nephotus when he heard a cock crow in the distance, thereby pulling him from his slumber. He bolted up from his bedroll, shaking, covered in sweat, and did his best to shove the remnants of the dream from his waking mind.

"Jaina, how I hate you! I wish I'd never found you!" he whispered harshly into the gloomy interior of his tent, but he knew the words rang hollow. He had secretly been thankful to find Nephotus, desperate even. Vlain wouldn't have changed any of it even if he could, and yet he simultaneously regretted the whole incident if such a blatant contradiction could make sense.

He grabbed his steel flask filled with Higorian whiskey and drank deeply. He swallowed the harsh liquor, then began his daily ritual of getting dressed, shaved, and presentable for morning formation. Vlain couldn't be late. He was, after all, second in command and had a reputation to uphold. He had to set an example for the rest of the 9th to follow. What's more, he couldn't give Prydus any excuse to curtail his power, limited as it was, by reducing his rank.

Despite arriving earlier than requested, Vlain saw that Caladin and Snill were already there, speaking with Commander Orilius. Vlain took a deep breath and bit his tongue as he walked up to the trio. He so badly wanted to call them kiss-asses, but he resisted the urge.

"Colonel Verous, reporting for duty," he said.

Captain Caladin glowered at Vlain. He clearly hadn't forgotten the savage beating the fighter had given him. Vlain smirked as he looked at the faint bruises on his face and his raw, red nose.

Although a cleric had accelerated the brute's natural healing process, it wasn't yet complete. Captain Snill glared at Vlain as well, but the fighter ignored the little, shrewish man. Captain Oudeteros appeared just then to witness the angry stares passing between Vlain and the others. He shook his head and sighed in disappointment. He had hoped the fight between Vlain and Caladin would have eased the tension between all of them, but it had apparently only aggravated the situation.

"I trust you and your men got plenty of sleep last night," Prydus replied.

Vlain nodded affirmatively. He was surprised the commander hadn't hurled a veiled insult his way or given him a dirty look like his underlings were doing. In fact, ever since the fight with Caladin, Prydus had acted professionally toward him, which he found more unnerving than the previously open animosity. However, his tone was icy, and his blue eyes cold, so Vlain knew he still didn't care for him.

"Good, because your division will be responsible for digging the foundation for two new fortresses, which will be built to the east and west of the current one. After you're done with that, you'll dig a wide trench, linking all the forts together. Then, you'll dismantle Hadrian's Wall and move the stone blocks to the sites for the new forts. We'll use the blocks to construct them."

"Captain Oudeteros, your division will remove the wooden wall surrounding Fort Faldin. All of the rotten, damaged wood will be set aside for firewood. Any salvageable wood will be transported to the mill in town, where workers will use it to make weapons and tool handles. Do you both understand your orders?"

Vlain hated to admit it, but Prydus's ideas actually made sense. "Yes, commander," he and Captain Oudeteros answered in unison.

"Dismissed," Prydus said with a wave of his hand. Vlain bit his tongue at the haughty, rude dismissal. If Oudeteros felt the same way, then he didn't show it.

"Something tells me we got the hardest jobs," Oudeteros said after they were too far away for the other men to hear them.

"No doubt. I guess that means Prydus thinks we're friends,"

Vlain said with a gruff laugh.

"How do you figure?"

"Prydus obviously hates me, which is why my men and I always get the shit jobs," Vlain answered. "He used to like you, though. I'm guessing he's seen us talking and now thinks we're pals and thus plotting and scheming his downfall." He rolled his eyes to drive home his point.

"I thought we *are* friends," Oudeteros honestly replied.

"We are," Vlain said, clapping him roughly on the back.

Oudeteros smiled in reply. "What do you think the rest of the legion will be doing while we carry out our orders?"

"I imagine Caladin and Snill's divisions will start renovating and expanding Fort Faldin. At some point, we'll finish our work and then probably assist them in building the two new forts."

"How long do you think all of this will take?"

"Considering there are over four thousand of us legionnaires and plenty of laborers and craftsmen in Faldin eager to earn our marks...a year...maybe longer."

"What if the woodlanders strike before the forts are completed?"

"Then we'll have to rely on our swords. I hope you've been practicing," Vlain replied. He flashed a reckless smile at Oudeteros, then turned and walked away.

MIDNIGHT MELEE

Chapter 3

Vlain pulled back on Viscol's reins, bringing the galloping, snow-white charger to a stop in front of a worn and weathered tavern. A sign reading "The Crow's Foot" hung over the heavy oak door. The fighter tied his horse to the hitching post, then entered the tavern just as the rest of his posse arrived on their horses. Meris, Belor, Hildin, Paetro, and Bollis dismounted, tied their horses to the post as well, then headed into the tavern in search of their leader.

"Good Jaina!" Belor exclaimed. "Would it kill you to lose a wager now and then?" He said as he sat down at a round table across from Vlain.

"He can't do that," Meris said with a secretive smile. Vlain shot him an alarmed look. "His ego's too damned big." Vlain visibly relaxed and smiled as the men laughed.

The table was located at the back of the dimly lit building, affording Vlain a perfect view of who came and went through the front door. It wasn't a large establishment like the Pig's Feast, a sprawling restaurant and pub, which they had passed on their first day in town. Nor was it tiny and claustrophobic like some pubs. It was somewhere in between, which Vlain thought was just right.

The Pig's Feast, on the other hand, was more for large gatherings. It had a generic feel, and Prydus and his posse had taken a liking to it. Word had it; he was wooing one of the waitresses there. Since Vlain didn't want to be around the commander and his sycophants any more than he had to, he had sought another watering hole for himself and his men. It hadn't taken long before he stumbled on the Crow's Foot, located on the rowdier northern edge of town, which was uncomfortably close to the Last Wild. Although the tavern had seen better days and would admit any riffraff with marks to spend, the ale was always cold, the food hot, and the service reliable, if not very friendly. Vlain and his men couldn't have asked for more.

"You should know by now not to bet against me," Vlain said to Belor.

"But I should have had you this time," he replied. "I don't get it. My horse is lighter and faster than your charger. I should have won the race from our camp to here." He shook his head in bewilderment.

"Every horse has his day," came Vlain's reply.

Belor pulled a small pouch filled with copper marks from his belt and was about to pour them onto the dingy tabletop when Vlain held up a calloused hand to stop him.

"Buy the first round, and we'll call it good," he said good-naturedly.

"Thank you, boss," Belor replied. He caught the waitress's attention from across the room. "Seven redheads, please!" he shouted, indicating they all wanted the tasty, red-tinted ale the Crow's Foot was famous for. "Oh, and a basket of pretzels, too."

"Why'd you order seven when there's only six of us here?" Bollis asked.

"Because our fearless leader mentioned back at camp that Captain Oudeteros will be joining us this evening. You should try paying attention rather than constantly stuffing your face."

"You're one to talk with all the pretzels you shove into yours."

"It's a miracle I get to eat any of them the way you inhale food..."

"Gentleman, please!" Meris exclaimed. "Vlain has something to share."

"Actually, Oudeteros is the one with the news."

Just then, a plump, middle-aged woman with a dour expression appeared at their table. She wore a soiled, black apron and bore a large tray containing a basket filled with thick, steaming pretzels and several mugs full of red ale. She quickly set the pretzels and beer down on the table.

"Thank you, Judi," Vlain said, flashing her a sweet smile.

"Yeah, yeah. Just try not to make a mess this time," she said before walking away.

"I think I'm wearing her down," Vlain said to Meris.

"I wouldn't hold your breath," he replied.

No sooner had Meris spoken then in walked Oudeteros. A few patrons were scattered throughout the tavern, so Vlain raised his hand to draw his attention to their table. He noticed the weary slump to Oudeteros' shoulders and how his pace was slower than usual. A month of intensive labor had taken its toll on him. Oudeteros was like himself in that he led from the front, so he had helped his men remove the unsightly and ineffective wooden barrier surrounding Fort Faldin. After much toil, a few accidents, and many splinters, they had finally pulled the last beam of timber from the ground. Most of it had already been hauled off to the mill for repurposing that afternoon.

Vlain and his men had spent the last month laying the foundation for the eastern fort. They had hired several masons from town to supervise their labor. Still, the legionnaires had done most of the back-breaking work themselves. Prydus had given the 9th Legion four days off due to the Midsommer holiday. Vlain, Oudeteros, and all the other legionnaires meant to take full advantage of their much-needed respite. Drinking, carousing, and fornicating were high on the list of many a legionnaire. Vlain hoped Faldin would survive the holiday.

"Greetings, gentlemen!" Oudeteros said as he took a seat next to Vlain.

"You'll find none of those here," Hildin said with a chuckle.

"Drink this. Looks like you need it," Vlain said, shoving a cold glass mug full of red, frothy ale at Oudeteros.

The southerner's eyes lit up as he lifted the mug to his mouth. He took a deep drink, then wiped his mouth with the back of his hand and set the mug down. "Delicious! What do they call it?"

"A redhead. Best in Taloria, if you ask me," Bollis piped in.

"I've had better in the capital," Vlain said with a sly smile.

"We're talking about the beer," Meris quipped back.

"I hear you finally finished with the timber wall," Vlain said, ignoring his comment.

"Thank Jaina!" Oudeteros exclaimed. "I have splinters in places you wouldn't believe. I heard your crew finished making the foundation for the eastern fort."

"Yes, and we have the bruises to prove it," Vlain responded. "After the holiday, we'll start dismantling Hadrian's Wall and then transport the blocks to the new foundation so we can start building the fort. Slow but steady progress."

"When you mentioned Hadrian's wall just now, you reminded me of what I wanted to share with you," Oudeteros said in a low tone as he leaned forward.

Vlain nodded at him, signaling he should proceed, then grabbed a hot pretzel and tore it apart so he could dip the pieces into his beer. Meris watched his actions with a disapproving look.

"Word has it that Tessen, one of Vorsord's ranch-hands, spotted a woodlander at Milner's Crossing the other day. The first one that's been spotted past the wall since we arrived."

"What did it look like?" Vlain asked.

"Said it was a hideous mixture of a bull and a man. An abomination straight out of a nightmare," the southerner said with a shudder. "Why Jaina saw fit to make such beasts is beyond me."

"Hmmm," Vlain replied. "Just one?"

"Yup."

"Did it attack Tessen?"

"Sure as Thania did! Lowered its horns and charged straight at him, but the youth was mounted, and his horse proved faster. He outran it, then headed back to Vorsord's plantation."

"Maybe all the commotion we've been making lately roused its curiosity," Meris said.

"Maybe," Oudeteros replied. "I also heard that the sentries standing guard on Hadrian's wall were all found dead this morning. Filled full of arrows that had been dipped in poison."

"How lovely," Vlain said.

"Some of the sentries were missing," Oudeteros continued. "They found pools of blood where they had stood guard, but no bodies."

"I hope that doesn't mean they're eating us," Bollis interjected.

"I told the commander not to station legionnaires on the wall! It's too vulnerable a location, and visibility is poor due to all the foliage," Vlain said, shaking his head in frustration.

"I remember. I was there," Oudeteros replied. "But you know how headstrong Prydus can be. Thinks he knows everything because of all the war lore he's read."

"Please tell me he didn't replace the sentries we lost on the wall," Vlain said.

"No, thank Jaina. The wall is now off-limits."

"Good. Any idea what his next move is?" Vlain asked. "I've only seen Prydus once since we started working on the foundation. He complimented me on the progress we'd made. I nearly fainted in disbelief," Vlain chuckled. "Then he rode off, and I haven't seen him since."

"I overheard him talking to Caladin and Snill the other day," Oudeteros began. "He said something about sending scouts out to hunt for the woodlanders' villages, but not until after the fortresses are complete and the trench has been dug."

"I doubt we'll ever see those scouts again," Belor said.

"If I know the commander, he'll press the woodlanders hard until he either draws them out of the Wild or destroys their homes," Oudeteros replied. "He needs to win this war to make a name for himself. Prydus has his sights set on becoming the next grand general."

"His unbridled ambition makes our mission all the more dangerous," Meris said gloomily.

"I'll do what I can to temper his eagerness," Vlain said.

After that, talk turned to timetables to complete the proposed fortresses and the wide trench that would link them all. Vlain and Oudeteros assumed Caladin and Snill's divisions would finish the expansion and repair of the existing fort within a few months. After that, their forces would assist.

Vlain and Oudeteros's so that the work would go faster. Vlain figured it would take the legion at least another year before all of the work was done, especially since their progress would slow down during the winter months. Oudeteros, however, held a different opinion. He thought the work could be completed in as early as six months. Vlain smiled at his optimism but said no more on the topic.

The evening wore into the night. Vlain, Meris, and Belor started playing a game of darts to pass the time. Despite drinking enough ale to stagger a horse, Vlain won three games in a row. He lost interest after the third win, then wandered over to the bar to hit on Judie, the surly waitress. Oudeteros, Hildin, Bollis, and Paetro settled into a game of Seld, a complex card game that relied on equal parts memory, strategy, and luck. Oudeteros found out the hard way that Paetro had an extraordinary memory and thus often dominated the game. The only one who could consistently beat him was Vlain, but Paetro finally got his chance to shine since Vlain wasn't playing.

They had just finished a game and were about to begin a new one when Tessen, Vorsord's farmhand, pushed the door open and raced into the tavern. He skidded to a stop in front of Vlain and Judi, who both stared in surprise at the wide-eyed youth. The teenager sported a shock of spiky blond hair and was covered in dirt, twigs, and had fresh bruises on his arms.

"Colonel Vlain! My liege, Vorsord, sent me to get you. The plantation is under attack!"

"Whoa, settle down, son," Vlain replied in a calm voice. "Start at the beginning. What exactly happened?"

An impatient look flashed across the boy's face. He took a deep breath then began anew. "Lord Vorsord's plantation is under attack by a group of woodlanders. They have the manor surrounded. Please come help before everyone is killed!"

"Men! Leave your games and follow me!" Vlain shouted.

"What about your bill?" Judi shouted.

"Put it on my tab," the fighter replied.

Vlain led the charge, pulling the men in his wake toward the door. They swiftly mounted their horses, then galloped behind Tessen as he led the way. The buildings and houses flashed by until they emerged into the rolling hills north of Faldin, populated by occasional clusters of pine trees. They rode hard until Vorsord's sprawling manor appeared in the distance. Vlain suddenly dropped back until he was riding beside Belor the Brave.

"Ready your bow and follow my lead," he shouted over the din of galloping hooves on the hard-packed dirt. Then he shot forward until he was right behind Tessen again.

No sooner had they rounded a curve in the road than they saw a ring of over twenty woodlanders surrounding the mansion. The full moon provided more than enough illumination to highlight their inhuman forms as they closed in. Vlain watched as Vorsord made a stand in front of the thick, iron door. He held a blazing torch in one hand and a short sword in the other. Two ranch-hands, armed with a pitchfork and an ax, stood to either side of the hunter as they faced a group of centaurs.

"Belor, get on the roof and start shooting! The rest of you with me!" Vlain shouted as he dug his heels into Viscol's sides to urge his steed on faster. "Hold on, Vorsord! Don't you go dying on me!"

The hunter looked over at Vlain in bewilderment, and then the lead centaur, a creature with the head and torso of a man and the lower body of a horse, was upon him. The centaur wielded an enormous, double-headed battle ax with one arm and had steel gauntlets on both forearms. His right shoulder was protected by a huge steel shoulder guard. The heavily muscled creature swung the giant ax at Vorsord, meaning to cut him in half. The hunter wisely chose to duck rather than block the ax with his short sword but was then knocked back when the creature's front legs kicked him in the chest. The hunter went flying backward to land a few paces from the front porch.

Vlain lost track of Vorsord as he focused on the closest centaur. It was slighter of build than the one that had attacked the hunter built more for speed than strength. The woodlander wielded two long swords and also wore a steel shoulder guard. As he got closer, Vlain realized a satyr, a creature with the head and legs of a goat and the torso of a man, was clinging to the centaur's back. The fighter barely had time to duck as it fired an arrow at his head.

Time seemed to slow to a crawl. The sounds around Vlain lowered in volume, and he acquired tunnel vision, which always preceded combat. He also began to sense the weaknesses of his adversaries, whether it was a lack of proficiency with their weapons, old injuries that hadn't properly healed, or just plain old fear. Another "gift" from Nephotus. Vlain sensed their weaknesses and ruthlessly exploited them. The satyr fired another arrow at him. Vlain swatted it out of the air with his sword. Viscol slammed into the centaur's left flank a split second later, causing him to spin around.

Miraculously, the fighter had decapitated the satyr at the moment of collision. His battle-scarred face was now covered in the creature's blood. He smiled grimly as he watched the satyr's corpse pitch forward and then fall lifelessly to the ground. The centaur cried out in anguish as he looked down at his former companion, then Vlain was upon him. Despite the recent brutal collision, the creature still had his wits about him. He let out a war-cry then thrust both long swords straight at Vlain, who parried with the sword in his right hand. The fighter simultaneously twisted to the right, thereby dodging the other sword, then pushed the tip of his other sword straight into the centaur's open, screaming mouth. The blade punched through the back of his head, and a thick torrent of blood silenced his cry. With blurring speed, Vlain sliced the centaur's head off, then threw it at the lead centaur that was about to bury its ax in Vorsord's chest. As soon as he realized what had just hit him, the brute bellowed in rage, then turned and charged straight at Vlain. The fighter let out a war cry and was about to collide with him when a muscle-bound minotaur with a broken horn and wielding a hefty ax slammed his armored shoulder into Viscol's side. Vlain went flying off of his horse and hit the ground so hard that he lost consciousness.

Hildin pulled both hatchets from the back of his belt as he bore down on a lumbering minotaur. The beast-man had just gutted a ranch hand with a bastard sword. The young man watched in shock as his bowels spilled out of the gaping wound in his abdomen to tumble onto the grass. A sound like boulders grating together filled the air as the minotaur laughed at the bloody spectacle. Before it knew what hit it, Hildin had buried one hatchet in the side of its head and severed its spine at the base of its neck with the other one. The brute pitched forward to land on top of the dying boy, but not before Hildin yanked his hatchet free of its head.

Paetro leaned back in his saddle and let out a whooping war cry right before he collided head-on with a centaur. The jarring impact threw both opponents back several yards. A few seconds passed by as they regained their bearings. Paetro studied his opponent. The creature had long black hair and a long beard. The face was utterly human as it sneered at him. He shot forward, then slashed wildly at Paetro with its ax. The legionnaire raised his wooden shield to deflect the blow. The centaur darted to the left while simultaneously swinging at him. Paetro ducked beneath the glittering, steel edge, then shoved his spear up through the centaur's throat and out through the top of his head. He turned his charger around and galloped away before the creature had fallen to the ground.

Oudeteros shook his head in bewilderment as he watched Vlain tear into the woodlanders with reckless abandon. He felt conflicted. Part of him wanted to aid his fellow legionnaire, but truth be told, it didn't look like Vlain needed any help. The other part of him thought Vorsord required assistance after getting kicked in the chest, so he decided to administer whatever aid he could. If nothing else, he could at least defend the farmer until the woodlanders had been defeated or driven off. The southerner dropped down from his steed and approached Vorsord.

"Vorsord! Are you still with me?" he asked. The hunter moaned in pain and opened his eyes to focus on Oudeteros's face.

"Think I broke some ribs when that oaf shoved his hooves into my chest," the hunter answered.

"I know this will hurt, but let's bind the break and then get you on your feet. The fight has only begun, and I want you mobile if it comes back this way."

Oudeteros helped Vorsord sit up. Working together, they rolled up his shirt. The legionnaire walked back to the horse and dug through a saddlebag until he found a thin blanket. He knelt down and wrapped it firmly around Vorsord's midsection, then pushed long daggers through the folds in the fabric to keep the wrappings in place. Oudeteros then helped Vorsord stand up. After the hunter was steady, he searched about until he found the man's discarded short sword.

"You may need this," Oudeteros said as he handed him the weapon.

"I'm in no condition to fight, captain," he answered through clenched teeth.

"You may not have a choice in the matter."

As if in answer to Oudeteros's last statement, an orange-skinned centaur with long brown hair and a long, braided beard suddenly came galloping at them from around the corner of the house. The woodlander had a steel scimitar in one hand and a wooden shield in the other. Steel armor protected his upper midsection. He narrowed his eyes as they closed in on the men.

"Get to the porch!" Oudeteros said. "I'll hold him off."

Without waiting for an answer, the legionnaire jumped onto his horse then turned to face the charging centaur. Oudeteros barely had time to pull his shield off his back and to pull his sword free of its sheath before the woodlander was upon him. His horse whinnied and snorted in alarm but bravely stood its ground. The centaur's furious attack soon forced the horse and rider back toward the front porch. They traded blow after blow for several exhausting minutes. Sparks flew from the ceaseless collision of steel on steel, and their shields became increasingly damaged as they absorbed hit after hit. Oudeteros knew he wouldn't be able to keep up the pace for much longer. He also knew he was fighting an opponent who was his equal and seemed to have boundless energy. The legionnaire was trying to figure out his next move when the unforeseen happened. He had just blocked a slash from the centaur's scimitar when several shards of steel from his sword flew into his eyes. Oudeteros reflexively shut them and fought the desire to drop his weapons so he could rub his injury. He slashed, thrust, and swung about wildly to drive his opponent away but encountered no resistance. The centaur withdrew from Oudeteros's reach, and it smiled when it saw tears of blood streaming down Oudeteros's cheeks. It sheathed its sword, then pulled a short spear from the holder on its side. The centaur was just about to throw the spear at the legionnaire when Vorsord, who had sneaked up behind it, thrust his short sword deep into the beast-man's rear leg. The woodlander snarled in pain, then whipped around to face the hunter. Unfortunately for Vorsord, the centaur's rapid, violent movement had wrenched the sword's grip out of his hands. He watched in dismay as the sword tumbled from the bloody wound to land on the grass. Vorsord closed his eyes and held up his hands as the centaur limped toward him with its spear held aloft. His heart wildly hammered away in his chest as he awaited his death. Then, all of a sudden, he heard what sounded like arrows slamming into flesh. He risked opening his eyes to see the tips of three arrows, which had embedded themselves in the centaur's back, shoulder, and head. The mighty beastman let out a bloody sigh, then sank to the grass. Vorsord's eyes scanned the roof of his manor until they found the figure of a man crouched in front of a chimney. He nodded and waved at him in gratitude, then walked over to Oudeteros's steed.

"Your archer on the roof took care of the centaur," he informed the legionnaire. "What happened to you?"

"Part of his blade or mine broke off, and those fragments got into my eyes. Can't see anything on account of all the damn blood! Are there any more woodlanders about?" he asked.

Vorsord quickly looked around. "None close to us. Here, I'll help you get down. Then we'll get onto the porch. If your legionnaires fail to win the battle, then we'll go inside my house and make our stand in there. My door is made of iron and three inches thick. Should at least buy us some time."

"Vlain and our men will win or die trying. That much I know," Oudeteros said as Vorsord helped him dismount.

The farmer ripped a strip of fabric off the hem of his shirt, then wrapped it around Oudeteros's eyes. He then guided the legionnaire up the porch stairs. Vorsord positioned Oudeteros and himself in front of the sturdy iron door, then tensely watched the battles unfold in his front yard.

Bollis gulped down his fear as he hefted his smooth, round steel mace and pulled his shield off his back. Although he loved fighting as much as the other men, he always felt a wave of panic right before combat. He powered through it like he always did, though, which was fortunate because a minotaur holding a massive stone war-hammer was charging at him. Bollis's mount bolted away in fright right before they could collide. The cook cursed in anger and then tugged on the right reign, forcing the animal back into battle. The beast-man sneered at him, then threw its hammer straight at the horse. Bollis heard a loud crunching sound as the huge hammer slammed into the unfortunate animal's chest, bringing it to an instant stop. Bollis had just enough time to hop off his mount before it collapsed to the ground. He shouted in fury, for he had liked that horse a great deal and rammed his shoulder into the minotaur. The beast grunted but didn't move in the slightest. It gave him a withering look to show how unimpressed it was, then punched at Bollis. The man blocked its fist with his shield, but he could feel the raw power of the blow even through the oak barrier. The woodlander then ran over to Bollis's fallen mount to retrieve its stone hammer. After it held its weapon aloft, it scanned the battlefield for its foe. A perplexed look formed on its face when it couldn't find the man. Bollis had slipped behind the behemoth while it had recovered its weapon. He slammed his mace into the back of the minotaur's head with all the force he could muster. The beast-man whirled around, took a threatening step forward, raised its hammer high above its head with both arms and then toppled to the ground. Bollis saw that he had cracked open the back of its skull with his mace, allowing blood and viscera to seep out from the ghastly wound.

"Thank Jaina," the portly legionnaire gasped. He slumped forward and put his hands on his knees as he struggled to catch his breath, but his break was short-lived. For there was already a centaur, with bronze skin, glowing, cat-like eyes, and long, pointy ears, bearing down on him. "I'd much rather be cooking," he gasped as he stood back up.

Bollis shouted at the top of his lungs as he charged the bronze centaur. Right before he was about to slam into each other, the centaur leaped over the legionnaire, skidded to a stop, and then kicked Bollis in the back with his powerful hind legs. The cook was caught entirely off guard by the woodlander's unconventional attack. Luckily, his backplate absorbed most of the blow, but one of the hooves cracked a bone in his mace-wielding arm. Before he knew it, Bollis was flying face-first from the force of the kick. He skidded across the grass before rolling to an agonizing stop. It was agonizing on account of the now aggravated break in his mangled arm. Bollis gritted his teeth, dropped his shield, picked up his mace with his left hand, then forced himself to stand. He teetered back and forth as the woodlander glared at him.

"Tanlindin voia Klim Caernos! Duer vandakin Maiva?" it said in a baritone voice.

When Bollis didn't answer him, he grew enraged, then gripped his steel spear with both hands and ran straight at him. The cook raised the mace with his good arm and then began praying to his creator, the Goddess Jaina. The centaur cocked its right arm back, then, right before it could impale Bollis with the spear, two things happened. The first thing occurred when the steelhead of an arrow suddenly protruded from the woodlander's left deltoid. The confused centaur looked back to see who had shot it. Its eyes soon caught sight of a man kneeling on the roof.

Thank Jaina for Belor and his uncanny aim! Bollis thought.

The second thing was the sudden appearance of Meris. The legionnaire slammed his broad shield into the centaur's exotic face, then pushed it back with all his might. The lieutenant's horse strove to overcome the woodlander's strength, but it was clearly a stalemate. Suddenly, Meris raised his shield up a few inches, then jabbed his long sword into the centaur's abdomen. The beast-man cried out in agony and reared back, but as he did so, he shoved the tip of his spear down at the legionnaire's head. Thankfully, the tip of the spear snapped off on his helmet, but Bollis saw that it had driven a deep dent into the metal. Blood oozed out from the wound to spill down Meris's face. He turned around to stare drunkenly at Bollis. There was a strange smile on his face.

"You always were more trouble than you're worth, Bollis. If not for your cooking..." he trailed off as his eyes rolled to the back of his head, and he swooned.

Bollis raced over to catch his long-time friend and colleague. Although his right arm dangled uselessly at his side, he caught Meris with his left arm before he hit the ground. He gently lowered his companion to the grass.

"Then you would have divorced me long ago. I know. I've heard it all before," Bollis said softly as he stared down at his unconscious friend. "Please don't die on me."

Bollis ignored the bronze-skinned centaur as it staggered toward him. Its face bore an expression that was equal parts rage and agony. The woodlander clutched at a bleeding wound in his stomach with one hand, and the other one hefted his spear. He pulled the spear back, then jerkily walked forward a few more paces. It raised the spear higher and was about to throw it at Bollis when an arrow suddenly flew out from its mouth. The centaur silently collapsed.

"Took you long enough," Bollis sighed as he stared up at Belor's silhouette on the roof.

A victorious smirk formed on Belor's face when he saw his arrow punch through the centaur's head. He had saved his friends from harm once more. The archer sighed in relief, then searched for Vlain on the battlefield. Unfortunately, he couldn't see the fighter from his current position. He'd have to move further down the roof, away from the front door, to lay eyes on his leader. Belor decided against moving because he knew Vlain could take care of himself and because he didn't want to leave his two friends alone in their wounded, vulnerable state. Furthermore, he could also cover Hildin and Paetro from his vantage point, should they run into trouble. He had just knocked another arrow to his string when an arrow suddenly plowed through his ear. The archer jumped back in pain and alarm. He felt hot blood oozing down his neck to pool in the space between his throat and chest plate armor. His first instinct was to inspect the wound with his hand to assess the damage, but the wiser part of him knew he needed to identify his assailant and return fire. Another arrow shot past his head. Belor steadied his frayed nerves and scanned the field below. After several tense seconds passed, he located three figures hiding behind a clump of bushes not far from the manor. Two of them were fawns, horned creatures with the upper bodies of men and the lower bodies of goats, and one of them was a satyr. A fawn suddenly stood up from behind the bush to take a shot at him. Belor loosened an arrow. It jumped back, dropped its bow, and massaged its upper arm before dipping back down behind the bush. Belor cursed in anger. It looked like he had only wounded the archer. The satyr then popped up and fired, narrowly missing him. Belor slipped behind a chimney for cover. After waiting a moment, he stepped out from behind the barrier, aimed, fired, and then stepped back behind the chimney. A volley of arrows soon collided with the chimney. Belor cursed his luck. He'd have to pick them off before he could cover his friends again.

The massive minotaur snorted in victory as it looked down at the unconscious man at its feet. A toothy smile formed on its bestial face, then it raised its huge ax in the air to deliver the killing blow. Vlain suddenly shot up off the ground to bury his hunting knife in the beast's groin. It bellowed in agony, staggered back, then dropped its ax and grabbed its injury with both hands. Vlain ripped the knife free, shot to his feet, then slit the creature's throat wide open.

He was about to retrieve his swords, which he had lost during the fall, but the centaur with the gigantic, double-headed ax was now upon him. Vlain sheathed his knife, then picked up the fallen minotaur's ax with both hands. The centaur snorted derisively, thinking the man too weak to wield such a large weapon, but Vlain maneuvered it with little difficulty. He whipped it about several times to gauge the weight and balance of the crude weapon, then nodded in satisfaction. The woodlander frowned, then charged him. Vlain ran straight at the galloping centaur, then, when they were almost upon each other, he threw the ax at his foe. The centaur predictably blocked the projectile with its ax and then searched for his adversary, but he was nowhere to be seen. Vlain, taking advantage of the brief distraction, had sprinted to the right of the centaur, then reached up to grab one of the leather belts around his upper waist. He hauled himself onto its back and withdrew his hunting knife in one blurring movement. Vlain repeatedly stabbed the woodlander in its side, then grabbed its chin with his free hand and shoved the knife hilt deep into the base of the centaur's skull. The beast-man collapsed like a marionette after its strings had been cut. Vlain leaped clear of the centaur right before he hit the ground.

Tessen, the farmhand, who had watched the entire episode from behind a nearby bush, shivered in fear. He didn't know what was more terrifying, the woodlanders or watching Colonel Vlain as he carved through them like a bloody hurricane. What's more, the fighter's eyes were glowing like simmering embers in a bonfire. The boy wondered if he was watching a demon in the form of a man or perhaps Endlin, the God of War, who had ascended to Taloria to fight once more. Or maybe the legionnaire was god-spawn, the result of a union between a god and a human? Tessen had no way of knowing what the warrior was. He just knew he was unnatural.

Vlain dropped the ax, then, after a brief search, located both of his swords. He picked them up from the short grass, then stalked off in search of more woodlanders to slay. As soon as he was gone, Tessen sank farther down behind the bush and prayed to Jaina for protection. He promised the goddess he would be good from this night forth if she would let him live to see the light of day.

Hildin urged his steed on as he closed in on the massive woodlander before him. It had the head and lower body of a bull and the torso of a man. The hulking beast-man was covered in short black fur from head to hoof. It bellowed out a challenge as it raised a spiked, black mace in its right hand. The weapon looked like it weighed nearly as much as a full-grown man, yet it wielded it with ease. The woodlander held a thick, black iron shield in its other arm. It pulled the shield close to its torso as it bore down on Hildin and swung the mace at his head, prompting Hildin to duck. The legionnaire tugged on the reigns, thereby guiding his horse to the left to avoid a collision. As he passed the woodlander on his right, he repeatedly hacked at its side with his hatchet. The beast-man snorted in pain, then brought its mace down onto the horse's back, right behind the saddle. The horse whinnied in pain as its vertebrae were crushed. Hildin barely managed to jump off the poor beast before its rear legs drooped uselessly to the ground. Before he could put the horse out of its misery, the woodlander slammed its enormous mace into the animal's skull. The warhorse fell to the ground without a sound. Hildin shouted in wrath as he ran at his adversary. The lumbering beast-man shoved its heavy shield into his face. The legionnaire hacked wildly but ineffectually at the iron barrier.

"Duck!" Paetro shouted as he hurled his spear at the woodlander's chest.

Hildin did just that. A second later, Paetro's spear shot through the air. Unfortunately, the beastman had also been warned by the legionnaire's shout. It jerked the shield into the spear's path at the last second, causing the weapon to bounce off of it. Without pausing, Paetro pulled his sword free of its sheath, then closed it with the mino-centaur. He hacked away on the broad shield with all his strength but made no progress. Hildin took full advantage of Paetro's sudden appearance by repeatedly burying his hatchets in the woodlander's side. The beast-man snarled in agony, then lashed out at Paetro with its enormous mace. The legionnaire instinctively raised his sword to block the weapon. The mace plowed through the blade, breaking it in half. Paetro's sword arm went numb from the force of the blow. He raised his shield to block the next strike from the mace, but the woodlander wheeled around to attack Hildin instead. It kicked Paetro's horse in the chest with its hind legs. The hooves buried themselves in the warhorse's flesh. Paetro heard the horse's bones break, and then he, too, was forced to jump from his steed to avoid getting pinned beneath it. The beastman then lunged at Hildin with his mace. The legionnaire dodged to the left, but a sharp spike sliced through his right calf as he did so. Hildin cursed in anger and pain, then threw a hatchet at the mino-centaur's chest, but it blocked it with its shield.

Paetro slammed his shield into the woodlander's side, but the blow left it unfazed. It swung its gigantic mace at him again. Paetro blocked the blow with his shield but went flying backward from the force. Hildin buried his hatchet in the beast-man's right front leg, then wrenched it free and dove to the ground to retrieve his other hatchet. The beastman bellowed in rage, then limped toward him. It swung its mace at him, but Hildin jumped back beyond its reach, then screamed as pain lanced through his calf. Blood flowed from the jagged wound even faster than before. He knew he couldn't afford to lose much more of it. The woodlander charged forward. Hildin wailed away at the iron shield, then ducked to avoid the incoming mace. The pattern repeated itself several more times. Hildin knew he couldn't keep it up much longer. He was losing too much blood, and the wounds he had inflicted on the beast-man didn't seem to be slowing it down. Suddenly, his wounded calf gave out. He dropped to his knees. The woodlander raised its mace high. Hildin threw his last hatchet at its face, but it deflected the weapon with its shield. The legionnaire closed his eyes as he prepared for his death.

"It's not your time yet," came a gruff voice.

Hildin opened his eyes to watch as Vlain leaped over him to collide with the woodlander. The fighter shoved one blade through the beast-man's throat while simultaneously lopping off its mace-wielding arm at the elbow. He dropped the sword in his left hand, grabbed one of the woodlander's horns, and repeatedly stabbed his upper torso while the woodlander tried to shove him away with its shield. He eventually succeeded, but the fighter landed nimbly on his feet. He was about to rush back in for the kill when he noticed the beast-man was tottering back and forth. The grievous wounds had finally caught up to it. A cold smile formed on Vlain's face when it finally crashed to the ground.

***

Vlain sheathed both swords, then knelt to inspect Hildin's ugly wound. He pulled his belt off his waist and used it to make a tourniquet. Hildin grunted in pain as Vlain tightened it around his bloody calf and then gasped as he hauled him to his feet.

"Quite a night, eh?" Vlain said as they made their way to the front porch.

"You can say that again," he replied. "Paetro needs help too..."

"I know. I saw him go down. I'll go back for him and the others after I get you to the porch."

Hildin shook his head in disbelief as he saw the wounded legionnaires scattered across the lawn. "I had no idea the woodlanders would be so strong," he said.

"What did you expect?" Vlain asked. "They have the forms of animals and are as cunning as we are. This was never gonna be a walk through a rose garden."

"And yet you managed to avoid injury," Hildin said.

"Not true," Vlain admitted. "Everything's a little blurry. Think

65

I got a concussion."

Vlain paused as an arrow thudded into a satyr not thirty paces away. He pulled his sword from its sheath with one arm while holding Hilden steady with the other. He soon realized that Belor had just killed the last of the woodlander archers. The two fawns already lay dead on the ground behind a dense cluster of bushes. The fighter waved his sword in the air several times.

"Come on down, Belor," he shouted. "They're all dead."

The archer waved back to him, slung his bow over his shoulder, then walked to the edge of the roof and began to climb down. Vlain resumed walking but kept his sword out. He and Hildin soon ascended to the front porch. Vlain looked at Captain Oudeteros, then let out a low-pitched whistle.

"What happened to you, captain?" he asked.

"Got into a sword fight with a woodlander. The metal from our blades got in my eyes," the weary legionnaire answered.

"Hell of a night, huh?" Vlain said.

"Hell of a night."

"What about you, Vorsord?" Vlain asked.

"Got some busted ribs, but I'll live."

"You wanna open the door and let us in so we can treat our wounds in the light?"

Vorsord nodded in agreement as he turned around, then grimaced as the pain in his ribs flared up. He banged the door knocker against the door several times.

"Open up, Hilga! We got wounded men out here." The sound of several locks and deadbolts opening up disturbed the still night air. A moment later, the door opened to reveal the pallid, troubled face of an older woman.

"Thank Jaina, you survived..." But she was interrupted by the sound of breaking glass and the piercing scream of a woman.

Vlain tilted his head to the right. It sounded like the scream had come from the western side of the mansion. The fighter shot off in that direction. He jumped over the balcony railing with a sword in hand and landed on the soft lawn. He stared up at the windows lining the manor and soon located the screamer. A young woman's head was sticking outside of a window on the third level. They locked eyes. Vlain's brow creased in uncertainty when he saw she had ram horns sprouting from her head.

A woodlander? He wondered as he gazed at the strange being. Vlain strode back to the front porch. He ran up the steps, then grabbed Vorsord by the shoulder.

"Why is there a woodlander on your property?" he asked.

"What are you talking about..?"

"Don't do that! My men and I just took a beating for you! Don't disrespect us by lying now," Vlain fixed him with a hard stare.

A sorrowful look slowly surfaced on Vorsord's weathered face. "They kidnapped my daughter a few years ago, so I...took one of theirs. I figured it was an even trade. She must have been someone important, though, because they never stop coming for her."

Vlain glared at him for several tense seconds, then pointed a finger in his face. "No wonder they were hell-bent on getting in here! You were holding one of their own hostage!"

"Colonel Vlain. Go easy." Belor said with hands raised as he approached him. "We're all battle-rattled right now, and anything you say could make its way back to Prydus."

Vlain took a deep breath, then shook his head in agreement. "You speak the truth. But you!" Vlain said, turning his attention back to Vorsord. "You withheld vital knowledge concerning the enemy from the legion. Your actions have placed the entire region in danger. I demand you release the woodlander into my custody."

"And what would you do with her?!" Vorsord asked.

"Release her. If she's as important as you claim, then freeing her could go a long way toward earning the woodlanders' trust. We might be able to avoid the whole blaeting war!"

Vorsord swore softly under his breath, then shook his head in disagreement. "No," he solemnly replied. "If I let her go, then they'll have no incentive to release my daughter."

"I'm not asking," Vlain said ominously. Vorsord grasped the hilt of his sword, but Vlain's fingers clamped around his wrist with vise-like strength. "You don't want to do that. You're in no condition to fight me, and even if you were, you'd still lose."

"Is that a fact?" Vorsord asked as he defiantly glared at him.

"As hard and cold as they come." Both men stared each other down for a moment.

Vorsord gradually relaxed. He released the sword hilt then let out a deep sigh. "I suppose there's been enough bloodshed for tonight."

"Wise choice. Now, bring her out."

Vorsord turned to his wife. "Go get her," he said. Hilga stared at him in bewilderment, then turned and walked down the hall. The woman reappeared a few minutes later, leading a feminine figure shrouded in a light blue cloak by the hand. Vlain first noticed the hostage had hooves rather than feet, then he looked up and saw there were ram horns on top of her otherwise human-looking head. Here was the woodlander he had seen from the window. The fawn's eyes were a deep, vibrant green, and her face was quite human in appearance. If not for her long, pointy ears and curling horns, she would have been considered beautiful by human standards.

"Do you know her name?" Vlain asked.

"She answers to Maiva," Vorsord said with downcast eyes.

"Come, Maiva, I mean you no harm," Vlain said in his gentlest voice while extending his calloused hand to her. Although his expression was kind and earnest, the fawn recoiled in fear. Vlain then remembered he was still covered in the blood and gore of his slain enemies. He cursed himself for a fool, then tried a different tactic. He placed his hand against his chest plate and then patted it several times. "My name is Vlain. Vlain," he repeated. "I'm here to set you free," he said while pointing at the treeline behind Hadrian's Wall.

Maiva stared at him suspiciously. She took a hesitant step forward and was about to take his hand when she caught sight of several dead woodlanders lying on the lawn. She let out a heart-rending shriek and was about to bolt back into the house when Vlain grabbed her by the waist and threw her over his shoulder. He turned and walked down the porch steps while Maiva uselessly kicked her hooves in the air and pounded her fists against his back. When that didn't work, she started screaming. Vlain ignored her antics as he walked to his horse. He set her down on the steed in front of the saddle, then pulled himself up behind her. He dug his heels into Viscol's sides, causing the horse to bolt toward Hadrian's Wall. Vorsord and his wife watched them depart with heavy hearts. Their hopes of seeing their daughter again appeared to be slipping out of their fingers.

"Where's he off to?" Bollis asked as he lumbered up to the front porch.

He had one of Meris's arms draped across his back, and the legionnaire's other arm was draped across Paetro's back. Meris was unconscious and deathly pale. The tips of his boots banged against the steps as the legionnaires carried him up to the porch.

"And who's that with him?" A battered and weary Paetro inquired.

"A woodlander by the name of Maiva," Hildin answered. "Vlain's going to release her back into the Wild."

"Aha," Bollis exclaimed as he and Paetro gently laid Meris down on the porch floorboards. "No wonder they fought so hard. They were trying to rescue one of their own."

Vlain urged Viscol into a swift canter. Maiva ceased struggling as the ground flashed beneath them, and the manor receded into the distance. Vlain figured she had given up hope of escaping and had resigned herself to her fate. He was careful to keep both arms around her to prevent her from jumping off the horse and so he could quickly immobilize her if she tried to harm him. The fawn, however, did neither. She just stared ahead with a stoic look fixed to her exotic face. The fighter pulled back on the reigns and slowly brought Viscol to a stop as they neared Hadrian's Wall. He dismounted, then reached up to help Maiva get down. The woodlander gasped in pain when one of his hands brushed her back, causing him to arch an eyebrow in concern.

"Are you hurt?" he asked softly as he turned her around. She stiffened when he placed a hand against her back. Blood seeped into the light blue fabric of the cloak which covered her back. "Looks as though someone's been beating you," he growled. "I have something that will help."

Vlain rummaged through his saddlebags until he found a jar of healing ointment that Edanus, one of the Jainin clerics, had given him during the long ride north. It was filled with various herbal and botanical essences and had been blessed in a temple devoted to the worship of the Goddess. The ointment sped up the body's natural healing process and caused wounds to heal more thoroughly than they otherwise would.

"That'll help you heal faster," Vlain said while pointing to the jar. "Please drop your cloak so I can apply it to your back." He then pointed to her back. The fawn narrowed her eyes in distrust but made no move to stop him as he pulled the cloak down off of her shoulders. "Jaina!" Vlain cursed as he looked at the numerous, angry welts and whip marks that lined her back. "I'll have words with Vorsord when I get back! Torturing captives is a vile practice!"

Tears of pain flowed from Maiva's eyes as Vlain gently applied the ointment to her lacerations and bruises. She knew he meant well, for the balm had already begun to soothe her wounds, but the application hurt nonetheless. He soon finished administering it, then picked up the cloak where it had fallen and draped it back over her slender shoulders. A faint, grateful smile formed on the fawn's face as she turned around to face the fighter.

"Prydus would have a fit if he knew what I was about to do," he said with a smile. "I suppose that alone makes it worth it."

"Pry...dus?" Maiva hesitantly asked.

"An arrogant brat who thinks he's my boss, and I've been kind enough to play along so far. Anyway, I think it's best to release you since Prydus would probably torture you to death. Besides, I don't see what harm you could possibly bring to the legion. Maybe you can even convince them to let Vorsord's daughter go when you get home." Maiva stared at him in uncertainty as she tried in vain to decipher his strange language. Vlain went back to his mount to untie a pack, which had been nestled among the saddlebags. He offered the bag to Maiva.

"There's a food bag, a water skin, and a blanket in here. It's not much, but it's all I have to give you," he explained.

"Tand lea," she said with a slight bow.

"If that means thank you, then you're welcome, and for what it's worth, I'm sorry for what my kind did to you," he said before mounting his horse.

Vlain took one last look at the fawn, who appeared otherworldly as she stood there in the moonlit meadow. Vlain dug his heels into Viscol's sides, prompting the horse into a gallop. Maiva bolted toward a gap in Hadrian's Wall. Tears of happiness flowed down her cheeks, and her plump lips formed a trembling smile as she left the world of man behind and stepped into the Last Wild.

FACES FROM THE PAST

Chapter 4

Vlain urged Viscol to maintain a full gallop all the way back to base camp. The light blue predawn glow filled the sky by the time he reached his tent. The fighter tied his steed to a hitching post, grabbed the first legionnaire he found and told him everything that had transpired at Vorsord's manor. He excluded the presence of Maiva the woodlander, however. The hotheaded commander would never forgive Vlain for releasing her and would love to punish him for the perceived transgression. He told the legionnaire, a young foot soldier, to report everything he had just shared to Commander Orilius, then grabbed a bag of provisions from his tent.

Vlain then woke one of his platoon leaders and told him to ready thirty men to ride out with him in twenty minutes. Next, he went to the tent of healing to speak to Edanus, the head of the Jainan clerics. Vlain asked the white-haired, older gentleman to provide him with several clerics so they could return with him to Vorsord's manor to heal his men. Not only did Edanus appoint nine healers for the task, but he volunteered to come himself. Vlain smiled and gratefully clapped him on the shoulder, then told him to gather all the supplies he'd need and to meet him outside when he was done.

The contingent of legionnaires and clerics rode out from camp right before the first rays of sunlight broke over the horizon. Vlain smiled in satisfaction. He had hoped to leave before too many men had awoken to question them regarding their activities. The last thing he needed was further delays. Although he longed to ride as quickly as possible back to Vorsord's, they had to go at a pace that the clerics' pack mules could match. Still, they made good time and got back to the sprawling manor in less than an hour.

The legionnaires swore in amazement when they saw the

bloody corpses of over twenty woodlanders scattered on the lawn in front of the great house. The huge beast-men looked even more intimidating in the cold light of dawn. Vlain told the men to bury the corpses in a mass grave and to form a circle of mounted cavalry around the property's perimeter in case more woodlanders arrived. He then escorted the clerics to the porch. Vorsord opened the iron door and greeted Vlain with a sheepish smile. He guided them to the living room, where the wounded men had all been made comfortable. Edanus and another cleric named Iollan tended to Meris, who was the most severely injured. The other clerics each began working on a man.

Vlain watched over Meris as Edanus carefully removed his dented helmet. The fighter bit down on his lip when he saw the crack that had formed in his friend's skull. A portion of his swollen brain had pushed up out of the ghastly wound. Edanus and Iollan, however, seemed unfazed, which heartened Vlain. They disinfected the injury and their hands with hot, soapy water, then lightly placed them on the wound and began to pray to Jaina. Although Vlain couldn't be sure, he thought he saw a faint white light emanating from the clerics' fingertips and palms. He was about to move in for a closer look when Hilga, Vorsord's wife, gently grasped him by the shoulder.

"You look a fright, colonel," the woman declared. "There's a washroom down the hall where you can clean up. After that, please join my husband and me for breakfast on the back porch."

"But my men..." he started to object.

"Are in good hands. You must be parched and famished. Please join us. Besides, there are things we must discuss."

Vlain nodded, then did as she asked. He found the washroom, then stripped off his weapons, armor, and blood-soaked clothing. Thankfully, most of the blood hadn't belonged to him. He had acquired a few cuts and bruises during the fight, but nothing too serious. Even his nagging headache and blurry vision were starting to improve. His healing had accelerated ever since the Change, a valuable gift for a man in his profession.

Vlain was thankful to see steam curling up out of the tall, graceful vase, which rested on the countertop before him. He and the rest of the legion had been deprived of hot water during the long march north. He poured it into a wide, white marble bowl, then splashed the hot water onto his face, shoulders, and chest. He stared hard at himself in the mirror as he washed the blood and grime off his skin with a towel.

"What have you gotten yourself into this time?" he asked his reflection. "Have your reckless actions gotten Meris killed? And what of the others? Will they be maimed?"

Vlain knew they were all career soldiers who had willingly followed him into combat. However, he still felt responsible for their injuries. After all, he had led them headlong into a battle against an unknown enemy who had outnumbered them two to one. What's more, they had proven to be a fearless and formidable force. Of course, they had been fighting to win the freedom of one of their own, which was something he planned to discuss with Vorsord.

The fighter emerged onto the stone deck behind the manor, looking more like his old self. He held his plumed helmet in the crook of his arm as he walked up to the table where Vorsord and Hilga sat. Two maids were laying out platters of scrambled eggs, bacon, hash browns, and sweet bread. Jugs filled with water, tea, and cranberry juice had also been set on the table.

"You should have the clerics lay their hands on those cracked ribs," Vlain said as he made eye contact with Vorsord.

"I intend to after we've eaten and discussed certain matters," the hunter replied.

"If you're worried that I'll tell Commander Orilius that you took a woodlander hostage, then worry no longer," Vlain assured him. "It wouldn't do either of us any good." The fighter placed some eggs, bacon, and hash browns on his plate, then generously sprinkled pepper over it all.

"That's a relief to hear," Vorsord said with a sigh.

"There is the issue of Maiva's wounds, however. How did she come by them?"

Vorsord shared a nervous look with his wife. "There were times when she attacked us or tried to escape. We had to discourage such behavior from happening..."

"Let me make one thing clear," Vlain cut in. "You're no longer to kidnap woodlanders, nor are you to engage in torture or slavery. Not while the 9th Legion occupies Faldin and not while I'm a part of it. I won't tolerate that behavior, not even from civilians. Is that understood?"

"Yes, colonel," Vorsord said with a grimace. "But I hope you realize that by freeing Maiva, you've deprived us of leverage..."

"At some point, the 9th will clash with the woodlander army. After we've defeated them, I'll do my utmost to locate your daughter and any other human captives they have. So you haven't lost anything aside from someone to whip and beat at your leisure," Vlain replied with a frown.

"We understand, Colonel Vlain. Thank you for your candor," Hilga said while placing her hand over Vorsord's.

"Tell me, how did this whole thing come about?" Vlain asked after he took a bite of food.

"I was leading a hunting party in the Wild," Vorsord began. "We brought down some game, then started to head back home, but we encountered a minotaur on the trail. The nasty-looking brute was blocking our path and wouldn't budge, so we cut it down where it stood. The next day, our daughter Rowan went out to tend her garden, but she never came back. I went to look for her and found hoof tracks leading up to the garden. There were signs of a struggle; scraps of her dress and strands of her hair were lying all about. We figured they took her in retribution for killing one of their own."

"What did you expect?" Vlain asked. "For them to just forgive you for murder?"

"You're out of line!" Vorsord angrily shouted. He tried to rise, but the pain in his ribs stopped him from doing so.

Vlain flashed him an amused smile. "Am I? You're the one with the missing daughter, so who's out of line?"

"Gentleman, let's try to remain civil..." Hilga interjected.

"When did relations between humans and woodlanders sour?" Vlain asked. "What other confrontations, aside from the one you just shared, occurred? Help me understand this conflict."

Hilga took a deep breath. "Truth be told, it's been building for years. The trouble first started when the woodlanders came out of the forest to gather in front of cairns and strange statues they made long ago. Maybe they were worshiping at these sites? I know not. Regardless of their reason, the people of Faldin, who had recently built homes near these structures, were spooked by their sudden arrival. They tried to discourage them from gathering at them by any means necessary. Eventually, the beast-men took the hint and stayed away, but not before blood was shed."

"That's not all," Vorsord added. "Hunters and lumberjacks started getting chased out of the Wild not long after those incidents. Nowadays, if you want to go hunting, you've got to gather up a posse of twenty or more men in case you run into hostiles. It's gotten so bad that even I rarely hunt in the forest anymore," the old hunter shook his head in dismay.

"If things have gotten so dangerous out here on the fringe of the Wild, then why didn't you have more muscle on hand to protect yourselves?" Vlain asked. "If my men and I hadn't been visiting the Crow's Foot last night, then you'd both probably be dead right now."

"We used to have several strong, well-armed lads in our employ," Vorsord replied. "But the woodlanders picked them off one by one. After a while, no one wanted to work for us, regardless of the pay we promised them. So, I spoke to Governor Worrington, and he told me he'd send city guards to protect us. The problem is, most of them are assisting you legionnaires in repairing Fort Faldin, so it'll be a while before Commander Orilius can spare any."

"I'll talk to the commander. I'm sure he can spare a dozen or so city guards. If he can't or won't, then I'll station one of my platoons here," Vlain said matter-of-factually.

Hilga smiled in relief. "Thank you so much, Colonel..."

"But my help comes at a price," Vlain cut in. "You're no longer to hunt in the Wild. It's gotten too dangerous. Nor are you to antagonize or confront any of the woodlanders. In fact, I want you to report all of your interactions with them to me from now on."

"Understood," Vorsord solemnly replied.

"Then we have an accord," Vlain concluded.

The talk at the table turned to mundane matters such as crop growth and the weather after that. Vlain devoured the food on his plate, then helped himself to seconds. Hilga ate very little, as did Vorsord, whose pain seemed to be increasing by the minute. Vlain read the man's body language and thus concluded the meal. He stood up, took his helmet off the table, and bowed before the couple.

"Thank you for the delicious repast and for sheltering my wounded men. I promise to remove them after they're stable enough to travel back to camp," he told them.

"You're welcome, colonel," Hilga replied. "And thank you again for intervening last night."

"Such is the mission of the 9th, my lady."

"I can see the exhaustion in your face. You'll find a guestroom across the hall from the washroom. Please rest in there while the clerics work on your men."

"Speaking of clerics, I think it's high time they placed their holy hands on my ribs," Vorsord said with a pained expression.

Hilga helped him stand up. All three of them walked back into the house. Vlain entered the guestroom while Hilga steadied Vorsord as he slowly made his way down the hall. Vlain shut the door, then laid down on the small bed. He placed a sword on either side of him and rested a hunting knife on his chest. He trusted the legionnaires who stood guard, but he always slept lightly whenever an enemy could be close by. The bed was hard and lumpy, but Vlain didn't mind. He had spent most of his career as a legionnaire and adventurer sleeping on the hard ground or on uncomfortable cots. He soon slipped into a light sleep.

***

A brawny fawn hammered away at a long, glowing, red-hot bar of iron he had just placed on the anvil. He repeatedly slammed the mallet down as red, white, and orange sparks flew in a flurry off the hot metal. The fawn's brown eyes reflected the fiery swirl of sparks shooting off in every direction. The woodlander's only protection and clothing was a heavy, brown leather apron covering him from just below the neck to just below the knees. He stopped hammering the cooling metal and used prongs to dip it into a tub of water. Steam

79

shot up to fill the air with clouds of mist. The fawn pulled the metal bar from the water to carefully inspect it. He ran a finger across the newly formed edge on either side, then smiled in satisfaction when a bead of blood appeared at the tip. He was about to return the metal bar to the forge when a shadow fell over him. An irritated expression formed on his goatish face as he looked up at the person responsible for blocking his light.

The fawn was totally unprepared for the sight which met his gaze. There, standing before him, was a female fawn he had known and loved all his life. How often had her beautiful face and beguiling green eyes haunted his dreams in the last few years? How he had missed her! He dropped the iron bar and prongs onto the anvil, then rushed forward to embrace her.

"Maiva!" he shouted in joy as they collided.

"Father!" she cried out as she wrapped her slender arms around him. "I have returned!" They hugged each other for a long time, then the male fawn stepped back so he could look her in her eyes.

"How is this possible?" he asked. "I heard the last war party sent to free you was defeated. What miracle brought you back to us?"

"A great warrior with eyes the color of the setting sun healed my wounds then released me," Maiva said as tears of joy ran down her pretty face. Her lips trembled from the force of her emotions.

"A man?!" the fawn asked incredulously. "Since when has their kind shown us anything other than hatred or scorn?"

"There's a first time for all things," Maiva replied. "Which means even Haephius the blacksmith must wrestle with the unknown from time to time," she said with a light, musical laugh.

"Yes, yes," he said with a wave of his hand. "What I want to know is if those savages hurt you or not. Did those hairless demons harm you?"

A shadow seemed to pass over Maiva's face while she remembered the cruel treatment she had received at the hands of her human captors. "I won't lie, father. I suffered many indignities and beatings at the hands of the red-headed hunter, but I survived by the Stag's grace. And as I said, the man who rescued me put a salve on my back that healed my wounds. Truth be told, I haven't felt this good in a long time," she said with a sweet smile.

"Well, you're far too thin, for one," her father said after turning her around and giving her an appraising look. "And I bet you need a good night's sleep in your old bed. Aside from that, you look healthy enough. "Praise the White Stag for returning you to us!" He shouted ecstatically.

"I'm sorry I interrupted your work. I know how important..."

"Oh, hush, child. It pales in comparison to your return! I'm taking the rest of the day off. What do you want to do? I'll make us a meal. We have so much to catch up..."

"How's mother?" Maiva innocently asked.

Haephius's face fell. It looked as if the fawn had just been kicked in the stomach. "I don't know how else to tell you this, but...well..."

"Oh no, no, no!" Maiva wailed. She buried her face in Haephius's chest, and soon her shoulders shook from the force of her sobbing.

"Your mother left over a year ago with a war party determined to free you at all costs. Odera fell in battle in front of the hunter's house. Thankfully, a centaur picked her up while he retreated. She was wounded at the time, but she died on the trip back here...." The fawn trailed off into silence as memories threatened to overwhelm him. Maiva moaned in grief as she rocked back and forth in her father's embrace.

"There, there, my girl. I'll take you home, and you can sleep in your own bed again, surrounded by your old belongings. Then I'll take you to Blessed Hill in the morning to visit your mother's urn. Would you like that?" Maiva nodded her assent but kept her eyes shut as tears flowed from them. "After that, we'll visit the king! He has missed you terribly, Maiva! Almost as much as I have."

Haephius could no longer contain himself. He began to weep as he clutched Maiva's head to his chest. The fawn lowered his head until it rested on top of hers. Father and daughter stood there late into the night, mourning the loss of a mother and wife.

***

Vlain watched intently as the healers Edanus and Iollan worked on Meris's head wound. The clerics had carefully moved him into the guestroom that Vlain had rested in yesterday because it was quieter and out of the way. They had also shaved his head so that they could better focus on his injury. Vlain could already see improvement. The swelling in Meris's brain had reduced enough for it to recede back into his skull. Now, Edanus was focusing all his energy on sealing the cracked bone shut.

Meanwhile, Iollan was busy reducing the brain swelling even further while also preventing infections from occurring. All of this was being done by the laying on of hands and by fervently praying to the Goddess Jaina.

"Will he make it?" Vlain asked tentatively.

"He's responding well to the treatment," Edanus replied. "I think he'll pull through, but I don't know yet if he'll have brain damage."

Vlain nodded in understanding. He appreciated the old cleric's honesty, but part of him wished he had just told him he'd be alright.

"Let's hope for the best," he replied. "I'm going to leave the room for a while. Do you two need anything?" The clerics both shook their heads "No."

The fighter stepped into the hall then walked to the living room. He was immediately comforted by what he saw. Bollis was showing Vorsord's female chef new culinary tricks in the kitchen. The rotund legionnaire was also shamelessly flirting with her. Suddenly, he flipped the contents of a frying pan in the air while simultaneously pinching the woman on the ass. The chef slapped him in the face, then shook her finger at him. Although she rebuked his advances, Vlain noticed that her slap seemed more playful than angry. He also saw that her eyes never left his. She was clearly entranced by the rakish rogue who had taken over her kitchen.

"What are you cooking, you old wolf?" Vlain asked.

"Truffles!" Bollis exclaimed. "Vorsord gave me a bag of them this morning. His way of saying thank you for saving his hide, I suppose. After they're done frying, I'm gonna dice them up, then mix them into a meat pie for us tonight. I'm telling you, it's gonna be heaven in your mouth!"

Vlain smiled in amusement. His eyes then fell on the sling on Bollis's arm. "How's the break coming along?"

"The clerics worked wonders," the cook said as he flipped the truffles again. "They said it's healed but that I should baby it for a few days to make sure."

"Glad to hear it," Vlain said before walking into the living room.

All of the other men were gathered there. Vlain spoke to each of them while inspecting their wounds. Belor's ear was bandaged up so Vlain couldn't look at it, but the archer told him it was almost fully healed. It would probably scar, but he didn't care. He was just glad he hadn't lost any of his hearing. Oudeteros's eyes had been flushed with blessed water several times, and the clerics had meticulously removed the metal shards with tweezers. They had laid hands on him after that, and it had worked miracles. His dominant eye had made a complete recovery, and his other eye had regained most of its former sight. The southerner was reclining on a divan while drinking wine and eating grapes. He offered Vlain the bottle. The fighter took a mighty swig then handed it back to him. Hildin's calf was recovering nicely. He no longer limped and was in high spirits while playing a game of six against

Paetro on the floor. Paetro had been badly bruised after being blasted into the air by a woodlander. The clerics had healed him completely the morning after the fight. Vlain smiled in satisfaction. Little by little, his men were returning to their former, healthy selves. He only needed to worry about Meris now.

Vlain was just about to sit down to join Hildin and Paetro in their game when a young legionnaire named Rivers entered the house. He walked up to Vlain, assumed the position of attention, and saluted him. "You can skip all that until we get back to camp," Vlain told him. "What is it?"

"Captain Snill just arrived, sir. He's speaking with the farmhand now and requested to speak to you next."

"I'll wait for him on the porch," he replied in a bored tone, but he was secretly surprised that Snill had visited them rather than Prydus. The Shrew, as he and Meris privately referred to him, rarely spoke to anyone other than the commander. In fact, he was far less interested in people than he was in matters concerning engineering. Word had it; Snill had gone to school to become a military engineer and had received high marks. He knew how to construct battle carriages, war boats, and fortresses, but he truly excelled at making engines of destruction. Vlain had once overheard him talking to Prydus about a new type of catapult he had designed in his mind.

Snill had made a technical drawing of his device during the conversation. Vlain had caught a glimpse of it when he walked past the men, and he had thought the catapult looked intimidating and formidable. In fact, there had been something vaguely familiar about the design, but Vlain had been unable to identify what it was.

Vlain followed Rivers out onto the porch. The young legionnaire walked down the porch steps and onto the front yard to check on the sentries stationed at the property's perimeter. The fighter sat down on a sturdy, albeit uncomfortable, wooden chair while he waited for Snill. Vlain figured Prydus must have sent Snill in his place to gather facts about the recent skirmish with the woodlanders. What he didn't understand, however, was why Prydus hadn't come himself.

Vlain could see Snill talking to Tessen, the ranch hand, from where he was sitting. Unfortunately, they were too far away for Vlain to overhear their conversation. Judging from Snill's dour expression, it looked as if he was interrogating the poor youth. Tessen looked like he would have preferred to be anywhere else in Taloria rather than answering Snill's endless barrage of questions. Finally, Snill dismissed the flustered youth, then the legionnaire turned on his heel and walked toward the porch.

"Fine evening, isn't it, Colonel Verous?" Snill said in his high-pitched voice as he walked up the porch steps.

"It beats last night," Vlain replied. He didn't rise to greet him. He didn't have to since he was second only to Prydus in command. Vlain did, however, point to a chair across from himself, indicating Snill should sit there.

"Ah, yes. Last night," Snill said as he sat down. "Let's talk about that incident, shall we?"

"Certainly, but I can't help but wonder why Commander Orilius didn't come himself. I hope he's not ill or otherwise indisposed."

"Oh, quite the contrary," Snill replied. "He's in a meeting with one of the locals."

"Ah, that sly dog," Vlain said with a wolfish grin. "Let me guess, Brinhilda, the tavern wench from the Pig's Feast?"

Snill fixed him with a stern, disapproving look. "That's a crude way to discuss your superior officer's consort, don't you think?"

"I'm right, though!" Vlain said with a hardy laugh. "I love women as much as the next man, but it troubles me that he'd rather fondle her right now than check on the condition of his legionnaires. For Jaina's sake, this is our first contact with the enemy!"

"I assure you, I'm more than capable of gathering all pertinent facts and writing the report myself," Snill replied while struggling to keep his composure. "Now, first question: how did Tessen know to find you at the..?"

"Crow's Foot," Vlain finished for him. "It's no secret my men and I like to drink there. One of the locals must have told Vorsord, who then told Tessen to check for us there."

"Of course, it would be you, wouldn't it?" Snill commented.

"What's that supposed to mean?" Vlain said ominously as he leaned forward in his seat. "It's just funny, remarkable even, how you're always at the heart of the action. No one can outdo Vlain the Victorious," Snill sneered.

"You're welcome to try, little man," Vlain said as he stood up and balled his fists. "You'll make my evening entertaining if nothing else."

"Oh no. I won't fall into one of your brutish traps," Snill quipped. "I may be smaller than Caladin but I'm also smarter. You may be the best fighter, but I can make engines of destruction that will outperform one hundred of you, "Snill said with a smug expression.

"I don't see any catapults here, Snill, so you'd be wise to watch your tone unless you want to lose some teeth."

"Always resorting to violence, eh?"

"Isn't that our profession?" Vlain asked as he sat back down.

"Yes, but so is thinking, planning, strategizing..."

"All things I employed when my men and I defeated the woodlanders while being outnumbered two to one."

"If you're so tactical in your thoughts, then why didn't you send one of your men back to camp to get help from the rest of the 9th?"

"Oh, come now, Snill! You're smarter than that," Vlain admonished. "We needed every man to win the battle. Besides, the fight would have been long over by the time reinforcements arrived."

"True enough," Snill grudgingly agreed. "Still, it was quite a risk to take."

"What is war if not risk?"

"What I don't understand is why Vorsord was singled out?" Snill said, ignoring Vlain's last statement. "There are many other houses this close to the Wild, and yet none of them were attacked. And why did they send such a large force? None of it adds up."

"If you had spent more time talking to the men from Faldin on the trip north, you would have learned that Vorsord frequently hunts in the forest. During one of his hunts, he and some other hunters killed a minotaur. The woodlanders have had it out for him ever since. Hell, they even kidnapped his daughter a while back."

"Fair enough. Then why send so many?"

"Up until recently, Vorsord hired extra muscle to keep his place safe. He also has a reputation for being a lethal hunter. Those are reasons enough for the woodlanders to bring plenty of warriors."

"When I asked Tessen that same question, it seemed like he was about to blurt out a different answer, then he thought better of it and said something similar to what you just said. I hope, for your sake, you're not lying to me. We both know the commander wouldn't take kindly to that."

"You can take my answers and shove them up your ass for all I care," Vlain shot back. He was growing angry again and made no effort to hide it. "Now, are we done here? My men and I are about to eat."

"What's for dinner?"

"Truffles and you're not invited."

"Come now, Vlain," Snill said with a sly smile. "There's no need for hostilities..."

"You could have fooled me," Vlain said as he stood up.

"Before I go, you should know the commander wants you and your men to return to camp as soon as possible."

"We plan to ride back tomorrow. All save Meris, that is. His condition is too fragile to risk travel right now. Two clerics will remain behind to treat him. I'll also keep a platoon here to protect Vorsord and his people, at least until the governor can send some city guards here."

"The commander wants all of the legionnaires, with the single exception of Meris, to return to camp no later than tomorrow."

"So he'll condemn Vorsord and his family to die?" Vlain asked incredulously.

"Of course not," Snill replied. "Despite what you may think, the commander isn't heartless. He's ordering all civilians who live north of Faldin to relocate to the safety of the village. After the war's over, they can go back to their homes. That way, we won't lose valuable legionnaires to guard duty."

"They'll have no homes to go back to, most likely," Vlain countered. "The woodlanders will put their houses to the torch as soon as they realize they're empty."

"That's not our problem," Snill countered as he stood up.

"Your compassion is astounding," Vlain replied.

"Compassion is a luxury of peacetime we can ill afford." Snill was about to descend the porch steps when Vlain's voice halted him in his tracks.

"I didn't dismiss you, Snill."

"Is there something more to discuss?"

"Not once did you ask about the welfare of my men." Snill was completely thrown off by his statement. He swallowed hard as his quick mind strove to come up with a suitable reply. "No, don't bother. I see now where your concerns lie." With that said, Vlain walked into the house and slammed the iron door shut with a resounding clang.

***

The Crow's Foot hummed and buzzed with an unusual amount of activity for a work night. Vlain sat at a table at the back of the dimly lit tavern with Belor, Paetro, and Hildin. The quartet happily munched on freshly baked pretzels while drinking obscene amounts of red ale. Meris, Oudeteros, and Bollis were missing from their ranks, however. Over two weeks had transpired since the woodlander attack on Vorsord's manor. Meris had finally recovered enough to be transported back to camp. He was now able to sit up in bed and feed himself, but the Jainin clerics still insisted on bed rest for another week or so. The healers had tested him in every way they knew, and he hadn't shown any signs of brain damage. Vlain had been ecstatic at the news and had tried to sneak Higorian mead into his friend to celebrate, but a cleric had seen the flask before Meris could take a drink and had confiscated it.

Oudeteros was busy supervising his contingent of legionnaires while they assisted Caladin and Snill's forces with renovations at Fort Faldin. Since his eyes were working fine, he had decided to put in extra hours to catch up for the time he had lost while he had recovered from his injury.

Bollis was currently romancing the chef at Vorsord's new house in town. No doubt, he was "sharing recipes" with her in a supply room or broom closet at that very moment. Vorsord wasn't happy with his frequent visits. Still, Vlain figured he owed the legion some hospitality after everything they had done for him and his wife.

"It seems awfully crowded tonight, doesn't it?" Belor thought out loud.

"The news about renovating Fort Faldin and constructing new forts has attracted the attention of laborers and artisans from far and wide," Vlain responded. "They've all come here, hoping to earn some of the marks the legion is so generously doling out."

"Nothing stirs commerce like war," Hildin gloomily replied.

"Truer words were never spoken," Paetro said.

"How much longer do you think it'll be before the work on Fort Faldin is complete?" Belor asked Vlain, but the fighter was too focused on a group of barbarians who had just sat down at a nearby table to reply. "Is everything alright, fearless leader?" the archer asked.

Vlain shook his head in uncertainty. "There's something familiar about the middle-aged one in the center," Vlain explained. "I wish Meris was here. He'd know who he was." Hildin and Paetro exchanged nervous looks.

Belor gazed at Vlain in concern. "I know you and Meris served in the 7th Legion years ago," he began. "I also know you were both nearly wiped out by the barbarian hordes when they breached the empire's northern border. Should we be worried?"

"Not as long as they behave," Vlain said with a wry smile.

"We're blaeted then. Barbarians never behave," Belor gloomily replied.

"They're trouble. I can already tell," Paetro said.

Vlain watched as Judi approached the table to take the order of the six barbarians who had just seated themselves. They each gave her their order. Then she walked away. Belor noticed that Judi smiled at Vlain as she walked by, and he smiled back. Belor also noticed the barmaid had applied make-up and was wearing a low-cut shirt, which revealed her ample bosom. He whistled softly to himself, shook his head, then looked at Vlain.

"Judi sure looks nice tonight," he said. "You wouldn't happen to have anything to do with that, would you?"

"Why are you asking me?" Vlain asked.

"Maybe because you've been hitting on her ever since we discovered this place."

"That was just harmless banter," Vlain said with a grin.

"Right."

The talk then turned to forecasts on when the work on the fortresses and trench would be completed. Each man had his own estimate of how long it would take. Belor noticed, however, that Vlain's amber eyes never left the barbarians' table while he talked. Although the fighter's voice remained calm, Belor saw that both of his hands had formed fists and his muscular shoulders were tense as if he anticipated a fight. Belor tried to tell himself his leader's body language was nothing to worry about, but the wiser part of him knew better.

"Anyone up for a game of darts?" he asked, hoping to distract Vlain from his dark thoughts.

Hildin scanned the targets lining the far wall. "Looks like they're all being used right now. We can sign up at the bar for the next opening."

"Nah. Too much bother," Vlain distractedly said.

"How about a card game of Seld, then?" Belor asked.

"Not in the mood," Paetro answered. He was also staring hard at the barbarians.

"Me either," Hildin said.

"Same goes for me," Vlain said.

The fighter watched as Judi returned to the barbarians' table, holding a platter loaded with huge steins filled with ale. A large pitcher, probably filled with more ale, occupied the center of the platter. All four legionnaires watched as Judi carefully set the drinks and pitcher down on the table. The barbarians snatched the steins up as soon as she set them down and drained them in a matter of minutes. The older barbarian used the pitcher to refill his stein, then passed it to the man closest to him. Everything was going well until Judi returned to their table with a bowl full of crackers and a large chunk of cheese. No sooner had she set the items down then the older man reached up to fondle her shapely buttocks. Judi jumped back in alarm, then slapped him soundly on his bearded face. Vlain was about to intercede but stopped short when he noticed two city guardsmen were already approaching the table. They had been drinking at the bar and had been watching the barbarians ever since they arrived.

"What's the problem here?" Vlain heard one of them ask Judi.

"This one here just felt me up!" she angrily replied while pointing to the older, pot-bellied barbarian who sat in the center of the group.

"What do you have to say for yourself?" One of the guardsmen asked him.

"I did nothing of the sort!" he exclaimed. "I was just trying to slip a copper mark into her back pocket when she bolted away. See? Here it is," he said as he held a large copper coin up for both of them to see.

"You should leave the tip on the table," the guard said.

"And you should leave my father alone," a clean-shaven, muscular barbarian with dark blue eyes, a scarred face, and long black hair said. He sat to his father's right.

"That's right, Kovan. Now be gone and let our father drink in peace," a huge man with long blond hair, a neatly trimmed beard, and bright blue eyes said. He sat to his father's left. The other three barbarians nodded in agreement while glaring angrily at the two guards.

Judi sighed in exasperation. "Just pay your tab and get out of here," she said in a huff, then turned and walked away.

"Hey, that's no way to talk to a paying customer!" the heavy-set barbarian shouted. The stout man stood up to stare angrily into the eyes of the nearest guard. His hair and beard were red, and his eyes gray. He wore a steel helmet that sprouted one broken horn and one that was still whole.

"I think you should do as the lady said," the guard replied.

"Or what?" the leader of the barbarians asked.

"That's our cue," Vlain said with a reckless smile. He stood up and beckoned for his friends to join him as he approached the barbarians' table.

"Or we'll escort you out of here," the other guard said with a scowl.

"I'd like to see that," the leader ominously growled.

All of the other barbarians stood up at once. Belor was amazed at how huge the blond-haired man was. He looked like he was over seven feet tall and was nearly three feet wide at the shoulders. The barbarian had an intricately designed war hammer strapped to his back. Hildin was focused on the chiseled physique of the dark-haired man with a scarred face. He had a long sword strapped to his broad back. The barbarian's dark blue eyes smoldered with hostility. Hildin gulped down his fear.

Belor's eyes narrowed to thin slits as he studied each of the barbarians at the table. Paetro just shrugged his shoulders and resigned himself to the coming fight. Vlain's smile grew wider and wider.

"Is everything alright here, gentleman?" Vlain asked the city guards.

"Endlin's beard! I know you! You're Vlain! Those hellish eyes have hounded me in my nightmares," the lead barbarian said as he stared hard at him. "In case you've forgotten, the name's Brenor Battleaxe. You killed scores of my kin during the border war! It's time you paid for what you did!" The man's face was livid with rage.

"As I recall, you and your horde killed many of my fellow

legionnaires as well," Vlain coolly responded. "But I suppose we can settle the score tonight, Brenor."

"Blaeting right we will!"

"One rule: no weapons!" Vlain shouted for all to hear.

"We won't need weapons to kill the lot of you!" Brenor snarled.

The city guard had heard enough. "All right, that's it! It's time you and your..." But he was cut off when Brenor punched him in the stomach, then kneed him in the face. The man stumbled backward. Vlain hit Brenor in the mouth, then tackled him. The men went flying over the table to land heavily on the stone floor. Belor, Hildin, Paetro, and the remaining guardsman squared off against the other barbarians.

Everyone in the tavern stopped what they were doing to stare at the brawl with wide eyes. Most patrons made a wild dash for the door, but a few started fights with whoever was nearby. Judi and the other barmaids ran behind the bar, then ducked down out of sight just as several mugs and plates collided with the wall behind them. The women had been through many a brawl before and had no desire to get caught up in one again.

"I remember how quick you are," Brenor said after spitting out a tooth. "You won't get the...," but he was cut off as Vlain pummeled the barbarian's bloody face. Brenor raised his thick forearms to protect himself, but Vlain's fists always found an opening. The fighter's eyes began to glow with a faint orange light as he steadily pounded his opponent into the ground. Vlain stopped hitting Brenor as soon as his arms fell limply to his sides. He stood up, wiped his bloody knuckles on his trousers, then smiled grimly as he watched his men wade into the barbarians.

Belor swung at the enormous blond barbarian with all his strength, but the man caught his fist in his huge hand and squeezed it, thereby forcing him to his knees. The archer grimaced in pain and punched his adversary in the groin. The barbarian released his fist, then hopped back out of reach. A cold smile formed on his bearded face as he glared down at Belor.

"No one lays hands on Wrothgar, little man," he growled as he kicked the legionnaire soundly in the chest.

Belor went flying backward. Vlain quickly realized his friend would land on the antlers of a stag that had been mounted on the wall. Patrons of the Crow's Foot used it as a coat rack. Vlain swore softly under his breath, then shot off to intercept his air-born friend. His feet blurred beneath him as he sprinted through the tavern. The fighter leaped into the air and caught Belor from the side. They both landed roughly on the stone floor.

"You alright?" Vlain asked as he helped the archer stand up.

"Wrothgar's stronger...than an ox," Belor gasped. "Think he busted a rib or two."

"Sit this one out. I've got him," Vlain said before rushing back into the fray.

Kovan threw a punch at Hildin's face. The spearman ducked beneath his fist, then repeatedly hit the man in the stomach and side. Unfortunately, his efforts only caused the big man to grunt in amusement. The barbarian slammed his elbow down into Hildin's shoulder. Stunned by the blow, the legionnaire fell to his knees. Kovan hauled Hildin to his feet, then punched him hard in the chin. As Hildin tottered back and forth, the city guard, who had been knocked back by Brenor, suddenly tackled the barbarian from behind. Both men went crashing into a nearby table, sending platters, plates, beer steins, and cutlery flying into the air.

Paetro launched himself at a shaggy-headed barbarian with lanky brown hair. The youth swung at him prematurely, allowing the legionnaire to dodge and then strike him in the side of his face. The two men exchanged blows for a minute. Although the young barbarian was stronger, it became apparent that Paetro was the better fighter. He relentlessly pounded away at his opponent, then staggered him with an uppercut. The young man backed away until a table stopped his retreat. Paetro snatched a thick, porcelain platter up from the table, then broke it over his head. The youth collapsed to the floor with a moan. He sat there in a daze as he rubbed his sore head.

"And stay down!" Paetro shouted.

The other city guard was fighting hard against a short, stout, bald-headed barbarian. They slammed into tables and sent chairs flying as they staggered back and forth across the tavern. The bald man suddenly kneed the guard in the groin, causing him to fall to his knees. Before the barbarian could knock him down, however, Storg, a huge, hunched-back man who served as the tavern's bouncer, barreled out from behind the bar to tackle him. Both men went flying until the far wall stopped them. Storg rained blow after blow down onto the barbarian until he lost consciousness, then stood up to search for another opponent.

Meanwhile, Kovan repeatedly slammed a city guard's head against the tabletop. The man had clearly lost consciousness, but the barbarian didn't seem to care. He lifted the guard's limp body up by the back of the neck and was about to slam him back down again when Paetro kicked him in the back. The barbarian grunted in anger, then threw the unconscious guard at him. Hildin caught the man, lowered him to the ground, and stood back up just in time to get punched in the chin. He went flying back, then slid to a stop on the floor. To his credit, he tried to get up but lost consciousness.

"You're gonna pay for what you did to my friend," Vlain said grimly as he strode up to Wrothgar.

The barbarian's head fell back as his booming laughter filled the air. "If you fight like him, then that's a hollow threat," he replied. "And let's not forget that I owe YOU for beating my father down."

"If you fight like your father, then it's me who has nothing to worry about," Vlain countered.

Vlain knew he couldn't overpower Wrothgar, so he figured he'd rely on his speed and the accuracy of his strikes to bring him down like he had done when he fought Caladin. Both men warily circled each other for a moment. Vlain feigned to the right, then shifted to the left to land a solid hit to the man's stomach. The barbarian grimaced in pain, then swung at Vlain's face. The fighter dodged at the last second, grabbed his wrist, then turned and flipped him over his shoulder. Wrothgar cursed in bewilderment as he went sailing through the air, only to demolish a table as it caught all 350 pounds of him. Vlain was on him before he could get up. He wrapped a muscular arm around Wrothgar's thick neck and tried to choke him out, but the barbarian proved to be more stubborn and powerful than Caladin. Wrothgar shot to his feet as Vlain hung from his neck. The huge man began running backward toward the wall. Vlain knew he meant to crush him between the wall and himself, so he extended his legs back to brace himself against the oncoming wall. Wrothgar grunted in surprise when Vlain's feet brought them to a stop, but then he redoubled his efforts. Each man strained against the other for one long, torturous moment. Unfortunately for the barbarian, he was steadily running out of air while Vlain could breathe freely. Wrothgar repeatedly elbowed Vlain in the sides. The fighter gasped in pain but refused to let go. Eventually, Wrothgar's face turned red, a mottled purple, then blue before he ceased struggling and collapsed to the floor. Vlain pitched forward with him to land on his back. He paused to take a breath, then ran off to help Paetro and the others.

Kovan had just felled the second city guard with one thunderous punch when Storg tackled him from the side. Both men collided with the bar. Storg grabbed the man's long dark hair with one hand and tried to slam him face-first into the countertop, but the barbarian planted his massive arms on the countertop to stop the movement. He then launched backward and head-butted the hunchback in the face. Storg's nose flattened, and his eyes rolled into the back of his head as he passed out from the pain. The barbarian turned around, raised an iron-shod boot, and was about to stomp on Storg's throat when Vlain tackled him. The men slammed into the countertop then fell back behind the bar. The women that had been hiding back there screamed in fright and raced toward the kitchen to get away from the wildly thrashing men.

Paetro faced off against the last of the barbarians. The man was tall and had a wiry, muscular build. His long brown beard was braided, and he had the blue image of a dragon with a long, ribbon-like body tattooed across his entire back and up onto his neck and arms. Both earlobes had wide steel gauges in them, and the bottom part of his nose was pierced with what looked like a wolf's canine tooth. The barbarian lashed out at Paetro with his stiff fingers. The man's long, jagged nails raked pieces of skin from the legionnaire's face. Reeling from the pain, Paetro stepped back, which allowed him to avoid a second slash from the man's talon-like fingers. Try as he might, Paetro couldn't land a blow on the quick-footed barbarian. Again and again, the man side-stepped his attacks, then clawed at his face with his strong fingers. Paetro's face was soon gauged and bloody.

Meanwhile, Vlain and the black-haired barbarian were trading blow for blow behind the bar. Blood flew from both of their mouths and noses as they mercilessly pummeled each other. Vlain marveled at the man's ferocity and unfailing energy. He hadn't been challenged like this in a long time. Just then, the barbarian grabbed a bottle off the shelf, smashed it against the counter-top, and shoved the jagged shards of glass at his throat. Vlain leaped back, ripped his belt off his trousers, and started whipping the man in the arms and face with it. The barbarian was forced to give ground as dozens of bloody welts formed all across his skin.

"That's enough!" a harsh voice suddenly shouted. "Put down your weapons and surrender! So, orders the city guard!"

Vlain risked a quick look at the door. A team of city guards was pouring into the tavern. They were all heavily armed with crossbows and wore steel armor. The tattooed barbarian who had been fighting Paetro made a run for the back door, prompting one of the guardsmen to point a loaded crossbow his way. A bolt streaked through the tavern and embedded itself in the door he was running toward. The man stopped abruptly, turned around, and raised his hands in the air.

"The next one goes in you!" the leader of the guards bellowed. "And you! Drop that bottle and step away from the legionnaire!"

Kovan scowled angrily but did as he was told. He realized Vlain's eyes were glowing. A look of fear formed on his scarred face as he stepped back from the fighter.

"Kron! Are you a devil?" he asked.

"Only to those who hurt my friends," Vlain said with a smirk. His eyes were already losing their eerie glow, shifting from burning embers back to amber. The big man muttered something about hating sorcery, then leaped over the bar. Vlain followed suit, landing nimbly beside him.

"On your knees, big fella, and put your hands behind your head," the captain of the guard ordered as he approached the barbarian with manacles in hand. "You alright, Colonel Verous?"

"Nothing a trip to the cleric won't fix," he replied. "Speaking of clerics, I need to get my men to them now."

"Alright," the captain replied. "I'll come by in the morning to collect your statement," he said as he bound Kovan in chains, then roughly hauled him to his feet.

"What are you going to do with them?" Vlain asked.

"They'll spend some time in the stockade, then they'll be barred from Faldin for life," the man replied. "They'll have a date with the gallows should they dare to return."

"If you ever come near our lands, then I'll be waiting for you, devil," Kovan said as he passed Vlain. The captain of the guard shoved him forward.

Vlain laughed and shook his head. "I don't plan on it, but I look forward to finishing our fight if we meet again." He watched as the city guardsmen collected all of the barbarians and dragged or carried them out of the tavern. He then wiped the back of his hand across his bloody face and flung the blood onto the floor.

"Hell of a night," he muttered as he walked over to Paetro. The battered legionnaire leaned heavily against a support beam as he gingerly touched the bleeding gouges on his face. Vlain stopped beside him, then beckoned to Belor, who was sitting across the room, to come over.

Paetro raised his eyebrows when he saw Vlain's bruised and bloody face. "Looks like you finally met someone who could challenge you," he said.

"He was quite a fighter," Vlain admitted. "Looks like you took a beating as well."

"His fingers were like pieces of iron. Feels like he ripped half my face off."

Vlain looked at both sides of his face. "Nothing the clerics can't fix. You'll be scoring with the ladies again in no time. But right now, I need you to help Belor get on his horse. He's got some busted ribs.

I'll wake Hildin up from his nap while you do that."

With that said, Vlain walked back behind the bar to get some water. He grabbed a jug, poured cold water into a mug, then turned around to come face-to-face with Judi. The woman was crying as she surveyed the ruined furniture and the broken dishes scattered all about. Even the stout timber walls had several deep gouges in them. She shook her head in disbelief.

"Business has been slow on account of the feud ragin' between the woodlanders and us Faldinites," she began. "We lost most of our customers but still managed to scrape by. We were thinking about closing right before the 9th Legion came into town. Even though most of your men prefer the Pig's Feast, we still got a huge surge in business. But now...now we've lost a year's worth of profit thanks to your fight. Couldn't you have taken it outside?"

"Now, hold on. I was defending your honor..."

"More like settling an old score."

Vlain was about to reply, but he paused, then nodded in agreement. "I'm sorry," he said with sincerity. "I've got to get my men to the clerics right now, but I'll return as soon as I can to help you clean this mess up."

"Don't bother. My sisters and I will handle it like we always do," Judi wearily replied.

"It's the least I can do after all the trouble I caused." But Judi was no longer listening. She bent down and began gathering up broken pieces of cutlery from the floor. Vlain sighed, then walked over to where Hildin was lying on the floor. The fighter poured water down onto his face. The legionnaire groggily shook his head, then sputtered in protest as the water splashed all over his bruised face.

"Up and at 'em," Vlain said cheerfully.

"Good Jaina," Hildin mumbled. The tracker slowly rose to a seated position. "Feel like I was kicked by a horse."

"Yeah, he sure can hit," Vlain agreed, regarding the barbarian named Kovan, whom they had both fought. "Can you get in the saddle by yourself?" he asked. Hildin shook his head "yes," then started massaging his sore chin. "Good. I'll meet you outside in a minute."

Vlain took one last look at Judi. The waitress had grabbed a broom and was busy sweeping up broken pieces of glass. He turned away and was about to leave when he caught sight of Storg, the bouncer, lying on the floor. He walked over to the big, unconscious man, squatted down, and picked him up.

"I'm taking him to the clerics," he informed Judi. "A night in the tent of healing will do him wonders." The waitress nodded absently while continuing to sweep up debris. The fighter carried him out of the tavern. The hunchback came to just as Vlain reached his snow-white steed. He mounted the horse, then reached down to help Storg get up behind him.

Vlain and his men made good time on the road and arrived back at camp in under an hour. Vlain placed each man in the care of a cleric and was about to return to the Crow's Foot when Edanus grabbed him by the shoulder. The elder cleric arched an eyebrow as he inspected Vlain's bloody face. "You aren't going anywhere until I've laid hands on you," he told him.

"My injuries are minor, and I'm a quick healer..." Vlain explained, but the cleric wouldn't take no for an answer.

Vlain left the tent of healing an hour later, looking and feeling much better than when he had first gone in. He jumped onto Viscol and was about to return to the Crow's Foot when he suddenly had an idea. The fighter rode to his tent instead. He jumped down from the saddle, entered his tent, then exited a moment later, carrying a small bag. Vlain urged his horse into a gallop and soon returned to the Crow's Foot.

Judi and her three sisters were still cleaning when Vlain walked back into the tavern. He went straight to Judi and held the small bag up to her. The waitress gave him a curious look, then took the bag and opened it. Dozens of rectangular silver marks glittered up at her. She stood there with her mouth wide open as she gazed at the money.

"That should easily pay for the damages," Vlain said with a smile.

"I can't take this...it's too much," Judi stammered.

"It's only money. Don't worry about it."

Judi flung her arms around Vlain. The fighter let out a startled laugh, then hugged her back as tears began falling from her face. She held him for a long moment, then stepped back and gazed appreciatively up at him. "You're full of surprises," she said.

"You have no idea," Vlain said with a chuckle. "But enough standing around already. Let's get to work."

Vlain and Hibert, the owner, chef, and Judi's father, spent the rest of the night hauling broken furniture out of the tavern. The women swept and mopped the floor, scrubbed stains off the walls, and threw out all the broken dishes. The pub almost looked like its old self when the first golden rays of sunlight peeked in through the windows. Hibert thanked Vlain for his generosity and help, then left with Judi's sisters.

Judi stayed behind to cook breakfast for Vlain and herself. They laughed and talked while they feasted on scrambled eggs, sausages, hash browns, and buttered biscuits. Vlain washed the meal down with a cup of milk, then pushed himself back from the table.

"Thank you for that," he said as he stood up.

"And where do you think you're going?" Judi asked.

"Back to camp."

"You could do that," she said in a sultry tone while running her hands through her long, auburn tresses. "Or you could stay for dessert. The choice is yours."

"What's on the menu?" he asked with a sly grin.

"You have to ask?" she said, batting her eyes at him. Judi ran her hand up his inner thigh until it rested on his crotch.

Vlain smiled from ear to ear. "Camp can wait," he replied.

***

"The commander wants to see you," Sergeant Rivers told Vlain right as he was about to dismount his horse and enter his tent.

Figures he would, he angrily thought, but all he said was: "Then, I'll be on my way."

He had just put in another long day of working on the new fortress located west of Fort Faldin. All he wanted to do was bathe and then get to bed so he could rise early for the next grueling workday, but it wasn't to be. At least not yet. He hoped the meeting wouldn't last long.

Vlain urged Viscol into a steady canter until the snow-white mount arrived at Prydus's elaborate pavilion, then he got down and tied him to a hitching post. He nodded at the two legionnaires who stood guard outside the tent, parted the flap, and walked in. The fighter was about to part the next flap, which led to Prydus's inner sanctum, when a pale, slender hand pushed it aside. Out walked Brinhilda, Prydus's girlfriend and former waitress at the Pig's Feast. Word had it; she had recently quit her job, which made Vlain wonder if he'd soon marry the girl. Brinhilda was a tall, beautiful, youthful blond, much like Prydus. She emerged from the inner tent, dressed in a light, white gossamer nightgown with ruffles around the neck and sleeves. A sweet perfume lazily drifted in her wake.

"Don't leave on my account," Vlain said with a wink and a smirk.

The young woman turned her nose up and looked straight ahead rather than making eye contact. "Vlain, I presume?" she asked haughtily.

"The one and only."

"Don't keep him up too late. We were in the middle of something important."

"I bet you were, but don't worry. I always keep our visits as short as possible," he said with a grin. Brinhilda no longer seemed to be listening, however. She pushed the folds of the outer tent open and stepped out into the night with her silver slippers. "Glad we had that talk," he said to her back.

Vlain pushed the flaps aside, then stepped through. The fighter was immediately struck by the strange decorum surrounding him. On the one hand, it was definitely the tent of a military man, for numerous maps of the region had been placed on the walls, indicating the recent movements of the woodlanders. Also, two gilded sabers had been hung in an x over the head of the mammoth bed that occupied the rear of the tent. On the other hand, it looked opulent and gaudy. The oversized bed was covered with fox and ermine furs, something Vlain would have expected to see in a high-class brothel in the capital. It was a strange mixture of worldly power melding with the decadently sensual. Vlain figured Brinhilda was sharing some of her own fashion ideas with the up-and-coming grand general.

"You wanted to see me, commander?" Vlain asked.

"At ease, Colonel Verous," Prydus said with a wave of his hand. The young man was sitting with one leg slung over the armrest of an oversized, wicker chair that resembled a throne of sorts.

Prydus was dressed in a blue silk tunic and held a dagger in one hand and a goblet of wine in the other. He looked intoxicated. Vlain struggled to stop himself from snickering at the scene.

"You appear to be living well," Vlain said with a faint smile.

"Yes, well, a man must look the part," he replied. "Take a seat. The *hero* of the empire shouldn't be forced to stand."

Vlain's amber eyes hardened when he heard the sarcasm in his voice. "I'm fine with standing. It strengthens the body," he said coldly.

"You're probably wondering why I summoned you here," Prydus said.

"The thought had crossed my mind."

Prydus took a sip of red wine then held his arms out wide. "Your famous good luck is about to manifest again, colonel," he calmly stated.

"How so?"

"After careful consideration, I've decided to place YOU in charge of leading an assault against the woodlanders. You have three days to prepare the men."

"Excuse me?!" Vlain asked in disbelief.

"We're going to fight the beasties on their own land! A stroke of genius, isn't it? It's the last thing they'd ever expect, which is why it'll work."

"But the other two forts are still under construction, and the trench still hasn't been com..."

"Yes, yes, but all that has lost its importance in light of new developments."

"Let me get this straight," Vlain began, struggling to control his temper. "You're proposing we enter the Last Wild, where the woodlanders have every tactical advantage and where they can marshal thousands of warriors to their aid. Meanwhile, we'll be cut off from Fort Faldin, our supply lines, and any help the village of Faldin can offer..."

"Have some faith in your leader!" Prydus angrily shouted. He threw his cup of wine at the supple wall of his tent. He then shot to his feet to glare at Vlain while brandishing his hunting knife.

Vlain's hands closed around the handles of his twin swords. His eyes narrowed to thin slits as he studied Prydus's petulant face. "I have faith in logic. Tell me you're employing it because all of our lives depend on you making the right choice."

Commander Orilius took a deep breath then turned away. He began pacing back and forth while slicing the air in front of him with his razor-sharp knife. "How long has it been since your fight with the barbarians in the tavern?" he suddenly asked.

"About three months," Vlain replied.

"I've been busy during that time," Prydus said with a sly, secretive smile. "While you and the other officers were working on the new fortresses, I was sending scouts and local trackers into the Wild. Regrettably, lives were lost, but we learned a great secret. There's a woodlander village only a few miles from Hadrian's Wall. The beastmen refer to it as Algos. You'll attack it then withdraw back to the safety of Fort Faldin. The enemy will undoubtedly seek retribution, which is when we'll use the legion's latest weapons against them."

"Let me guess. Snill finally made his war engines," Vlain replied.

"Yes, and let me tell you, their effects are awesome to behold!"

"That may be, but I'm more concerned about what happens while we're in the Wild. Catapults and ballistae are too big and cumbersome to take with us. We could be ambushed, outmaneuvered, overwhelmed. It's too great a risk," Vlain countered.

"Not if you consider another brilliant creation of Snill's," Prydus excitedly proclaimed.

"Do tell," Vlain unenthusiastically replied.

"You're obviously familiar with a typical crossbow, but you probably haven't heard about a repeating crossbow. I'm telling you, it's an ingenious design," Prydus said. He paused to pick a long, wooden crossbow up from his desk, then handed it to Vlain. "The magazine holds twenty bolts, which are gravity-fed down onto the tiller. The shooter has only to push this arming lever back and up to reset the drawstring before it's ready to shoot the next bolt. Go on. Give it a try," Prydus said, pointing at a small target, which had been placed in front of a pile of sandbags by the tent wall.

Vlain held the crossbow up to his face, pulled the trigger, and watched as a bolt shot out of the tiller at an incredible speed. The ten-inch long, steel dart plowed through the wooden target then buried itself in the sandbags behind it. Vlain pushed the arming lever in the rear back and then up to reset the drawstring. As soon as he had done so, another bolt dropped down from the magazine to land snugly in the tiller. He fired and rapidly pushed the arming lever over and over again until all of the bolts had been spent. It had taken him less than thirty seconds to shoot all twenty bolts.

"Not bad," Vlain grudgingly admitted. "What's the range?"

"It's most effective from one hundred to two hundred feet out, with a maximum range of five hundred feet. Have you ever heard of such a thing? I'm telling you, it's a war changer!"

Vlain nodded in agreement. "So you plan to arm all of us with these for the attack on Algos?"

"Precisely, which is one of the reasons I don't think we'll lose. You'll be able to fire much faster than even their best archers, and the steel bolts are swift enough to punch through light armor and thin shields at close range."

"You said, 'I'll be able to fire much faster than even their best archers'." Vlain quoted. "Tell me, dear commander, do you intend on staying in the rear and thereby miss all the fighting?"

"With such capable leadership guiding my legionnaires, there's no need for me to be there," Prydus explained. "I'll stay here with the maps and models and guide your movements with the help of a mage mirror. Besides, in the rare event that the battle goes against us, it will be up to me to lead the remaining twenty-five hundred legionnaires."

"It's so strange," Vlain said with an amused smile.

"What's that?" Prydus asked.

"To meet a wanna-be grand general who's afraid of fighting."

For a second, it looked as if Prydus was about to lunge at Vlain with the knife, but if he was, he soon rethought it and abruptly turned away. He turned back around a moment later with a furious, trembling scowl. Vlain knew he would have died on the spot if looks could kill.

"I assure you, colonel, I'll wield my sword when the time comes. And let me assure you. It'll be like nothing you've ever seen," he said with a smirk.

"Is that so?" Vlain asked in a bored tone. "And what was your second reason for believing we'll win?"

"The timing of our assault," Prydus resumed. "One of our mages accompanied the scouts and tracker I sent in. He cast a spell that allowed him to understand two woodlanders while he eavesdropped from behind a tree. Apparently, the beast-men worship an animal god called the White Stag, whom they honor every autumn in a celebration called Walperen. We'll attack the morning after they've been up all night drinking and doing Jaina knows what. They'll be so hungover and tired that you should easily overcome them! Especially when you factor in our new, magnificent crossbows."

"I see," Vlain said with a nod. He hated to admit it, but Prydus's plan had some merit. "How many woodlanders live in Algos?"

"Our scouts estimate around one thousand."

"Estimate?" Vlain asked with a sour expression.

"They couldn't exactly walk from hut to hut to count them all," Prydus said, rolling his eyes. "They had to watch their comings and goings while not getting caught and while trying not to recount the same individuals. That is their best estimate, given those limitations."

"So we don't know their true strength," Vlain said, arching an eyebrow.

"It's around one thousand," Prydus said decisively. "I trust my scouts."

I'm glad to know you trust someone besides yourself, Vlain thought. "And what will our troop strength be on this assault?" he asked.

"Come, take a look," Prydus said, beckoning Vlain over to a map that he had laid out on his desktop. "You'll lead a force of five hundred men up this forest road, which leads directly into the village. Even after partying all night, the woodlanders will eventually rally. But worry not, Captain Caladin will emerge from the west of the forest with a force of five hundred, and Captain Oudeteros will do so as well, but from the east. You'll crush them between your combined forces!" the young commander slammed his knife down into the "village" on the map.

"It's a sound enough plan," Vlain admitted. "But there's still a lot that can go wrong. Caladin and Oudeteros could get lost in the forest while trying to rende..."

"Not likely," Prydus cut in. "They'll be guided by scouts who've been out there already."

"Well, you said you lost some scouts while trying to acquire this information. What if they were tortured into sharing your plans with the woodlanders."

"Not possible," Prydus said. "I hadn't formed this plan yet when they were lost."

"That's good to know, but our mere presence in the forest indicates a hostile intent. The woodlanders might be on greater guard than before."

Prydus shook his head in disagreement. "Unless it's a truly massive force, then we have nothing to fear. Our crossbows will enable us to defeat an army several times bigger than our own."

"For the sake of the men, I hope you're right," Vlain said uneasily.

Prydus stared at him doubtfully for a second. "Vlain, I chose you to lead the primary assault force because you have experience fighting the woodlanders and because of your illustrious reputation.

Tell me, have I chosen wrong?"

Vlain gave him a hard look. "We both know I'm the best man for the job. It's just a big risk to take. We'll be leaving the safety of our fort far behind while advancing deep into enemy territory. If the woodlanders can assemble a big enough force while we're there, then..."

"We won't be there long enough for them to coordinate a large counter-attack," Prydus cut in. "After you've cut down all opposition, you and the other officers are to retreat from Algos as quickly as possible."

"What's the point of taking the village if we're just gonna give it up?" Vlain asked. "To kill exhausted revelers in their sleep for sport?"

"As I mentioned earlier, the foremost reason is to instill a desire for revenge in the woodlanders. Their need for retribution will drive them out of the safety of the forest and south of the Wild. Once they come out into the open, our catapults and ballistae will devastate them. The second reason is to acquire prisoners to press for information, which will shape our future actions. You must admit, it's a daring plan."

"Daring? Yes, but there's also much that could go wrong."

"Of course, that's the nature of war." Vlain opened his mouth to object, but Commander Orilius cut him off. "You have your orders, colonel. Train your men to use the new crossbows in the morning and start getting the supplies you'll need for the assault. You leave in three days. You're dismissed," Prydus said with a wave of his hand.

Vlain wanted to throttle Prydus due to his haughty tone, but he contained his anger. He nodded, saluted him, then turned on his heel and left. Vlain looked up at the sky after he had left the tent and its sentries behind.

"Jaina, if you're up there listening, I have a favor to ask. Please protect my men during this assault. They don't deserve to die just to further Prydus's ambitions. Can you do that for me?"

Vlain studied the sky for several moments, but if She had heard his words, She gave no indication. He sighed in frustration, then walked back to his tent.

As soon as Vlain left, Prydus sat down in front of his desk and opened the bottom drawer. He reached down to snatch a small, golden tincture jar, unscrewed the lid, and gazed in wonder at the glistening, translucent powder within it. He shoved his little finger into his mouth then dipped it into the tiny, see-through crystals. Prydus put his finger back into his mouth and sucked the powder off. Several seconds later, his breath caught in his throat, and his pupils rapidly dilated. It felt like lightning was coursing through his veins, but instead of burning him, it strengthened him.

The cells in his body cried out in ecstasy as an empowering warmth radiated throughout them.

"When the moment's right, Vlain, I'll defeat you and take your title of invincibility. Your time has come and gone, but mine has only begun," he said in a hard voice.

THE BLESSING

Chapter 5

"By the White Stag! You look just like her," Haephius said in a voice raw with emotion. The fawn stepped back to stare at his daughter with a mixture of adoration and sorrow. Adoration for the spirit and form of his late wife that now resided in his daughter, and sorrow for the constant reminder of her loss. Odera was gone forever and yet ever-present.

Maiva twirled around several times, showing off the sky cloak Haephius had created with the help of magic. The enchanted fabric reflected the current conditions of the sky and displayed all the familiar constellations in stunning detail. Silver white pinpricks of light twinkled with bewitching beauty across the black cloak as the young fawn danced about in the cottage.

"Please don't cry, poppa!" Maiva said when she saw the tears glistening in her father's eyes. "I won't wear it if it brings you pain." She started to take the cloak off, but Haephius stopped her.

"No. It's yours now. Wear it with pride, and dance with joy tonight! Celebrate your mother and honor the sacrifice she made." His eyes were still glistening, but no tears fell. The blacksmith had regained control of his emotions. He was more enamored with the sight of the sky cloak on Maiva than the grief it had brought to the surface.

"We should be going," Maiva said, pulling him from his thoughts. "I promised Zenda we'd meet her by the old birch."

"I know," the middle-aged fawn replied. "Here," he said as he handed her a green candle. He grabbed a brown one from the mantle above the fireplace, then turned and led them to the door. "We're not forgetting anything, are we?"

"No, poppa," Maiva said as they stepped out into the night.

They were immediately swept into a steady stream of woodland revelers as they poured through the village road on their way to the Meadow of Knowing. Maiva's eyes were wide with excitement, and her smile was full of mirth as she spoke to friends and neighbors she hadn't seen in years. They were so happy to see her after her long absence from the Wild. She had spoken to many of them in the days preceding the Walperen festival. However, they still made her feel like royalty by nodding deferentially at her. Woodlanders placed high honor on those who survived harsh ordeals with their integrity intact. Thus, Maiva had become a local celebrity.

The young fawn jumped up and down when she saw her dear friend Zenda waiting patiently beneath the branches of a birch tree. Zenda was one of those rare woodlanders who lacked horns and had the spotted hind legs of a deer. She wore a wreath of fragrant wildflowers, and her long, red hair flowed down to her lower back. As always, her large, doe-like eyes were bright and alert.

"Maiva!" she exclaimed as she raced forward to embrace her long-lost friend. The fawns held each other for several moments. Haephius cleared his throat and reminded them they had a timetable to stick to. Maiva reluctantly stepped back, which allowed Zenda to see her shimmering cloak.

"Oh, how beautiful!" Zenda exclaimed. "Wasn't that your mother's?"

"It was," Maiva stated proudly. "She'll be at the ceremony tonight in spirit if not in body." With that said, she took her friend by the hand. The two of them skipped down the old woodland path together. Haephius struggled to keep up. Most of the woodlanders were either drunk, high, or in a forgiving mood, so they didn't mind being jostled about by the young, exuberant fawns.

Maiva took a deep breath and suddenly stopped when she saw

the familiar, starlit Meadow of Knowing. Zenda gave her hand a reassuring squeeze, prompting her to continue on down the trail. "Come along, we mustn't keep Him waiting," she said teasingly.

Maiva gave her a wide smile, which caused dimples to form on her round cheeks. She squeezed Zenda's hand, then looked back at her father. He nodded, which was his way of saying: "Go on ahead. I'll find you." That was all Maiva needed. The two of them raced off into the meadow.

Several druids stood in the center of the clearing. They wore dark, green hooded cloaks, which obscured their faces, and were huddled together as they fervently chanted prayers to their forest god. The woodland revelers streamed into the meadow then formed a vast circle around the druids. Maiva and Zenda exchanged excited looks as the chanting grew in volume. Their ears began to buzz from the noise while spatial distortions flickered in and out of existence all around them. The air was pregnant with magic, and a rainbow sheen hovered just above the glistening grass.

The young fawns were about to lend their voices to the cacophony when an old satyr druid approached them, bearing a basket full of wild mushrooms. He reached down to grab a clump of them with gnarled fingers, then offered them to Maiva and Zenda. They thanked him, tossed them into their mouths, chewed them up, and swallowed them. Since neither of them had eaten that night, it didn't take long before they felt the effects. Maiva gradually began to see the multi-colored auras of all those around her. Her eyes were dazzled by the rich, liquid lights as they trailed along behind the ecstatic dancers. Zenda felt like she was floating above the ground as they danced in a ring around the druids.

Suddenly, the druids clasped hands, then tilted their heads back to stare up at the star-studded sky. They called out to the White Stag in one magically amplified voice. A hush fell over the revelers as they watched the stars rearrange themselves to form a new constellation resembling that of a buck with huge antlers. Maiva could barely believe her eyes when the star Stag began running through the black sky as if it were a field. It grew darker in the meadow since the Stag's image had been formed by absorbing all of the stars. The celestial "animal" suddenly stopped running to look down at the woodlanders. Without warning, it leaped down from the sky to plummet to the ground like a silvery-white meteor. Many of those assembled held up their arms to shield themselves from a violent collision, but none came. The glowing Stag landed gently and nimbly on the grass, then began to run around the meadow with boundless energy.

Maiva's jaw dropped open in amazement while Zenda sighed in wonder. Maiva realized the star animal was several times larger than an actual stag after it ran past a section of revelers. Her eyes now had something known and familiar to gauge the star being's size. It continued to leap and frolic about the meadow as the druids lifted their voices in song. They raised their arms to encourage the gathering to sing with them:

"The forest has all that we need.
We live in the paradise of Findalora
where the White Stag reigns,
where the Hart of the forest dwells!

Why should we ever leave?
The mighty trees shelter us,
and the animals nurture us.
Paradise is a life in the forest!

I sing praise to the White Stag!
May He rule Findalora forever,
where the redwoods grow,
and the unicorns run free!

I was born in this forest
and I will die here as well.
My last breath will be spent
in the White Stag's green halls!"

Tears of joy streamed down Maiva's face as the assembly sang the last stanza. She looked over to see that Zenda had also been moved by the song and by the radiant beauty of the star animal whose silver light suffused the meadow. Suddenly, it turned, then gracefully bounded straight toward Maiva.

The young fawn was transfixed as the celestial being stopped in front of her. She was mesmerized by its luminous, glowing body, which consisted of thousands of tiny silver and white lights. They churned and sparkled like miniature suns as the star animal lowered its snout until it gently touched Maiva's forehead. A warm, pleasant sensation flooded through her entire being. She felt so alive at that moment!

The living constellation slowly backed away from Maiva, turned around, and began running at an incredible speed. For a second, it looked like it was about to run straight into the knot of druids, but it leaped into the sky before it could do so. Its star body blazed with silvery-white energy as it flew up into the heavens. It "landed" in the black field of the sky once more, then looked down at the revelers below. With a blinding flash of light, the stars forming its body shot outward to resume their normal positions in the night sky. All of the old, familiar constellations were visible once again. It was as if the celestial Stag had never existed.

Most woodlanders cheered in wonder, but Maiva felt a stinging sadness now that He was gone. She didn't know how much of what she had witnessed was a product of the mushrooms she had ingested or was a result of the illusory spell cast by the druids. She only knew the emotions she felt were real. She felt deeply connected to the White Stag; a burning kinship and a fierce love had sprouted in her heart when it had touched her head. Maiva didn't understand the connection yet, but that was all right. She knew it would take time to process the miracle she had just been at the heart of.

"Maiva!" Zenda whispered. "There's an image of a star on your forehead!"

"What?" she asked in disbelief.

"It's violet and delicate and beautiful!"

Suddenly, her father was there. He leaned forward to stare in bewilderment at the star on her forehead. Haephius backed away while shaking his head in awe.

"You've been blessed!" he exclaimed. "The White Stag has smiled upon you!"

"What does that mean?" she asked with a mixture of elation and uncertainty.

"Only time will tell," Haephius replied. Soon, dozens of woodlanders were crowding Maiva, trying to get a look at the glowing star on her forehead. They all jostled for position as they tried to touch it while others knelt before her and began to pray. An old male centaur begged her to bless him. Maiva was quickly becoming overwhelmed by all the attention.

Haephius, who had seen her growing look of alarm, grabbed her by the hand and pulled her out of the throng. Haephius, Maiva, and Zenda ran out of the meadow and into a deserted section of the forest. They didn't stop until they had put considerable distance between themselves and the other woodlanders.

"Are you alright?" Haephius asked after they stopped.

"Yes," Maiva answered. She was winded but relieved to be away from the crowd. "But with all of the people gathered there, why did He choose me?"

Zenda reached for her hand and smiled encouragingly at her. "Trust in Him, and all will be revealed," she said.

Haephius took her other hand and squeezed it. "Perhaps it's because you suffered so long at the hands of Man, and this is your gift for enduring such pain. Or maybe it's because He sensed your pure heart and thus knew you were worthy. Either way, it's the highest compliment one could receive. Don't fret over the meaning right now. Tonight is for celebrating, and this holy sign gives us all the more reason to do so."

"Yes!" Zenda exclaimed. "Let's head back to my cottage! I have six bottles of wine and a bushel of Lanin weed waiting for us. Let's drink and smoke, then dance around the White Stag's statue in my garden until sunrise!"

"How can I resist such an offer?" Maiva asked.

Maiva hugged her and then hugged her father. The three of them set off in the direction of

Zenda's cottage. Maiva began to feel like her old self again as they made their way through the dense bushes and red ferns that covered the forest floor. The trio soon began singing the song they had heard when the druids had called the White Stag down from the heavens. Maiva had never felt so happy or so at peace as she did just then.

***

Her dream started out with a burst of silvery, white colors, reminiscent of the miracle she had experienced in the meadow, but then it took a dark turn. The White Stag vanished among the trees as Maiva tried to catch up to it, then a cloying fog enveloped her. The fawn lost sight of her father, Zenda, and all the other woodlanders in the meadow. She stood alone and shivering in the cold, unnatural mist. It was then that she saw a pair of eyes glowing

121

with a harsh, orange light. They kept drawing closer to her no matter how fast she ran.

"Who are you?!" she called out. "What do you want?" But the only answer she received was cruel, heartless laughter. "Stay away!" she shouted as she ran, but she lost her footing and fell. Maiva was just about to get up to resume running when a hand clamped around her wrist and roughly hauled her up from the ground.

"You're mine now, little fawn!" the hard voice said. The man's eyes were the color of the setting sun. "I only released you so I could track you back to your den!"

Maiva bolted up from the soft, fragrant grass where she had collapsed after downing a bottle of huckleberry wine. She shook her head from side to side to shake the effects of the dreaded dream and to help herself wake up. Her father was snoring loudly as he slept blissfully beneath an old, bent sycamore. He cradled an empty bottle in his arms that had been filled with cloudberry wine. Haephius had a lecherous smile on his face as he moaned in pleasure. Maiva frowned at the sight and looked away. She then stood and gazed up at the sky, trying to gauge what time it was. It felt like early morning, just a few hours past midnight.

A sharp pain lanced through her forehead. It radiated out from the spot where the god-given star had formed on her skin. A vision of slaughtered woodlanders lying in the streets of Algos filled her mind. She heard the cries of the dying and wounded. She smelled their blood on the wind. The awful premonition hit her with such force that it left her reeling. Maiva instantly knew what she had to do.

"Get up!" she shouted at her father. Haephius jerked in his sleep. Maiva knelt down, then shook him by the shoulders until his eyes finally snapped open. He stared at her in bleary-eyed confusion. "Father! I need you to get up!"

"What's the matter?" he asked groggily.

"The village is under attack, or at least it soon will be," she exclaimed.

"How? How could you possibly know that?" he asked with wide eyes.

"I...I can't explain, but I know it to be true. Where's Zenda?"

"I don't know..." Maiva scanned the backyard until she saw her slumbering friend. Zenda had passed out in a flower bed next to a gurgling fountain. The fawn raced over and shook her until she woke up.

"Is it morning already?" Zenda asked sleepily. The foggy-headed fawn was regretting having drunk two bottles of strawberry wine.

"I can't tell you how I know, but our village will soon be attacked. I need you to get up and come with us." Maiva's urgent tone roused Zenda as much as her dire words did.

"We're under attack? By who?"

"By Man. They sent soldiers to kill us."

"But how could you know…?"

"I just know," Maiva said as she extended her hand to Zenda. She took it then Maiva pulled her up from the ground.

"Do you have any weapons?" Haephius asked Zenda. He was still rubbing the sleep out of his eyes, but his mind was starting to process the situation.

"Just an old hunting knife, a bow, a quiver full of arrows..."

"Go get them. We'll leave for our cabin as soon as you return."

Maiva smiled warmly at him. "Thank you for believing in me," she said.

"You're my daughter, and you were blessed by the Stag last night," Haephius replied. "I'd be crazy not to." He walked over to the fountain, squatted down, cupped his hands, and plunged them into the cool water. The fawn took several drinks then splashed some water on his face. "Come, drink. You'll need it after all the wine you had." Maiva did as he said. The water soothed her parched throat and helped sharpen her mind. She drank as much as she could, then dunked her face beneath the surface. The fawn pulled her head out a few seconds later and then used her cloak to dry off.

"I'm ready," Zenda said. She had buckled a leather belt to her waist from which hung a sheath containing a knife and had strapped a quiver full of arrows to her back. The fawn held a longbow in her hand. Her expression was fearful yet determined.

The trio stealthily made their way through the forest until they came upon the outer limits of the village. It was dreadfully quiet.

A wave of despair washed over Maiva. *Have we arrived too late?* She wondered. Her fears were soon allayed when she saw the sleeping forms of dozens of woodlanders passed out on the grass. Maiva sighed in relief. Some of the revelers still held bottles of wine in their hands, and some even clasped half-eaten turkey legs. Most of them had fallen asleep beneath the trees, but others had passed out beneath tables, on benches, and in chairs. Some even slept on low-lying tree branches. Such was the after-effect of the autumnal holiday known as Walperen.

"We should wake them up," Maiva said as she moved toward the sleeping figures.

"No," Haephius replied. "It would take too long, and many of them wouldn't believe us. "We need to sound the Bell of Warning. Then they'll know the danger is real. But there's something I need to get from home first."

Haephius took the lead, then guided them to the cabin he shared with Maiva. The trio quietly slipped into the small, shadow-swept dwelling. The blacksmith headed straight back to the bedroom.

Maiva ignited an oil lamp in the living room, then paced back and forth as she waited for her father.

Zenda stared nervously at her. "Are you going to tell me what's going on?" she asked.

"I had a dream. No, a premonition. Well, both," she began. "Anyway, I saw hundreds of dead Findalorans lying in the streets of our village. It was awful."

"Sounds like it, but how do you know it will happen?"

"Because of this," Maiva replied, pointing to her forehead. Zenda's eyes narrowed, and her brow furrowed as she grabbed Maiva by the shoulders and brought her to a stop. She leaned close to inspect her forehead, then shook her head in confusion. "What is it?" Maiva asked.

"It's gone," Zenda replied.

"That can't be."

"I'm telling you, there isn't the faintest trace of it on your skin. It's as if it was never there."

Maiva was dumbfounded. "Well, maybe you can only see it in the dark," she wondered.

Zenda turned the oil lamp off, thereby plunging the room back into inky darkness. She sighed in amazement as the star reformed on Maiva's forehead. The lines forming the image were spidery thin and gave off a faint, violet light. "You were right," Zenda said. "I can see it plain as day again." She turned the round knob on the lighter, then reignited the wick with a match. The room glowed with warm light once more.

Maiva was about to say more when Haephius walked back into the room. The fawn was holding two medium-sized wooden boxes, and he was clad from head to hoof in leather and steelwood armor. He had another set of armor draped over his shoulder. Steelwood was an extremely hard wood that was almost as tough as tempered steel yet much lighter. It was greatly prized due to its remarkable durability and thus made excellent armor, shields, weapons, and tools. Haephius handed Maiva one of the boxes, then gave her the armor.

"What's this, poppa?" Maiva asked as she took the box.

"Open it and see."

Maiva set the box down on a nearby table, then opened the lid. She gazed down at an elegantly carved wooden slingshot handle connected to a length of animal sinew that formed the sling. A pair of steel-mesh gloves rested beside it, and a bulging black velvet bag rested beside the gloves. Maiva was about to open the bag when Haephius placed his hand on hers.

"Not so fast," he cautioned her. "Put the gloves on first." Maiva did as she was told. The gloves fit her perfectly. She then opened the velvet bag and peered down at what must have been over a over a hundred steel balls, each of which were covered by sharp spikes. The balls were roughly the size of cherries. She plucked one from the bag, then held it up to study it from every angle. She felt a fluid sloshing back and forth within the ball as she shook it.

"What's in there?" she asked.

"Viper venom," Haephius said with a wicked grin. "It'll kill someone in less than a minute. There's a reservoir inside the balls that holds the poison. When one hits its target, the sudden stop causes the venom to shoot out of the hollow spikes and straight into your enemy. Never handle them without first putting on the protective gloves, or it could be your last mistake. The venom probably won't exit the spikes unless the ball stops abruptly, but I still wouldn't risk it."

"Thanks for the warning," Maiva somberly replied.

"I made it for you because I remembered how good you were with a slingshot when you were little. I was going to give it to you on your eighteenth birthday, but you were taken from me before I could do so," he finished sadly.

"But I'm back now, father. That's what counts," Maiva replied.

"We should hurry up," Zenda said. "If there's going to be an attack, then every second counts."

"Right you are," Haephius said. "We'll leave as soon as your armor's on, Maiva. I'd give you some as well, Zenda, but the rest of it's stored at the armory."

"That's alright. I'll take cover behind the trees," she replied.

"What's in the other box?" Maiva asked as she set her shimmering sky cloak down on a chair, then wiggled and squirmed into the suit of wooden armor.

"I thought you'd never ask," Haephius replied excitedly. The blacksmith set his box on the floor, then opened the lid to reveal two black, steel mesh gloves similar to the ones in Maiva's box. The most notable difference, however, was the symbol of a lightning bolt on the backside of each glove. Haephius slipped each glove on, then held both hands above his head and said the word: "Genlin!" The air around the gloves crackled and hummed with energy, then two bluish-white bolts of electricity formed in his palms. Maiva and

Zenda stared at his hands with wide eyes. Haephius let the bolts continue to flash and crackle for a few seconds. Then he said the word: "Danlin." The bolts shimmered out of existence, leaving behind thin wisps of vapor in the air. The smell of ozone permeated the cabin as he lowered his hands to his sides.

"A potent weapon, indeed!" Maiva said in awe.

"You have attained the power of the gods," Zenda said.

"Well, I wouldn't go that far," Haephius said with a triumphant smile. "I call them lightning gloves. When I throw the bolts at a living thing, it brings instant death."

"I'm ready, poppa," Maiva said as she finished adjusting her armor.

"Right, but why do I feel as if I'm forgetting something?" he asked himself while nervously tapping a hoof against the hardwood floor. "Aha, shields! I think I have enough for all of us." With that said, he raced back down the hall to his bedroom. He soon returned, holding three circular steel wood shields. He handed one to Maiva, one to Zenda, and slipped the last one onto his forearm. "I'll go ring the bell in the village square while you two warn the king," With that said, the trio exited the cabin.

"Be safe, father," Maiva whispered right before they parted ways.

"And you as well, love," Haephius shot back, then he was gone.

Maiva and Zenda raced down the road. They had almost reached the great lodge in the center of the village, which served as the king's quarters whenever he visited when the Bell of Warning shattered the still morning air. The ominous sound caused the two burly centaur sentries, standing guard before the door, to spring to attention. They were anxiously looking around when Maiva and Zenda skidded to a stop before them.

"Who are you? State your business!" one of them barked.

"I'm Maiva Delinor and this is Zenda Tallow. We have an urgent message for the king," Maiva informed him.

"Which is?"

"We will soon be attacked."

"I assume this is linked to the tolling bell?" the guardsman asked.

"Yes. Now, please let us in. There isn't much time!" Maiva pressed.

"We should do as she asks," the other guard said. "She's a favorite of the king's, and word has it she was blessed by the Great Stag last night. Just look at the star on her brow."

The centaur guard leaned closer to stare at the star mark in fascination. "You may enter, blessed one." He pushed the heavy, oak door open with a brawny arm, then stepped back.

Maiva and Zenda dashed to the far back of the lodge, where a fire burned low in the fireplace.

The lodge was dimly lit with candelabras that hung from the rafters. An old, diminutive satyr sat in a roomy, cushioned seat in front of the fire. Maiva had never seen such pure white fur on a Findaloran before. The elder wore a strange metal frame on his goatish face. The frame contained two circular pieces of glass through which the satyr viewed the world. Maiva marveled at the strange contraption. What was even stranger was that this odd, little satyr was staring at ink marks on sheets of paper that had been bound together between two leather covers. Maiva had heard about a thing called reading that Man did, but she had rarely seen one of her own kind engage in the activity. She wondered what other oddities the strange old satyr would reveal to her.

"How may I help you?" the old Findaloran asked without looking up from his book.

"We're here to see the king, sir," Maiva replied.

The satyr arched an eyebrow, then placed a marker in his book, closed it, and looked up to study her. His eyes narrowed as he took all of her in.

"You're the fawn who was blessed last night," he stated matter-of-factually.

"Yes. I'm Maiva Delinor. What's your name?"

"Oshur Whitehoof," he said. He raised a hand to stroke the long goatee that hung down his chin. "I'm the king's personal assistant and scribe."

"It's an honor to meet you," Maiva said with a curtsy. Zenda smiled and followed suit.

"The honor is mine, blessed one. Pray, what requires the attention of the king?"

"I recently had a vision in which Algos was attacked. Many Findalorans will die should it come to pass. Please inform the king so that we may mount a defense against the coming danger."

"Thus the tolling bell," the satyr said with a nod. "And who was the aggressor in your vision?" he asked.

"Man," Maiva stated simply.

Oshur set his book to the side and quickly stood up. "Wait here while I fetch the king."

Maiva and Zenda watched as the small satyr walked over to a nearby door. He wrapped on the stout oak barrier three times. "My king, we are under attack!" he shouted through the barrier. There was no reply at first. Oshur raised his fist to knock again, but before he could do so, a supernaturally deep voice rumbled out a response.

"I shall be out shortly," the voice said.

"You must excuse us. The Bell of Knowing hasn't been sounded in so long that I'm afraid we've all grown quite complacent. And, of course, the effects of last night's festival doesn't help matters," the satyr explained as he walked back to the fawns.

Just then, the door soon opened and out stepped a massive centaur. The king had the lower half of a draft horse and the upper torso of a muscular man, and his face was veiled in shadow. His pupil-less eyes glowed with an eerie white light, and thick ram horns curled down from the top of his head. He was covered from head to hoof with short, gray fur. A bone-white crown had been perfectly cut to accommodate the ram horns on his head. Maiva and Zenda felt an overwhelming power and authority radiating out from him. They immediately bowed to him.

"Rise, oh blessed one," the king said with a booming voice. Maiva did as she was told. The king walked over to her and spread his arms wide. She rushed forward to embrace him. Her face sank into the soft fur that covered his chest. A dimpled smile formed on her face as she heard his strong heartbeat thundering away. "I have missed you, little fawn," The centaur rumbled.

"And I have missed you, King Caernos," Maiva replied.

He stepped back to look down at her face while resting his calloused hands on her slender shoulders. Maiva could almost make out his noble, leonine face; however, the perpetual plane of shadow that lingered there prevented her from doing so. It was a well-known fact that shadows clung to King Caernos the way frost clings to a stone in winter. This strange attribute had earned him the title of the Grey King. It was, however, a valuable trait to have because it rendered him virtually invisible in shadow and in darkness. Some said it was an enchantment his mother had placed on him at birth. Others said it was simply a natural trait. Maiva didn't care one way or the other. She just wished she could see his smile because she felt he had one just then.

"I would have come for you myself had I not been battling dragons in the north," Caernos confided.

"I understand," Maiva replied.

"I heard the news about your mother. I'm so sorry for your loss," he said.

"Thank you, my king. She must now live on in my thoughts and actions."

"Then you shall accomplish wondrous things, for Odera was an exceptional shield-maiden. Boudika will miss her greatly. Now, why did I awaken to the Bellof Warning?" he asked.

"I received a vision this morning that warned me of a battle that will be waged in these very streets. Algos will soon be attacked by Man."

"Ah, I see. The Stag's star has given you far sight."

"It must have. I never had prophetic visions or dreams before."

"Then it would appear I have arrived in Algos just in time to defend her," the king said. He looked over at the young fawn, who was still kneeling to Maiva's right. "Rise, child of Findalora," he rumbled. She did as he commanded. "What is your name?"

"Zenda, your majesty," she said with a curtsy.

"Well met, Zenda," he replied. "Now, I have a task for each of you. Maiva, I want you to gather as many younglings as you can. Take them through the green gate north of the Meadow of Knowing. It will take you to a safe place hundreds of leagues from here."

"Yes, my king," Maiva responded.

"Zenda, you shall gather the old and infirm and take them through the green gate by Tellin's Pond. It leads to caves that are full of provisions. Your charges will be comfortable there for many weeks. You both have your orders; now go!" As soon as the fawns had left the hall, the king focused his glowing gaze on Oshur. "Tell the sentries to spread the word that we're under attack. After that, go to the armory and tell them to start arming the people."

"Yes, my liege," Oshur said. He bowed, then raced out of the lodge to carry out his orders.

King Caernos let out a deep, disappointed sigh. *"Is there no end to the violence and bloodshed? How many wars must I fight during my reign?"* he thought. He then walked back into his room to don his weapons and armor.

Chapter 6

"It's dark as Thania's heart out here!" Bollis harshly whispered.

"Quiet!" Vlain growled as he looked back at him.

The cook sunk into a sullen silence after that. Vlain understood his frustration, but he couldn't risk using torches or magical light sources without giving away their position. To do so could mean walking straight into an ambush. Unfortunately, the forest was incredibly dark on account of it being a moonless night. Only the stars offered any illumination, but it was faint, to say the least. Luckily, Vlain's scouts could navigate with little difficulty since all they had to do was follow the smooth dirt road until it led them into Algos. Vlain felt bad, however, for Captain Oudeteros and Captain Caladin's forces because they would have to navigate through the dense, pathless forest. Then again, they had brought along local scouts to help them find the way.

Vlain's thoughts were interrupted when a fiery, silver streak shot down from the night sky to plunge into the forest. The fighter thought it was a flash of lightning at first, but then he remembered it was a clear, cloudless night. He tried to gauge how far away the silver bolt had been from their location when it hit the ground. Perhaps, three or four leagues? It was hard to be sure since distances could be deceiving at night.

Suddenly, it got darker. It had already been dark, but now it looked like they were all marching in a cave. Vlain could barely see the ground below as he rode along on his white charger. He looked up to search for the twinkling stars he knew must be overhead, but they were nowhere to be found. It was as if someone had snuffed them all out at once. He shook his head in bewilderment and tried to figure out what was going on when he noticed a bright light emanating from a section of the forest. He wasn't sure if he could trust his eyes, but it appeared to be coming from the area where the silver streak had landed. Vlain wondered what in Taloria could have produced such a powerful light. Even the combined glow from a thousand torches couldn't have equaled it, and besides, torchlight would have been the color of fire. No, this was something else altogether. Was it magic?

They plodded along in the inky darkness for about twenty minutes. Suddenly, the silvery-white light shot up from the forest as abruptly as it had descended. There was an explosion of light in the heavens. Vlain had to look away, for his eyes had grown accustomed to the unnatural darkness. He risked looking up again a few seconds later, only to see that the stars had all returned to their previous positions. Vlain shook his head in confusion. It didn't make any sense.

They rode along for a few more uneventful hours. Although the wind sometimes blew the sounds of merry-making their way, they didn't encounter a single soul on the road. Vlain figured the woodlanders were all in one location for a ceremony or a feast in honor of their holiday.

Vlain soon realized one of his scouts was riding back to him. He came to a stop mere inches away, then leaned forward in his saddle.

"It looks as if the whole village is awake, and most of the woodlanders are armed," the legionnaire said. "They must have gotten wind of our plans, colonel. What do you want to do?"

"Jaina's light!" Vlain swore softly under his breath.

They had clearly lost the element of surprise. Now, Vlain and his force of five hundred legionnaires would be marching straight into an armed and ready populace. That meant their deaths and casualties would be much higher than anticipated. The question was, could their new crossbows erase the woodlander's advantage of being prepared? Vlain had confidence in his men. He knew they were a well-trained and disciplined force that could quickly adapt to new fighting conditions. The fighter had also been impressed by Captain Snill's crossbow when he had tested it in Prydus's tent. Snill may have been unlikable, but he did have a mind for machines.

"We take the village as planned," Vlain said, thereby committing his men to a pitched battle in the dark. *We've come this far, and Prydus's plan has some merit,* Vlain thought. *If this attack draws the woodlanders out into the plains where we can defeat them with Snill's war engines, then they'll be more likely to sign a treaty. This means the war could end sooner rather than later, and with less loss of life for the legion,* he reasoned.

He told the scout to tell all of the platoon leaders what to expect in the village. The platoon leaders would, in turn, pass the information down until all five hundred men had been informed. Thus, both armies would be expecting the other tonight. The odds were getting more and more even by the minute. Vlain didn't care for it. He always sought to gain whatever advantages he could, but sometimes fate took them away.

"Shields up!" Vlain bellowed as they entered the village. "Expect archers on the rooftops!" he warned. "Bring your horses to a gallop. Close ranks with the enemy as quickly as you can! Attack! Attack!"

No sooner had the words left Vlain's mouth than he dug his heels into Viscol, urging the horse into a sprint. Arrows rattled off his shield as he shot past what looked like buildings and huts to either side of him. It was still so dark it was hard to be sure what they were. Vlain raised his repeating crossbow to fire at the dark figures that came together to block his path, but he decided not to fire at the last second. Instead, he prodded the warhorse to leap over the first line of defenders only to land right in their midst. Viscol crushed bones and savagely stomped on those beneath him. Before the woodlanders could recover, Vlain leaned down to whisper into his steed's ear.

"Rage!" was all he said, and it was all that was needed. Viscol's training took over. He reared back on his hind legs, and crashed his hooves down into the unfortunate souls in front of him. The horse shifted his weight to his front legs, then kicked back with his hind legs, sending broken fawns and satyrs flying away in all directions.

While Viscol raged, Vlain leveled his crossbow at the woodlanders, who surged toward him.

Steel bolts flew into their chests and faces, causing them to fall back in agony. Vlain squeezed the trigger and pumped the lever until all twenty bolts had been spent. Then, he dropped the crossbow, which was connected to the pommel of his saddle by a thin rope, pulled one of his orichalcum swords from its sheath, and charged forward. Again and again, he thrust his sword down into their teeming ranks until they fell back from him in terror. The beast-men and women didn't just fear his skill with the blade; they were terrified of his eyes, which had begun to glow with a harsh orange light.

Suddenly, Haephius appeared at the back of the throng. He smiled victoriously as he raised a hand into the air. The fawn said a word that Vlain was too far away to hear, and a bolt of lightning formed in his gloved palm. Haephius threw the lightning bolt while Vlain raised his steel shield to block it. The crackling bolt seared the darkness with an angry blue light. Vlain's broad shield absorbed the massive charge. The fighter clenched his teeth in pain as raw voltage overloaded his system. Fortunately, the interior of his shield was lined with a thick layer of leather to help absorb the impact from strikes. The forearm grip and strap, known as enarmes, were also made of leather. All of this insulation offered Vlain some protection, but he still received the shock of his life. His hair stood on end, his eyes shot wide open, and he tried to scream, but his vocal cords wouldn't obey him. He felt like his whole body was on fire. The fighter could only cling to his saddle in agony and wait until the shock subsided. Viscol shivered in pain as Vlain unknowingly shared the charge with his steed.

Plumes of steam rose off of Vlain's armored body. His breathing was labored and strained, and his heart beat erratically. Haephius smirked in victory, then raised his other hand. A bolt formed in the blacksmith's hand. He hurled it straight at Vlain. The fighter hadn't yet fully recovered, but he launched sideways out of his saddle none-the-less, thereby evading a shimmering lightening bolt. He then twisted in mid-air, dropped his sword, grabbed his crossbow, and a loaded magazine from his saddlebag.

Haephius marveled at the man's speed. He had never seen anyone move so fast in his life. The fawn raised his hand again, thereby summoning another bolt into existence. Vlain slammed the magazine down onto the crossbow's tiller, then started rapidly firing from where he had landed on the ground. The first three bolts struck the fawn in his steelwood armor, but the fourth one grazed his side. Haephius grunted in pain as the bolt rent the leather armor and sliced him open. The lightning bolt slipped out of the blacksmith's hand to land on a nearby satyr. The creature writhed in agony as a massive surge of voltage shot through him. Haephius fell back against a stone building and left a bloodstain on the wall as he did so. He grabbed his wound with a gloved hand and summoned a faint electrical current between his fingers to cauterize it. Haephius grunted in pain as the heat burned the wound closed.

Vlain smiled grimly, then pulled the trigger on his crossbow. Haephius raised his shield just in time to block the bolt, then ran away as quickly as his hooves would allow. Vlain shifted his attention from the fleeing fawn to the horde of woodlanders that had surrounded him. He snatched up his sword and leaped onto his steed. The fighter pulled his other sword from its sheath and plowed into the oncoming wave of villagers. Luckily for Vlain, the other legionnaires had finally fought their way to him. Belor and Paetro appeared on either side to help him drive the enemy back.

All of a sudden, the first rays of sunlight lit up the sky. The much-needed light allowed Vlain to see that they were in the center of the town square. The sunrise heartened the legionnaires, causing them to fight even harder. They finally got a good view of the battlefield, and who they were aiming at.

However, as they started to rally, Vlain saw several spears of blazing light shoot down from a nearby rooftop to land in a knot of legionnaires. Haephius had climbed up there and was now raining death down onto Vlain's troops. The fighter growled in anger as he watched a dozen men fall beneath the ceaseless, withering assault. Something had to be done about the fawn.

"Belor!" Vlain shouted.

"Over here, colonel!" came the reply.

"Kill that one with the glowing gloves!" he snarled while pointing at the fawn on the roof.

"Consider it done," Belor said.

The legionnaire and his steed shot off toward Haephius's silhouette. Vlain was glad to see Belor held a crossbow. He had objected to using the new weapon at first. Vlain figured it probably made the old-fashioned archer feel threatened, so he had tried a different tactic. He asked him to "test" it out for him, then critique it after the battle. Belor had grudgingly agreed, but Vlain could tell that the crossbow was growing on him. The archer was just as accurate with it as his longbow, but it had significantly increased his range.

Vlain figured the pesky fawn was as good as dead, considering

Belor's uncanny aim. Hence, he focused his attention back on the woodlanders. To his happy surprise, most of them had been driven down the street, away from the square. Vlain was about to join his troops in routing the villagers when he heard a commotion behind him.

He turned Viscol around just in time to witness King Caernos and his entourage of fifty centaur warriors as they poured out of a lodge and out onto the street. The woodlander king was a sight to behold in the gray morning twilight. He was clad in thick steelwood armor, with black leather beneath it, and a black, velvet cloak billowed out behind him as he reared back on his hind legs. His face was covered in shadow, his eyes blazed with a fell white light, and he wore a pale crown carved from the bone of some gigantic beast. Even from a distance, Vlain could feel the king's commanding presence.

The mighty centaur let out a long, booming war-cry, causing many a legionnaire to shudder in fear. The men heard their death in that primal challenge, and it turned their blood cold. Not all of the legionnaires were daunted, however. In fact, a force of over a hundred men suddenly rounded the lodge to come face to face with the centaur king and his royal guard. At first, Vlain watched with pride as his men fearlessly tore into the beast-men, but his expression soon turned to one of dismay.

King Caernos held a black sword aloft, resembling a claymore in design, but it looked like it had been carved from a single, massive diamond. The mighty king raised the glittering sword and brought it down onto the men again and again with devastating results. The dark blade carved through shields, helmets, chest plates, and swords as if they were all made of fragile ice. Nothing could withstand the lethal weapon, which the king wielded with a combination of animalistic fury and surgical precision. Vlain watched in numb rage as the proud monarch felled ten of his men in less than a minute.

Vlain spurred Viscol into a gallop, when he saw that Meris and Bollis were about to fight the king. He knew there was no way they could beat him, even if they fought as a team. The king's sword was simply too deadly. Vlain figured the black blade was either enchanted or made out of something unimaginably tough or maybe both. It looked heavy, but the king wielded it as if it was nothing more than a dagger. Vlain marveled at the centaur's strength as he and Viscol sped straight at him.

"Your village is surrounded! Fewer will die if you surrender," Meris said right before he swung his sword at him.

"There will be no surrender, invader! Now, prepare to meet your god," King Caernos rumbled as he swatted Meris's sword away.

Meris was surprised to hear the king speak in perfect Emblin, which was the official language of the Elamaran Empire. He was also surprised that he felt compelled to submit to the centaur's will. In fact, he fought a powerful urge to throw down his weapons and bow before him. The legionnaire shook his head to clear his thoughts, then parried an incoming thrust. He gritted his teeth from the strain as he turned the black blade aside. Unfortunately, it cut halfway through his own blade in the process. Meris swore in anger and threw his damaged sword at the king. The centaur batted it away with his shield, then lunged in for the kill. Meris, however, had since leveled his repeating crossbow at him. He pulled the trigger and cocked the lever several times, sending six bolts into the king at point-blank range. The centaur blocked three bolts with his wooden shield, but the other three slipped past his guard. Meris watched in disbelief as the bolts stopped in mid-air, mere inches from the king, then fell harmlessly to the ground.

"Careful, Bollis!" Meris shouted out to his friend, who was approaching King Caernos from the side. "This one's a coward. He has a magical, protective ward on him, so he can't be hurt."

"Then we'll just have to blast through it!" Bollis exclaimed.

He swung his mace at the centaur, but the black blade sliced it in half. The cook dropped the remains of the mace and swerved away while he readied his crossbow. Meris fired more bolts at the king, but those also failed to penetrate the invisible ward surrounding the centaur.

Vlain was just about to reach both men when a group of the king's royal guards suddenly converged to block his path. He tried to evade them, but they were too nimble. The fighter belted out a war cry, then tore into them with his flashing swords. He swung his blades so quickly that they were merely a blur, making it impossible for the guards to block all of his strikes. Eventually, Vlain slipped through the defenses of a centaur, scoring a lethal hit on his exposed neck. Down went the guard, but two more rushed forward to take his place. Vlain drove his blurring blades straight into them. He sliced a hand-off of one and disarmed the other one. Vlain then abruptly reversed the direction of his spinning swords. His tactic caught the unarmed one off balance. The centaur was instantly decapitated. The other guard cradled the bleeding stump where his hand had just been, allowing Vlain to stab him in the side. The fighter shot past the falling guard, only to encounter more of them. He furiously parried and blocked the thrusts from his new attackers' spears and axes.

Meanwhile, King Caernos reared back and raised his ebony sword high for a strike. Meris continuously fired the crossbow at the centaur, but the bolts all stopped short of hitting him, then fell to the ground just as the others had. The ward still held firm. Meris raised his shield to block the king's glittering, black blade. Vlain cursed in frustration. He knew the strange weapon would plow straight through his friend's shield. The sword seemed unnaturally sharp, and the king appeared stronger than even the minotaurs they had fought, as evidenced by how he casually flung the legionnaires out of his path. Vlain cursed again and tried to force the centaur guards back with a flurry of vicious attacks, but Meris and Bollis remained beyond his reach.

***

Hildin hurled his hatchet at a fawn that was about to throw a spear at his twin brother. The hatchet buried itself in the side of the woodlander's head. The legionnaire yanked it out, then rode back into the fray. Paetro continued fighting a female centaur, unaware that his brother had just saved his life. The woodlander charged forward and hurled a knife at him. Paetro dodged to the right, then fired his repeating crossbow twice. The centaur staggered back as two bolts sank into her chest. A bloody cough escaped her lips as she crashed to the ground. Paetro looked down at the pile of bodies on which she had fallen. The legionnaires were slowly winning, at least in this part of the village.

Just then, Hildin and Paetro heard a familiar voice rallying his men to attack. They both looked at the far end of the street as Oudeteros and his men burst out from the forest. He held his crossbow with one hand and the horse's reigns with the other as his rowan steed barreled down the road. Paetro smiled because he knew the stubborn knot of woodlanders they were fighting would soon be caught between themselves and Oudeteros's men.

Oudeteros signaled to Paetro, Hildin, and the other legionnaires to move to the side as he drew closer. The men had just gotten clear when a cloud of steel bolts filled the air. Oudeteros and his men fired again and again until only a score of woodlander were left standing. The captain drew his sword, raised his shield, and tore into the survivors. His men swiftly followed suit. Within a few seconds, all of the villagers had either fallen or fled into the forest.

"You make it look easy," Hildin said as he rode up to him with a wide grin.

"Nah, we just mopped them up after you all did the hard work,"

143

Oudeteros replied. "To be honest, though, I hadn't expected this much resistance. Looks like they were ready for us," he said suspiciously as he gazed at the fallen villagers.

"They were," Paetro gloomily replied. "We don't know how it happened, but word got out about our attack. The beasties were armed and ready to fight when we arrived."

"I wonder how they..." but Oudeteros was cut off by a booming sound behind him. The legionnaires turned to look at several massive shapes as they strode through the forest just beyond the road. The man-shaped creatures were made of wood and ranged from eight to twelve feet tall. They had long, thick limbs and dagger-like fingers, and their eyes glowed with an eerie green light that flickered like fire in their dark eye sockets. The wooden creatures trampled all the bushes and plants in their path, and even bent trees out of the way so their bulky bodies could squeeze through the forest. The first of them lumbered out onto the road, took one look at the legionnaires, and ran straight at them. The earth quivered from its weight as it ran. It stood over ten feet tall, and its body was covered in glowing green runes. Moss and lichen hung from its bark-like skin, and a massive rack of deer antlers sprouted from its head. Shrubs and flowers grew on its over-sized shoulders and arms, and an eldritch green light glowed deep within its chest.

"Fall back!" Oudeteros shouted as he leveled his crossbow at the monstrosity. He repeatedly fired into the creature's wooden hide. The steel bolts sank several inches deep but had no effect on it. The wooden giant raised a mighty fist as it quickly covered the distance between Oudeteros and itself. The captain had just enough time to lift his shield before the creature's fist collided with it. A massive dent formed in it as Oudeteros was launched backwards. Hildin and Paetro watched him fly away from them with a look of bewilderment on his face. The southerner landed roughly on the road and moaned in pain as he stared up at the sky.

"What in Taloria is it?!" Hildin asked his twin.

"Looks to me like a wood golem," Paetro replied. "I've heard stories about them, but I didn't think they were real."

"What's a wood golem, and how do we kill it?"

Paetro was about to answer when the creature pulled back its leg to kick him. The legionnaire deftly turned his horse to the side, thus avoiding a lethal blow by the breadth of a hair. The behemoth then shifted its focus to Hildin. It bent low as it lumbered after him, trying desperately to snatch him out of the saddle with its grasping hands. Hildin knew it would be futile to engage the creature with his hatchets, so he lead it on a chase up and down the road. His plan was simple: keep the golem engaged long enough for his fellow legionnaires to formulate a plan. Hildin knew his horse could maintain the pace for quite some time. He just hoped nothing and no one would get in their way, or the golem would be on them in seconds.

Oudeteros painfully pushed himself up from the ground and inspected his shield arm. It was bruised but thankfully not broken. The same couldn't be said for his shield. It was dented so deeply he could barely extract his forearm from the leather straps. He tossed it aside and scowled as he watched the wooden creature chase poor Hildin down the road. Suddenly, a thought came to him. Oudeteros knew he had to come up with a plan before the horse tired or stumbled. He also knew the other golems would soon emerge from the forest to attack them. Oudeteros had learned his repeating crossbow was useless against a golem, and he figured swords and spears would take too long to destroy one. They needed something that could quickly damage their hardy wooden bodies.

"Men! Listen to me!" he yelled so that all of the legionnaires, as well as those from Vlain's force, could hear him. "Gather axes from the fallen woodlanders, then hack the tree monsters' legs off!

That will slow them down and give us time to pick them apart. We'll also cover them with cooking oil and shoot them full of burning arrows. You have your orders!"

Over two dozen men jumped down from their horses to scour the dead villagers for axes, while some dug through their packs to find bottles of cooking oil. Others put away their crossbows and pulled forth longbows and quivers full of arrows. A few of them ignited the tips of their arrows when two other golems burst out of the forest. The largest was over twelve feet tall, with long arms and hands that ended with wickedly sharp talons. Its body was covered with moss, mold, and mildew, and it moved with alarming speed. It backhanded a legionnaire off his horse, then savagely stomped on his chest. It then turned and ripped a galloping horse to shreds with its talon-like fingers. As soon as the horse fell, the golem snatched up its rider and crushed him in its merciless grip. It tossed the broken man aside then ran toward another legionnaire.

The third golem to arrive looked like someone had shoved a pile of mismatched logs together until they crudely resembled the shape of a man. Its smooth, bald head was too small for its long body, it had a permanent scowl carved into its face, and an angry, green light danced in its narrow eyes. The golem's fingers looked like huge prongs on one hand and like jagged knives on the other. It rushed at Oudeteros with its crab-like legs.

A legionnaire tossed the captain a battle-ax and a discarded steelwood shield. He caught the weapons then spurred his horse forward. The golem slashed its knife-like fingers at him. Oudeteros blocked the wild slash with his shield, then whipped his horse around and swung his ax at the creature's leg. The sharp edge sliced deep into its wooden body. Oudeteros yanked it free and would have hit it again, but the golem slashed at him with its prong-shaped hand.

Seven other golems emerged from the forest while Oudeteros

and others fought against the first three. The last few golems to step onto the road looked more like mixtures of men and animals and thus resembled their creators. Some of them had the hind legs of dogs or deer, and the trailing moss and bushy leaves on their faces made them look like they had green beards. The last one to leap onto the road was enormous. It had a dog-like body, and its giant head looked like a flared shield with long, sharp, wooden spikes that protruded from the back.

"Douse them with oil!" Oudeteros shouted. Over a dozen legionnaires hurled their glass jars at the enchanted creatures. The jars shattered against the golems' bark-like skin, allowing the oil to ooze down the length of their bodies. "Archers! Fire!" Oudeteros commanded. The air was filled with flickering red, orange, and yellow lights as a hail of burning arrows shot forth to bury themselves in the golems' thick hides.

The fierce elementals continued to attack the legionnaires even though they had become walking torches. Although the flames weren't causing them pain or dissuading them from fighting, Oudeteros knew the fire would eventually consume them. Unfortunately, the writhing flames made the golems even more dangerous in the meantime. Some of them snatched legionnaires off their horses, then pressed them against their burning bodies. The men's horrific screams filled the morning air as they were burned alive.

Paetro grabbed an ax handle and wrenched the ax free of the legionnaire that its woodlander owner had felled in the initial melee. He rode to the nearest golem and hacked away at its tree-like legs as it chased after his twin brother. The golem suddenly stopped, then whipped around to grasp at Paetro. The legionnaire ducked beneath the giant hand, then rode away from it. Hildin seized the opportunity to hack at the wooden brute's arm with his two hatchets. He managed to cut off several of its fingers right before a jar of oil slammed into its jagged back. Hildin jerked on his horse's reigns, causing it to bolt to the left just as a burning arrow set the golem ablaze.

Oudeteros smiled in satisfaction. His hastily constructed plan was working. Little by little, they were picking the golems apart with fire and steel. He had lost far more men than he would have liked, but if they kept at it, they'd eventually destroy them. The captain hefted his ax and was about to attack another golem when he saw several figures wearing dark green, hooded cloaks emerge from the forest. One of them stopped in front of him, raised a slender blowgun to its mouth, and blew. A tiny dart shot forth. Oudeteros raised his shield, but he was a split second too late. The dart buried itself in his forearm. He glowered at the hooded figure as he felt a potent toxin invade his system. The captain clumsily dropped his ax then reached for his crossbow, but his arm wouldn't obey him. Even thinking was difficult. All his brain wanted to do was shut down. Oudeteros tried to urge his horse into a gallop with the hope of trampling this new, sinister-looking enemy, but his hands and feet refused his commands. An overwhelming drowsiness suddenly gripped him. Oudeteros valiantly fought it, but he eventually blacked out and pitched foreword in his saddle.

***

Maiva watched the raging battle between the legionnaires and wooden golems from the safety of the forest. A group of nearly fifty children and several young mothers hid in the tall grass and bushes behind her. The fawn anxiously bit her lower lip as she scanned the road and the forest beyond it. She couldn't risk the legionnaires seeing the younglings, or her mission to get them to safety would be jeopardized. Maiva had to figure out a way to get them all across the road without being spotted since the Meadow of Knowing was in that direction, and the closest green gate bordered the meadow. She just didn't know how to conceal such a large group. On top of that, the golems might mistake them for the enemy and tear them to shreds. If they skirted the road rather than crossing it, they would have to travel for an additional half-hour through a chaotic battle zone.

The fawn took a deep breath and prayed to the White Stag for guidance. As soon as she opened her eyes, she saw a human druid materialize in front of her. Maiva was startled by her sudden appearance, but she was also relieved to see her. The fawn and human locked eyes. She knew, as did all woodlanders, that a small population of brown-skinned, peace-loving humans occupied Findalora. Most of the time, the human tribes stuck to themselves, but now and then, one of them chose to live with woodlanders and vice versa. Sometimes, romantic unions even occurred between them.

"You're Maiva Starmark, right?" the druidess asked.

Maiva was still adjusting to her newfound fame. "Yes, my first name is Maiva, and I bear the starmark," she answered. The druidess bowed low before her and didn't rise until Maiva returned the honorary gesture.

"May I approach you to gaze upon the Stag's blessing?" the human asked.

"It's invisible in the light," Maiva informed her. "But should we meet again at night, then I'll gladly show it to you."

"I would like that very much," the woman replied.

"I have a favor to ask of you," Maiva said.

"Yes, Starmark?"

"The Grey King put me in charge of getting these younglings to safety," she said, pointing to the group of woodlander children behind her. "We need to cross the road so we can get to the nearest green gate, but it's too dangerous so could you..?"

"Help you cross unseen? Yes, blessed one. I would be happy to do so," the druidess said. Maiva could only see her hazel eyes due to the dense shadow cast by her hood. "I'm going to cast a spell which will make all of you blend in with your surroundings. I'll need you to bring all of the children close together for it to work."

"And what of the golems? Can you keep them away from us?" Maiva asked.

"Yes," the woman calmly replied. "You should hurry, though, for I must soon return to help the other druids control them." Maiva nodded in understanding then softly called the children and their mothers to gather together as closely as possible. When they were all huddled before the druid, she silently mouthed the words to a spell and held up her hands. The air began to shimmer around the group. Maiva watched the strange rippling and warping distortions for a moment, but she soon had to shut her eyes. The odd effect was starting to make her feel dizzy and sick to her stomach.

"It is done," the druidess said matter-of-factually. Maiva looked down at herself and gasped in surprise. Her clothing, skin, and even her hair were the same color as the forest around her. She looked around at the children, and they perfectly blended in with the background as well. Those who stood beside the trees now partially looked like them as well as the nearby shrubs and bushes. Maiva could only tell the younglings were there when one of them moved. The fawn reminded herself that she had known they were all there before the spell was cast. Had she not known what to look for, then her eyes could have easily missed the entire group.

"How long will it last?" Maiva asked.

"An hour, perhaps less," the druidess replied. "But you must all stay together for it to work. Since I didn't have time to cast a spell on each of you, I placed it on the entire group. Should one of you get separated from the rest, then that person will be visible."

"I understand. Thank you for helping us... what's your name?"

Maiva asked.

"Iolee," the woman said.

"I'll remember your kindness today, Iolee," Maiva said.

"Travel safely, Maiva. I hope we meet again," Iolee said.

"If it's the Stag's will," Maiva said. She gave the druidess a quick hug and walked away from her. "Come on, kids!" She whispered. "We all blend into the environment now, but we have to stay together for the spell to work," she explained. It felt strange talking to the group, considering she could barely see them even though they were staring right at her. Now and then, she detected an eye or the contour of a body, but these little giveaways continuously blurred in and out of view.

Maiva swallowed her fear and then stepped onto the road. There was a knot of legionnaires battling two hulking golems less than fifty feet away. She stopped and turned to wave at one of the young mothers. Unfortunately, the camouflage effect prevented her from getting the woodlander's attention.

"Ganymay!" Maiva whispered to the satyr, prompting her to come forward. "You lead the children across the road while I bring up the rear. Remember to pack them close together!"

"Yes, Starmark," the woodlander said.

Ganymay led the children out of the forest. At first, first, everything was fine. The legionnaires were so focused on the burning golems that they probably wouldn't have noticed the younglings even if they hadn't been magically camouflaged. It wasn't until over half of the children had crossed the road that things began to fall apart. One of the children, a little male fawn, tripped on a rock, fell, and rolled several feet away from the group. He immediately became visible. Maiva held her breath as she raced forward. She was careful to run right beside the children to maintain her own camouflage. Maiva had to eventually depart from the group, however, to get close to the little fawn. The clumsy youngling jumped up and started running straight toward Maiva. By now, Maiva had also become visible.

They were about to rejoin the group's safety when a flailing golem suddenly knocked Paetro off his horse. The legionnaire sailed through the air, then skidded to a stop a few feet away from Maiva and the youngling. The young man grimaced, then slowly stood up. He was about to race back into the fray when he saw Maiva crouched down on the road with her arms wrapped around the youngling.

Maiva's heart hammered away in her chest as she stared into the man's eyes. A shiver of fear mixed with a strange feeling of familiarity passed through her. She tried to place the man's face, but was unable to do so.

Paetro studied the fawn's face for a second as he, too, realized there was something familiar about her. He then remembered she was the woodlander that had emerged from Vorsord's manor. Neither of them moved as they stared at each other for a few tense seconds. Eventually, Paetro stepped backwards and pointed to the forest bordering the road, indicating she should go in that direction. He then turned and ran back to his horse.

Maiva sighed in relief, and ran to catch up with her camouflaged group. The spell of concealment flowed back over Maiva and the youngling as soon as they returned to the back of the line. The sounds of the fearsome battle on the road gradually faded as they hiked through the dense underbrush. Maiva half expected to see the black armored forms of legionnaires spring out at them at any moment, but they failed to materialize. Maiva resumed her place at the front of the group and had Ganymay bring up the rear. She was on high alert and thus kept a spiked ball loaded in her slingshot. Finally, the Meadow of Knowing came into view. Maiva crouched down then scanned the wide-open space to make sure no legionnaires lurked nearby. She soon felt confident that none were around, so she shifted her focus to the green gate across the meadow. Although planted separately, two aspen trees had grown together over the years. Their slender trunks had met some ten feet above the ground to form an archway. Strangely enough, the trees grew in opposite directions above the meeting point. Druids had carved ruins into the tree trunks on both sides of the arch and had imbued the ruins with magic during a ceremony. They had thus created an artificial addition to the preexisting green gates that had naturally formed throughout Findalora. The green gates linked separate and distant locations together whenever they were activated. By using them, one could walk directly from one area to another without traversing the space in between.

Maiva smiled in relief as she gazed at the dormant green gate. Once activated, the magical tunnel would allow her and her party of younglings to instantly travel hundreds of leagues away to another meadow at the heart of the forest. It was a definite path to safety, but they had to reach it first.

"Once we get to the gate, I'll stand guard until everyone goes through," Maiva whispered to Ganymay. "I'll slip in behind the last youngling."

Ganymay nodded in understanding, then went to the front of the line. Maiva stepped out into the meadow, holding her slingshot in case any legionnaires arrived. Any onlooker would have only seen a vague, rippling distortion in the shape of a long line as it crossed the wide, flat field.

They soon arrived at the green gate. Maiva positioned herself in front of it and began chanting a phrase to activate the spatial doorway. Ganymay soon joined her in the chant while the younglings looked on with curious eyes. "Geross Gon Dorom tor Barum Follos," the two Findalorans said in unison, which meant,

"Open, Gate of Knowing, to Barum Field."

Nothing happened at first, then shimmering, green energy began to form in the space between the two aspen trees. The portal soon resembled a waterfall, but instead of being made of water, it was a cascading, iridescent green light that never reached the ground. Maiva shook her head in wonder. No matter how many times she watched a green gate form, it always amazed her. Haephius called them "glorified shortcuts" and was only mildly interested in them. Maiva, on the other hand, was mystified by the swirling tunnels of energy that could instantly transport you to distant places.

"Go ahead, Ganymay, lead them in," Maiva told her.

Ganymay nodded, then grabbed the hands of two younglings. "Come along now. I want you to all follow me through the gate," the satyr said in a cheerful tone.

"Where are we going?" a young female centaur asked.

To Barum Field, deep within Findalora," she replied right before she stepped into the cascading curtain of green light. The younglings followed her into the glowing portal. Over half of them had gone through when Maiva suddenly saw a small group of horse-mounted legionnaires appear in the distance. They were chasing a golem that was burning like a bonfire. The blundering behemoth ignited every tree it touched. The men hacked at it with axes whenever it tried to attack them. Now and then, it succeeded in knocking a man from his horse, but the legionnaires never relented. Eventually, it fell in the center of the meadow. The golem had been reduced to a charred and smoldering ruin by now.

One of the legionnaires scanned the meadow to see if any other threats lurked nearby. His eyes passed right over the camouflaged younglings but were instantly drawn to the shimmering portal. He rode closer to inspect the otherworldly light, and as he did so, he saw Maiva crouching down beside one of the tree trunks.

"Hey there!" The legionnaire called out to his fellows. "There's a beastie hiding by this glowing thing over there!"

The ring of men moved away from the burnt golem to look where he was pointing. Maiva's heart raced as the men urged their steeds toward her. Several more younglings still needed to get through the green gate before she could get in line behind them. She knew she had to buy them time, so she shot a warning shot at the lead rider. The spiky ball sailed over the legionnaire's helmet with only a few inches to spare. The man responded by pulling a long crossbow from a holder on his saddle and leveling it at her. Maiva doubted the man could hit her from there, but something told her to shoot anyway. She lined up her sights and fired a second round. The spiked ball shot forth with the speed of an arrow, making an angry buzzing sound as it clove through the air. The legionnaire gasped in surprise as the spikes sank into his cheek. The viper venom instantly shot into the hollow tips and was swept up into the man's bloodstream. He reflexively pulled the projectile off of his face and tossed it to the ground. The skin around the puncture wound began to swell and blister. His breathing became shallow and labored. The legionnaire fired his crossbow at Maiva, but the shot went wild. The steel bolt buried itself in the tree trunk to the right of the green gate.

The man slumped forward in his saddle, prompting the other legionnaires to call out to him in concern. Hildin leveled his crossbow at Maiva. Just then, the fawn saw that the last of the younglings had just gone through the green gate. She fired another shot at the approaching legionnaires, then turned and sprinted into the rippling portal. A hail of steel bolts shot forth from the men's crossbows. One of them passed through the air where Maiva had just been. Several of them went wild, but a few bolts flew straight into the green gate.

The legionnaires pulled back on their reigns as they neared the portal. Hildin jumped down from his horse, pulled out his sword and crossbow, and wondered what to do when the curtain of energy abruptly dissipated. A swooshing sound filled the air as the green light flickered out of existence. Hildin jumped back in alarm. After several uneventful seconds went by, he muttered a curse and walked away from the deactivated gate. He was disappointed that they hadn't captured the woodlander but thankful that whatever strange sorcery had been at work was now over.

***

Captain Caladin smiled wickedly as he pushed through the pine trees and maple saplings to emerge onto the road just west of Algos. He and his men had spent the night riding through the forest, hoping to reach the village before sunrise. The sun had risen, but it was still early morning. Still, the captain considered their mission a success. He could already hear the chaotic sounds of warfare emanating from the village, which meant Vlain was carrying out his role as the tip of the spear in the assault. The arrogant fighter and his lackeys would break the spirit of the beasties, and then Caladin and his men would ride in to finish the job. He smiled at the brilliance of Commander Orilius's plan.

The giant of a man looked down at the war dogs that circled his draft horse. They were a mixture of Rottweilers and Pit-bulls and had been bred on the choicest meats. Caladin had poured all of his extra time and energy into training the six dogs, which he referred to as his War Pack. The animals could track prey as effectively as bloodhounds and could outfight wolves. Caladin had even paid armorers in Faldin to fashion special armor for them. The sun glinted off the steel helmets, plates, and connective fish mail armor on the panting beasts. The captain planned to christen them in the blood of the beasties today.

Caladin crossed the road and entered the village with his force of five hundred legionnaires in tow. Vlain's force was already in

156

heated combat with the defenders of the town. The huge man smiled in anticipation of the upcoming battle. Ever since he had lost the duel to Vlain, he had been aching for a chance to prove himself as a capable warrior and leader. Perhaps he would get an opportunity to outshine the brash fighter today, or better yet, maybe Vlain would meet his demise. The big man suddenly turned his black horse around to address his men.

"Hear me! Today, you forge yourselves into the men of war you were meant to be. Remember, no mercy, no forgiveness, no restraint! Give your all or give me nothing!" With that said, Caladin turned his horse back around, then charged forward.

He pulled his shield off his back and held his battle-ax aloft. A long, sharp pike protruded from the opposite end of the ax head. The pink glow of the sunrise highlighted the wicked-looking weapon, making it look like it was made of molten steel. Caladin laughed maniacally as he closed in on a group of woodlanders that had surrounded Vlain. He chopped the beastmen and women apart with his ax until their blood filled the air like crimson rain. None of their weapons could harm him. His armor was too thick, and the adrenaline coursing through him made him all but painless. He hacked away with his giant ax, bashed heads in with his heavy shield, and watched in glee as his horse stomped on the dead and dying with its iron-shod hooves.

He had lost himself in the bloody carnage when he heard the roar of an animal, or was it a man? He couldn't be sure. All he knew was that it came from behind him. Caladin turned around to search for the one who had made the war-cry. That was when he saw the minotaur, but this one had the head and hind-legs of a buffalo. The hulking beast was covered in long, brown fur, and wooden plates of armor covered his enormous body. An iron crown terminating in sharp spikes rested on his enormous head, and he held an immense, double-headed battle-ax. Caladin saw there were at least a hundred other minotaur warriors standing behind their king. The legionnaires immediately engaged them in battle.

A furious frown formed on Caladin's face as he watched the beastman slaughter his legionnaires. His men fought ferociously and with coordinated precision, but it didn't matter. Their repeating crossbows and other weapons were all useless against him. The minotaur king appeared to be invulnerable, for no bolt or sharp edge could touch him. The bolts always fell short, and no one could connect their blades to his flesh, no matter how hard they tried.

A legionnaire suddenly threw a spear at the king's chest, but it inexplicably slowed down and fell to the ground before it could connect. Caladin had seen a bright red spark where the tip had almost hit the minotaur just before the spear had slowed down. He arched an eyebrow as he scrolled through his memory. The captain had once heard a tale about a mage who had placed a ward of protection on himself. The magical barrier had sparked red whenever someone had attempted to bypass it. Every ward, however, had a limit to how much force it could absorb before it dissipated. Other wards were time-sensitive, evaporating after their allotted time had run out. Caladin decided then and there that he would break the minotaur's ward regardless of how it operated.

The giant of a man balanced his ax on the neck of his mount, then put his fingers to his mouth and whistled shrilly. The muscle-bound war dogs all stared up at him, waiting for the command they knew was coming. "Attack!" Caladin shouted while pointing at the minotaur king.

The entire pack turned to glower at their new enemy, then sprinted forward as if they were one animal. They closed the distance in less than a minute. The lead dog launched itself at the minotaur's thick neck and tried to clamp its jaws down on his throat. It only succeeded in bouncing off the invisible ward protecting the king and then fell to the earth. The minotaur pinned the dog to the ground with its hoof, raised his ax, then brought it down. The blade sliced through the dog's neck. The beast king roared in victory, then stepped back and kicked the dog's head at the approaching pack. The second dog to attack was impaled by the spike protruding from the top of the king's ax head. The third was killed when the minotaur stomped a hoof down onto its neck. The rest of the pack was obliterated by continuous, sweeping hits from the ax blade. The minotaur had made a sport out of slaughtering them.

Pieces of the dogs had been scattered all around the towering king when Captain Caladin arrived to challenge him. The two warriors sized each other up and then ran toward each other. The minotaur snorted out blasts of steam from its nose when it reached a full sprint. Caladin urged his horse to gallop faster and shot bolt after bolt from his crossbow at the charging beastman. Bright red sparks formed wherever the steel bolts encountered the ward. The king swung his ax into the stallion a split second before they collided. The broad blade plowed into the horse's heart, killing it instantly, but the animal's momentum pushed the minotaur back against the trunk of an oak tree. A bright red flash filled the air, signaling the demise of the protective ward surrounding the minotaur. Caladin grunted as he jumped clear of his falling, dead horse. The beastman shoved the broken animal back, then stepped away from the tree.

Man and minotaur met with a fearsome clash of arms. Caladin was the first to swing his ax. The woodlander blocked it with the steelwood handle of his own ax, then shoved Caladin with such force that he went flying backward to fall on the ground. The king blasted steam from his nose, lifted his ax high, and ran toward the downed legionnaire. Caladin raised his shield to block the lethal, downward strike. Sparks flew, and a deep dent formed in the shield. The minotaur repeatedly raised his ax to batter the steel barrier until it was a mass of mangled metal. Caladin was desperately trying to think of a way to get out from under the relentless assault before the ax blade bit into his arm.

Suddenly, a legionnaire rode up and fired bolt after bolt at the minotaur king. Most of the bolts bounced off the beastman's steelwood armor, but two of them lodged themselves in the brown leather connecting the wooden plates. The king gave no indication he had been wounded, however. He surged forward to cut the horse down with his mammoth ax, then cut its rider in half. The well-timed intervention had given Caladin time to rise, however. He tossed his ruined shield away, grabbed the discarded one from the freshly killed legionnaire, and charged the minotaur again. He was determined to either kill the beast king or die in the process. He needed this victory if he was to regain favor in Commander Orilius's eyes.

***

Belor cursed under his breath as bolt after bolt of lightning streaked down at him and the other two legionnaires who were taking cover beneath a wagon. It was like being caught in a lightning storm. Belor had to admit the fawn's aim was almost as good as his own. In the short time he had been hunkered down under the wagon, he had watched over ten men get blasted to the ground by the brutal barrage. The archer was waiting for the fawn to rest so he could return fire. He knew the goatman was injured because he had watched as one of Vlain's bolts had torn open his side. The fawn had cauterized the wound, but it must still be hurting him. Belor figured the adrenaline of combat must be responsible for the beastie's remarkable endurance.

Finally, the electrical assault paused, prompting Belor to slide out from under the wagon to search for the fawn's silhouette on the roof. He almost took an arrow in the eye for his trouble, for a couple of woodland archers had joined Haephius on the rooftop. One of them fired at Belor, but the satyr's aim was slightly off. An arrow thudded into the dirt, not two inches from Belor's head. The legionnaire rapidly discharged and cocked his crossbow four times, then rolled back under the wagon. A satisfied smile rose to his

160

handsome face as he watched the two archers plummet from the rooftop to land heavily in the road. The steel bolts from his crossbow stuck out of the woodlanders' chests. They moaned in pain as they succumbed to their injuries.

No sooner had the archers fallen than the fawn reappeared on the rooftop. A storm of hissing, electrical bolts rained down on the wagon that protected Belor and the two other legionnaires. So savage was the assault that for a moment, it looked like the spears of lightning would punch through the wooden wagon bed. Belor instinctively rolled to the side to avoid getting hit. His quick thinking served him well, for a bolt of energy zapped the spot he had just been lying in. Smoke drifted up from the charred wagon bed. Belor sniffed the air. Flames flickered and danced at the edge of the blackened hole in the wood.

"Jaina's living light!" Belor cursed as he shot out from beneath the burning wagon to challenge the woodland sniper.

Haephius raised his hand and summoned another bolt into his palm when he said the word" "Genlin," but Belor shot two steel bolts at him before he could hurl it. The first bolt ricocheted off of Haephius's steelwood shield, and the second one bounced off of one of the fawn's horns with such force that he went tumbling back to land on the clay roof tiles. He somersaulted backward due to the pitched angle of the roof, and fell off of it.

Haephius landed painfully on the hard-packed dirt on the far side of the building. The twelve-foot drop had knocked the wind out of him. He desperately tried to breathe even as Belor ran around the building to engage him. The fawn forced himself to stand up and was about to flee when the archer fired another two bolts at him. Haephius raised his shield. The barrier blocked one bolt, and the other one bounced off of the fawn's wooden armor. He threw several lightning bolts at Belor in reply, but the archer was running before the first bolt flew his way. He dove behind the corner of the building. Two nearby legionnaires, however, hadn't been so quick. One of them blocked a lightning bolt with a steel shield, just as Vlain had done, but this one lacked leather enarmes and padding to protect him from the shock. The man shook and danced about as if he was having a seizure, then pitched forward to land dead and smoking on the ground. The other legionnaire, Sergeant Rivers, blocked a shaft of lightning with a steelwood shield he had salvaged from a woodlander's corpse. The lightning bolt singed and blackened the spot where it struck the wood, but it was only lightly damaged, and Rivers remained unharmed. The fawn threw several more bolts at the men, then sprinted into the nearby forest.

Belor had watched the exchange with rapt attention. "Legionnaire!" he shouted at Rivers.

"Yes, lieutenant?" The young man asked.

"I'll need that shield while I pursue the goatman," he told the enlisted man. "In the meantime, I want you to return to Vlain and help him bring down the centaur king."

"Aye, aye," the legionnaire said as he handed the parma shield to Belor.

"You have your orders, now go," the archer said.

"Yes, sir," Rivers replied before dashing off.

A cold smile formed on the archer's lips as he plunged into the forest after Haephius. The fawn had a slight lead on him, but Belor figured he could quickly catch up since his legs were longer. He soon realized he had underestimated his opponent. Even in a wounded state, the woodlander's lead was steadily growing. Belor shook his head in disbelief.

"Do you have wings on your hooves?!" he asked the fawn as he watched him slip through the trees. The archer knew he wouldn't be able to catch him at this rate, so he raised his crossbow to his cheek, took careful aim, and fired. The steel bolt swiftly flew through the forest, only to plow into a tree trunk an inch away from the fawn's head. Belor cursed his bad luck because he had lost the element of surprise. The woodlander knew he was there now.

Haephius ducked and skidded to a stop. He whirled around a split second later and began lobbing lightning bolt after bolt at Belor. The archer slipped behind a thick pine tree just in time. Haephius had had enough. He was exhausted, enraged, and heartsick after having seen his village reduced to a bloody battleground. The fawn poured all of his anger and grief into the withering assault. Soon, the mighty tree had a smoldering crater in it. Flames danced to life in its center, and the ominous sounds of cracking wood filled the air.

Belor stepped away from the tree in alarm. It was swaying in his direction, and the unmistakable sound of falling timber rose to his ears. The archer began to run as the tree fell toward him, but he ran in a straight line to confound the fawn. Haephius swore in frustration. He figured the man wanted to either be crushed by the great tree or was too stupid to get out of its way. Regardless of the reason, the fawn couldn't score a lethal hit as long as the forest giant remained between them. At the last second, Belor leaped to the left of the plunging tree. A booming crash resounded within the forest, and the ground quivered from the violent impact. Belor scrambled to take cover behind another tree just as Haephius resumed throwing bolts of hissing energy at him.

Haephius hurled several more lightning bolts at the tree behind which Belor stood, and was about to throw another when he saw movement out of the corner of his eye. The blacksmith turned his head to get a better look and was amazed to see Zenda crouched down in the tall grass, not fifty feet away. His eyes widened when he saw a large gathering of elderly, sick, and injured woodlanders crouched down behind her.

"What are you doing out here, girl?" he asked as he skidded to a stop in front of her.

"The king told me to get as many elderlings and infirm villagers out of Algos as I could. We're trying to get to the green gate near Tellin's Pond," she explained.

"I see," he responded. "It'll take you to the Cave of Sanctuary, which is filled with provisions. A wise move," he admitted. "But what of Maiva? Why isn't she with you?"

"The king ordered her to take all of the younglings she could find to the green gate at the Meadow of Knowing. I pray she reached it," Zenda replied in a worried tone.

"Stag willing," Haephius said as an anxious look formed on his goat-like face. He was about to say more when a steel bolt suddenly sliced through the air above his head.

"Who's shooting at you?" Zenda asked in alarm.

"The most stubborn man I've ever fought!" Haephius angrily replied. "You're all in danger until I bring him down. Run! Go that way, then veer toward Tellin's Pond," he said while pointing in the opposite direction of the legionnaire.

"But what about you?!" Zenda asked. "We can't just leave you out here all alone."

"I'll join you just as soon as I kill this hairless ape!" he growled.

"You better," Zenda whispered. "Or Maiva will never forgive me."

"Go! I'll catch up!" Haephius shouted as he turned to throw lightning bolts at Belor. Zenda nodded, then signaled to the group to resume following her. She knocked an arrow to the string on her bow and began jogging toward the green gate. The elderly and infirm struggled to keep up with her then started falling farther and farther back. Zenda was forced to slow her pace or risk leaving them behind.

The sound of the battle between fawn and man grew fainter as Zenda and the villagers moved farther away. Part of Zenda wanted to help Haephius fight the legionnaire, but she knew her mission was to protect the villagers. The king had given her an order, and she wasn't about to let him down. She'd just have to hope Haephius survived his battle with the outlander.

The dark green body of Tellin's pond gradually came into view between the trees. Zenda led the woodlanders out of the forest to stand before it. She figured they needed a break after their long walk from the village, so she let them sit down to catch their breath. While they rested, Zenda focused on a huge granite boulder that had been set upright in the clearing, not thirty paces away from the pond. A deep, smooth depression had been carved into the center, where the green gate would form when activated. She had only to stand in front of it, speak the gate's name, and where she wished to go, to form the portal.

Zenda gave the group a few more minutes to recover, then cleared her throat and spoke loudly: "Come! We've rested long enough. Man lurks nearby, so it's time we departed. The oldest and most injured will go first. The rest of you will wait in the rear with me." Zenda waited for the throng to arrange itself, then nodded at the elderlings in front. Having received the signal, they started chanting in unison: "Open, Gate of Tellin, to the Gate of Sanctuary."

A brilliant green radiance filled the clearing. The gate had formed. Zenda smiled as the witch light formed a vibrant, shimmering curtain, which now prevented her from seeing the depression in the boulder's face. Those at the front filed into the portal only to vanish into the seething green light. Zenda was about to step through it herself when the sounds of a struggle suddenly intruded into the clearing. She turned to look into the forest. Streaks of lightning filled the air, as well as the incessant whine of arrows.

Haephius leaped into the clearing while hurling bolt after bolt of energy into the trees behind him. Zenda crouched down, raised her bow and arrow to her cheek, and searched the tree-line for signs of the legionnaire. It didn't take long before a man clad in black armor with the symbol of a white eagle painted on his chest plate appeared at the edge of the glade. He held a longbow with one hand and notched an arrow to the string with his other. Zenda was about to shoot at him when Haephius frantically waved at her to get away.

"Run! They're counting on you!" he shouted. Zenda nodded in reply, then turned and ran toward the green gate. Belor aimed his arrow at her just as Haephius hurled another bolt of lightning at him. The man raised his steelwood shield in defense while partially stepping behind a tree. Zenda disappeared into the green curtain of light. Haephius turned and began running toward the shimmering portal even as Belor drew back on his bowstring. The fawn was about to leap forward when Belor shot an arrow at his back. His legendary aim held true. The wooden shaft lodged itself between the rigid plates of Haephius's body armor, causing him to gasp in pain. He twisted in mid-air, then threw a bolt of energy at the tree behind which Belor stood. The outer edge of the tree trunk exploded into jagged shards of smoking wood. The archer cursed as shrapnel pelted his face, chest, and arms. Despite his fresh injuries, however, he still held his bow aloft while he searched for the fawn. The woodlander sailed through the flickering green gate.

Belor was about to send more arrows through the fading green curtain of light, but he stayed his hand. Whatever magic had activated, the portal was ending now, so he figured there was no use wasting arrows. All he could do was hope his shot had proved lethal.

Belor sighed in frustration, then gingerly touched his stinging, swollen face. He pulled his fingertips away and saw they were covered with blood. The shrapnel had peppered his once handsome face. Hopefully, the clerics could heal him in the coming days. The archer wearily slung his bow onto his back turned away from the dormant gate, and began the long trek back to the village.

FIRE AND WATER

Chapter 7

Sparks flew into the air as King Caernos drove his ebony sword down through Meris's steel shield. Thankfully, the blade narrowly missed the legionnaire's forearm. Before Meris could react, the woodlander king wrenched the shield toward him, thereby ripping the man straight out of his saddle. Meris struggled to extract his bruised and aching arm from the enarmes within the shield while the king tossed him aside. The legionnaire flew through the air and was caught by Vlain as he rode up on his white charger. Vlain had just fought his way through the king's bodyguards, and not a moment too soon. He set Meris on the ground, then bent down to speak to him.

"The king is mine," he said in a low voice. "Keep his guards at bay while we fight." Before Meris could answer, Vlain squeezed Viscol's sides with his legs, prompting the horse to charge forward. He held one sword high and the other low as he closed in on the massive centaur. The king narrowed his eyes as he scrutinized his new enemy.

"Know this, invader. You face King Caernos, protector of Finadalora. Who are you, and why do you court death?" the king rumbled in perfect Emblin.

"Vlain Verous," the fighter answered with a smirk, even though he was surprised to hear the woodlander flawlessly speak his language. "And we'll all die, but today is not my day."

"How do you know that?" Caernos asked, and although Vlain couldn't see his face, he sensed the centaur was smirking.

"You're about to find out."

The king surged forward like an avalanche. He brought his black sword down onto Vlain's again and again. The fighter's blades began quivering as they dissipated the energy from each strike. They didn't break, nor were they damaged.

Caernos raised an eyebrow in wonder. He was surprised and startled to see Vlain's copper-colored weapons take hit after hit from Svartur without getting a scratch.

Since the king's standard attack was failing, he abruptly shifted tactics. He slammed his sword down onto Vlain's again, but this time, he held it in place with both hands and bore down with all his might. The fighter's eyes began glowing like molten iron as he struggled against Caernos's elephantine strength. He sheathed one of his swords and then gripped the handle of his active sword with his second hand. Both warriors vainly struggled for several seconds as they circled each other in the town square. The centaur warriors and legionnaires watched their leaders battle with wide eyes.

Although Vlain's enchanted vision showed him the weaknesses of those he fought, there were precious few when it came to Caernos. He could see a strange blue glow emanating from a steel armband on his right arm. The runes of power on it glowed with a steady, bewitching light, which indicated it was a magical item. Perhaps it was multiplying the monarch's strength? Aside from that, he could make out the ward that protected the centaur from injury. Glowing red lines highlighted a geometric pattern that encapsulated the proud centaur. Strangely enough, the king's black blade appeared to be non-magical. Although Vlain detected a weakness within the crystalline weapon, he instinctively knew he couldn't summon the force required to shatter it.

Despite his considerable strength, Vlain knew he couldn't resist the king much longer. He let out a high-pitched whistle, signaling Viscol to move to the side. As soon as the horse responded, he lowered his sword while twisting it to the side. The king's blade harmlessly sliced through the air. However, before the centaur could pull it back up, Vlain pulled his second sword from its sheath and attacked him with high and low strikes. Meris, who had been watching their fight while fending off the royal guards, noticed Vlain wasn't trying to hit any vital areas. Instead, he was wearing down the king's protective ward. It took several minutes and a multitude of hits before a red flash sprang into the air, signaling the demise of the enchantment.

Vlain swung his blade at the centaur's armband before he could react to the loss of his protection. Bright blue sparks exploded into the space between them. The deep cut in the metal had done the job. The king would have to use his natural strength for the rest of the fight.

"Now we fight with only our true abilities and skill," the centaur said in his booming baritone as he warily circled Vlain.

"So it would appear," Vlain cryptically answered.

"You should pray to your gods that you'll survive."

"I'm not worried. Are you?"

Caernos's glowing, white eyes narrowed as he studied the crafty fighter. The centaur growled angrily, then came at him. Vlain let him take the offensive for several minutes. He was patiently waiting for the king to slow down so he could slip past his defenses. In the meantime, he realized the centaur was using a surprising combination of Talorian fighting styles. Sometimes, he fought like the southern men who preferred downward slashes with their scimitars. Then he'd switch to the refined, measured thrusts favored by fencers, only to give in to berserk, hacking fury for which the barbarians were well-known. The monarch had clearly been schooled in various fighting methods.

After several minutes had passed, the Grey King began to slow down, which prompted Vlain to attack. Meris shook his head in awe as the fighter parried, thrust, slashed and hacked at his opponent. None of the strikes were conventional. Vlain either rolled his wrists at the last instant to throw the king's next strike off, or he used the vibrating edge of his blades to push the centaur's sword off course. Despite the king's raw power, skill, and confidence, he was slowly losing. As always, Vlain was assuming control of the battlefield.

***

Two druids ran up to Oudeteros's horse and then pulled him down from the saddle. The bigger druid draped the legionnaire over his shoulder and ran off into the forest while the second one followed him. Paetro and the other legionnaires were so intent on fighting the golems that they didn't witness the abduction. The lieutenant furiously hacked away at the huge, dog-shaped golem with his hatchets. He was scoring major hits on its burnt body, but the heat from the flames was singeing his skin. Paetro sheathed his hatchets, jumped down from his horse to grab a discarded ax, and was about to mount his horse again when a dart thudded into his neck. The legionnaire whipped around to see a tall, slender druid dressed in a hooded green cloak, holding a blowgun.

"Legionnaires! There's a new enemy at hand!" he shouted for all to hear. A few of the men heard his cry and saw the druid standing in the road, but most of them were too busy fighting to heed him. Paetro ran straight at the druid with his ax held high. He was about to chop the woodlander down when someone shoved a steel wood staff out from the bushes to trip him. Down he went. The druid jumped onto his back before he could push himself up. He struggled mightily for a few seconds, but the powerful drug was overriding his system. Hildin ceased thrashing as he lost consciousness. He was promptly carried off by the druid.

"Paetro!" Hildin screamed as he and his men returned from the Meadow of Knowing, where they had encountered Maiva. "Get back here with my brother, you beastie scum!" he shouted as he jumped down from his horse and raced after the druid who had taken Paetro.

Hildin ran into the dense forest in hot pursuit but soon came face-to-face with a druid. The wind blew the green cloak tightly against the woodlander's body, revealing the shapely figure of a woman beneath it. Hildin pulled his sword from its sheath, then ran at her. The druid raised her hands into the air and whispered a word too softly for Hildin to hear. Suddenly, several vines hanging from nearby branches began writhing like snakes. The vines shot forth to wrap themselves around the legionnaire's wrists and ankles. Hildin violently fought against them and managed to rip his sword-wielding arm free. He hacked at a vine on his ankle and had almost severed it when a low-lying tree branch slapped him hard in the face. It, too, had come to life, seemingly on its own. As Hildin lay there, reeling from the stunning blow, more vines crept out from the trees to twine themselves around his limbs. When he had been fully immobilized, the druidess stepped forward to blow a dart from her gun at the exposed flesh on his neck. Hildin's eyes widened in alarm. He tried to break free one more time before the toxin could overwhelm him. It was no use, however. His mind went dark as the back of his head thudded against the ground.

Hildin's men had watched him rush into the forest after his brother and were about to join him when a burning golem suddenly attacked them. The legionnaires valiantly hacked and stabbed the lumbering monstrosity as it bore down on them. One of the men, named Denin, chopped an arm off the golem and was about to cut the other one off when several druids suddenly emerged from the forest. The cloaked and hooded figures formed a semi-circle behind the legionnaires even as more golems came running up to fight them from the front.

"It's no use!" Denin shouted to his fellow legionnaires. "We can't fight them on two fronts."

"What do you suggest?" one of the men asked.

"We should lead the wooden monsters back to the village square. In their damaged state, maybe they can't tell friends from foes and might kill some woodlanders before they burn up. If not, then at least Vlain and his men can help us fight them."

"And what about these new foes?" another man asked him as he pointed at the druids.

"Leave them be," Denin answered. "I don't like the look of them, and who knows what sorcery they can use against us." No sooner had Denin spoken than one of the druids raised a blowgun to its mouth and shot a dart at one of the legionnaires. The tiny projectile embedded itself in the man's neck.

"What in Jaina's name was that?" the legionnaire said as he reached up to pull the dart out of his skin. He took a moment to scrutinize it. "It's covered in some kind of white sap..." he lost consciousness a few seconds later and slumped forward in his saddle.

"Retreat! We're doomed if we stay here! Retreat!" Denin screamed as he dropped his ax and grabbed the horse's reins that belonged to the unconscious legionnaire. Denin spurred both horses forward while narrowly avoiding the grasping hands of a burning golem that suddenly sprang at him. He risked a quick look back as both horses attained a steady gallop. It took all of his skill as a rider, but he evaded the other golems and soon gained the open road.

Two legionnaires fired their crossbows at the druids, but the steel bolts bounced harmlessly off the red-tinged wards surrounding them. The druids responded by blowing darts at them from their blowguns. The other legionnaires prompted their steeds into a full gallop while trying to avoid the grasping talons of the golems. Most of them succeeded, but the last two legionnaires and their mounts were dragged to the ground and ripped to shreds. The men who had fired their crossbows at the druids had since passed out and were now being pulled from their saddles by the cloaked figures.

Denin intentionally slowed down so his fellow legionnaires could catch up and so the golems would continue to give chase. Thankfully, the druids remained where they were and thus receded farther and farther into the distance.

Denin turned to address the men when they drew up alongside him and his two horses. "Ride on ahead! I'll bring up the rear," he shouted. The men did as he asked. Their lead on him grew wider, and they soon disappeared behind the curve in the road. Denin slowed down even more, hoping to draw the attention of the closest golems. The wooden monsters predictably gave chase, prompting the others to do the same. Denin was careful to always stay just beyond their crushing grasp while never getting so far ahead that they gave up chasing him. Thus, he slowly but inexorably led them toward the village square. He could only hope that Vlain and his men were winning the fight against the woodlanders and that they could defeat the burning monstrosities behind him.

***

Caladin swung his ax at the minotaur king's head, but the wily beast-man side-stepped the curved blade at the last instant. He then slammed the butt of his ax handle into Caladin's shoulder. Even though his shoulder was protected by armor, the huge man grunted in pain. The minotaur blasted steam out of his wide nostrils, then swung his ax at the legionnaire. Caladin blocked the strike with his shield, but a deep pain lanced through his brawny arm. He had never been struck so hard in his life! The captain winced, then shook his head to clear it.

Both opponents warily circled each other as a dozen desperate battles raged all around them. Although the minotaurs were bigger and stronger than the legionnaires, they were outnumbered five to one. Still, they fought fearlessly as they formed a protective ring around their towering monarch. Caladin was the only man who had gotten close to the king and was determined to make the most of the opportunity.

Suddenly, the king lowered his head, scrapped a hoof against the ground, and charged him. Caladin firmly planted both feet in the moist soil and raised his ax for a strike. Before he could bury the blade in the beast-man's skull, however, the minotaur shoved the spiked head of his ax into Caladin's breastplate, thereby denting the armor and sending the big man flying. He hit the ground hard, spraying mud and pebbles all about. The legionnaire regained his feet before the minotaur could hit him again, but he was off-balance. He thrust his shield out to stop the minotaur's incoming ax. Sparks flew as steel collided with steel. Caladin fell back from the brutal blow. He raised his ax, but the minotaur was on him before he could strike. The first hit glanced off Caladin's shield, but the flat side of the ax smacked soundly against his knee cap.

The legionnaire wanted to howl in pain, but he gritted his teeth instead. "You'll pay for that, you beastie scum!" Caladin growled.

The minotaur king let out a deep, rumbling laugh, then spat at his feet. Caladin came at him with everything he had. The screech of steel on steel filled the air as the legionnaire hacked at his opponent. Caladin soon realized that the last hit had dislocated his knee. The pain took his breath away each time he put weight on it. He prayed the king would fail to notice that he was now limping.

The burly minotaur waited until Caladin grew tired, then made his move. The curved head of his ax blade embedded itself in Caladin's chest plate. The big man cried out in pain as the sharp edge bit into his flesh. Blood flowed down his chest to drip onto his leather boots. Even though it hurt, the chest plate had absorbed most of the force. Only a quarter-inch or so of the blade had bit into his skin. Caladin punched the hulking monarch in the face right before he wrenched his ax blade free. The woodlander gave no indication he had felt the blow. He swung at Caladin's head, prompting him to duck. The legionnaire swung back, but the king blocked him with the broad side of his ax head.

Caladin was panting and shaking now. Adrenaline still coursed through his veins, but his muscles were growing numb from fatigue. The beast-man swung at him again. Caladin deflected the ax with his shield, but the savage blow caused an explosion of pain in his forearm. He swung at the minotaur, but he twisted out of the way and then delivered a heavy blow to Caladin's already damaged chest plate. The cloven steel caved in, causing several of the man's ribs to break. Caladin wheezed in agony and swung at the king in retaliation, but his mind was on Endlin, the god of war. He prayed to his deity for the strength to kill the minotaur. The king raised his ax high. Scenes from Caladin's life shot through his mind as he watched the huge blade descend. He instinctively raised his shield, even though he knew it was a useless gesture. His bruised forearm would probably buckle from the force. Then, the next strike would end his life. Caladin inwardly cursed his fate and hoped his death would be quick and painless.

He was about to close his eyes when a legionnaire suddenly careened off a minotaur's shield and stumbled toward him. Caladin seized the opportunity by shoving the hapless, terrified man straight at the minotaur king. Instead of hitting Caladin, the beast-man's ax plowed through the legionnaire's helmet. The man died the instant the hefty blade sank into his skull. The king wrenched it free from the legionnaire's head, but not before Caladin swung his ax blade into the minotaur's back. The king reflexively jerked away, thereby wrenching the ax out of the big man's hands. Caladin watched in dismay as the mighty minotaur reached back to pull the ax out of his broad back. The king bellowed in rage and pain as he raised both weapons, then charged Caladin. The captain drew a knife from a sheath on his belt and was about to slash at the king's neck when the minotaur finally stumbled and fell at Caladin's feet. The captain stooped low as he buried his knife to the hilt at the base of the minotaur's neck. He wanted to make sure he was dead. When the king failed to respond, Caladin straightened up and raised his hands in the air.

"Praise be to Endlin! I am victorious!" he roared for all to hear. A cheer went up among his men when they saw he had defeated the king of the minotaurs. Caladin smirked in satisfaction as the remaining minotaurs fell back in fear and uncertainty. Clearly, they had never thought their fearsome king could fall in combat, least of all to a man. Caladin was only too happy to disappoint them.

"Cut them to pieces!" he growled. "But be sure to leave a few alive. Remember, the commander wants prisoners."

With their spirits raised by their leader's victory, the legionnaires soon overwhelmed the smaller minotaur force. Eventually, several of the beast-men turned to flee into the surrounding forest in hopes of escaping death or imprisonment. Caladin limped over to the oak tree that he had pinned the minotaur king against earlier in their fight. He leaned heavily against it as his injures ached and throbbed. Caladin couldn't recall the last time he had been so exhausted, but he put on a tough front as he watched his men take ten minotaurs captive. After the legionnaires subdued them, they stripped them of their weapons and bound them with heavy chains.

"Well done, lads!" he shouted in approval. "Now onward to the village square. We can't let Vlain and his boys take all the glory for themselves," Caladin shouted.

***

Caernos grudgingly gave ground as Vlain's relentless assault drove him farther and farther from the town square. The centaur was amazed at the man's stamina. Although both combatants were covered in sweat and dust, Vlain showed no signs of tiring. Caernos, on the other hand, was panting for breath, and his arms ached from repeatedly fending off the legionnaires' lightning-fast strikes. He was slowly, inexorably, running out of energy while Vlain's movements appeared to be speeding up.

The king didn't know how much longer he could maintain his defenses. Up until now, the proud centaur had never been defeated in battle. He hated to admit it to himself, but he had finally met his match. In retrospect, he realized he had become overly dependent on Svartur's ability to slice through an opponent's weapons and armor quickly. Try as he might, though, he couldn't damage Vlain's blades. He figured they either held a mighty enchantment or were made out of some wondrous metal. Either way, he couldn't even scratch them. Caernos also realized he had relied too much on his protective ward and the strength enhancement spell on his armband. Although the centaur was naturally stronger than Vlain, he still couldn't overpower him. Whenever Caernos locked blades with the battle-hardened legionnaire, Vlain quickly disengaged only to attack from a different angle. On top of that, Vlain's uncanny speed more than compensated for the centaur's strength advantage. Caernos knew it was only a matter of time before he was too slow to block a strike, and then his life would end.

Caernos's rear leg encountered resistance behind him. He risked a quick look back to see that he had bumped into a wooden fence skirting the edge of a cliff. The king knew there was nothing beyond the barrier except a steep drop down into white-water rapids. The rough rapids eventually flowed into the mighty Rendel Falls. Caernos could hear the roar of the waterfall even over the chaotic din of combat. The centaur surged forward, seeking to overcome Vlain's defenses, but it proved useless. The legionnaire was simply too experienced and seasoned a swordsman to provide even the smallest opening. In fact, he fought like a tireless machine.

Vlain smiled grimly, and his glowing eyes narrowed in

anticipation of the coming kill. He could sense the end of the fight was rapidly approaching. He had finally succeeded in cornering the wily centaur and was already planning how he would kill him. First, he'd use both swords to disarm him. Then he'd stab him through the heart. Vlain's last cut would decapitate the centaur. However, part of Vlain already regretted the centaur's imminent death because the proud king had fought with honor, intelligence, and skill. The fighter so rarely encountered a worthy opponent these days, but he had found one in King Caernos, and now he was about to end him.

Vlain took a deep breath, then launched his final attack sequence. Using both swords, he trapped the king's glittering blade between his own. He was just about to fling the strange weapon into the air when a wooden golem suddenly slammed into him from behind.

Unbeknownst to Vlain or the king, more druids and the golems they controlled had recently entered the fray. One of the druids saw King Caernos was in danger, so she used her golem to intervene. She had only intended to harm the legionnaire with the glowing eyes, but in her fearful haste, she had made the golem attack with too much force. She watched in helpless horror as the wooden monster pushed man, horse, and centaur through the fence and out into the air beyond the cliff's edge.

Meris and Bollis, who had been desperately fighting to prevent the king's royal guard from assisting Caernos, watched in horror as their friend and leader plummeted toward the raging rapids far below. The golem tried to steady itself at the last instant but failed. Then it, too, toppled forward to join Vlain, Viscol, and the king as they fell toward the river's frothy surface. Viscol whinnied in terror as he twisted helplessly in the air. Vlain pushed himself clear of the flailing horse, sheathed both swords and dove head-first into the water. Meris squinted as he searched for Vlain's form amongst the white-tinged waves. Several seconds went by, but he failed to break the surface. Caernos let his sword go and unsuccessfully tried to angle his hooves toward the river. He ended up hitting the water back-first, then sank out of sight.

The druidess, Meris, Bollis, and the king's royal guards all raced to the edge of the cliff to watch as the four combatants disappeared into the rolling rapids. Plumes of water shot into the air to mark the spot where each of them had landed. At first, the river appeared to have swallowed them whole, then, after a few tense seconds, Meris and Bollis saw the golem and Viscol bob to the surface. The wooden monster thrashed about wildly, but neither man could tell if the horse was moving or not. They all stared at the river for one long moment, but Vlain and Caernos both failed to reappear.

It suddenly dawned on the legionnaires that they were surrounded by enemies. Meris and Bollis dug their heels into the steeds' sides, prompting them to close with the distracted centaurs. Some of the beast-men were heart-sick since they had just lost their king, but others were filled with a white-hot fury. The enraged guardsmen fought Meris and Bollis with such ferocity that they would have soon overwhelmed them if not for Belor's timely intervention. The archer had recently returned from Tellin's Pond, where he had battled Haephius. Although his face was still bloody and filled with splinters, his aim was as true as ever. Using his longbow, he fired arrow after arrow into the centaurs' ranks until they were forced to retreat.

The druidess silently wept while she watched the river for any signs of her king. She was so distraught she ignored the raging battle between the legionnaires and centaurs, even though it was only a few yards away. Then, after Belor succeeded in driving most of the guardsmen off, she turned to face Meris and Bollis. The fawn reached into a pocket on the inside of her hooded cloak and pulled out a blowgun. She aimed it at Bollis and blew while Belor simultaneously fired an arrow at her. The tiny dart buried itself in Bollis's hand even as the archer's arrow bounced off the red-tinged ward surrounding the druid. Bollis pulled the projectile from his hand while Belor fired a volley of arrows at the druidess, prompting her to run away before the ward could dissipate. Bollis soon lost consciousness. He passed out in his saddle and would have fallen off his horse had Meris steadied him.

"Bollis! This is no time for a nap, you blaeting idiot!" Meris yelled at him, hoping the cook was merely jesting. He grabbed him by the hair and pulled his head back, then placed his ear next to his mouth and listened for his breath.

"What's the prognosis?" Belor anxiously asked as he came running up to them.

"He's breathing, but it's faint," Meris replied. "Looks like he's in a deep sleep."

"I'm glad to hear that," Denin said as he brought his horse to a stop beside Meris's mount. "Captain Oudeteros and Lieutenants Hildin and Paetro were shot by darts, too. Hopefully, they're all still alive as well."

"You're Sergeant Denin, right?" Meris asked. "You serve under Captain Oudeteros?"

"That's right, lieutenant," Denin replied. "At least, I did."

"Where are they now?" Belor asked.

"I don't know," Denin answered with a frown. "Several of those cloaked figures grabbed them, then ran off into the forest. We were about to go after them, but then those wooden creatures attacked us," Denin said, pointing at the burning golems that rampaged through the village square, attacking legionnaire and woodlander alike. "I led the remnants of Captain Oudeteros's force here, hoping those monsters would follow us, and they did."

"Why in Taloria would you want to lead them here," Meris

asked.

"I figured they might not know friend from foe in their damaged state. Apparently, I was right," Denin said with a grin as they watched one of the golems pick up a picnic table and launch it at a group of fleeing centaurs.

"You were indeed, sergeant," Belor said with an amused smile. "Good instincts."

"Thank you, sir," Denin replied, then focused on Meris. "We're to report to Colonel Verous now that Captain Oudeteros is gone. Where can I find him?" he asked.

Belor and Meris exchanged bleak expressions. "You must have just missed it," Meris gloomily replied. "You see that break in the fence?" Meris pointed at the gaping hole in the barrier.

"Yes?" Denin asked with a perplexed look.

"Vlain, and what we think was the king of the woodlanders, broke through it and fell into the rapids below."

"Jaina's living light!" Denin exclaimed. "I'm sorry. I didn't know..."

"It's alright, lad. None of us saw this coming."

"Do you think he survived?" Denin asked. "Did you see him come up for air?"

"Neither he nor the king came to the surface," the sharp-eyed Belor replied.

"What should we do?" Denin asked Meris.

"I'll lead Vlain's forces for now, and Belor, you'll lead Captain Oudeteros's men."

"Understood," Belor replied.

"What the hell happened to your face?" Meris asked the archer.

"I almost got hit by lightning." Meris gave him a side-long look. Belor shrugged his shoulders and added: "It's a long story."

"I'll listen to it later," Meris replied. "In the meantime, I'll order the men to wipe out the pockets of resistance in the square while a platoon combs the river for Vlain and..."

"But reinforcements could arrive from other villages to aid the woodlanders at any time," Belor cut in. "And it sounds like this section of the Rendel feeds a waterfall downstream. We have no idea where Vlain could have..."

"I know all that!" Meris snapped as he jumped down from his mount and tied Bollis to his saddle so he wouldn't fall off. "But we can't just leave him to die in this Jaina-forsaken forest!"

"I want to find Vlain as much as you do," Belor replied. "But we don't have time to mount a proper search. For Jaina's sake, we don't even know where the river leads..."

"Sure we do," Meris said as he swung back up into his saddle, took Bollis's horse by the reigns, and led it away from the cliff. Belor and Denin followed him. "We know it travels south, splits into two, and flows west of Fort Faldin. A platoon can follow it all the way back to Hadrian's Wall, then veer west to return to the fort. Hopefully, they'll encounter Vlain somewhere along the way."

"He may be dead for all we know," Belor bluntly stated. "You must have thought of that."

"You don't know Vlain like I do," Meris said in a strange tone.

"I'm not sure what that means," Belor replied. "But right now, we have problems of our own. For example, we still don't know where Caladin's force is..."

A platoon of Captain Caladin's men suddenly entered the

village square on horseback as if on cue. They drove nearly a dozen bound and chained minotaurs before them. Soon, several more platoons streamed into the village, followed by Captain Caladin, who brought up the rear. The big man wore a victorious smile on his broad face, but a well-trained eye could tell he was in great pain. Meris's eyes narrowed as he focused on a bandage around Caladin's knee. He also noticed one of his arms was in a sling, and the dent in his chest plate was impossible to miss.

"Looks like somebody kicked his ass again," Meris said in an amused tone.

"True, but judging by his smile, I'd say he won the fight," Belor replied.

Captain Caladin stopped his horse once he reached the center of the town square, then called his lieutenants over to him. Meris and Belor couldn't hear him from that distance, but they figured he was giving them orders. Sure enough, the lieutenants soon raced and told their men to attack the few remaining knots of woodlanders who still refused to surrender or flee.

"Go lend them a hand," Meris told Belor and Denin. "I need to speak with Caladin." The men nodded obediently, then galloped off to help subdue the dwindling defenders of Algos. Meris guided his and Bollis's horses across the town square, then stopped them in front of the giant legionnaire. Caladin raised an expectant eyebrow and looked down at Meris from his tall draft horse.

"What happened to you, captain?" Meris asked

"You should see the other guy," Caladin said with a smirk. Meris forced himself to form a wan smile. "Truth be told, I defeated the king of the minotaurs in single combat. You should have seen it. It was glorious," Caladin elaborated.

"The king of the minotaurs, you say," Meris responded as he

shook his head up and down. "Truth be told, I didn't know they had one."

"Clearly, there's much you don't know about the enemy," Caladin haughtily replied.

Meris bit his tongue. He knew Caladin hadn't known anything about a minotaur king either until he had encountered him on the battlefield, but he didn't want to argue. Not while there were more pressing matters to discuss. He was about to ask for Caladin's leave to search for Vlain, but the big man spoke before he could get the words out. "What happened to that one?" Caladin asked, pointing at Bollis's slumbering form.

"Oh, don't mind, Bollis," Meris replied with a sigh. "One of the woodlanders shot a dart at him earlier. It was apparently laced with a sleeping potion."

"Amateur," Caladin replied with a scornful look. Once again, Meris had to bite his tongue for fear of lashing out at his superior. "Where's Vlain and Oudeteros? I would speak with them."

Meris took a deep breath. "Vlain was pushed over the edge of that cliff there while he fought the king of the woodlanders," he sorrowfully replied while pointing across the square at the broken fence bordering the cliff. "As for Captain Oudeteros, Sargent Denin informed me he too was drugged by a dart and then carried off into the forest. Another amateur, I'm afraid," he said sarcastically.

Caladin narrowed his eyes as he studied Meris's face. "You mean to tell me Vlain's dead?" he asked incredulously. Try as he might, he couldn't hide how happy he was to hear the news. Meris scowled at his inappropriate response.

"That's not what I said," Meris replied. "He may have survived the fall. In fact, let me have a platoon to search for him along the banks of the Rendel..."

"Out of the question," Caladin snapped. "It's too dangerous on account of the recent battle. In fact, this whole area will be crawling with beasties soon. Any platoon you send after Vlain's corpse will only end up dead, and then I'll have to explain my actions to Commander..."

"But he's alive," Meris insisted. "I know it..."

"How?" Caladin pressed. Meris shook his head in frustration, and his eyes seethed with anger, but he remained silent. "That's what I thought. It's only a pipe dream. I understand, though. You were friends, and it's hard to lose..."

"He's alive, damn it!" Meris said with conviction. "Just let me have a few men, and I'll find..."

"Permission denied, lieutenant!" Caladin barked. "Now, that's quite enough. We'll have to manage as best we can without Colonel Verous or Captain Oudeteros in our midst. It was clearly their destiny to die in service of the empire today. I can't imagine a nobler end. Can you?" Meris took a deep breath but said nothing. "Words fail you. I understand. Grief is never easy." Meris gritted his teeth and looked away. Silence reigned as both men watched the legionnaires mop up the remaining woodlanders who still fought in the square.

"If I can't look for Vlain, then I might as well help the men wrap things up," Meris said in a hard voice. He thought about asking Caladin to watch over Bollis while he fought, but then he thought better of it. He didn't trust the self-absorbed man to look after his friend. He was about to find a quiet place where he could leave Bollis when Caladin spoke again.

"Don't bother," the big man rumbled. "We will soon be victorious. I have a special job for you in the meantime."

"And what is that?" Meris asked.

"I want you to supervise a team of men with the task of setting Algos ablaze," Caladin casually stated. "If we burn the village to the ground, then the beasties will be even more likely to attack Fort Faldin. The sooner they attack, the sooner we can deploy Snill's catapults and ballistae against them. We'll either eradicate them or force them into signing a treaty in our favor. Such were the commander's orders. Genius, is it not?"

A look of disgust formed on Meris's face. "Genius isn't the word I'd use," he replied.

"Be careful, lieutenant..."

"There's no need to burn the village down! We've clearly won the day," Meris objected.

"Are you refusing a direct order?" Caladin asked. "I'll have you up on charges for insubordination."

Meris waved his words away as if they were bothersome gnats. "Tell me, did Vlain know the commander wanted the village to be torched?"

"What does it matter?"

"Just answer the question..."

"Watch your tone, lieutenant!"

"I bet he didn't," Meris said. "He'd never agree to something like that. In fact, I doubt you'd be ordering me to do it if he was still..."

"Alive?" Caladin asked with a smug expression.

"Here!" Meris resisted the impulse to draw his sword and attack him.

"So you're refusing a direct order?" Caladin asked.

"You're damned right I am!" Meris said in a rush. "Get one of your lackeys to do your dirty work. I'll have nothing to do with it!"

"I should cut you down where you stand!" Caladin shouted.

"You're welcomed to try!" Meris shouted back. "Judging by your condition, I have no doubt I'd win. So what are you waiting for, big man?"

"Legionnaires!" Caladin suddenly shouted at two men as they passed by.

They ran over to stand at attention in front of the captain. "Yes, sir?!" they asked in unison.

"Arrest this man!" he snarled as he pointed at Meris. "Get him out of my sight."

One of the legionnaires grabbed the reigns of Meris's horse while the other one pointed his crossbow at him. For a second, Meris was tempted to prod his horse into a gallop in hopes of getting away. Once he was clear of Caladin's men, he'd search for Vlain in the river below. He quickly decided against such a rash course of action, however. It was one thing to refuse a direct order, which carried the punishment of a few days confined in the brig and a reduction in pay and rank. It was another thing to desert the legion, which carried the heavy penalty of death. He knew Caladin and Prydus wouldn't shy away from hanging him even if he found Vlain. In fact, he figured his punishment would be even worse if he did because he knew neither Prydus nor Caladin liked Vlain. He was simply too famous, charismatic, and formidable for their comfort. Vlain's star shined too bright, and thus, he highlighted Prydus and Caladin's failings as men and as leaders. So, Meris did the sensible thing by raising his hands and surrendering.

Caladin's men stripped him of his weapons, then bound his wrists together behind his back. They then attached a rope from one of their horses to his to control his movements on the march back to the fort.

Belor, who had just defeated a centaur on the other side of the square, watched Caladin's men with his hawk-like gaze as they arrested Meris. He nodded at Meris, which was his way of saying: "Do you want me to fill those fools with arrows?" Meris shook his head from side-to-side, thereby declining his offer. The movement of his head was subtle, almost imperceptible, but Belor saw it. As much as Meris would have loved to watch the archer shoot Caladin and the men who had just arrested him, he knew no good would come of it. Belor would probably be killed soon afterward, and Meris would be as well. Their deaths would be pointless and meaningless.

Caladin shouted the order for all legionnaires to gather their prisoners and begin the long march back to Fort Faldin. He then summoned ten of his most trusted men and tasked them with setting the village on fire. The men wasted no time carrying out his orders. Half of them rode about the village square lobbing glass jars of cooking oil at every wooden structure, while the other half ignited the tips of their arrows and then fired them at the designated targets. Billowing clouds of smoke rose into the air as the 9th Legion left the burning village behind.

Meris and Belor hung their heads in shame. They both felt the 9th was behaving in a deplorable and dishonorable manner. It was one thing to defeat an enemy in battle and quite another to destroy their homes and livelihoods after they had already been defeated. Meris knew Vlain would never have allowed Caladin to torch Algos, but he wasn't there to stop him. He cursed himself for not being the man Vlain was, but then he remembered his friend had a significant edge over him. Meris, unlike Vlain, could be defeated, so it wasn't a fair comparison. Still, he felt helpless at that moment and wished he could have done more.

AN UNDERSTANDING
Chapter 8

Vlain felt a surge of panic as the wooden golem pushed him, Viscol, and Caernos through the fence bordering the cliff's edge. He twisted around in his saddle and contemplated leaping off his horse and back onto solid ground. Vlain knew in his heart, however, that even he couldn't make such a leap. He also loathed the idea of leaving his gallant steed to die alone. The wind roared in Vlain's ears as he fell like a stone toward the raging river, and the sun glinted off his razor-sharp blades. His logical side told him to sheath his swords to avoid accidentally stabbing himself, nor did he want to risk losing his irreplaceable weapons. Somehow, he managed to sheath them while falling headfirst through the air.

A raven squawked in protest as it flew past his head. He ignored the startled bird, then used his legs to push himself away from Viscol. He assumed a diving position as the water rushed up to meet him, then shot down into the roiling rapids. Vlain angled his upper torso toward the surface so his dive would carry him horizontally through the water rather than straight down. He figured the river wasn't deep enough to slow him down in time to avoid hitting the rocky bottom. All Vlain could do was hope his upwardly angled body would level out before that happened. Clang! His helmeted head glanced off of a submerged boulder, causing him to nearly lose consciousness. Before he could stabilize himself, the undertow grabbed him and raked him along the stony river bed. His oxygen-starved lungs burned for air, but try as he might, he couldn't reach the surface. He then remembered he was clad in heavy, steel armor, which prevented him from floating. Vlain hastily undid the clasps connecting his chest plate to his backplate and watched as the armor sank to the gravely bottom. He tried to reach the surface again but still found it difficult.

Vlain still wore steel bracers on his forearms and greaves on his shins, but their combined weight shouldn't have prevented him from rising. Bam! The current slammed him back, first into another boulder. Although the impact was jarring, it hadn't hurt as much as it should have. Then, he remembered his steel shield was strapped to his back. It had absorbed most of the impact from the hit, but it was also responsible for weighing him down. A whirlpool spun him around and then launched him toward another boulder. Vlain raised his feet and braced for impact. As soon as his feet collided with the rock, he pushed upward with all his strength. His face only broke the surface for a few seconds, but it was enough time for him to fill his lungs with fresh air. He pulled the shield off his back and was about to drop it when he suddenly became airborne.

The roar of the Rendel Falls was deafening. Vlain flailed helplessly about as he fell over a hundred feet. He slipped his arm through the leather enarmes within the shield, then curled up in a ball behind the barrier in case he encountered a boulder at the base of the falls. Wham! Sure enough, the outer rim of his shield had slammed against a submerged rock. The current pulled him out into deeper water. Vlain dropped his shield into the watery depths before the heavy piece of steel could drag him down. Now, he was only weighed down by his long swords, bracers, greaves, and a hunting knife. Despite the weight of those items, he was still able to swim to the surface.

The fighter filled his lungs with as much air as they could contain, then swam toward the shore farthest from Algos. The swirling undertow and numerous whirlpools made it all but impossible, but Vlain was a powerful swimmer and refused to give up. After much toil and frustration, he finally won free of the dangerous currents and reached the muddy shore. The shallow water was covered with marshy reeds, and tall weeds lined the riverbank, affording Vlain a measure of concealment.

For a moment, Vlain lay there on the gravel, striving to catch his breath. The severity of his injuries gradually made themselves known as the adrenaline in his system died down. His vision was blurry, and the waterfall's sound was strangely muddled, indicating he had a concussion. On top of that, Vlain's shield arm was badly bruised. He attempted to move it, then realized his arm was dislocated. The fighter muttered several curses, then sat up to look around for a boulder or a tree that he could use to force it back into position.

Vlain's thoughts, however, were interrupted by a loud splash. He turned to look at the river. At first, he thought he was looking at an upright log, but then his eyes made sense of the image. He was gazing at the wooden golem that had pushed all of them off the cliff. The huge creature had just descended from the falls and was now swimming to shore. Vlain wisely eased back into the water, thereby hoping to stay out of sight. Although he still had his swords, he didn't like the prospect of battling the golem with a dislocated arm. He'd fight, but only if he had to. Thankfully, the golem failed to see Vlain's submerged form as it lumbered toward the shore. It strode up onto the riverbank, then paused to look around. Although Vlain was only a stone's throw away, the tall weeds and river lilies provided enough concealment to hide him. After a moment, the golem walked into the forest and was soon blocked from view by the trees.

Vlain's head slowly broke the surface as he raised himself up to search for the golem. He didn't stand up until he was convinced the danger had passed. The pain from his dislocated arm suddenly flared up, causing him to nearly pass out. Vlain clenched his teeth so he wouldn't give voice to the pain, then tossed his heavy, dented helmet to the ground. After he got control of the pain, he started walking toward a Y-shaped tree bordering the forest. He placed his limp, dangling arm at the intersection of the Y, angled himself away from the strangely shaped tree, and then quickly pushed his shoulder toward his immobilized arm. An excruciating pain shot through his upper arm, signifying the ball joint had gone back into its socket. It took all of Vlain's willpower to prevent himself from crying out. He took a moment to get his breathing under control, then pulled his arm free of the tree and gently massaged it.

"What now?" he asked himself as he gazed at the turbulent river. No sooner had Vlain asked the question then he heard another loud splash in the distance. He involuntarily shifted into a fighting crouch and pulled both swords from their sheaths. His injured arm throbbed, and he had a pounding headache, but he would fight if need be.

Soon, a vague, white shape appeared in the river. It was larger than a man, but he couldn't make sense of it. Then, suddenly, he knew exactly what it was. He was gazing at Viscol, his trusted steed and friend. The warhorse was clearly dead as it drifted face down in the water. Vlain waded out into the water, despite his pain and exhaustion, to gently wrap his arms around the dead horse's head and neck. Tears streamed down Vlain's scarred face as he pressed his forehead against Viscol's. The fighter swore to himself after he scanned the horse's broken body. It looked like the animal had landed on a boulder after the terrifying fall from the cliff. Viscol's neck was obviously broken, and his hips were tilted back at an unnatural angle. Vlain cursed himself for sending his trusted friend and steed to a watery grave. Although Viscol had loved him and had willingly served him, Vlain had still been responsible for placing the horse in a situation that had gotten him killed.

"I'm sorry, my friend," Vlain said as he pushed the horse away from him and back out into the river current. Although Viscol deserved a proper burial, Vlain lacked the time and energy to do so. In fact, all his body wanted to do was lie down and rest. Vlain waded out until the water reached his neck. He watched Viscol float away until a bend in the river took him out of sight. "You deserved better than this," he said before turning and swimming back to shore.

Vlain sat down on a log facing the river and took stock of his situation. He was alone, on foot, and way behind enemy lines with only two swords and a knife. Truth be told, he had been in worse situations before and emerged victorious, but it still wasn't a great scenario. He figured the 9th Legion had already left Algos or would soon do so. The legion had been winning before Vlain's disastrous fall, so it was reasonable to assume they had won the day. Prydus's orders had been to take what prisoners they could, then leave the village after defeating the woodlanders. Perhaps Meris or one of the others would organize a search for him. However, they were unlikely to get permission since Caladin was now the senior officer in charge. Vlain knew the big man would be glad to be free of him. In the end, Vlain decided the best course of action was to follow the Rendel south until it flowed past Hadrian's Wall and out into the grasslands. Once there, he'd be able to see the fort from a distance and could quickly make his way there.

Vlain stood up and began following the river's course southward. He had only traveled a short distance when his thirst got the better of him. He walked over to the swiftly flowing river, squatted down, cupped his hands together, and raised them to his mouth. As he drank, his amber eyes ceaselessly scanned the opposite side of the river. Vlain stopped drinking to stare at an oddly shaped boulder lying next to the water. The fighter soon realized he wasn't staring at a boulder at all. He was actually looking at the gray fur covering a centaur's muscular body, which belonged to the king of the woodlanders! King Caernos appeared to be completely still, at least from a distance. Vlain would have to swim across the river to determine if he was merely unconscious or dead.

The fighter squared his shoulders, took a deep breath, and waded out into the water. The cold current was strong and relentlessly pushed him downstream as he swam, but it only threw him off course by a few feet. Vlain's injured arm throbbed and ached, but he did his best to ignore it. He walked out of the river to stand on the grave shore, then walked upstream until he reached the centaur's inert form. Vlain had to admit that King Caernos was impressive to behold, even when he was just lying on the ground. His bone-white crown was missing, and the spell which had obscured the monarch's face with shadow was now gone. Vlain marveled as he gazed at the centaur's regal, leonine features. His nose looked like it could have belonged to a lion, as did the upper lip and the furry lower jaw. However, the forehead and high cheekbones resembled those of a human being. The king's entire face was covered with short, gray fur, and his curling ram horns looked even bigger up close. The last thing of note was his pointy, elf-like ears. Vlain had never seen such a curious mixture of features brought together in one being.

The legionnaire got down on his knees and placed his ear over the centaur's mouth. He strained to hear the faintest of breaths, to feel the gentlest stir of air. Vlain was just about to conclude the king was dead when he suddenly saw his chest rise and fall. He placed his index and middle finger together, then rested them on the centaur's carotid artery. Sure enough, he felt it throb as the blood surged through it. Against all odds, the king yet lived!

Vlain stood up, then surveyed the centaur's bruised and battered body. It looked like several of his ribs were either broken or dislocated on his right side. An angry-looking, swollen knot had formed above Cacrnos's left eye, and there were numerous cuts, scrapes, and bloody gouges lining the left side of his body.

Vlain sighed as he grudgingly pulled his swords from their sheaths. He positioned one blade above Caernos's throat and the other over his heart. Vlain took a deep breath to steady his nerves. He hated to kill a defenseless adversary, but the king was too important to be allowed to live.

***

Maiva walked softly through the lush forest. The young fawn held a basket full of roots, tubers, wild spices, mushrooms, and berries. She held her slingshot with her other hand and was careful not to step on any sticks or twigs in her path. Maiva was hoping to find a deer or at least a rabbit. The foraged food in her basket would dull the younglings' hunger pangs, but it wasn't enough to sustain them for long. To do that, she needed to bring down the big game. Maiva had gathered a score of smooth, round stones from a dry riverbed to use in her slingshot. She couldn't use the spiked balls because they would pump an animal full of viper venom.

The fawn stopped for a moment and set the basket and slingshot down. The dull ache in her back was starting to act up again. Thankfully, her steel-wood armor had blocked the legionnaire's bolt from penetrating her back, but the impact had bruised her. Maiva wanted to take the armor off and massage the sore spot. However, she refrained from doing so because she didn't know who or what she would encounter in the Wild. Maiva wanted to be fully protected in case she ran into a dangerous predator.

Maiva picked up the basket and slingshot, then resumed hunting. She tried to focus on finding a game as she crept through the dense underbrush, but her mind always returned to her fight with the legionnaires. Maiva could still see their angry, snarling faces right before she had sprinted through the green gate. Worst of all was the memory of the pained, terrified expression on the legionnaire's face when she had shot him with a poisoned, spiked ball. She had little doubt he had died soon after, and the thought of his blood on her hands greatly pained her. Maiva had known it was either him or her, but it hadn't made his death any easier to handle.

Fortunately, none of the others in her group had been injured by the legionnaires' bolts. One youngling had received a scratch on her face, and one mother had gotten a small cut on her arm after two bolts streaked through the portal. However, their luck took a turn for the worse after locating the supply shed in Barum Field. Some huge animal or monster had broken the stout wooden doors. It had devoured all of the emergency rations, leaving them with plenty of tents, blankets, sleeping rolls, pots, pans, and utensils but no food. Maiva and Ganymay had told the younglings to fill jugs with water from a nearby river, but aside from that, they hadn't had any nourishment in days.

Ganymay had suggested they all return to Algos since there was probably food there. The satyr figured the battle was probably over by now, so it would be safe to go back. Maiva had balked at the idea, however, because she thought the legionnaires might be occupying Algos. She didn't want to lead the younglings into a trap. Ganymay had been disappointed by Maiva's reply but had understood her logic.

Maiva then suggested using the green gate to travel to a gate in Valaren, the closest village to Barum Field. They had tried that, but Barum's green gate was too depleted to function since it had just transported such a large group. It would need several days to recharge, which meant the younglings would have to live off what Maiva and the other adults could forage in the forest.

Suddenly, Maiva heard what sounded like a deer crashing through the underbrush. The fawn set her basket down, fit a smooth stone into her slingshot, and waited. To her delight, she soon laid eyes on a doe. The deer froze as soon as they made eye contact. Several tense seconds passed. Maiva aimed at the doe's head, pulled back the sling, and was about to release it when she heard a voice behind her.

"I would nae do that, lassie!" someone shouted. Maiva jumped in fright just as she released the stone. The shot went wild, hitting a tree trunk only to ricochet off into the bushes. The deer bolted back into the underbrush. Maiva swore in frustration, then turned to search for whoever was responsible for ruining her shot. Strangely enough, there was no one there.

"Hello?" she asked while passing her hand through the air in front of her. "Is anyone there?" She was starting to think she was going crazy when she heard someone speak again.

"It's a good thing you missed! She's one of Irial's friends," the disembodied voice said. It spoke Findaloran with a strange accent Maiva had never heard before.

"Where...where are you...and who are you?" the fawn asked.

"I'm right in front of ya, lass. Heh, heh, and as for who I am? Well, I'm sure you've heard my name before."

Suddenly, a small being popped into view right in front of Maiva. At first, she thought it was a child, but the odd, little figure had a black, curling mustache and a short, sharply pointed goatee. He wore a purple overcoat with long coattails, purple trousers, purple gloves, and a purple cavalier hat pulled up on one side. His leather belt and Corinthian boots were a deep, glossy black. His shirt was bright white and frilled around the throat. He held a slender, black, metal walking stick topped with a multi-faceted, purple diamond that was nearly as big as an apple. The small being snatched his hat off his head to reveal his shortly cropped, pitch-black hair, then bowed low before Maiva with a theatrical flair. Although his expression was solemn, his movements were highly animated and comical, which instantly endeared him to her. "Allow me to introduce myself; I'm..."

"Oisin Corcra!" Maiva exclaimed. "My father told me tales about you when I was young." She could hardly believe she was looking at the same being whom Haephius had fashioned expensive, magical items for when she had been a tender youngling.

"And who might yer dah be?" Oisin asked.

"Haephius, blacksmith of Algos," she proudly stated.

"Ah, dear old Haephy!" Oisin chirped. "How is the old goat

these days?"

Maiva was taken aback by the informal way in which he talked about her father. She didn't know if she should be offended or just laugh it off. Little did she know, this was always Oisin's effect on those he met for the first time.

"He's...well, I honestly don't know," Maiva said as her throat tightened. The fear and anxiety from the past few days threatened to overwhelm her. It took everything she had to resist crying.

"There, there, lass," Oisin cooed as he approached her. "You've got a story ta tell, and I want ta hear all about it, but first and foremost, what're you doing way out here all by yer lonesome?"

"Algos was attacked by Man a few days ago," Maiva began. "The king tasked me with getting as many younglings out of the village as I could. We needed a safe place to take them, so we chose Barum Field. Unfortunately, someone or something ate all of the rations in the supply shed, so we've been..."

"Algos was attacked?!" Oisin blurted out. His little face became flushed with anger at the news. He started pacing back and forth. "So the Faldinites finally struck, eh?"

"Yes, we barely escaped in time," Maiva replied.

Oisin clenched his little fists and shook them in the air with rage. "Oy, if only I'd been there! I'd have shown 'em all what a Lillen can do!" he shouted defiantly.

Maiva tried to keep herself from laughing. Despite his dower expression, his diminutive size made him look more comical than threatening. "What's a Lillen," she asked.

"What's a Lillen?" he repeated. "I'm a Lillen, lass! Are ye daft?" Before she could answer, he continued. "I'm from a race of wee folk called the Lillen," he explained. "Granted, there aren't many of us left naow. A few hundred or so last time anyone bothered countin'."

"Oh, that's right," Maiva said. "I remember my father telling me about your people when I was little. I always hoped I'd meet one of you, and now my wish has come true. But tell me, why couldn't I see you at first?"

Oisin's lips formed a cocky smile. "Full of magic, I am. Positively full of it! I can do things that'd make yer head spin," he proudly stated as he placed both fists on his hips and puffed out his little chest. His dramatic pose caused his overcoat to fall back, allowing Maiva to see a sheathed rapier and dagger hanging from his belt.

"In that case, we could really use your help," Maiva admitted. "The younglings haven't had much to eat in the past few days, and..."

"Why haven't ye gone back to check on Algos?" Oisin interrupted.

"For all we know, the men could still be there, and besides, the green gate won't work. I think we overwhelmed it by taking such a large group through it. We can't get so much as a flicker of light from it now," she explained.

Oisin shook his head and chuckled softly as a knowing smile formed on his face. "Yer da clearly didn't teach ya how the gates work, or praps he forgot. Or maybe he was nae payin' attention when I splained it to him, back when he made me trinkets," he said while pointing at a bright, flat, purple diamond that was pinned to his overcoat. It had been intricately carved to resemble an open-faced flower. "Anyway, a gate usually needs a few days ta recharge after handlin' so much mass, but I know a way to kick-start her sooner," he stated matter-of-factually.

"Wonderful!" Maiva exclaimed. "I'll lead you back to our camp so you can get the gate working again."

Oisin thoughtfully tugged on his pointy goatee as he looked up at her. "I was in the middle of findin' emeralds for Irial, with tomorrow bein' her birthday an all, but I spose I can spare a moment ta help ye. Can't have the wee ones starvin', naow."

"Thank you, Mr. Corcra," Maiva replied. "Our camp is only a few leagues away. We should be able to walk there in..."

"Walk?" Oisin spat the word out with distaste like a sour lemon. "I thought ya were in a hurry ta get back to yer camp."

"I am," Maiva replied in a confused tone.

"Then I'll show ye a faster way o' gettin' there," he said with a devilish smile. He held his little, gloved hand out to her. Maiva hesitantly reached out to grab it. As soon as she had done so, Oisin held his walking stick aloft and began skipping down the road. Maiva was forced to quicken her pace to keep up with him. She was about to ask Oisin if he had meant skipping was his faster method of getting them there. However, before she could do so, the gem on top of his walking staff began to give off an eerie purple glow. "And now it begins," he said with a giggle.

"What begins?" she asked, but she promptly received her answer when the world began to warp and shimmer all around them.

***

Vlain stopped the tips of his blades from puncturing the king's body when they were only a hair's breadth away. Try as he might, he couldn't bring himself to kill the defenseless centaur. To do so would mean robbing the world of a majestic being destined to rule a savage but beautiful land. Obviously, the Elamaran Empire was at war with the woodlanders, and thus, he was compelled to kill their leader. However, another side of him saw such an act as cowardly and cruel, given the present circumstances. King Caernos couldn't protect himself in his unconscious state, so where was the honor in taking his life? Not to mention, he had survived a fall from the cliff, a trip through the rapids, and a second fall over the Rendel Falls just as Vlain had. Had the king survived against all odds only to be slain now?

He sheathed his swords, then placed his hands on his hips while thinking about what to do next. He figured there were two possibilities. Vlain could leave the king here, and no one would ever know he had spared him. Of course, Caernos could die before his people found him. Such was the risk of walking away. On the other hand, he could assist the king, but Vlain would then be responsible for all the legionnaires he might harm in future conflicts. Vlain shook his head in frustration. He felt bewildered by all the consequences of his actions.

"There's really only one thing to do," he said to himself as he bent down. "Wake up!" he shouted while vigorously slapping the centaur's bestial yet noble face. "Time to rise!" The king murmured incoherently, and his eyes fluttered open, but Vlain could tell he wasn't fully awake. The legionnaire slapped his palm hard against Caernos's cheek, then stood back. The centaur raised a hand to absently swat at Vlain, but his eyes remained closed. The fighter swore in frustration, then stood up and walked to the river. He bent down, cupped both hands and plunged them into the water. Vlain returned to fling the water at Caernos's face. The king sputtered several times, then bolted up from the ground with a dazed expression.

"Khon...khon dalig mn?" the centaur asked groggily. "Tuol Dano vre ling?"

"Emblin, remember?" Vlain said. "You're speaking to an outlander, a man from the southern empire of Elamara."

"I remember now," Caernos said as he painfully rose to a standing position. "You are Vlain Verous, the man with eyes like molten metal."

"They only get like that when I'm fired up," Vlain casually replied. Still, his expression was stern and severe as he peered into the king's pupilless, white eyes. He had to make sure Caernos was lucid and not in the grips of delirium brought on by head trauma. "You just survived falling off a cliff, followed by a ride over the falls. Can you make it back to Algos? Back to your people?"

The King stared at him incredulously for a moment, then teetered forward and would have lost his balance had Vlain not rushed forward to steady him. "What is this? Are you sparing me, outlander? If so, then why?"

"Can you make it or not?" Vlain asked.

"I think so," the king replied. He took a few steps forward and would have fallen if Vlain hadn't caught him by the arm again.

"I'm going to take that as a solid no," Vlain said with a sigh.

"I don't understand," Caernos prodded. "You're in better condition than I am, and you are armed. Why not just kill me? Isn't that what your empire wants?" he asked.

"It's no longer that simple," Vlain explained. "At least not for me."

"What has changed?" Caernos asked as he angrily shoved Vlain away.

"I'm not entirely sure," Vlain admitted. "Stay there for a moment," he said while holding his hands out before him. He walked over to a dead tree, ripped a long, straight branch from its trunk, then walked back to Caernos and handed it to him. "Here, this should help." The king stared distrustfully at Vlain for a second but still took the proffered piece of wood. He used it as a staff to help steady his wobbly gait while he walked across the gravel bed.

Caernos turned to address Vlain when they reached the edge of the forest. "Whether you intended to or not, you have placed me in your debt," the king told him. "If I am to retain my honor, then I must also spare your life."

Vlain shook his head in disagreement. "Just pretend you never saw me after the fall. No one needs to..."

"No," Caernos rumbled. "I will do no such thing. You spared my life, so I shall return the favor for as long as you remain in the forest."

"And how exactly do you intend to do that?" Vlain asked.

With that said, "By granting you safe passage out of Findalora, which Man refers to as the Last Wild," the king said. "I will tell my people to spare the life of the man with the burning eyes should they encounter you. The edict shall last for three days. That should give you enough time to get back to your fort." With that said, Caernos turned away from Vlain and walked into the woods. Even with the help of the staff, he only made it a short distance before one of his front legs gave out, and he pitched forward. He would have fallen again had Vlain not rushed to his side to lend support.

"I appreciate the thought, but you could die out here if I leave now," Vlain said.

The king fixed him with a questioning gaze. "And why should that bother you? Are we not enemies?"

"Of course," Vlain replied.

"Then why do you care if I die? If memory serves, you were trying very hard to make that happen just a short while ago. So, what's changed?"

Vlain's brow creased in frustration as he sought the words to explain his change in behavior.

"Something told me not to kill you" was all he could come up with. "And... well...the clerics are always going on about how Jaina wants us to be merciful to each other. So, there you have it."

"Jaina is your goddess?" Caernos asked.

"She's the most powerful and well-known of our gods," Vlain explained.

"And what is a cleric?"

"A person who channels Jaina's power to heal the sick and injured."

"Are you a cleric in addition to being a warrior?"

"Jaina, no!" Vlain said with an amused laugh. "I just see the wisdom in their teachings from time to time."

The woodlander king gave Vlain a long, hard look. "If this is some ruse to gain my trust so you can spy on me, then I will..."

Vlain held up his hands and took a step back. "That's not at all what this is, but you know what? I wouldn't believe me either. In fact, I'm gonna leave before..." But he was interrupted by the sudden arrival of a group of druids.

"Klim Caernos! Mol nae grae! Wom toll yuin ix ne Man!" One of them shouted as he ran toward Caernos and Vlain. The druids fanned out into a semi-circle as they drew near. Several of them pulled blow guns out from the pockets lining the inside of their forest green cloaks. Despite his injuries, Vlain pulled both swords from their sheaths in the blink of an eye. The druid closest to Vlain took a deep breath and was just about to blow a dart at him when Caernos raised his fist into the air.

"Chon danir tolu tonnin vlin!" the centaur boomed. Although Vlain couldn't understand the language, he could tell from Caernos's tone that he was issuing a command. The druids reluctantly put their blowguns away, then bowed low before the king. Caernos spoke to them again, causing them all to rise. One of the druids pulled back the hood on her cloak to reveal she was a brown-skinned human. She ran over to the king and embraced him. The two of them spoke quietly and intently for a moment.

Vlain sheathed his swords and stared intently at the human druid. He had assumed all of the woodlanders were nonhuman, but he had obviously been wrong. Vlain wondered if she was merely an anomaly or if her existence signified a human presence in the Last Wild. Of course, the empire would still wage war against the woodlanders even if their ranks consisted of humans, but it made doing so less palatable, at least to Vlain than it had been before. He very much doubted Prydus would care about killing fellow humans, however.

Suddenly, Caernos and the druidess turned to face Vlain. "This is Iolee, one of our most gifted druids," the king said as he placed a hand on her shoulder.

"Vlain Verous," Vlain said as he gave her a slight bow.

The woman smiled in return, although it appeared forced. In fact, she looked like she would have loved nothing more than to kill him on the spot. Vlain couldn't really blame her, given the circumstances. However, despite the hostility in her eyes, he had to admit she was beautiful. Her shoulder-length hair was pitch-black, and it framed her perfectly proportioned face. He found her delicate nose to be endearing, and her hazel eyes twinkled bewitchingly at him.

"Although your injuries are less serious than mine, please let her heal them. I will then supply you with a bag of provisions for your journey back to your fort. In this way, I can repay my life debt to you," the king said in his booming voice.

The paranoid part of Vlain wondered if this was some type of ruse to lull him into letting his guard down so they could kill him without a fight. However, the trusting side of him believed in the sincerity he had detected in King Caernos's voice. Furthermore, he secretly knew the woodlanders couldn't defeat him even though he was outnumbered. However, his victory would be painful and hard-won since he was already in bad shape and the druids looked quite formidable.

"Well, this is definitely a first," he said with a dry chuckle. "Normally, I'd be leery of letting my enemies heal me, but the offer fits right in with how strange the rest of the day has been."

"So, we have an accord?" the king asked.

"Sure, my head is throbbing, and my arm is aching. Bring it on, I say."

Caernos directed them all to a small meadow covered with soft, lush grass. As soon as he stopped, two druids approached him from both sides and gently placed their hands on him. Vlain watched as the druids' fingertips began glowing with a soft, green light. The scene reminded him of the times he had watched clerics heal people, except the color of their light was white.

"This will be easier if you remove your weapons," Iolee said with a thick woodlander accent.

"Yeah, that's not happening," he replied with a smirk.

"Very well," the druidess said. "Will you at least sit down?" she asked while pointing to a smooth, weathered log.

"That I can do," Vlain said.

As soon as he got comfortable, Iolee placed both hands on his head. Vlain relaxed as a tingling sensation followed by a soothing warmth flowed from her fingertips. It felt terrific at first, but then it became painful as his head began healing at an unnaturally fast rate. However, the pain gradually grew more bearable and then slowly faded away. The druid had used magic to cram a week's worth of healing into just a few moments' worth of time. Iolee then placed both hands on his inflamed shoulder. The same order of sensations occurred as his previously dislocated arm was healed in an astonishingly short time. After she was done with his arm, the druid placed one hand on Vlain's chest and one on his back. She closed her eyes, and her breathing slowed as she concentrated on healing all of the other cuts, scrapes, and bruises that lined his body. The fighter sighed in contentment when she finally removed her hands.

"You could teach our clerics a thing or two," he told her with a sincere smile.

"Clerics?" she asked. "What does it mean?"

"They're skilled healers like yourself," he replied.

"I see," she replied with a thoughtful expression. "You are welcome."

"Tell me, where did you learn to speak Emblin?" he asked.

"The king's scribe, Oshur, taught all of us who wished to learn," she answered.

Vlain watched her as she knelt down and pressed both palms to the ground. The green light that had emanated from her fingers and palms when she had healed him now flowed upward from the ground and into her hands. Vlain stood up to test his previously injured shoulder by rolling it about and was delighted at how good it felt.

"Why are you doing that?" he inquired.

"I must replace the energy I just gave you," she explained. "Findalora shall restore it."

Vlain was about to reply when Caernos, who was now fully healed as well, stared at the space above Vlain's head with a look of amazement. The king pointed his finger at something that had captivated him and spoke rapidly to the druids in the Finadaloran language. A similar look of wonder formed on all of their faces.

Vlain turned around to search for what had captivated them. His eyes soon found it. A glowing white dove was perched on a branch a mere foot above Vlain's head. It gave off a soft, radiant light akin to the glow the clerics emitted whenever they healed someone. Vlain stared at the bird for a moment, then reached up to touch it. However, the motion startled the ethereal dove, and it flew from its perch and up into the trees until it was lost from view. Vlain turned back to face the king.

"Do you know what this means?" Caernos asked him.

"That some of the birds here can glow?" Vlain said, clearly at a loss.

"It means you have brought peace to our land. We just witnessed a great omen!" the king informed him.

"Me, the bringer of peace?" Vlain asked with an incredulous laugh. "This is truly a day of firsts!"

"This is no joking matter," the king stated. "You just saw Amani, an emissary of the Great Stag. Where ever she goes, peace soon follows."

"How can I bring peace when I just led an assault against your village?" Vlain asked.

"I know not," Caernos rumbled. "I only know the Stag doesn't make mistakes, nor do his emissaries. You have been marked by the dove, Vlain."

"So, what happens now?" Vlain asked in a befuddled tone.

Before the king could answer, one of the druids rushed forward to whisper something in his ear. The exchange only lasted a few seconds, but after the druid pulled away, Caernos fixed Vlain with a hard, angry look. Vlain shifted uncomfortably beneath his withering glare, and his hands instinctively moved toward his swords.

"Your army set Algos on fire before they left! Did you know of this?" the king demanded.

Vlain took a deep breath as he shook his head from side to side. "No," he honestly replied. "I wasn't given orders to torch the village. Perhaps it was started by accident during the..."

"How can I trust you to speak the truth?!" the king raged. "And why?! Why would you burn our village after you had already won? What did you hope to gain by destroying our homes?"

Vlain heard the heart-rending anguish in Caernos's voice, and it made him feel ashamed of the actions of his fellow legionnaires. "I don't know why they did it," was all he could say. A confused expression formed on Vlain's face as he mulled over this new development. Prydus had never given him an order to torch the village, nor had Vlain heard him even mention it. Had this been the commander's plan all along, but he had kept Vlain ignorant of it to avoid a fight? He had no way of knowing. Vlain would have to ask him when he saw him again.

The centaur snatched a bag from one of the druids and tossed it at Vlain's feet. "Here are the provisions I promised you," he said in a bitter tone. "Take it and leave. You are no longer welcome here." The king and the druids turned away and walked uphill toward the village.

Vlain snatched the bag up from the ground, slung it over his shoulder, and started walking back to the river so he could follow it south out of the forest. He took two steps, then stopped and gazed at the retreating forms of the woodlanders. "King Caernos!" he shouted. "Please listen to me," he implored him.

The proud centaur stopped, then turned around to glare at Vlain. He crossed his muscular arms over his broad chest as he stared expectantly at the man who had invaded his land. "What do you have to say, outlander?" he boomed.

"Let me atone for the actions of my fellow legionnaires by helping you fight the fire," Vlain said. "Or I can search for those who still cling to life in the ashes. Although I'm only one man, I'm a tireless worker. Please, give me a chance to redeem the honor of the 9th Legion."

Caernos glowered at Vlain while the druids shouted curses and pointed accusingly at him. "Even if I agreed to such a strange proposition, I couldn't guarantee your safety once you're among my people. They are grieving the fresh loss of their loved ones and are filled with rage. Any one of them could kill you before I could prevent..."

"I have an idea!" Vlain cut in. "I could dress like one of your druids. That way, the villagers won't know an outlander is among them. I'll pass unseen right under their noses while I work to undo some of the harm I've caused. Please, let me do what I can."

The king stared at him for a long moment, and as he did so, his expression slowly changed from one of wrath to one of surprise. "But what if someone discovers your ruse? Are you prepared to die for your act of atonement?"

"Yes," Vlain answered succinctly. "But I won't be in any danger."

"And why is that?"

"Because I'll have a ward of protection on me," Vlain said with a sly smile.

***

Haephius moaned in agony, prompting Daedra, an elderly druidess, to lay her hands on him for the fifth time that morning. Zenda watched as a pale green light emanated from the elderling's fingertips. Daedra had retired from druidic service several years ago because her body had gotten too old to use magic properly. She had helped ease Haephius's pain but was unable to heal him. Zenda sighed in frustration as she gazed down at the arrow that was still lodged in the fawn's back, a parting gift from the archer whom he had fought at Tellin's Pond. She had asked Daedra why she hadn't removed it. The retired druidess had told her it was too dangerous since it was so close to an artery. She feared removing it would tear it open and cause the fawn to bleed to death.

"I can't just stand here and watch him die," Zenda blurted out.

"What other options do we have?" Daedra calmly asked.

"I'm going to search for help. Maybe I'll get lucky and run into someone."

"Who would be wandering these caves and tunnels besides monsters?"

"I heard that the gnomes pass through here now and then."

"Their kingdom is several leagues south of here if memory serves, and there's precious few gems or gold to lure them out this way."

"I don't care," Zenda replied. "I'm useless just standing here. I have to try something."

212

"In that case, be sure to take several others with you," Daedra said as she used a rag to dab at the blood that had seeped out of the angry-looking wound. "It's easy to get lost in these twisting tunnels, and predators roam the dark."

"I will," Zenda said as she slid the strap of her quiver down over her chest. The fawn picked up her longbow and left the alcove. She walked over to the milling group of elderlings and wounded woodlanders in the center of the cavern. Zenda scanned the throng for the healthiest beastlings she could find. In the end, she had to settle for an aged centaur, a limping minotaur, a feverish fawn, and a satyr with his arm in a sling. "I know none of you are in good shape right now, but Haephius needs magical assistance. He'll die if we don't find help soon."

"Then, by all means, let's get on with it," the centaur, a male with cloudy cataracts, replied.

Zenda led the rag-tag group out of the cavern. She couldn't walk very fast due to the minotaur's limping gait and the decrepit centaur's unsteady steps. Still, they made decent time. The sickly fawn had the idea of scraping an X on the wall whenever they left one tunnel and entered another. With these markers in place, they'd hopefully be able to find their way back to Sanctuary.

Zenda held a magical lantern aloft to light the way. The other members in her party each had an unlit torch, as well as a tinder, should they need to set them ablaze. At one point, Zenda passed a doorway to her right. The deep darkness within stubbornly resisted the light from her lantern. Zenda quickened her pace as she walked past the opening. The foul smell of rotting meat wafted out of the room, if such it was, and the fawn heard what sounded like a gigantic serpent's scales as they slid across the stone floor. She knew her imagination was probably populating the dense darkness with monsters, but she hurried on nonetheless, as did the other members of her party.

The group had been walking for over an hour when a faint, repetitive sound gradually came to Zenda's ears. She stopped and tilted her head to the side as she listened intently. It sounded like hammers or pic-axes hitting stone. Her lips formed a hopeful smile. She led the group toward the sound, and as they got closer, Zenda became certain that she was hearing miners as they labored.

Zenda turned a corner in the tunnel, which allowed the light from her lantern to shine on a group of twenty or so gnomes as they toiled away. The fawn waved her hand in a sign of greeting while she approached the one-foot-tall miners. Each gnome wore the same outfit: red suspenders, red shirts, red, pointy hats, and brown leather boots. They ranged in age and build, but they all had long beards, though some were brown while others were graying or snow-white. The tiny miners looked up at Zenda with a mixture of alarm and surprise. Some of them backed away even as others raised their pick-axes as if they meant to strike her.

"Greetings, I'm Zenda of Algos, and these are my friends," the fawn said as she gestured back at the other members of her party. "We come in peace."

One of the oldest-looking gnomes fixed her with a stern look as he wiped the sweat off his brow. "You're a long way from home, sapling. What brings you down into the deep dark?"

"Our village was attacked by Man," Zenda replied, prompting several gnomes to murmur fearfully amongst themselves. "We came through the gate in the Cave of Sanctuary. One of our people is gravely injured. Are there any clerics among you?"

The eldest gnome shook his head from side to side. "Nay, but Hilberg can guide ye back to our kingdom," he said as he pointed to a lanky gnome with a dark brown beard. "There, ye can have an audience with the queen, and if it's her will, you'll get the clerics ye need."

Zenda nodded in understanding. "Thank you, kind sir. We're sorry to have disturbed you. We'll be on our way now."

"May the good Stag watch over ye," the old gnome said as Zenda walked past him.

"And may His light shine upon you," she said, thus completing the ancient Findaloran saying.

Zenda and the others left the miners behind as they followed Hilberg down the tunnel. It eventually led them to a gigantic cavern filled with mushrooms that ranged from a few inches to several feet tall. Hilberg paused every so often so the woodlanders could catch up. Zenda was thankful for the gnome's patience because she knew it would be easy to get lost in the maze-like mushroom forest.

As they walked along, Zenda caught occasional glimpses of what looked like huge rats scurrying between the mushroom stalks. However, she couldn't be sure if they were really rats since the skittish creatures always stayed beyond the light of her lantern. Only their red eyes were clearly discernible in the shadows. The only other wildlife Zenda saw were scores of black, horned toads the size of cats. The sinister-looking amphibians were perched on top of oversized mushrooms and stared menacingly at Zenda whenever she passed them by.

After another hour of walking, they came upon an ancient-looking, arched stone bridge that spanned a shallow, sluggish river. A bat as big as a crow swooped down at Zenda when she reached the apex of the bridge. She screeched in terror, causing the gnome to race back to check on her.

"Are ye alright, ma'am?" he asked.

"Ba...bat!" she stuttered as she pointed up. Hilberg looked up, but the bat was long gone. A smile spread across his face and he began laughing uncontrollably while holding his sides. Zenda glared at him. "It's not funny," she said defensively. "It was huge...the size of an eagle," but her words only made Hilberg laugh harder.

"There's plenty o' bats round here, I'm afraid," the gnome said. "Come along, now. We mustn't dawdle on account of yer injured friend and all." With that said, Hilberg retook the lead.

That's when Zenda realized he didn't have a light source of any kind to guide him, yet he seemed to be navigating without any trouble at all. *Must be magic*, she thought. *Or maybe gnomes see better in the dark than us surface-dwellers.*

The mushroom forest continued on the other side of the bridge, but Zenda no longer saw any toads or bats. Her eyes were now drawn to a green, phosphorescent moss that grew on the cavern's floor, walls, and the ceiling far above. The bright patches of moss reminded Zenda of stars and even formed their own 'constellations' as she gazed up at them. In fact, the moss gave off so much light that if she had turned her lantern off, she would still have been able to see without much difficulty.

The light from the moss allowed her to make out enormous stalactites that jutted down from the ceiling, as well as stalagmites that rose up from the cavern floor. She was beginning to enjoy the scenery when a black centipede as big as a snake suddenly ran over her hooves. Zenda was tempted to shriek, but she didn't want Hilberg to laugh at her again, so she clamped a hand around her mouth and remained silent.

They left the colossal cavern a few minutes later and entered into a tunnel that led them into what appeared to be the outskirts of the gnome kingdom. At first, the woodlanders only saw a few miners here and there, but the little people became more and more numerous as they progressed. Soon, Zenda saw male and female gnomes scurrying about on countless unknown missions. Some looked like merchants and tradesmen, while others appeared to be dignitaries and administrators. Zenda came to these conclusions based on how refined and expensive the gnomes' clothing looked, in addition to how they carried themselves. Hilberg waved at several of the gnomes in a congenial manner, indicating he knew them well.

The gnome led them to a gigantic set of iron doors, then told them to wait there as he slipped through a gnome-sized door on the side of the tunnel. Zenda looked back to make sure all the Findalorans in her party were present. One by one, they came limping or shuffling into the foyer in front of the grand doors. They had only been waiting there for a few minutes when the iron doors opened to reveal a group of white-robed gnomes.

"Greetings, travelers from the world above," a female gnome said as she bowed before them.

"Greetings, good people of the Deepdark," Zenda replied.

"Queen Pietra instructed us to heal your companions while you speak with her in the Chamber of Awakening," the gnome informed her.

"Are you all alright with that?" she asked the four Findalorans. They eagerly shook their heads in agreement.

"My name is Grislin," the female gnome said with a slight bow.

"And I'm Zenda," the fawn said with a curtsy.

"Come, I'll take you to the queen." Zenda watched as the white-robed clerics each chose a woodlander to treat. Their tiny hands soon emitted an unmistakable white, healing light. When Zenda was satisfied that her companions were well being cared for, she turned and followed Grislin through the massive iron doors.

***

Vlain swore softly under his breath as he stared at the smoking

217

and charred ruins of the once-great lodge that had bordered the town square. All the other structures in the area had been similarly devastated by the raging fire which had swept through the village. Vlain turned to look at the smoke billowing above the tree line. After destroying most of Algos's houses and buildings, the fire had leaped into the forest and was now running riot amongst the towering trees. Vlain had initially asked to help fight the fire, but Caernos had told him he'd be better utilized searching for survivors in the village. The king had appointed two druids to watch over him and assist with the rescue operation. Caernos had ordered the rest of the druids and the remaining wooden golems to fight the forest fire.

Caernos had then rounded up all able-bodied villagers and split them into groups, each tasked with looking for survivors in Algos. Vlain's group consisted of several hulking minotaurs, a score of fawns and satyrs, ten or so centaurs, two golems, and the two druids and himself. They had been working for several hours straight to extract trapped woodlanders from the burnt remnants of their former homes.

Vlain was growing wearier by the second, but his pace never faltered. One of the druids watching over him, an aging male satyr named Dinn, had just cast a spell that enabled him to sense the presence of survivors hidden in the rubble. The satyr pointed at the area where the woodlanders had been buried, indicating Vlain's work detail should dig there. The disguised legionnaire and three muscle-bound minotaurs clambered over the mangled remains of the lodge and then got to work.

Vlain grabbed a steaming hot section of masonry with his bare hands, then chucked it aside. For the hundredth time that day, he was grateful for the protective ward surrounding his body. His hands and arms would have been badly burnt by now if Iolee hadn't formed the magical barrier around him. The two druids accompanying him had also summoned wards to protect themselves during their dangerous and challenging work. Iolee, who stood to Vlain's left, had insisted that the king also wear a ward in case Vlain tried to harm him. Caernos had agreed, but not just because of Vlain's presence. Like Vlain, the king figured he could work faster to extract buried survivors if he didn't have to worry about getting sung by hot debris.

"The life signs are coming from your left, Garis. Dig there," Iolee told a minotaur.

The huge beast-man grunted in acknowledgment, then did as the druidess had instructed him. Vlain had been able to understand the Findaloran language Iolee had just spoken on account of a magical construct called an understanding. It was a necklace made from hundreds of enchanted, small gray stones strung together, which gave off a rainbow sheen when the light hit them. The necklace had the ability to translate any language for the wearer. Speaking an unknown language back to others was trickier, but Vlain was slowly getting the hang of it. Iolee had told him the necklace would accelerate his ability to learn their language. Vlain had only been wearing it for a few hours, yet he already knew hundreds of words in Findaloran. When Vlain had asked Iolee what the woodlanders called the necklace, she had informed him there was no direct translation for the word in Emblin. She told him to just refer to it as an understanding. Of course, after Vlain put the necklace on, he understood the Findaloran word for it, but like her, he was unable to find an Emblin match for it.

The fighter had asked Iolee, who had crafted such a magnificent and helpful tool. She had told him that the understandings, for there were many of them, had been invented by the renowned blacksmith and inventor named Haephius. Vlain was floored after she described the master blacksmith's appearance because he realized Haephius was the fawn with the lightning gloves he had fought earlier.

In fact, the genius inventor had almost killed Vlain when he hurled a lightning bolt at him. Vlain now felt remorseful for injuring him and for ordering Belor to kill him. He secretly hoped the archer had failed to do so, which in turn caused him to feel even more conflicted about the war.

Fortunately, none of the woodlanders suspected Vlain was anything more than the druid he was pretending to be. At least so far. Vlain had to constantly remind himself not to outdo the others in his work detail for fear of activating the powerful enchantment within him. If he relaxed his self-control for just a second, he'd outperform even the inhumanly strong minotaurs. His strength wouldn't eclipse theirs; he'd simply summon the energy needed to remove debris faster than they could. In such an event, his eyes would glow with an unnatural light, and he'd be discovered for what he truly was.

The minotaur named Garis pulled a charred beam of timber from out of the ashes. Once it was clear, Vlain moved forward and grabbed the blackened remains of a chimney stack. Another minotaur came over to help him with it. They were just about to pull it up when a male fawn came running up to their group.

"Iolee! Dinn! My house is on fire, and my children are trapped inside! Please, come quickly. I need your help!" he frantically shouted.

"We'll be there right away," Iolee told him.

Vlain jumped down from the mangled wreckage. "Lead the way," he said to the fawn. Without waiting for Iolee or the others, they both raced away.

"Hold on!" Iolee shouted. "Let me call the golems so they can..."

"There's no time," Vlain shouted back over his shoulder.

"Seconds count. Just meet up with us as soon as you can."

"But your ward is getting old. It won't last much longer!" Iolee shouted back. Vlain and the fawn were already out of earshot, however. "Damn it!" she cursed. "Percheron! Ardennais!" she called out to two powerfully-built centaurs who were working at the far end of the ruins. "Come here, quick! Dinn and I need a ride to Figler's house."

The centaurs dropped what they were doing, then galloped over. While she waited for them, Iolee mentally summoned the two golems. The giant wooden creatures had been busy moving debris on the opposite side of the square. They, too, dropped their burdens and then started walking toward her. Iolee and Dinn jumped onto the backs of the centaurs. The druidess telepathically told the golems to follow them as the centaurs galloped off.

Vlain was surprised at how fast Figler could run. If not for his enchantment, he would have been left far behind. The two of them sprinted past the outskirts of town and down a well-worn dirt road until they came to a solitary, two-story cabin. Flames billowed out of the upstairs windows and had already spread to the trees in the backyard.

"Where are the children, and how many of them are there?" Vlain asked Figler.

"They're upstairs. There's two of them."

"Alright, I'm going in."

"I'll come with you," Figler said.

"No, you wait here!" Vlain sternly replied. "I've got a ward protecting me, but you'll be burnt alive. Just wait. I won't belong." Vlain took a deep breath to steady his nerves, then raced into the burning house. Although the ward protected Vlain from the flames and heat, it still allowed smoke to pass through it. Vlain used a section of his cloak to cover his nose and mouth. He was halfway up the stairs when part of the ceiling fell down to block his path. Vlain swore in anger, pulled his swords from their sheathes, and hacked through the wooden barrier. He then raced up the stairwell.

The smoke was even worse upstairs. Once again, Vlain used his cloak to cover his face as he searched for the fawn's children in the gloom. He was about to call out for them when he saw both of their inert forms lying on the floor in the hallway. Vlain tucked one diminutive fawn under each arm, then turned and ran back toward the stairs. He was about to step onto the first step when the entire staircase collapsed to the ground floor. Vlain cursed, then, with no other option at hand, he leaped down onto the burning stairs. As soon as he landed, a bright red flash filled the air, signaling the demise of his ward. Vlain cursed again, then sprinted toward the front door while deftly avoiding crashing timber beams as well as sudden bursts of flames. He was almost to the door when the entire door frame collapsed in on itself. Vlain angled his shoulder toward the hot debris, then ran full speed into it.

Figler jumped in fright as Vlain burst through the burning mass of wood to emerge into the clean sunlight. The fighter set each youngling on the ground, then ripped the dark green cloak off his body. It was now writhing with flames. He threw it to the ground, then stomped on it until the fire went out. Vlain knew Figler could now see the swords on his belt as well as his legionnaire outfit, but it couldn't be helped. Thankfully, Figler was so focused on his children that he didn't see Vlain's weapons, unusual clothing, or even his blazing, reddish-orange eyes. Just to be safe, Vlain stepped behind a tree. The fighter gently touched the burnt skin on his neck, shoulders, back, and arms. Even though he'd only worn the burning cloak for a few seconds after the ward had vanished, it had still been enough time for the fire to hurt him.

"Thank you so much!" Figler said as he pressed the younglings to his chest. "Where did you go?" he asked Vlain, but he soon lost interest in him as he inspected his children for burns. One of the fawns started coughing, a sure sign she had inhaled plenty of smoke. The other child, however, remained limp and unconscious. Figler looked up at the centaurs and druids as they rode up to him.

"Please!" Figler said as he lifted the still youngling up to Dinn. "Heal him!"

The druid jumped off Percheron's back, took the fawn child in his arms, and closed his eyes as he summoned the energy to heal him. Soon, a faint green light emanated from his hands, which he placed on the youngling's forehead and chest. Iolee and Ardennais searched for Vlain while Dinn healed the youngling.

"Where did the other druid go?" Iolee asked Figler.

"I...I don't know. He disappeared right after he rescued my children," Figler explained.

"Pssst! Over here," Vlain whispered as he stuck his head out from behind a tree.

Ardennais trotted over to him, and Iolee jumped down from his back.

"Of all the foolhardy things you could do..." she berated him.

"I saved the children, didn't I?" Vlain asked.

"One of them. We don't know about the other one yet. Dinn's healing him." Just then, the boy fawn began to cough and sputter. Dinn smiled from ear to ear, and Figler laughed in joy. Dinn continued healing the youngling while Figler stroked his hair.

"Make that two," Vlain said with a pained smile.

"Come here, hero," Iolee said. "Let me look at those burns." Vlain grimaced as she touched them. "I knew the ward wouldn't hold. You wore it too long and used it too heavily."

"It lasted long enough for me to get the children out. That's what matters."

"What about your own safety?" Iolee asked as the green, healing light sprang from her hands. She placed them on Vlain's burnt back.

"I always muddle through somehow," he casually replied.

"You certainly do. Ardennais and Percheron told me it looked like you were about to beat the Grey King before you both tumbled off the cliff. You should know up until now, he has never been defeated. After that, you survived the fall, the rapids, Rendel Falls, and now this. What's your secret?"

"Lucky, I guess," Vlain answered.

Iolee moved her hands from Vlain's back, which was now fully healed, up to his shoulders. "I might believe that if not for your glowing eyes. Are you a sorcerer?"

"Jaina, no!" Vlain said with a laugh. "I wasn't born a sevlin, and even if I had been, I don't have the patience for all that studying."

"What's a sevlin?" Iolee asked.

"Someone who can sense and control magic."

"I see," Iolee said. "We refer to magic-users as findoree."

"Then you must be one."

"All druids are, but don't think I haven't noticed that you changed the subject," she said with a smirk. She moved her hands to Vlain's muscular arms.

Vlain laughed good-naturedly. "Let's just say I'm enchanted and leave it at that."

"Determined to remain mysterious?" Iolee said with a smile as she moved her hands to his chest. She was starting to like the outlander despite herself.

"All part of my rugged charm, I suppose."

"That's the second time I healed you today," she said as she stepped back. "Try not to get hurt again. As for our conversation, I'd like to continue it when there's more..."

"Good afternoon, Iolee," Oshur Whitehoof, the king's scribe and servant, said as he rode up to them on a tan-colored pony. The pure white fawn wore an immaculate red shirt, brown leather vest, and woolen trousers. Vlain thought it an odd outfit for a woodlander, considering it was the standard attire for Elamara's scholars.

"Good afternoon, Oshur," Iolee replied.

"Pardon the interruption, but the king requested the outlander, Mr. Vlain, join him for dinner."

"Alone?!" Iolee asked.

"Of course not," Oshur replied. "His royal guard and others will be on hand."

"Good," Iolee said. "I still don't trust you," the druidess said to Vlain.

"I wouldn't either," Vlain replied. "Besides, it'll take you time to realize I'm actually a lecherous rapscallion. That was a joke, by the way. Well, not entirely."

"Quite amusing," Oshur said. Iolee rolled her eyes, then walked away.

"Iolee, before you go, ask Dinn to give Mr. Vlain his hooded cloak. We don't want to scare anyone by parading an outlander about," Oshur said. Iolee nodded in agreement, then walked away.

"It's just Vlain, by the way. You can drop the mister," Vlain said as he extended his hand to Oshur. The goatman tentatively sniffed it. "You clasp it," Vlain said, trying hard not to laugh.

Oshur cautiously gripped his hand. "Then you shake it like this," Vlain said as he shook his hand.

"What a curious greeting," Oshur said. "I shall remember it." Iolee soon returned bearing Dinn's forest green cloak. Dinn didn't look happy at having to part with it, but he said nothing. After Vlain was again concealed, Oshur waved for Ardennais and Percheron to join them. "The king's guesthouse is only a couple of leagues outside Algos, but the journey will go quicker if you ride one of the centaurs," Oshur suggested.

"I'm fine walking," Vlain replied. The idea of riding a centaur just didn't sit right with him. "What about Figler's house? Shouldn't we stay to help put the fire out?"

"We'd only get in the way," Oshur replied. "Take a look."

Vlain did just that and was glad to see Iolee and Dinn were using magic to suffocate the flames somehow. He also saw that the two golems had finally arrived, and each one carried a huge barrel of water in each arm. They threw the water onto the burning house then started demolishing it. Vlain smiled in satisfaction, then turned back around. He was sad that Figler and his children had lost their home but relieved that the fire wouldn't spread out into the forest.

DINNER WITH THE KING

Chapter 9

The odd quartet made good time as they followed a game trail through the forest. Vlain looked up, more than once, in awe at the enormous trees. They reminded him of the towering turrets that surrounded the royal palace back in the capital, but, of course, the trees were each distinct, living beings that contributed to a vast, green sea.

Vlain also noticed neither of the centaurs would look his way. The white-haired Percheron, who was nearly the size of Caernos, had a hostile expression on his handsome face, while the smaller, brown-skinned, and brown-haired Ardennais looked surly and angry. Vlain could feel the aggression radiating out from them. At one point, Percheron trotted up to Oshur and began berating him for allowing the invader to live. He was outraged that Vlain was permitted to dine with the king when he thought he should be rotting in a grave. Percheron snarled in wrath as he mentioned how many woodlanders Vlain had killed that morning and how many orphans he had created in that short time. He then begged Oshur to look the other way while he slew the outlander.

The bitter words stung Vlain's heart because they were all true and therefore justified Percheron's hatred. The fighter figured the centaur had either forgotten he could understand their language now that he wore an understanding or naively assumed they were out of earshot. Or perhaps he didn't care whether Vlain overheard him or not. There was no way Vlain could know what was going on in his head. Regardless of his reasoning, however, Vlain heard everything.

The druidic cloak concealed Vlain's hands as he reached for his sword grips. The centaur's angry words had triggered the fighter's tactical mind. He envisioned a scenario in which he would swiftly kill all three woodlanders. Since Ardennais was behind Vlain, he'd turn and kill him first. He'd then engage Percheron while keeping a watchful eye on Oshur. Although the fawn was physically unimpressive, he seemed quite intelligent and could be a magic-user. As soon as Percheron was dead, Vlain would move on to Oshur, and unless the fawn had some devilish tricks up his sleeve, he imagined he'd go down quickly.

Vlain began to relax when he heard Oshur's reply. The little fawn reminded Percheron that he and Ardennais had killed many legionnaires right in front of Vlain. The centaur seemed to take great pride in that fact as he trotted beside the eloquent scribe. Oshur then reminded him that the Elamaran Empire and Findalora were at war, so what else should he expect the 9th Legion to do? Percheron scoffed at his statement and was about to argue his case further when the fawn finally lost his patience with the hulking guardsman.

"Percheron! I'll never gainsay the king!" he whispered harshly while furtively looking back at Vlain. "I don't care if you hate him or not. The outlander is the king's guest and should be afforded respect until we're told otherwise! Is that understood?!" When Percheron objected, Oshur launched into his own tirade. "Has it ever occurred to you that perhaps the king and the outlander can negotiate a peaceful solution to our long-running conflict with Man?" Percheron was at a loss at how to answer. "I swear, you muscle-bound warriors are only good for one thing," Oshur grumbled. "Now quit your griping and leave the statecraft to those of us with a brain!"

For a moment, it looked like Percheron might knock the fawn off his pony for his outburst. He took a deep breath instead, then moved back behind Oshur and remained sullenly silent for the rest of the journey. Vlain released his sword grips and sighed in relief. He was glad he hadn't been forced to kill the guardsmen. There had already been more than enough bloodshed.

A turn in the trail suddenly brought them within sight of several buildings. Towering pine trees ringed a medium-sized clearing, which contained a long, low lodge, as well as three small cabins in its center. Oshur guided Vlain to the cabin farthest from the lodge. He got down from his pony then told the fighter to follow him inside. Vlain was surprised at how well decorated the cozy cabin was. There were colorful quilts hanging on the walls, and a fire cheerfully blazed in the fireplace.

"First off, I want to apologize for Percheron's inane outburst..." the fawn began.

"There's no need," Vlain said as he held up his hands. "As a warrior and a leader, I know what it's like to watch an enemy kill your men. And let's not mince words, I am your enemy, and you are mine. Unless that dynamic changes, I'll expect enmity from your people."

Oshur nodded in agreement. "Be that as it may, I think the oaf forgot you wore an understanding," he said with an embarrassed smile.

"Or he was seeking to provoke me," Vlain countered. "I care not for his reason. Just know that I'll remain peaceful unless someone attacks me. This I promise."

"Your outlook shall serve you well for, believe me when I say, you're surrounded by King Caernos's protectors, some of which are unseen."

"Understood," Vlain responded. The fighter knew his enchantment would prevent him from losing a fight regardless of the odds. Still, he remained silent since there was nothing to be gained by sharing such knowledge.

"There's hot water in the bathtub and clean clothes on the bed," Oshur informed him in a hospitable tone. "Please join the king for dinner when you're ready."

"Thank you, Oshur. I shall do so."

The little goatman bowed his head, then left the cabin. Vlain collapsed onto a chair as soon as he was gone. The heavy toil of pulling survivors out from the ashes of Algos had exhausted him. It felt wonderful to sit down, rest, and catch his breath. All was quiet save for the melodic calls of birds outside. Vlain lost himself in the soothing silence and would have fallen asleep had he not stood up.

He knew it would be rude to keep Caernos waiting, so he decided to wash up and get dressed for dinner. He walked to the back of the cabin, where he found a circular, claw-footed, iron bathtub.

Wisps of steam curled up invitingly off the surface of the water. The fighter eagerly stripped off his dirty clothes, then sighed contentedly as he slipped into the hot bath. However, he was careful to keep his sword belt within quick and easy reach. After soaking for a while, Vlain grabbed a soap bar from a nearby table. He stood to lather up, then sank back into the water.

Vlain forced himself to get out of the tub and used a towel to dry off. He walked over to a small bed to look down at the clothes which had been laid out for him. The garments were silk, a fabric that Vlain hadn't thought the woodlanders were privy to. Perhaps they had stolen it from one of the trading caravans? The long-sleeved shirt was a teal green, while the trousers and leather shoes were a walnut brown. When combined, the colors reminded Vlain of the giant trees which formed the surrounding forest. Vlain donned the clothes then strapped his sword belt over them. He smiled in pleasant surprise at how well the clothes fit, and wondered how Oshur could have known his sizes. Vlain covered himself with the druid cloak to complete the ensemble and then exited the cabin.

Although Vlain didn't see anyone during his short walk to the lodge, he could sense multiple presences close by. The fighter tried to act as if he was unaware of the king's hidden protectors as he stepped up to the lodge's front door. He was just about to knock when Oshur suddenly opened it. The fawn took his cloak from him and hung it on a peg on the wall. He then nodded at Vlain's sword belt with a disapproving look.

"They stay with me," Vlain said in a tone that left no room for dissent. Oshur looked at King Caernos, who stood in front of a tall table.

"It's alright," the king rumbled. "Let him keep his weapons. It's only fair."

Oshur nodded obediently, then ushered Vlain to the table. The fighter's mouth watered as the smell of roasted pheasant, pan-fried trout, and baked potatoes filled the air. His eyes grew wide when he sat down in front of the table in a tall chair. All the foods he had smelled were there, in addition to a big bowl of fresh salad. Vlain's enchanted vision informed him that the food didn't contain any poison or drugs. He felt a pang of disappointment, however, when he saw there wasn't any alcohol. There were pitchers filled with water, milk, and what looked like apple juice but no spirits.

Caernos seemed to read Vlain's mind when he broke the silence. "Normally, my table would be laden with an assortment of wine, mead, and ale, but in light of our recent tragedy, it doesn't seem fitting. This is a night of mourning, after all, so the least we can do is abstain from drinking. Besides, you and I need to think clearly, don't we?"

Vlain noticed a magical layer of shadow once again covered Caernos's face. His glowing white eyes and ultra-deep voice were now the only metrics by which Vlain could gauge his mood. The fighter studied the massive centaur. He wore a black leather vest over a white silk shirt. Vlain also noticed two black iron swords hung from either side of the king's slim waist. Black iron was a harder form of iron, which was rare and so dark in color that it almost looked black. Vlain smiled. The king appeared to be adapting to Vlain's fighting style by carrying two swords. Of course, Vlain's orichalcum blades would eventually cut through even black iron, but it would take time.

"I suppose we do," Vlain said as he lifted a napkin off the table, then draped it over his lap.

"Please pray with me before we partake," Caernos's deep voice rumbled in the gloom. Vlain closed his eyes and bowed his head as the centaur began. "Lord Stag, we ask you to guide the souls of all those who perished in Algos today into your blessed paradise. Also, please bless this meal, and protect us from our enemies," Caernos pointedly finished. A sad look formed on Vlain's face as he ripped both drumsticks from the roasted pheasant on his plate. "Are the accommodations to your liking?" Caernos asked.

"They are," Vlain replied. "Thank you for your hospitality. I do, however, have a question," he said right before he bit into one of the drumsticks.

"Yes?" the king inquired.

"Earlier, you told Oshur I could keep my swords because it would only be fair. What exactly did you mean by that?"

King Caernos secretly smiled as he cut into a baked potato. "Surely, you know I'm surrounded by my royal guard and hidden bodyguards as well."

"Oshur said as much," Vlain said.

"Then suffice it to say, you'll have to defeat a small army before you could harm me."

"Then my swords hardly make it a fair fight," Vlain countered.

"You understate your skill, Colonel Vlain," Caernos boomed. "I know firsthand how deadly you are with those remarkable swords."

"Deadly enough to defeat a small army all by myself?"

"I'd rather not find out."

Vlain swallowed a bite of meat then washed it down with milk. "Speaking of remarkable weapons, I assume you lost your black sword in the Rendel after we fell?"

"It's probably resting on the river bottom as we speak," Caernos mused. "I appointed several druids to look for it tomorrow, along with my crown. I trust they'll be found and returned to me."

"What exactly is your sword made of?" Vlain asked.

"Svartur is its name, and it's made from a rare element called ebonite. Have you heard of it?"

"As a matter of fact, I have," Vlain replied between bites of food. "Doesn't it have an opposing stone...ivorite or something like that?"

"I'm impressed," Caernos admitted. "Ivorite is both its sister stone and its antithesis, in that both minerals become soft and malleable when they're close to each other."

"I assume ivorite was used to soften a piece of ebonite so it could be sculpted into Svartur?"

"It was," Caernos said with a nod. "Without ivorite, it's impossible to alter ebonite, or vice-versa. They're both far harder and tougher than diamonds when they're kept apart. Even dragon fire doesn't faze them."

"Speaking of dragons, was your crown carved from a piece of dragon bone?"

"You don't miss a thing, outlander," Caernos said with a rumbling laugh. "It was carved from a section of Raisszann's skull after my great grandfather slew him in the Battle of Endless Autumn. Are you familiar with the dragon or the battle of which I speak?"

"Just the battle," Vlain answered. "My grandfather told me tales of the Endless Autumn. He said the cold spell lasted five years before the other seasons finally returned to Taloria."

"My grandfather told me similar tales, and he believed the Long Fall only ended because of Raisszann's death," Caernos finished proudly.

"So, we have your great grandfather to thank for breaking the dragon's spell?"

"Yes."

Vlain cut the fried trout on his plate into pieces then speared one with his fork. "Although the old worm is dead, I think his bones still have glamour magic in them. I could feel a sense of command, of authority coming off the crown, which was hard to resist when we fought."

"You have a knack for unraveling my secrets," Caernos admitted. "So, it's only fair I ask about yours. Tell me, why couldn't Svartur damage your swords? What are they made of?"

"They're made of several different alloys, along with an extra ingredient, which together forms a metal called orichalcum," Vlain explained. "Orichalcum is incredibly durable and has the unique property of vibrating when it's struck. By doing so, it dissipates the energy in a strike rather than absorbing it. Your sword may be the hardest thing in Taloria, but it'll never cut through mine due to this property," Vlain finished.

"Incredible," Caernos admitted. "And what is the extra

ingredient you mentioned?"

"You'd have to ask their creator, Phaelos the philosopher, the most brilliant mind of our age. Good luck, though; he never reveals his secrets," Vlain said with a chuckle. He was lying, of course.

The secret ingredient was a saffron-colored substance called the philosopher's stone, but Vlain never shared that information with anyone, let alone an enemy.

"What a pity," Caernos replied. "Then perhaps you can at least tell me why your eyes glow whenever you fight? Are you a magic-user?"

"Of sorts," Vlain cryptically replied.

"Come now, speak plainly."

"I use magic, but like you, I'm not a mage or, as you say, a findoree."

"I use enchanted items to enhance myself. You're implying you do the same?"

Vlain took a sip of apple juice then piled salad onto his plate. "We'll have to sign a peace treaty, and you'll need to earn my trust before I tell you more."

"How is that fair?" Caernos grumbled. "You know my secrets, but I don't know yours."

"Oh, I'm sure you haven't told me everything."

"Of course not."

"Then allow me to keep my secret," Vlain responded.

"Fair enough," Caernos said as he pushed his plate away. He clapped his hands together, prompting Oshur to emerge from the kitchen bearing a tray, which held a teapot, a bowl of sugar, and two cups. "Would you care for tea?" the king asked.

"Sure," Vlain said.

The fawn served them both then went back into the kitchen. Caernos dumped an ample amount of sugar and milk into his tea then took a sip. Vlain took his tea black. He always had. He sipped it and marveled at the fact he was having tea with a centaur who was king of the woodlanders. What's more, the hulking beastman drank his tea in the same refined manner as the lords and ladies of the capital! Vlain would have to share this story with his children and Gailin one day. He wondered if they'd believe it, though.

"Since you brought up the subject of a peace treaty, I must ask if you're able to sign on behalf of the Elamaran Empire," Caernos inquired.

"No," Vlain admitted. "I'm second in command of the 9th legion. I report to Commander Prydus Orilius, whose signature bears the full weight of the emperor's authority."

"Where is this commander of yours now?"

"Fort Faldin," Vlain answered with a frown.

"What type of commander waits in a fortress while his soldiers fight?" Caernos asked in an incredulous tone. "A true leader leads from the front!"

Vlain took a deep breath before answering. As much as he wanted to agree with the king, he knew it was the wrong thing to do. He had to present a united front when it came to the legion and the empire, or their negotiations would start out on the wrong foot.

"Prydus has a unique style of leadership that works for him," he carefully answered.

"I see," Caernos rumbled. "Tell me, what kind of man is he?"

Vlain drank some tea before answering. "I won't mince words. Prydus is young and headstrong, but he's not unreasonable. If you give me your terms for peace in writing, I'll deliver them to him. However, I ask that you share them with me tonight, so I can tell you if he's likely to accept them."

"Very well," Caernos said after he used a clay teapot to refill his cup. "My conditions are simple. Number one, I want all hostility directed at my people to cease immediately. I have lost so many to your cruel traps and poisonous snares over the years. This must stop! Number two, I want us to be free to visit the burial cairns in the open plains south of the forest as we have done since time immemorial. Number three, you shall only hunt in designated sections of Findalora and at certain times of the year. Number four, if the aforementioned conditions are met for at least a year, I'll consider trading with the merchants of Faldin. Trade would be good for both of our people."

Vlain nodded in agreement. "All of your conditions sound reasonable. There is, however, the issue of prisoners. We were given orders to take captives after we attacked Algos, and I'm assuming you also captured some of my legionnaires. Are you willing to exchange prisoners if my commander's open to the idea?"

"I am," Caernos rumbled. "I'm glad you brought up the subject of prisoners. There's a hunter among your kind named Vorsord. He led a hunting party into my forest a few years ago and killed one of my people."

"A minotaur, if memory serves," Vlain put forth.

"So, you know of Vorsord and his heinous act?" Caernos asked.

"I do," Vlain admitted. "My men and I responded to a call for help from one of his servants a few months ago. Regrettably, we killed over twenty of your people while defending his home from an assault. Only later did I learn that Vorsord held a woodlander there against her..."

"You speak of Dame Maiva, whom we call Starmark now," Caernos finished for him. "In fact, she told me a man fitting your description set her free. Is this true?"

"It is," Vlain answered. "You know, releasing Vorsord's daughter would go a long way toward showing your sincerity when it comes to these..."

"I cannot do that," Caernos interrupted.

"Why?" Vlain asked.

"Because Vorsord's daughter, Rowan, doesn't wish to leave," the king bluntly replied. "I offered to let her go after she had been with us for a year, but she declined. Rowan prefers our way of life now. She wants to stay in Findalora."

Vlain's eyes grew wide. He hadn't expected such an answer. "Then perhaps you could arrange for Rowan and her parents to meet soon? Surely, she'd like to see them again, and Vorsord would jump at the..."

"I'll ask her," the king replied.

"Good, that's a start," Vlain said with a satisfied sigh. "Are there any other terms you wish for me to present to the commander?"

"No, that's the bulk of it. We can assemble the finer details later."

"Very well," Vlain said after he swallowed a mouthful of tea. "With any luck, my commander will be open to your terms." He was about to stand up and excuse himself from the table when Caernos suddenly clapped his hands. Out came Oshur, bearing a pie of some kind. The little goatman set it down on the table, then looked up expectantly at the king.

"Would you care for dessert, colonel?" Caernos rumbled.

"What is it?" Vlain asked.

"Rhubarb pie."

"Then, by all means," he said with a nod. Oshur placed a slice of pie on a small plate then handed it to the king. He gave the next piece to Vlain, then disappeared back into the kitchen as was his custom. "You know, you surprised me tonight," Vlain admitted.

"How so?" Caernos asked.

"I figured centaurs ate like horses. You know? Grass, hay, oats, and all that."

Caernos's rumbling laughter caused the windows to quiver in their panes. "We aren't horses, Vlain," he said. "Although we bear a similar design on the outside, we're quite different on the inside."

"I realize that now," Vlain said with a smile. "I also didn't expect to see you drink tea with the poise and grace of one of our Elamaran dignitaries."

Caernos laughed again then fixed Vlain with an earnest look. "You also surprised me, outlander. Not only did you spare my life at the river, but you helped us pull villagers from the wreckage of Algos all day and rescued two younglings from a burning house. Either you're the most convincing spy I've ever encountered, or you're actually a good man."

Vlain raised his teacup in the air. "I'll drink to the latter," he said with a wink.

Their talk soon shifted to mundane matters like the weather. Caernos told Vlain winter wasn't far off and that it was no small matter in Findalora. The pace of daily life slowed to a crawl, and the Findalorans became shut-ins as the foul weather made travel dangerous and difficult. Neither of them relished the idea of fighting each other amidst the frigid snowstorms that would come. The unspoken hope in both of their hearts was that Prydus would agree to Caernos's demands so the conflict could soon reach a peaceful end.

After they finished off the pie and drank all the tea, Vlain pushed his chair back from the table and stood up. "I thank you for your hospitality, King Caernos, but I must excuse myself before I fall asleep."

"Ah, so you aren't god-spawn after all?" Caernos asked with a chuckle.

"No," Vlain replied. "Nor would I ever make such a claim."

"Before I bid you goodnight, let me tell you what shall transpire tomorrow. At first light, I'll take you to meet a group of druids who live a few leagues away from here. They have something I want you to see. After that, I'll give you a horse and a bag of provisions for your journey back to Fort Faldin. How does that sound?"

"A bit mysterious, but I'll play along."

"Good night, Vlain. Sleep well."

Vlain bowed low before the monarch then walked out of the lodge. He wondered what the king intended to show him tomorrow. His mind spun with possibilities as to what it could be during the short walk back to his cabin. In the end, he pushed the whirling thoughts out of his mind because he was simply too tired to wrestle with the mystery.

***

Maiva could hardly believe her eyes. Oisin and herself shot through the countryside at an insanely fast pace. Every few seconds, they'd slow to an actual skipping pace, only to shoot off again at a dizzying speed. As time went by, Maiva realized they weren't moving at all. A rippling, translucent tunnel surrounded them while they skipped along, thus separating them from the outside world, and it was this strange tunnel that was moving. However, the effect paused every hundred yards or so, allowing them to take one normal step before being thrust back into the bizarre, spatial tunnel.

The young fawn tried to clear her head by shaking it back and forth, but it did no good. Her stomach was tied up in knots, and she was growing more and more nauseous by the second. She was just about to lean down to ask Oisin, who was laughing and reveling in the sensation, to stop when her camp came into view. Maiva gave the Lillen's hand a squeeze, so he knew not to shoot past it. He nodded in understanding and struck his walking stick hard against the ground. The eerie purple nimbus of light surrounding the gem at the top gradually dissipated, as did the weird spatial tunnel around them. Maiva soon realized they had come to a stop, even though her body still felt the sensation of movement.

"So, what do ya think o' skip walkin', lass?" Oisin asked her. "Fastest way to travel, aside from the green gates, and damn fun too!"

"How...how does it work?" Maiva asked as she waited for her stomach to settle down.

Oisin looked up at her as if she had gone soft in the head. "For every step ye take, the staff shoves ye forward a hundred steps. Ye get to skip all the space in between; that's why it's called skip walkin'. Get it naow?"

"My stomach doesn't care for it," Maiva answered.

"That's to be expected first few times, but you'll get the hang o' it in..."

"Have you made a friend, Maiva?" Ganymay asked as she approached them.

"I have," Maiva replied. "This is Mr. Corcra..."

"Just call me Oisin, lass. Me da was Mr. Corcra."

"Greetings, Oisin. I'm Ganymay Greycoat," the satyr said as she bowed.

"Pleased ta make yer acquaintance," Oisin said, returning her bow.

"He's here to fix the gate..." Maiva began.

"Well, it ain't technically broken," Oisin corrected. "I'm just gonna give it extra power so you and yourn can get ta another village without havin' ta wait for it ta recharge."

"And how will you do that?" Ganymay asked.

"Take me ta the gate, and I'll show ya," Oisin cheerfully replied. The younglings immediately surrounded him. Looks of wonder formed on their faces as they stared at his garish clothes and possessions. Some of the bolder ones even reached out to touch his hat, overcoat, and gloves. A fawn boy was about to touch the purple gem on top of the walking stick when Oisin jerked it out of his reach.

"Can't have ye touchin' that, wee one. Ye could activate it and send me shootin' off to Stag knows where!"

Maiva led Oisin to the green gate, while Ganymay did her best to restrain and corral the mob of younglings who trailed behind them. The motley group reached the solitary stone ring in a few minutes. Ganymay told the younglings to stand back, so Oisin would have enough room to study the green gate from all angles.

"This un was made by druids long ago," he told Maiva as he

patted the runes inscribed on it with his small, gloved hand. "Fine craftsmanship," he said, nodding in approval.

"You seem to know a lot about the green gates," Maiva said.

Oisin stared at her with a look of disbelief. "Well, I certainly should, lassie! I'm the Portal Master, after all!" he exclaimed.

"Portal Master?" Maiva asked, at a loss.

"As in the one who maintains the portal system, makes new maps o' it, and advises folks on how ta build, repair, and use 'em. No one knows more about the green gates than I do, lassie! Been studin' 'em longer than yer da's been alive," he finished proudly.

"Then how fortunate it was for me to meet you," Maiva replied.

"Indeed, it was," Oisin said as he gave the portal ring a hearty slap. "Well, gather up the younglings. We can leave whenever yer ready."

Maiva turned to address the group. "Listen up," she shouted. "I want you all to line up just like you did in the Meadow of Knowing. We're going to travel by gate again, so I want you to be on your best behavior."

"But I thought it was bwoken," a little fawn girl said.

"It was only sleeping," Maiva said with a smile. "And now our good friend, Oisin, the Portal Master, is going to wake it up so we can go to the village of Valaren."

"Do they have food there?" a centaur boy asked. "My stomach hurts."

"They do. Now follow me," Maiva said as she turned and walked toward the gate.

Oisin tapped his skipping staff hard against the ground. Once again, a purple nimbus of light flowed out of the gem on top of his staff. He closed his eyes. Suddenly, the gate came to life. A green curtain of energy flowed down from the top of the ring until it filled the entire space. Maiva gazed at Oisin in wonder. The Lillen had somehow activated the gate without even speaking. She hadn't known such a thing was possible.

"Alrighty, in we go naow," he calmly stated. Maiva watched as he disappeared into the rippling, energy curtain, then stepped in after him. For a split second, she felt herself becoming undone. A horrid nothingness enveloped her, no sight, no sound, no awareness, just a dreadful null state. Then, just when she was convinced she was dead, she emerged from the other end of the magical wormhole, safe and sound. She blinked several times. It was unsettling yet strangely exhilarating at the same time. The sun was shining brilliantly here, unlike Barum Field, which had been overcast and gloomy.

Maiva waved at the huge minotaurs that had stopped to stare at her and the others who filed out of the green gate. Valaren was primarily a minotaur village, save for a few other Findaloran races. The muscle-bound creatures waved back at her. She followed Oisin down the ramp and into a small gathering of minotaurs who stood in the town square.

"Greetings, good people of Valaren. I'm Maiva Starmark," she said with a bow. "We have come from Algos, seeking sanctuary."

"Greetings, Maiva. I'm Charolais," a brawny, white-furred female minotaur said. "Why do you flee Algos? Is something amiss?"

"I have much to share with your king," Maiva answered. "Would you please guide me to him?"

"Follow me," Charolais replied. Maiva looked back to make sure the rest of the group had emerged from the portal. She watched as the last of the younglings, a female centaur, and her mother, emerged from it. She was just about to follow Charolais when she remembered Oisin. Maiva wanted to thank him for helping them in their hour of need, but the Lillen was nowhere to be found. Suddenly, he popped into view a few steps behind Charolais.

"Lookin' for me, lassie?" he asked with an amused expression.

"Thank you for all you've done..."

"Think nothin' of it. Golar vinder konin gint," he said, which means: "We are all one people."

"So true. Can we count on you to help in the struggle against Man?" Maiva's heart fell when he suddenly vanished from sight.

"Of course! Just open any green gate and shout me name! I'll come a skippin'," the disembodied voice answered.

"Fare thee well, Oisin, 'til we meet again," Maiva replied. She turned to wave at the group behind her, indicating they should follow her out of the bustling town square. She then fell in step behind the towering Charolais.

***

Vlain woke to the peaceful melody of birdsongs, which drifted in from outside of the cabin. He had fallen asleep while leaning against the wall. Both of his orichalcum swords were lying on his lap. His neck and back were stiff due to the awkward angle he had slept in, but he'd had no choice. Had he slept on his back, he would have slept too deeply and may not have heard the stealthy approach of an enemy. Vlain trusted Caernos and the other woodlanders only so far. One could never be too careful when sleeping alone behind enemy lines.

The fighter stood up, sheathed his swords, and buckled his sword belt. He then walked to the back of the cabin, poured water from a jug into a washbasin, and splashed the cool water on his face until he was fully awake. He had just taken a drink from the pitcher when he heard a knock on the door. Vlain opened it then looked down into Oshur's serious face. The diminutive goatman wore his signature spectacles and was dressed like a dandy gentleman fresh off the streets of Elamara. Vlain shook his head at the strangeness of the scene.

"Good morning, colonel. I trust you slept well," the fawn said.

"As well as can be expected," he replied.

"I think you've shown remarkable aplomb, considering you've been surrounded by enemies for the last two days."

"Thank you," Vlain replied with a look of surprise. "Jaina, and the White Stag willing, we won't be enemies for much longer."

"Wouldn't that be nice," Oshur said. Vlain detected a note of doubt in his voice, but the fawn spoke again before Vlain could question him about it. "Come, we mustn't keep the king waiting."

Vlain and Oshur walked side by side until they reached the front yard of the king's lodge. Percheron and Ardennais greeted Vlain by nodding in his direction. Their stony expressions, however, prevented him from reading their emotions. Vlain nodded back at them then turned to look at King Caernos as he emerged from the lodge.

"Greetings, outlander," he said in his booming baritone. "I trust you're ready for a jaunt through the countryside?"

"Why not," Vlain replied. Oshur pointed at a brown horse. The fawn's pony stood beside the horse as it ate the lush grass.

"Let's go get your steed," Caernos said.

"I'm surprised you keep horses in Findalora since most of you have your own...built-in transportation," Vlain responded.

"Although we centaurs don't need horses, the fawns and satyrs often use them. They're also used for plowing fields and hauling heavy loads. No self-respecting centaur would ever agree to do either of those tasks," Caernos said with a derisive snort.

Vlain smiled at the king's comment as he grabbed his horse by its long mane, then pulled himself up onto its back. The woodlanders hadn't provided a saddle, but it didn't bother him. He had ridden bareback many times, so it was a simple adjustment to make.

After Oshur mounted his pony, the motley group followed a winding trail that led them deep into the forest. As they trotted along, Vlain sensed unseen presences, hovering close by. However, he pretended not to notice them and focused instead on the vibrant beauty all around them. The giant trees stretched so high that Vlain's neck ached whenever he tried to find their topmost branches. Large black, brown, and gray squirrels scampered amongst the trees, pausing to stare at Vlain and the others now and then. At one point, Vlain thought he saw a small, human-like figure with dragonfly wings flitting through the upper branches of a tree. He blinked several times and tried to find the little creature again, but it had disappeared.

To pass the time, Vlain asked Caernos about the history of his people. The king told him the various races of Findalora had lived in the forest since time immemorial. At first, the tribes of centaurs, minotaurs, fawns, satyrs, cyclopes, and a shy, ape-like race called keti, had all lived separately. Over time, however, the tribes began to mingle and collaborate to form a diverse society. Although each tribe still had villages dominated by a particular group, it was becoming less common.

Caernos told him his great grandfather, Staevis the Strong, who had slain Raisszann, the great red dragon, had been the first elected king of Findalora. Although it was now considered a birthright of

Caernos's family, the Findalorans were intolerant of inept leaders and would depose any ruler who didn't do right by them. Typically, the right to rule was given to the eldest male child, but exceptions had been made over the years.

Vlain asked how many humans such as Iolee lived in Findalora. The king told him they numbered in the hundreds and were scattered throughout the vast forest. Some stayed in exclusively human tribes, but many also lived with nonhumans. Some of these humans became druids, shamans, or herbalists, while others lived a simple life as hunters and gatherers. As Caernos spoke, Vlain realized how much the king valued the human tribes' contributions to Findalora. The king did not, however, understand the humans who lived within the Elamaran Empire. Their concept of land ownership and exclusivity were bizarre and foreign to his communally-shaped mind. Caernos, as well as most Findalorans, thought there was plenty of land, game, and natural resources for all so long as no group became greedy or controlling. He was willing to share the rich bounty of Findalora with the Faldinites, so long as they extended the same courtesy to his people.

"After all, we were here first," Caernos finished. Vlain was about to respond when they suddenly emerged from the forest to stand in a large, flat meadow. There were several thatch-roofed huts in the center. The other notable feature was the many well-tended gardens. Vlain saw corn, potatoes, pumpkins, squash, and other vegetables, thriving in the dark soil. He was about to ask who lived there when the answer suddenly presented itself.

Two druids abruptly appeared on either side of Caernos. They looked like they had been walking through the forest, matching the group's pace, ever since they had left the king's lodge. The druids had only been a stone's throw away from either side of the king the whole time. At first, Vlain wondered if they had just teleported there. Vlain had witnessed powerful magic-users cast such spells before. Then, as he watched a druid's cloaks change color, he realized that he hadn't been able to see them because they had been so well camouflaged.

Several druids soon emerged from the large, central hut. As soon as Vlain and the others stopped, one of the druids, a female fawn, ran straight toward the king with outstretched arms. The sudden movement spooked Percheron and Ardennais, but they relaxed as soon as they recognized the druidess.

"Praise the White Stag!" the fawn shouted. "I'm so sorry, my liege!" she said as she buried her face in the king's chest. Although Caernos had been caught off guard, he still folded his thick arms around her.

"What's all this about, Xerlith?" he asked.

"It was me, my king," the fawn sobbed. "I almost killed you by sending my golem after the invader. It sensed my fear and ran too quickly, thereby pushing you all off the cliff. My actions almost got you..." but the fawn fell silent, and her eyes grew wide when she saw Vlain.

"You have no need to fear the outlander," Caernos reassured her. "In fact, you are all to treat him with respect, for he is my guest."

"I don't understand," Xerlith said. "Aren't we still at war with Man?"

"Yes, but Colonel Vlain and I have been discussing the possibility of a treaty," Caernos explained. "We hope it will lead to a peaceful resolution to our conflict," Xerlith said nothing; she just stared at Vlain with a mixture of hatred and fear. The king moved away from her to address the others. "Greetings, my druids!" Caernos boomed. They all bowed before him. "Of course, you already know Iolee and Dinn," Caernos said as he looked at Vlain. "But you have yet to meet Ibin," he said, pointing to a middle-aged satyr. "And Batutta," he said with a nod at a young female centaur.

"Greetings, Colonel Vlain," the satyr and centaur said in unison. Their tone was civil, even though their eyes were full of suspicion and distrust.

Vlain nodded at each of them. "A pleasure to make your acquaintances," he replied. Iolee and Dinn nodded at him also, prompting him to return the gesture.

"Come inside, Vlain. I have something to show you," Caernos rumbled as he walked toward the hut from which the druids had emerged.

Vlain did as the king asked. He noted none of the others followed them inside. Although it was a cool day, it was warm inside the hut. It was also dimmer, so Vlain's eyes needed a few seconds to adapt. However, as soon as they did, his breath caught in his throat. There, sitting on the floor in a semi-circle, were several legionnaires. Oudeteros, Paetro, Hildin, and four of Oudeteros's men were blindfolded, and their hands had been tied behind their backs. Some of them leaned against the wall and appeared to be sleeping, while others were tilting their heads as they listened to the sounds around them. Caernos pressed his finger against his lips, signaling Vlain to be silent. The fighter nodded in agreement then inspected each of his men. He was looking for bruises, cuts, or any evidence of illness. Vlain could find no such signs, however. Caernos started walking toward the door and waved for Vlain to join him outside. The fighter followed him out of the hut.

"As you can see, your men are being well cared for," Caernos rumbled.

"Aside from being deprived of their vision and freedom," Vlain countered.

"Now, now. Your legion took many of my people captive as well."

"What are you proposing? An exchange?"

"Eventually," Caernos said. "In the meantime, this gives you more incentive to convince your commander to negotiate with me. But that's not the only reason I showed them to you." Caernos paused to fix Vlain with his glowing white, pupilless stare. "I was moved by the fact that you freed Maiva when you didn't have to. I wish to reward your kind act by letting you take one of your men with you. So, which one will it be?"

For a second, Vlain was tempted to pull out his swords and start fighting. He knew he could beat the woodlanders due to his enchantment. Vlain started choreographing the fight in his mind. A moment later, however, he sighed and banished such thoughts. Although he'd win, he could receive severe injuries in the process. Some of Vlain's men could also get hurt or killed. More importantly, such a rash act would eliminate the prospect of both sides signing a peace treaty. The Findalorans would be enraged by the death of their king and would thus push for war.

Who should I choose? Vlain asked himself as he stared up at the cloudy sky. He had known the twins, Hildin and Paetro, longer than the others, but Oudeteros was highest in rank and a friend as well. The truth was, no matter whom he chose, he'd feel guilty for leaving the others behind. Then again, if Prydus was open to negotiating a peace treaty with Caernos, it might not be long before all of them were freed. "I choose Oudeteros, the dark-skinned man," Vlain said before he could rethink his answer. It made the most sense since Oudeteros knew the most about the 9th Legion's tactics, battle strategies, and troop strength. If the druids pressed the captives for answers, Vlain would be depriving them of the most well-informed legionnaire.

"Very well," Caernos rumbled. He nodded at Ibin and Batutta. The druids entered the hut then emerged with Oudeteros a moment later. "Wait here while we find a horse for him to ride," the king told

Vlain.

Ibin untied Oudeteros's wrists and removed his blindfold. The captain squinted and blinked several times as his eyes adjusted to the daylight. "Vlain, is that you?" he asked.

"It is," Vlain replied as he placed a hand on his shoulder. "You ready to get out of here?"

"But...what about the others?"

"We'll have to get them released through diplomatic means," Vlain said while trying to keep the disappointment out of his voice. "I won't give up on them, but I can only secure your release today." Oudeteros nodded agreeably, but he looked confused and anxious. Just then, the druid known as Dinn walked up to them, holding the reigns of a tan-colored mare in his hands. The satyr handed them to Oudeteros.

"Colonel Vlain," Caernos boomed. "This is for you," the centaur said as he gave him a hand-sized, rectangular mirror. Vlain took it from him. "We can communicate through this enchanted mirror. Are you familiar with such a device and how they operate?"

"I've used them before. We call them mage mirrors," Vlain replied.

"If your commander is open to negotiations, then use it to contact me, and we'll set up a time and place for our meeting. If he's not, then let me know, then destroy the mirror."

"Simple enough," Vlain said.

"You may now leave Findalora under my full protection. I only ask two things: present my terms to your commander, and let my horses go when you reach Hadrian's Wall."

"I will do so, King Caernos," Vlain said with a bow. "Thank you for your kindness and hospitality. I'll do all I can to encourage

Commander Orilius to negotiate."

Vlain helped the stiff-jointed Oudeteros mount his horse, then mounted his own. He nodded at Iolee as he passed her on the way out of the meadow. She nodded in return. The druidess was disappointed to see the outlander leave. She liked his unpredictable, fiery spirit. Not to mention, she sensed powerful magic at work in him even though he wasn't a findoree. Vlain embodied a mystery she would love to unravel should the opportunity present itself.

The other Findalorans were stone-faced and somber as they watched the legionnaires leave.

Caernos hoped he had placed his faith in the right man. His heart told him he had, but he knew how treacherous Man could be. Only time would tell if he had pinned his hopes to a duplicitous spy or to a true bringer of peace.

***

The tunnel beyond the thick, iron doors was much brighter than the ones on the outskirts of the gnome kingdom. Glowing crystals, which gave off a warm light like the sun, had been placed on the wall every fifty feet. Zenda was thankful for the ample light, not just because it was easier to see but because it brightened her mood. She had been so fearful ever since she and her fellow Findalorans had escaped from Algos. Now, for the first time in days, she finally felt like she was safe again.

Grislin led Zenda through several long, curving corridors until they reached a tall, wide door made of bronze. The gnome knocked on it three times then stepped back. Although Zenda hadn't hear anything, Grislin turned around and motioned to the door. "You may enter now," she told the fawn.

"Aren't you coming in with me?" Zenda asked.

"Oh no, not during an awakening," Grislin replied. With that said, the gnome turned around and walked away.

The fawn took a deep breath then grabbed the door handle. She expected it to be heavy and difficult to move, but it was so perfectly balanced it hardly took any effort. What she saw inside took her breath away. There was a massive stone golem, chiseled from granite, lying on the floor in the center of the room. An elderly female gnome, dressed in a glittering, silver-white robe, stood on the golem's enormous chest. She held a silver staff with a glowing sapphire affixed to the top. She was facing Zenda, but her eyes were closed. Suddenly, she began chanting in an eerie voice.

"Rise up from your earthen bed, child of stone! Rise to walk the land! Rise to serve and protect your mistress." The queen then slammed the bottom of her staff down onto the stone golem's chest.

A deep rumbling sound filled the cavern. Zenda couldn't make sense of it at first. One second, it sounded like an avalanche, and the next, it sounded like the stones in the cavern were trying to speak. The golem sat up without warning. The queen climbed onto the stone giant's shoulder as it rose to its full height of twelve feet. A fierce blue light emanated from the golem's perfectly carved eye sockets and blazed from a strange sigil that looked like three overlapping triangles in the center of its forehead.

The blue light also issued forth from a narrow slit carved where a mouth would be. The golem raised its mighty fists into the air and struggled to speak in its strange, booming voice.

"Yes! You live, my fearless servant. Now be still. Silence your earthen voice and set me down."

The golem's mighty voice rumbled one final time, then it slowly raised its segmented arm up to its shoulder so the queen could step onto its giant palm. It then lowered the queen to the ground.

"Remain here until I call upon you," the queen said. Queen Pietra smiled in satisfaction as she made eye contact with Zenda for the first time. "Isn't he magnificent?" she asked.

Zenda didn't know what to say, so she blurted out her first thought. "You just brought a stone golem to life."

"Why yes, dear," the queen said with a chuckle. "Don't your people animate wood golems?"

"Yes, but I've never seen it done before," Zenda admitted. "Such power, there's such power in his voice. He's incredible."

"Wait until you see him in action," the queen said as she walked to her.

"Why did you make him?" Zenda asked.

"Oh, the same reason as all the others: to defend our kingdom from monsters that roam the Deepdark, assist with construction, and to repair our tunnels."

"I'm sure he'll perform admirably," Zenda replied.

"Now, onto business," the elderly queen said. "As you've probably guessed, I'm Queen Pietra."

Zenda bowed low before her. "My name is Zenda..."

"Yes, I know. Hilberg told me. He also told me you have a wounded fawn in your midst."

"Haephius!" Zenda almost shouted. She felt ashamed for forgetting about him after watching the gnome queen animate the stone golem. "He's bleeding badly from an arrow wound. Please send healers to..."

"Relax, child. I've already sent a team of healers to help him and any others in your group who require assistance," the queen calmly answered. "I also arranged to have food, blankets, and other supplies sent to your people."

"Thank you so much!"

"Now, I have a request for you. Two, actually."

"Yes?"

"Please sit down. I'm getting a crick in my neck looking up at you," Pietra said with a laugh.

Zenda complied. "Secondly, tell me what happened to your village." Zenda pulled her knees up to her chest, hugged them, and rocked back and forth as she told the queen about the attack on Algos. The matriarch's heavily lined face grew thoughtful as she listened, but she didn't say anything until the fawn had finished speaking. "So, Man has finally decided to invade Findalora," she said softly. "I wish my husband, King Stenos, had lived to see this day. He would have relished the chance to battle men."

"I'm sorry for your loss," Zenda somberly replied.

"And I'm sorry for yours." The queen sighed. "Now off with you," she said as she shooed her away. "I must train my new golem while you take a meal in my royal kitchen. After you've had your fill, ask Grislin to take you to the bathhouse. You could do with a long soak," Pietra said with a wry smile while plugging her nose.

"Yes, your majesty," Zenda said as she blushed in embarrassment. The fawn stood up and was about to leave when the queen's voice stopped her.

"One more thing. Tell the Grey King that when the war starts, he can count on my support."

"I will," Zenda happily replied. She then opened the door and slipped out of the cavern.

HARD CHOICES

Chapter 10

A smokey haze filled the commander's spacious tent as Caladin, Snill, and Prydus sat in front of a checkered board populated with multi-colored stones. They had been playing a game of Six for nearly an hour. As they played, Prydus and Snill frequently drank Higorian hooch from a clay jug while Caladin furiously smoked a strain of the local weed called Faldin Haze. Prydus was irritated by the skunky smell of the weed and by the far-away look that had formed on Caladin's face, but he kept it to himself. He reminded himself that the big man's preoccupation with the local drug had so far diverted him from the Higorian hooch, which meant there was more for Snill and himself. Prydus waved a cloud of smoke out of his face, then moved a stone onto one of Caladin's squares and plucked his last stone off the board.

"I'm afraid you're out of the game now," Prydus smugly stated. "Methinks the potent weed has made you a worse player."

"I don't care if it has," Caladin dreamily replied. "It takes me to a nice place. Who cares if I lose a few coppermarks on the way there."

"Let him celebrate victory in his own way," Snill told Prydus. "No other legionnaire can boast about single-handedly slaying a minotaur king."

"True enough," Prydus admitted. "You've earned that smoke and many others."

"Thank you, commander," Caladin said with a belch. "I wish you had both been there to see our battle. It was spectacular! He was a full foot taller and at least two hundred pounds heavier than me. If not for my..."

"Giant blood you would have fallen before his might," Snill finished for him. "We know. We've heard your story many times since you got back."

"But it gets better with each telling, does it not?" Caladin said.

"It definitely gets more elaborate," Prydus said as he rolled his eyes.

"And although you weren't there in person," Caladin continued as if he hadn't heard Prydus. "Let's not forget your contribution to our victory," the big man said as he looked at Snill. "Those crossbows worked like miracles! The bolts shoot farther and faster than any arrow from a bow ever has. And their accuracy! By Endlin, it's uncanny! Tell me, how did you dream up such a design?"

Snill looked down at his feet in discomfort, then his thin lips formed a faint smile. "It took me years, and I made many mistakes along the way, but I finally perfected the gearing mechanism after we arrived in Faldin," Snill explained as he captured one of Prydus's stones.

"What was it about Faldin that enabled you to do that?" Prydus asked.

"A conversation with a clock-maker in Faldin's trade district of all things," Snill said with an uneasy laugh. "The old man showed me the complications in his latest clock, and suddenly it all came together in my mind."

"How fortunate for the 9th," Prydus said as he moved one of his stones toward Snill's. "Did his complications help you make the ballistae and catapults as well?"

"No, those designs came from a dream," Snill replied.

"Would that I'd have such dreams," Caladin rumbled.

"Perhaps all that weed you've smoked will bring them to you," Prydus sarcastically replied as he captured one of Snill's stones. "Anyway, I'm just glad we won the first battle, even though it cost us more than I would have liked."

"You refer to the loss of Vlain?" Snill asked. Now it was his turn for sarcasm.

"I was actually referring to the two hundred legionnaires who fell in Algos," Prydus clarified.

"As for Vlain, although he was an insufferable showoff, he was also a valuable weapon I would have rather not lost so early in the war."

Neither Snill or Caladin said anything in response, but their expressions betrayed their thoughts. They looked as pleased as foxes that have just devoured a brood of hens.

"I shall be your champion now," Caladin said.

If Prydus had heard his comment, he ignored it as he moved a stone onto a square occupied by one of Snill's. He snatched up his opponent's stone as a smug smile bloomed on his handsome face. "That's game," he happily announced.

The commander looked better than ever. His skin glowed with health and vitality. Even Snill and Caladin had noticed the change after they had returned from the Last Wild. His hair was a lighter, purer shade of gold, and he moved faster and more fluidly than before. In fact, the men had taken to calling him Prydus the Golden.

"So it is," Snill admitted. "I must say, commander, frontier life seems to agree with you. You've got a glow about you now. What's your secret?"

"Ah, the usual: plenty of good food, sleep, and of course, the tender ministrations of a fair damsel," he added with a chuckle. Both men knew he was alluding to his girlfriend, Brinhilda, the former tavern wench from the Pig's Feast.

"I'm sure all of that's true," Snill replied. "But there's something else at work, isn't there? Come now, your secret's safe with me."

Prydus stared intently at the shrew-faced man, then he sighed and appeared to drop his customary guard. "Alright, I'll tell you, but it mustn't leave this room," he said, prompting both men to lean forward in anticipation. He took a deep breath and was about to speak when a messenger suddenly entered the tent.

"Permission to speak, Commander Orilius," the young legionnaire said. All three men looked over at him in irritation.

"It better be good," Prydus snapped.

"Colonel Vlain and Captain Oudeteros just climbed over Hadrian's Wall. The night sentries intercepted them and are leading them here now. They should be here in a few minutes." The messenger's words hung in the air for several seconds as all three men struggled to process them.

"Vlain survived?!" Prydus finally shouted. "And Oudeteros too?"

"Yes, commander. Do they have permission to enter your tent?"

"Of course, you dolt!" Prydus snapped. "I must know what happened to them. You're dismissed," he said, waving the messenger away. "As are you two," he said to Caladin and Snill.

"I don't understand," Caladin groggily replied. "The men saw him go off a cliff."

"Clearly, he survived the incident," Prydus snapped again. "Now, as I said before, you're both dismissed." Prydus stood up to straighten out his uniform as the men withdrew from his tent. He then buckled on his sword belt for good measure and sat back down on his throne-like seat. The commander tried his best to look unflustered, even bored, while waiting for the two men to arrive. Finally, the tent flap parted, and Vlain and Oudeteros walked into his inner sanctum. They stopped in front of Prydus, assumed the position of attention, and saluted him.

"Colonel Verous and Captain Oudeteros reporting for duty, sir," Vlain's smooth voice broke the heavy silence.

"The reports of your demise were greatly exaggerated," Prydus replied. "What happened after you were pushed off the cliff?"

Vlain took a deep breath then told him all that occurred after he and Caernos had fallen into the Rendel rapids. He changed specific facts, however. Instead of admitting to sparing the king's life, he told Prydus he was about to attack the centaur after he found him wandering downstream of the waterfall. King Caernos had begged for him to stop and listen to his proposal, and Vlain had only done so out of curiosity. The king had surprised him by asking to negotiate a peace treaty with Commander Orilius. Of course, that part was all a lie, but Vlain knew Prydus would otherwise despise him for sparing the king's life. The commander was not known for his mercy, after all. Vlain had memorized the king's terms, then Caernos guided Vlain to a hut where Oudeteros and other legionnaires had been kept as prisoners. The king had allowed Vlain to take Oudeteros as a sign of good faith. Then the king loaned them horses and provisions to get back to Fort Faldin.

"I see," Prydus said while thoughtfully rubbing his chin. "And what is your account?" he asked as he shifted his gaze to Oudeteros. The captain told him all about the terrifying wooden golems that had emerged from the forest to kill dozens of legionnaires. He then told him about the mysterious cloaked and hooded figures who blew darts, laced with a powerful sleeping agent, at his men. Oudeteros told Prydus he had woken up blindfolded and tied up in what had smelled like a grass hut. He had seen nothing but darkness until the blindfold had been removed to reveal Vlain standing there before him.

Prydus nodded in understanding. "You're dismissed, Captain Oudeteros. Report to Fort Faldin for duty first thing in the morning." Oudeteros nodded obediently, then walked away. "Well, well, Vlain," Prydus said after he was gone. "You gave the men quite a scare."

"Why is that?" Vlain asked as he narrowed his eyes in uncertainty.

"I know it sounds ridiculous, but some of them were beginning to think you're invincible," he said with a derisive snort. "So, after they heard you had fallen in battle, it made them all feel as if death could take them at any time."

"It still can," Vlain said with a gruff laugh. "This is war, after all."

"True enough," Prydus admitted. "Tell me, what is the centaur king's name again?"

"Caernos. He also goes by the title, the Grey King."

"How amusing," Prydus scornfully replied. "And he's the king of the entire Last Wild?"

"Yes, although he refers to the forest as Findalora."

"Findalora! Ha! What fanciful names the beastmen give things." Prydus stood up, placed his hands behind his back, and began pacing back and forth. "After spending time with this king, do you honestly think he speaks for all of the beasties?"

"I do," Vlain answered.

"Then tell me, what are his conditions for a peace treaty?" Vlain relayed the four conditions Caernos had laid out for him. Prydus stopped his pacing to listen carefully. After Vlain had finished, the commander violently shook his head in disagreement.

"Absolutely not!" he spat the words out. "Can you imagine how terrified the Faldinites would be every time the Findalorans, as you call them, travel south to visit their burial cairns? Battles between the species would inevitably erupt. As for the hunting restrictions, our people would outright disregard them. Who wants to receive orders from little more than talking animals when it comes to where and when you can hunt?! And the notion of trading with them is utterly preposterous. The Elamaran Empire has plans for the forest, plans that don't include honoring the beasties' claim of ownership. No, I cannot entertain these unrealistic requests," Prydus said with a dismissive wave of his hand.

"What is so 'unrealistic' about them?!" Vlain angrily asked. "And the 'beasties,' as you call them, claim ownership of the forest because it is THEIR home and has been so for millennia! We are the newcomers, and the Faldinites have been cruel to them on more than one..."

"We just won the first battle against them!" Prydus objected. "Why sue for peace now?!"

"We only defeated one village, and look how many lives it cost us! Besides, there are many other villages in that vast forest. What happens if they all unite against us? How well will our meager force of four thousand legionnaires fair then?"

"Whose side are you on?!" Prydus shouted.

"On our men's side, which means I'll fight for peace because it'll spare their lives!"

"And how do we know King Caernos will honor his own terms?" Prydus shot back.

"We don't, and he doesn't know if we will either, but we'll never know if we don't give him a chance to..."

"I can't believe we're even having this discussion," Prydus cut in. "Here you are, the premier warrior of the empire, pining for peace on behalf of an unknown and untrustworthy enemy! You've revealed yourself to be quite the dove! Are you going soft on me, Vlain?"

"Raise your sword against me and find out!" Vlain fired back.

Prydus glared at him, and for a second, it looked like he was about to do just that. As usual, however, he turned away from Vlain's burning gaze and began pacing again."I will not sit down with this...beast king...to discuss anything other than his complete and utter surrender. Is that understood?"

Vlain took a deep breath and tried to calm down. Due to his enchantment, he knew he could win the argument if he persisted, but he'd have to do so every time Prydus's desire for war flared up. On top of that, he'd have to continuously argue with Caladin and Snill, who no doubt shared Prydus's hawkish stance. He knew it was ultimately hopeless, but he wasn't done speaking yet.

"What I *understand* is that you need this war to make a name for yourself," Vlain coolly replied. "I also *understand* Findalora is loaded with natural resources that will make many of the noblemen in Faldin and Elamara wealthy. We can't have the natives getting in the way of all that now, can we?"

"You forget yourself, colonel!" Prydus shouted. "One more comment like that, and I'll have you demoted and thrown in the brig!"

"Demote me if it pleases you," Vlain replied as he rolled his eyes. "But if you or anyone else tries to jail me, you'll get a taste of my swords."

"Even you can't beat all of us, Vlain," Prydus sneered.

"I can paint your tent red with the blood of anyone foolish enough to try me," Vlain ominously replied as his hands inched toward his sword handles. "And that's a promise."

"So you're being insubordinate just like Meris was?" Prydus asked.

"What's Meris have to do with any of this?"

"He refused to set Algos on fire when Captain Caladin ordered him to."

"As he should have," Vlain said. "That was a callous and unnecessary order."

"That order came from ME!" Prydus screamed.

"It doesn't matter who it came from! I would have disregarded it as well."

"Then you would have ended up in the brig, just as he has," Prydus smugly replied.

"You placed my lieutenant in the brig for disobeying that vile order?!" It was Vlain's turn to become red-faced and outraged.

"Absolutely, and I'd do it..."

"I want him out, now!"

"Who are you to give me..."

"Meris put his life on the line for you and fought with honor and bravery in Algos while you stayed back here in safety! How dare you jail him for disobeying such a cruel order! Get him out now, or I'll go to the brig and do it myself!" Vlain squared his shoulders and grasped his sword handles. Both men stared each other down.

Finally, Prydus broke the tense silence. "I'll release Meris," Prydus acquiesced. "But not because you asked me to," he quickly added. "No, I'll release him because I've already made an example of him. He spent two days in the brig, and I demoted him to sergeant. Word has already spread throughout the 9th that that's what happens when you disobey me. You would be wise to remember..."

"Are we done, commander?" Vlain icily asked.

"How dare you interrupt...!"

"I just returned from a hostile land. I'm tired, dirty, and hungry. You received my full report, so I'm going to my tent now," with that said, Vlain turned on his heel and left.

Prydus stared at his back with wide eyes and mouth agape. As soon as Vlain was gone, he began shaking and trembling with rage. Part of him wanted to order a platoon to strip the arrogant fighter of his weapons and throw him in the brig, but the wiser part of him knew it would cause unnecessary bloodshed. Vlain would kill many a legionnaire before he went down, and Prydus needed all the able-bodied men he could get in the upcoming war. In the end, he simply let Vlain walk away. The time wasn't yet right for him to challenge the brash fighter, but it was drawing closer and closer.

***

Charolais walked so quickly it was hard for Maiva to keep up. They soon encountered a rowdy group of minotaurs preoccupied with some spectacle in the field beyond. As Maiva got closer to the throng, she saw what held their attention. A few minotaurs were competing in what looked like games of strength and endurance. The players were big, even by minotaur standards. A team was hurling stones, another threw javelins, and two others were engaged in a wrestling match. Maiva's eyes lingered on one of the wrestlers. He had the build of a titan, and his face looked like a cross between that of a buffalo and a bull. The other athlete was smaller and had typical bullish features.

An old minotaur shouted for them to start the match. Both players collided in a burst of ferocity and aggression. Maiva watched as they pushed each other back and forth across the field. However, as time went by, the larger minotaur with buffalo-like features began to gain the upper hand. Although his rival wrestled with cunning and guile, he was eventually overwhelmed and pinned to the ground. The crowd went wild as the massive minotaur seized victory.

"All hail Prince Vulkas!" they chanted in unison.

The victorious bull, whom Maiva assumed was Prince Vulkas, sprang from the ground to pump his fists up and down in sync with the crowd's primal chant. Maiva had never seen a minotaur move with such confidence and self-assurance. Despite his brutish appearance, he had an air of nobility about him.

"That would be Prince Vulkas," Charolais said, thereby confirming Maiva's earlier assumption. "You'd better talk to him before he goes to the mead hall to celebrate his victory over Xaxis," she said with a knowing smile.

The towering prince strode into the crowd. As he brushed past Maiva, she found her nerve and reached out to grab one of his bulging arms.

"Prince Vulkas?" she asked.

The minotaur blasted steam out of his wide nostrils and gave her a curious look. "And who might you be, little fawn?" he asked in a rumbling baritone.

"I'm Maiva Starmark," she said, hoping to capitalize on her newfound fame.

"Never heard of ya," he responded.

She immediately changed tactics. "I bear news from Algos."

Those words stopped him dead in his tracks. "Algos, you say?"

"It was recently attacked by Man."

Vulkas guided her off to the side. "My father, King Hez, went there with King Caernos to celebrate Walperen," he said. "I assume you're here to bring me news of his victory against the invaders?"

"I wish that was the case, but truth be told, I don't know the result of the battle," she admitted.

"Then why are you here?" he asked with a puzzled expression.

"To tell you he's in danger, as are all of those who remained in Algos."

"I wouldn't worry about my father," he said with a rumbling laugh. "There are none mightier than him on the battlefield."

"That may be, but Man brought a host out of the south. They outnumbered our people, who were still recovering from a night of celebration. You should check on him."

Prince Vulkas stared hard at Maiva. "I assume you hail from Algos?"

"I do."

"Then why didn't you stay to defend her?"

"King Caernos asked me to take as many younglings as I could through the green gate, so they would be spared the carnage."

A look of concern formed on the prince's face. "I see. Well, why haven't you been back to check on things?" He held up his hand to stop a couple of enamored female minotaurs from approaching him. The cows' smiles faded away, and they turned around in disappointment.

"We couldn't get our gate to work again, and we're still not sure if it's safe to return. I was hoping you could lead an assault force there."

"Hmmm. Strangely, no one told us of this attack before you."

"That's probably because we depleted the two gates closest to Algos," Maiva said.

"'We?'" Vulkas asked.

"My friend, Zenda, was tasked with taking elderlings through another nearby gate."

"The timing couldn't be worse. We're in the middle of our annual strength games..."

"With all due respect, Prince Vulkas, are strength games more important than your father's well-being?" Maiva was getting impatient with his questions, and it finally came through in her tone.

The prince gave her a side-long look, then chuckled. "You have spunk, little one. I like that, and what's more, you're right. The games can wait." Vulkas took a deep breath and cupped his hands around his mouth. "Listen up, all you bulls and cows," he bellowed. "The village of Algos has been attacked by Man! As of this moment, the strength games are canceled. I'll soon lead an assault force of three hundred warriors through the green gate. You have one hour to get your armor and weapons, then meet me back here. If Man is still in Algos, then we'll send him straight to the Black Boar and earn our place by the Stag's side! You have your orders; now go!"

A hush fell across the crowd as Vulkas's words sank in. Some of the minotaurs murmured and muttered in bewilderment, but most left to gather their weapons and armor per the prince's instructions. Maiva was impressed at how the minotaurs had stoically received the disturbing news.

"Well said, my prince," Maiva said with an approving nod.

"Will you come with us?" he asked.

"I would if King Caernos hadn't charged me with watching over the younglings."

"I understand." The prince was about to leave when he suddenly stopped and looked at Maiva. "If your green gate was depleted, then how did you travel here?" he asked.

"I was fortunate enough to run into the Portal Master, Oisin Corcra," Maiva replied with a grin.

"Aha, how is the little scamp these days?" Vulkas asked.

"The only words that come to my mind are hyper and strange."

Vulkas chuckled. "That sounds like Oisin," the prince rumbled as he walked away.

"Please look for my father when you get to Algos," Maiva called out after him. "He's Haephius, the blacksmith. I last saw him when he was going to sound the Bell of Warning. Knowing him, he probably did something heroic and foolish when the fighting began."

"I know of Haephius," Vulkas replied. "I'll keep an eye out for him." Maiva watched the prince lumber away, then turned and left. She had done what she needed to do. Although she wanted to accompany the minotaurs, she was duty-bound to remain with the younglings. Maiva would honor the king's edict, and she'd also pray to the White Stag to spare her father from harm.

***

Vlain swore under his breath as he stomped away from Prydus. He angrily pushed the heavy flap of fabric aside, which allowed the cool evening air to wash over him. The two sentries standing to

270

either side of the entrance jumped in alarm as Vlain emerged, but he paid them no heed. He needed a quiet place to think and gather his thoughts. He also required privacy to use the mage mirror to communicate with Caernos.

But where should I go? he wondered as he strode past several legionnaires. Fortunately, it was the week's end, which meant most legionnaires were in Faldin spending their hard-earned coppermarks.

Vlain decided to head to the supply sheds on the outskirts of the camp, which were only frequented when the legionnaires were issued gear. The sun was setting when Vlain spotted a deserted area behind a warehouse. He pushed his way through dense bushes surrounding a small clearing. Vlain sat down and leaned back against an old oak tree that occupied the center.

I might as well get this over with, he thought as he pulled a thin, rectangular metal holder out of its hiding spot behind his chestplate. Vlain pulled a mage mirror out of the holder and passed his hand over it three times, which was customary when dealing with communication spells. No doubt, King Caernos had an identical mirror. If he couldn't answer his vibrating mirror, then Vlain's would remain occluded. The seconds ticked by. Vlain found himself hoping the king wouldn't answer so he wouldn't have to share his gloomy news. He was just about to shove the mirror back into its steel holder when the cloudiness on the surface coalesced into a gray likeness of King Caernos.

"Greetings, King Caernos," Vlain solemnly said as he nodded at the mirror.

"Greetings, Colonel Vlain," the centaur king rumbled. "I take it, by your expression and tone, that Commander Orilius isn't interested in my proposition?"

"I'm afraid not," Vlain sadly replied. "He wasn't swayed by any argument I threw at him. I honestly thought Prydus would be more reasonable. I'm sorry for giving you false hope."

"It's not your fault, colonel," Caernos said with a sigh. "It was always up to him. I hope he savors his recent victory, for it shall be his last. Algos fell because we learned of your coming only shortly in advance and because we were recovering from a celebration. There are, however, many villages, such as Algos, scattered throughout the forest. There are also other species and other kingdoms in Findalora with their own rulers who owe fealty to me. Although they are kings and queens of their own realms, I am THE king of the forest. They will all come when I call, and when they do, we'll amass an army so vast it'll obliterate your legion."

"I tried to tell Prydus as much, but he still wasn't swayed," Vlain responded.

"That's unfortunate because there's no way you can win this war, at least not without the intervention of other legions. I must tell you, in all honesty, however, that calling for reinforcements would only drag the conflict out and increase the death toll on both sides. We'll still defeat you. We'll do so because we fight for our homeland, our loved ones, and our freedom. We would rather die than surrender to Man or anyone else."

"I figured as much," Vlain said with a heavy sigh.

"Not even your skill with the blade or your legion's deadly crossbows will change the outcome. You will all fall in the end. Expect no mercy when we meet again."

"What about the prisoners? Can't we at least negotiate an exchange?" Vlain asked.

"Do you think Commander Orilius will actually honor it?"

"I'm not sure..."

"That's what I thought," Caernos rumbled. "Farewell, Vlain." King Caernos's gray image dispersed into a cloudy vapor that billowed out behind the mirror's surface. The communication spell had been severed.

Vlain swore, then slammed his fist down into the dirt. He had fought for peace, but it hadn't worked out. He was tempted to throw the mirror at the back of the supply shed but resisted the urge because he might need it in the future. He shoved the enchanted mirror back into its holder, then slipped it behind his chest plate and stood up. He decided to head back to his tent, where he could drown his sorrow with Higorian whiskey.

Before Vlain knew it, he had arrived back at his tent. The walk from the supply warehouse was only a dim blur in his memory. He had walked dejectedly through the darkness, consumed by gloomy thoughts. However, as he closed in on his tent, he was pleasantly surprised to see Sargent Rivers and Sargent Denin sitting and talking in front of a fire.

"Good Jaina, the rumors are true!" Rivers exclaimed when Vlain drew close enough for the firelight. "I thought you said he fell off a cliff!?" Rivers asked as he looked at Denin. Both men stood up to greet him.

"Meris and Belor saw him go over it with their own eyes," Denin replied. "The Goddess must have been protecting you," he said as he clasped hands with Vlain.

"Welcome back to the land of the living," Rivers said as he, too, shook his hand.

Vlain wanted to smile and laugh and make small talk, but his heart was heavy because he knew what the 9th legion would soon face. However, despite his dark thoughts, he tried to be sociable and appreciative of their concern. "Glad to be missed," Vlain said with a half-smile. "As for the Goddess, I've kept her busy looking out for me ever since I joined the military," he admitted. "I imagine she'll have some choice words for me when I enter her realm one day."

"Let's hope that day is far off," Rivers said as he and Denin sat back down. "Will you join us for a drink, colonel?" he asked as he proffered him a clay jug.

"I've never been one to turn down spirits," Vlain said, taking hold of the jug. He sat down on a log across from the men, took a deep drink, then handed it back to Rivers.

"I must know, colonel, how did you survive the fall?" Denin asked.

Vlain took a deep breath as the terrifying memory came roaring back. He could hear the shrill whistle of the wind in his ears, feel the cold embrace of the water, and hear Viscol's fearful...Vlain cut the memory short lest it overwhelmed him. "I dove into the water at just the right angle," he said in a tired voice. "Hit a boulder, but my helmet took the brunt of it. Going over the falls was tricky. Used my shield to deflect another boulder waiting for me at the bottom. Let me hit that jug again," he said.

"Good Jaina, I wouldn't wish that on my worst enemy," Rivers said with a shutter.

"Say, where's your horse? Viscol's his name, right?" Denin asked.

Vlain bit his lower lip. "He didn't make it."

"I'm sorry, colonel. I have a talent for sticking my boot in my mouth. He was a magnificent horse. We'll all miss him."

Vlain nodded absently, then took another drink of the hellish hooch. He wiped the back of his hand across his mouth, then tossed the jug to Denin. The young man caught it.

"Where's Bollis and Belor?" he asked. He wanted to change the subject and genuinely wanted to know their whereabouts.

"Bollis got hit by a dart covered with a sleeping potion," Rivers answered. "He's still recovering in the healing tent. Belor's there too. He got a face full of wooden shrapnel. The clerics have been working on him for a while."

"Hope it didn't hurt his looks. He was always a bit vain, that one," Vlain said with a chuckle.

Denin took a drink from the jug then passed it to Rivers. "We heard Meris got released..."

"And not a minute too soon," Meris said as he walked up to the trio. Vlain shot to his feet, clasped hands with him, and was about to clap him on the back when Meris stepped back beyond his reach. "Not yet, boss. Back's still raw."

Vlain stared at his back. He soon noticed faint traces of red staining Meris's white tunic. Vlain also saw he wasn't moving as freely or as fluidly as usual.

"You were whipped in the brig?" he asked as fiery anger welled up in his chest.

"Only a few lashes," Meris tried to sound upbeat. "Thanks for getting me out, by the way."

"But they cut deep. Can tell by the way you're moving. Did Caladin hold the whip?"

Meris sighed and looked at the ground between his feet. "I hear the fury in your voice, boss, which is why I wasn't going to tell..."

"So, it *was* Caladin," Vlain said through clenched teeth. "That muscle-bound ogre!" he shouted as he rose. "I'm going to carve his heart out..."

"Please sit, Vlain," Meris said as he patted the log the fighter had been sitting on. "I disobeyed a direct order..."

"It was an immoral order! You were right to..."

"You know how it is. He had to prove he was in charge..."

"He thought I was dead!" Vlain exclaimed. "He didn't think he'd have to answer to me, so he tortured you. I'll rip his blaeting head off...!"

"And what will that accomplish?" Meris asked. "He's under the commander's protection. Always has been. Commander Orilius is the face, Snill is the brains, and Caladin is the muscle. They climbed the ranks together and always look out for each..."

"I don't care," Vlain shot back. "He has to answer for..."

"What he did to Algos?"

"What he did to you," Vlain answered.

Meris looked away as his emotions threatened to overwhelm him. After he got control of himself, he looked back at Vlain. "I think you and I need to walk down to the river to have a..."

"We're going to the healing tent. You need a cleric..."

"I'll go there afterward, but we need to talk first," Meris said as he stood up.

"You always were stubborn," Vlain grumbled. "Alright. Let's go," he said as he began walking toward the Rendel. "Good night, boys," Vlain said as he waved at Denin and Rivers. "Don't bother waiting up."

Their pace was slow because of Meris's injuries. Still, they eventually reached the stony shore, where they often came to bathe. Thankfully, no one was around at that hour to eavesdrop. Meris stiffly sat down on a smooth boulder, but Vlain remained standing.

There was too much angry energy in his system. He needed to pace for a while to burn it off.

"Try to calm down, my friend," Meris said. "Violence is coming, one way or another, but right now, we need to have cool heads."

"Oh, yeah? Why's that," Vlain asked.

"Because we need to plot a course of action, but before we can do that, I need to know what's going on in your mind. Besides, the desire to kill Caladin."

Vlain stopped pacing, took a deep breath, and locked eyes with Meris. He then told him everything that had happened from the time he and Caernos had fallen off the cliff right up to the conversation they had just had via the mirrors.

Meris shook his head and let out a low whistle. "The king of the woodlanders called you a bringer of peace! I've heard it all now," he said with a pained smile.

"I had the same reaction," Vlain said with a gruff laugh.

"So, what do we do?" Meris asked.

"I honestly don't know," Vlain replied. "All of our options are bad."

"True, but whenever I'm wrestling with tough decisions, it helps me to state them out loud. Give it a try."

"Well, the first and most obvious option is to do nothing. We follow Prydus's orders and eventually get overwhelmed by the woodlander army."

"At least you'll survive," Meris bleakly replied.

"That's not good enough," Vlain said. "The second option is to desert. We gather up our crew after everyone's recovered from their injuries, then leave at an opportune time, never to be seen again."

"And spend the rest of our lives using fake names, moving from village to village, always looking over our shoulders for bounty hunters. Not to mention, we'd never get to see our families again. Oh, and the war would still happen, and most, if not all, of the 9th legion will be wiped out."

"Yeah, I'm not a fan of that one either," Vlain said with a mirthless laugh. "I could, however, send word to the emperor, via a messenger, that Prydus is unfit to lead and request that he promote me to the position of commander."

"If the messenger ever gets there, and that's a big if, considering Prydus may send men to intercept him. And we know how dangerous the journey to the capital is, even when you're not being pursued. The return trip will be equally dangerous, and so the emperor's reply may never be heard."

"True. Prydus could kill the messenger and destroy the message."

"And after that, he wouldn't rest until you and everyone who supports you is dead or forced to flee."

"The emperor would see him hang for that," Vlain countered.

"Prydus will make up any excuse he needs to get out of trouble, and even if the emperor sees through them, justice will come too late for us."

"True again," Vlain conceded.

"You could always debate Prydus until you win the argument," Meris suggested.

"I already thought of that, and the problem is, I'd have to do it forever. And not just with him, but with Snill, Caladin, and anyone else who supports the war."

"Yeah, it's exhausting just thinking about it."

Vlain nodded in agreement. "And eventually someone might catch on to the fact I never lose a debate, then all hell would break loose."

"Well, since you always win, perhaps you should lead an uprising against Prydus," Meris said.

"Thought of that too, but there are some problems with that. The first is, Caladin's never been more popular with his cohorts than now due to him besting a minotaur king in battle. Secondly, Snill's still riding high in the minds of the legionnaires due to his ingenious crossbow design. Thirdly, Prydus is well-liked due to our victory at Algos and because he treats everyone other than us civilly. Lastly, and we both know this from experience, my...winning streak only pertains to me. It doesn't extend to a cause, no matter how much I support it."

"We certainly found that out during the Great Rebellion," Meris stated glumly. Vlain sadly shook his head in agreement as painful memories of that desperate struggle filled his mind. "Alright, scratch that last one. What else have you got, boss?" Meris asked.

"The only option left is a doozie."

Meris gave him a knowing smile. "I waited patiently, and I know it'll pay off because you always save the best for last."

"We join the woodlander army," Vlain said.

***

Zenda smiled as she looked down at Haephius. He was seated on a cot, happily shoving spoonfuls of hot mushroom and toad soup into his mouth. Although the dish was a gnome delicacy, Zenda found its pungent smell repulsive. Haephius, however, couldn't get

279

enough of it, which was a good sign. The gnome healers had extracted the arrow from his back and then spent many hours healing the wound. He had fallen into a deep sleep after the surgery and had woken up with a ravenous appetite the following day. One of the gnomes had then presented him with their favorite soup, and he had gotten hooked.

"I'm glad to see your appetite has returned," Zenda said.

"I'm willing to share some with you," Haephius replied as he proffered her the bowl.

Zenda's pretty face scrunched up in disgust. "I already ate, thank you."

"Oh, that's right. You got to eat in the queen's royal kitchen, didn't you?" Zenda nodded up and down. "Tell me, what was on the menu?"

"Roasted goose, caramelized yams, buttered mashed potatoes, blueberry pie..."

"By the White Stag! They spoiled you," Haephius exclaimed.

"Well, you asked."

"And I'd be jealous if not for this delicious stew they gave me," he said, licking his lips.

Zenda sat down on the edge of his cot. "I'm so thankful for what the gnome healers did for you. Perhaps in a few more days, you'll be strong enough to return to Algos," she said.

Haephius's face fell at the mention of his village. "If it's safe to return," he replied.

"We'll never know if we don't try."

"But if Man's still there, we'll be killed or taken captive," he countered.

"Queen Pietra offered to send stone golems and gnome mages with us, and we can always return here if we need to."

"True enough," Haephius admitted. "My hope is that Maiva and the younglings got to the green gate before the soldiers got them."

"It would be unthinkable to lose her again after we finally got her back," Zenda said.

Haephius set the empty bowl down on the floor, then grasped her hand. They both fell silent for a moment as terrifying memories of the attack swirled through their minds. "On the bright side, I had an idea for an invention that I can't wait to work on when I get back to my workshop. Your red hair gave me the idea," he said as his eyes gleamed with a mischievous light.

"What is it?" she asked.

"Oh, no," Haephius said, wagging a stubby finger in her face. "I never reveal an invention until after it's been forged. I will, however, let you be the first to test it out. How's that?"

"I'd be honored."

"Good," Haephius replied. "After spending time with the queen, do you think she'll aid us in the coming war against Man?"

Zenda nodded up and down. "She told me she would."

"Excellent," Haephius said as he leaned back against the wall. "I don't know how big the human army is, but if all the kingdoms in Findalora gather as one beneath the Grey King's banner, we'll surely win!"

"But has such a thing ever happened?" Zenda asked as she watched a bat land on a stalactite.

"Not since I've been alive," Haephius admitted. "But Oshur told me it happened when Raisszann and his dragon horde attacked our people."

"But that was two hundred years ago," Zenda replied. "Do you think it can happen again? I mean, the merfolk wish to stay isolated in their underwater kingdom in Kristlin Lake. The cyclopes won't let us enter their village, and the ape-like keti are rarely seen these days. How are we all supposed to come together?"

Haephius placed a hand on her shoulder and gave her a knowing smile. "It's always been our way to remain separate until necessity forces us to unite. Don't fret, young one. The White Stag will bring us together when the time's right."

"I hope so," she replied.

"Do you know what time it is?"

Zenda fished a small, enchanted sundial out from one of her pocket. "One of the gnome miners gave me this the other day. It works like a sundial on the surface, except the shadow cast by the gnomon is fainter. Can you see it?"

"Well, I'll be," Haephius said, shaking his head in wonder. "The shadow is on the nine, but how do I know if it pertains to morning or evening?"

"It has two sides," Zenda explained. "The one on top, with the symbol of the moon, pertains to night. The one underneath, with the symbol of the sun, is for daytime."

"Aha, so it's nine at night," Haephius said with a laugh. "Flip it over. I want to see what the day side shows." Zenda did as he asked. They saw the gnomon on the day side didn't cast a shadow. "Those clever gnomes," He suddenly yawned. "I'm spent. I'm going to get some sleep."

"Alright," Zenda replied. The young fawn stood up, took a couple steps, then looked back at Haephius. "I'm so thankful to the Stag for sparing your life."

"As am I, dear girl. Now, remember what I told you. The people of Findalora may be proud, stubborn, and even ridiculous at times, but we always come together in the end."

"I'll take your words to heart," Zenda said before she walked out of the alcove.

***

Meris looked at Vlain for a moment, then smiled and shook his head in disbelief. "So, you think King Caernos will just let us waltz into the Last Wild and join..."

"Findalora," Vlain corrected. "They call their forest home, Findalora."

"Very well, you think the king of Findalora will welcome us with open arms?"

"What better option do we have?" Vlain asked.

"None, but this idea is foolhardy. He may reject us..."

"Why speculate on what his answer will be when I can just ask him?"

"And if he says it's fine, how many of our fellow legionnaires will agree to leave the Elamaran Empire to permanently live among the Findalorans?" Meris asked with a skeptical look.

"Who said anything about it being permanent?" Vlain said. "My thinking goes like this: we defect to King Caernos's side, convince the other kingdoms in Findalora to join us, and then display that mighty host to Prydus. He'll be in such awe of our superior force that he'll either agree to sign a peace treaty, or he'll flee with the remnants of the legion or surrender on the spot."

"And if he doesn't do any of those?" Meris pressed. "What if most of the legion stays with him, and we're forced to fight our old friends and allies?"

"In that case, we'll do what we must," Vlain grimly replied.

Meris shook his head. "There has to be a better way," he said.

"Then share it with me."

"I got nothin', boss."

"Then I'm gonna contact Caernos and ask him if we can..."

"You didn't answer my earlier question."

"Which was?"

"How many legionnaires do you think will defect with us?"

Vlain took a deep breath as his mind worked on the question. "Although Prydus, Snill, and Caladin, are popular right now, they still have their detractors. Not to mention, I've always been popular as well. And let's not forget, my popularity will grow when the men learn about the ordeal I just survived. Lastly, I think I can convince Oudeteros to join us, and some of his men will probably follow suit. So, I hope to bring at least a few hundred legionnaires with us. Perhaps more."

Meris nodded. "If King Caernos lets us join him, there's the possibility Prydus will call for reinforcements from the capital..."

"He's unlikely to get them," Vlain cut in. "The emperor took Prydus and me aside back at the capital and told us no reinforcements would be coming. The empire is embroiled in numerous conflicts across Taloria, which means the emperor can't spare any legions to help Prydus. He's on his own, and therein lies our key to victory."

"I see, but what if, by some miracle, Prydus wins? Or he simply withdraws from Faldin and leaves the region in our power? Either way, all the legionnaires who side with us will be forever barred from returning to their families, their homes..."

"Not so," Vlain stated.

"How do you figure?"

"Emperor Justus owes me a favor, and it's a big one," Vlain said with a sly smile. "I'll call it in and get all of our men pardoned after the war is over."

"Would this have anything to do with the foiled attempt on his life a few years ago?"

"You guessed it. I was the one who stopped the would-be assassin from killing him. The emperor didn't publicly announce the attack because he didn't want to give his enemy any attention or validation."

"Still, you really think the emperor will side with you? He's bound to lose some face when the people get wind of all this."

"Unlike his father, Justus and I have always seen eye-to-eye. And since he's emperor, he can put whatever spin on this he wants to," Vlain replied. "Now, please turn around, and be my lookout while I contact King Caernos."

"You got it, boss," Meris said as he carefully swiveled around on the smooth stone. Vlain crouched down behind a bush and fished the mage mirror out from behind his chestplate. He pulled the mirror out of the holder then passed his hand over its cloudy surface three times. This time, he only had to wait a few seconds before the billowing clouds coalesced into Caernos's face.

"Colonel Vlain, please tell me your commander has

reconsidered the peace talks," the centaur's voice boomed.

"No, but I have good news for you," Vlain replied.

"Go on."

"I'm willing to fight for you, and I can probably bring hundreds of legionnaires with me. What I need to know is, will you accept us, and can you guarantee our protection?"

The silence was deafening as King Caernos struggled to make sense of what he had just heard. Eventually, the centaur cleared his throat and spoke. "Did I just hear you right? You want to fight for me? If this is some type of ruse, I swear I'll..."

"There's no ruse here, no deception. I'm speaking plainly and honestly."

"Why would you even consider fighting for me?"

"First off, I know a losing cause when I see one, and I don't want to go down with the boat. Secondly, my commander is incapable of seeing reason, and my men shouldn't suffer for his blindness. Lastly, I trust you. I'm not entirely sure why, but I do."

Caernos stared at him for a long time before he spoke again. "If I do this, then you and all of your men must undergo a blood oath ceremony in which you swear undying fealty to me. I assure you, it isn't pleasant, but it is required if you join us. Will you do this?"

"I will, and I'll require it of all those who come with me."

Caernos nodded approvingly. "Very well. In return, I'll tell my people to accept you and treat you with respect. When can you come?"

"Tomorrow afternoon," Vlain said before he even knew what he was saying.

"Very good. Take the same road you used to reach Algos but continue past it by a league. I'll send my people to guide you to a village called Orrn."

"We shall do so," Vlain replied. Caernos must have placed his mirror back in its holder because his gray image dissolved into smokey, swirling chaos then went black. Vlain sheathed his mirror in its holder, tucked it behind his chest plate, and stood up. He walked over to Meris then smiled. "King Caernos will take us in," he said.

"Jaina, I hope this isn't a trap to get us all killed."

"My gut tells me he can be trusted."

"Then I'll follow you," Meris said with conviction.

"Let's get you to the healing tent," Vlain said as he lent him a hand.

"When do we leave?" Meris asked as Vlain hauled him to his feet.

"Tomorrow, so you better heal quickly."

* * *

Maiva watched as Prince Vulkas and his three hundred warriors emerged from Valaren's green gate. The prince carried a dead minotaur in his mighty arms. The minotaur had the features of a buffalo rather than those of a bull. It took Maiva a moment, but she soon recognized the corpse of King Hez.

Something was different about his appearance, however. Maiva soon realized the minotaur king was missing his horns. Someone had crudely removed them, as evidenced by the jagged cuts. Her breath caught in her throat, and she raised her hand to her mouth as tears formed in her eyes. She hadn't thought it possible for one as formidable as Hez to fall in battle. She had clearly been wrong.

Vulkas walked to the center of the field where the strength games had occurred and set his father's body down. He took a knee and reverently lowered his head. Maiva, and all those present, also got down on one knee, bowed their heads, and remained silent for a moment. The prince was too proud to cry, but Maiva could see the sorrow in his eyes and the pain in his face.

Vulkas stood up to address the crowd. "People of Valaren, you see my father's broken and desecrated body before you. This hateful act is the work of Man! I promise to avenge my father and all those who died in Algos!" he shouted in a fury.

The crowd roared to life. They shouted, bellowed, cursed, and raged with one, strident voice. Maiva watched as the minotaurs banged their weapons against their steelwood shields and rhythmically stomped their hooves. Her ears buzzed as they were overloaded by the din. She felt swept up in the sea of seething anger. Prince Vulkas picked up his father's body then walked off the field. All of his warriors trailed along behind him in one long, solemn procession.

Maiva grabbed Charolais by her brawny arm." Please tell me, is it safe to return to Algos?" she asked the shieldmaiden.

"Safe?" the minotaur asked. "It's never been safer." Maiva gave her a perplexed look. "Man burned Algos to the ground. There's nothing there now save ashes, death, and a few grieving survivors."

"By the White Stag!" Maiva replied. "Why would they do such a thing?"

"Who knows how the mind of Man works?" Charolais asked.

"Did you happen to see my father, Haephius, the blacksmith, while you were there?"

The minotaur's forehead creased in thought as she scrolled through her memories. "No. We only encountered a few fawns, but your father wasn't among them." A look of sorrow formed on Maiva's pretty face, and her lower lip trembled. "Perhaps he fled into the forest and is still hiding out there. Don't lose hope just yet."

"I'll round up the younglings at first light. Then we'll return to Algos."

"You're welcomed to stay here as long as you want to," Charolais said.

"Your people have been kind and hospitable, but I must find my father."

"I understand."

"What will Prince Vulkas do now?" Maiva asked.

"He'll bury his father in the morning, as is the custom. After that, we go to war. I'll accompany the prince since I'm a shieldmaiden of Valaren and thus honor-bound to fight. But I'd go even if I weren't obligated. What happened to King Hez and your village was despicable. It must be avenged."

Maiva nodded in agreement. "King Caernos will be pleased to have all of you with him in the days to come."

"It will be good to see the Grey King again," Charolais replied. "I must go now. Take care, Maiva. I hope you find your father."

"Thank you. May the White Stag watch over you." The fawn and minotaur embraced, then Charolais walked away.

MY ENEMY, MY FRIEND
Chapter 11

Vlain and Oudeteros sat on their horses and watched from a hilltop as their men engaged in a mock battle in a field just south of Hadrian's Wall. Each side consisted of one thousand legionnaires. The objective was to outmaneuver the opponent, using military formations and wooden swords and shields. They had been there since sunrise. Prydus had been surprised to hear Vlain and Oudeteros wanted to sharpen their men's battle prowess, considering they had won the day in Algos. Vlain had told him they lost too many men during the battle, which indicated further training was required. Thankfully, Prydus had believed him and had even admonished Caladin and Snill for not following suit. Vlain had chuckled when he saw their angry expressions.

"Are you going to tell me the real reason we're out here?" Oudeteros asked Vlain.

A sly smile formed on the fighter's face. "I was wondering when you'd ask."

"Well, wonder no longer." A cold wind had been blowing all day, and the warm weather-loving southerner was none too pleased to be out in the open where he was at its mercy.

"King Caernos wants peace, but Prydus insists on war," Vlain began.

"No surprise there," Oudeteros replied. "He's ambitious, wants to become grand general..."

"At the expense of our lives," Vlain finished. "That's unacceptable. Our legionnaires shouldn't die for one man's ambition. I won't stand for it. Will you?"

"What's the alternative?" Oudeteros asked.

"We join the woodlander army..."

"What did you just say?! We side with the enemy?! That's desertion! Betrayal!"

"Lower your voice," Vlain admonished. "It's survival. We were victorious in Algos because they were ill-prepared and only had a last-minute warning. We can't withstand the combined might of the Findaloran kingdoms. We'll be crushed underfoot."

"Prydus will ask for more legions..."

"There's no help coming," Vlain cut in. "The empire is already stretched too thin."

"If that's true, then why doesn't Prydus meet with Caernos?"

"Because he's blinded by pride. He thinks he's too smart to lose and is too inexperienced to see how wrong he is. What's more, he needs this win so badly he's prepared to risk all our lives to get it. Do you really want to throw your lot in with such a leader?"

Oudeteros stared hard at Vlain. "Then why not stage a coup? The men have..."

"It wouldn't work," Vlain answered. "If by some miracle it did, too many legionnaires would die in the process, which is exactly what I'm trying to avoid."

"But if I throw in with you and join the beasties..."

"Please don't use that word. You're better than that."

Oudeteros took a deep breath to calm his nerves. "Very well. If I fight for them, then I may have to kill those men down there," he said as he swept his hand out to indicate the legionnaires below them. "How could you ask me to do that?"

"I'm hoping it won't come to that," Vlain answered. "I'm hoping King Caernos, and I can present Prydus with such a powerful, opposing force that he feels compelled to sign a peace treaty."

"What if you can't?"

"Then we'll do what needs to be done."

Oudeteros grew quiet. He felt conflicted as he looked down at the men he had led from one danger into another for the last few months. They had responded valiantly each time. The prospect of deserting them was more than he could...

"I know it's a lot to take in," Vlain admitted. "And I'm sorry to..."

"No," Oudeteros cut in. "I'm sorry Prydus didn't heed your counsel. I'm sorry the two of you couldn't have gotten along from the beginning. I'm sorry it came to this."

"As am I," Vlain sadly replied. "I still need your answer, though."

Oudeteros sighed. "What would you do if I said no?"

"I'd leave you out of it, of course."

"When I received my officer commission, I pledged my undying support to the legion, to the empire, to..."

"None of which means anything if you're willing to throw your men's lives away for the political ambitions of an amoral man."

"Can I think it over? There's so much..."

"No," Vlain flatly replied. "I need your answer now."

"Why? Why can't I take a...?"

"I just do," Vlain forcefully said. "I just do," he repeated in a softer tone. "I respect you, Oudeteros, and I would greatly prefer you to be on my side..."

"So, you won't have to kill me later?"

"It won't come to that if you join us now."

"Us? You mean your core group, right?"

"Yes."

"Of course," Oudeteros said. "They'd follow you into Thania's lair itself."

"The question is, will you?"

"Yes," Oudeteros answered before he knew what he was saying. "I'll come with you." He shook his head from side to side as if he was waking from a dream. "Jaina! What is it about you? It's like you're magnetic," he said with a laugh.

"All part of my charm, I suppose," Vlain said with a crooked smile.

"I'm assuming you didn't pose the same question to Caladin or Snill?"

Vlain let out a harsh laugh. "No, but Snill did his best to win me over last night," he confided.

"Do tell."

"He was waiting for me in front of my tent after I returned from taking Meris to the clerics. He congratulated me on surviving my ordeal in Algos, then threw a business proposal at me," Vlain said as he rolled his eyes. He then imitated Snill's squeaky voice. "'I hope you realize the tremendous financial opportunities that can be extracted from the Last Wild after the locals have been dealt with. I hear there are trees in the forest with incredible properties. Some have bark that can be turned into potent medicine, while other trees make a sap that can kill a man. In addition to the trees, there are exotic animals we could sell for a fortune to the game masters who run the gladiator arena. In fact, you faced a native of the Last Wild when you fought a fearsome chimera years ago." Vlain finished with a chuckle.

"Let me guess, you turned him down?" Oudeteros asked.

"Actually, I told him I'd think it over."

"Why's that?"

"I didn't want to hurt my chances," Vlain explained. "If I'd told him to blaet off, he'd have scurried away to tell Prydus I was a dangerous liability. Then I might not have had the chance to do this."

Vlain urged his horse forward, then reached down to grab a steel horn from a saddlebag, raised it to his lips, and blew. A long, crisp note filled the air, bringing the thousands of men in the field below to a stop. "Gather round, I have something to share with you," Vlain shouted through his cupped hands.

Oudeteros was impressed at how quickly the legionnaires obeyed the command. He also noted that over fifty of Vlain's men arranged themselves in a tight semi-circle around the base of the hill. Meris led the group of hardened veterans. He looked imposing as he crossed his arms over his chest.

Vlain resumed speaking after the legionnaires were all focused on him. "As most of you know by now, I had a rough time of it in Algos, but by Jaina's grace, I survived. What's more, I learned something important while I was there. King Caernos, the king of the woodlanders, wants to negotiate a peace treaty with the Elamaran Empire, but Commander Orilius opposes the idea. He prefers to wage war and to risk all of your lives rather than strive for a mutually beneficial peace." The fighter paused to let the words sink in. Most of the legionnaires stared at him with dumbfounded expressions. "Well, I, for one, won't follow such a leader, especially since he'd rather remain behind in the safety of Fort Faldin during the fighting." Dead silence reigned, save for a few bewildered murmurs. "When I spoke to King Caernos, he informed me there are many kingdoms within the Last Wild, and when they all unite in her defense, we'll be annihilated. Emperor Justus can't send reinforcements. Our legions are already stretched thin enough as it is. So, I'm asking you to leave with me today and to cast your lot in with the woodlanders." Alarmed shouts erupted from the men. Vlain raised his hands, signaling for them to quiet down. "King Caernos has promised us protection. Although I can't guarantee your survival in the coming conflict, I can at least improve your odds if you join him now. What say you? Who will come with me?!"

The host of legionnaires looked up at Vlain with wide eyes and stunned expressions. They began whispering amongst each other while others jeered at Vlain. Eventually, a legionnaire shouted out a reply.

"Why haven't you asked Captain Caladin and Lieutenant Colonel Snill's men to join with you? Is the invitation not open to them as well?" he asked.

"Unfortunately, they both side with Commander Orilius on this issue, so their men are unlikely to be sympathetic to our cause," Vlain responded. Someone began to chant the word "traitor" several times, but his voice died down when no one else took up the chant.

Another legionnaire soon spoke up. "We all swore oaths to the empire when we joined the legion, and now you expect us to just walk away?"

"Yeah!" Another man shouted. "If we join with the beastmen,

then we'll never get to go home. We'll never see our families again!" The crowd murmured and nodded in approval of his words.

"After the war's over, I'll do my utmost to get you pardoned so you can resume your old lives," Vlain said. "Now, let those who wish to side with me and King Caernos walk behind the hill on which I stand. Those who wish to stay with Commander Orilius are free to return to camp. You have five minutes to make up your mind. After that, we ride into the Wild."

"Captain Oudeteros," one of his men shouted. "Will you desert with Vlain?"

Oudeteros urged his horse forward until it was standing beside Vlain's steed. "I side with Vlain in this conflict, and I urge all of you to follow your conscience at this crucial moment. Furthermore, we aren't deserting the legion; we're siding with those who fight for peace rather than self-aggrandizement. You heard the colonel; make your decision now. We ride out soon."

Vlain noticed two things at that moment. The first was that a score or more of legionnaires in the back of the assembly broke away and began riding back to camp. He figured they were about to tell Prydus what he had just said. Of course, he had counted on such an occurrence, which was why he planned to ride out so quickly. He didn't want to get into a fight with the legion until the Findaloran army could back him up. The second thing he noticed was the steady approach of an angry mob. A group of thirty or so men looked like they were about to clash with Vlain's band of loyalists at the base of the hill. However, Meris and the others leveled their crossbows as they drew closer. The aggressors stopped dead in their tracks. Vlain had ordered all legionnaires, save those who were unquestionably loyal to him, to only bring wooden swords to training today. Thus, he had granted his trusted men an advantage should fighting break out. The angry men scowled at Vlain and his supporters, then merged back into the assembly.

"We're down to two minutes," Vlain bellowed. "Who's coming with me?" None of the legionnaires moved, which caused his heart to sink. Eventually, a score of men broke away from the throng and walked to the back of the hill. Vlain's heart soared as more and more men joined them. He tried to count them but lost track after he reached three hundred. Vlain also noticed a sizeable group, which appeared to be over two hundred strong, broke away from Oudeteros's cohort to join the growing force behind the hill. *I had hoped for more, but five hundred will do,* Vlain thought. He took a deep breath then addressed the men who had chosen to remain behind. "To those of you who chose to stay, know this, Commander Orilius is leading you to your doom. However, if you change your mind and decide to fight with us, ride into the Wild and ask for me. The woodlanders will guide you to me. It was an honor to serve with you. Farewell!"

Vlain turned his horse around and rode down the hill with Oudeteros in tow. The fighter's loyal entourage of fifty legionnaires fell in behind him, followed by the five hundred legionnaires who had just renounced the 9th Legion. Vlain led them swiftly across the flat, grassy plain until they passed through a gap in Hadrian's Wall and disappeared into the forest. The legionnaires who had chosen to stay behind watched with stunned expressions as they galloped out of view. They turned and rode back to their camp with heavy hearts after the last of Vlain's men had been swallowed up by the Last Wild.

***

Caladin scowled as he sat on the back of his huge warhorse while it trotted down the old forest road. He wore his customary armor with one new exception. His steel helmet now had the two buffalo horns he had taken from the fallen minotaur king sprouting from the sides. He held the lower haft of his battle-ax with one hand and let the upper haft repeatedly fall into his other palm as he scanned the dense underbrush for movement. So far, he and his force of one thousand legionnaires hadn't encountered a single woodlander, which he found unsettling, to say the least.

The foul weather had put him and his men in an equally bad mood. It had started raining in the mid-afternoon and hadn't abated since. What's more, mosquitoes, the size of dragonflies, incessantly bit them as they traveled through the Last Wild. It didn't matter how vigorously the men swatted at them; the insatiable insects would always return to bite again and again. Large, purple welts had already formed on Caladin's arms, neck, and face. He had long since given up shooing the greedy, flying pests away. It only wasted precious energy, which he might need at any moment. For the thousandth time, the big man wondered how Vlain and his men had been able to repel the mosquitoes during the journey from Elamara to Faldin. He would have killed to know the brash fighter's secret. In fact, he longed to strangle Vlain because it was his actions that had forced Caladin and his legionnaires to enter a hostile, mosquito-infested land during a rainstorm.

Prydus had been livid when he had learned of Vlain's sudden betrayal. His pride was obviously wounded because the fighter had outmaneuvered him, thus making him look like an incompetent leader. On top of that, Vlain had taken over five hundred men with him, thus considerably weakening the 9th Legion. Prydus had snarled orders at Caladin like a man possessed after he learned about the mass desertion.

"Find Vlain and his fellow deserters!" Prydus had screamed at Caladin. "Find them and drag them back so we can hang them in Faldin's town square for all to see! If he puts up too much of a fight, then slay him where he stands, and bring me his head!" Prydus had snarled as flecks of saliva flew from his mouth, and his face turned beet-red.

Of course, Caladin had had no choice but to obey. Unfortunately, it required him to reenter the Last Wild. Knowing

Vlain, he had anticipated being followed, which meant he could attack at any moment. The thought of clashing with an armed and determined Vlain made Caladin extremely nervous because, despite his unusual strength, Caladin knew he couldn't beat him. Their brief fight had more than proven that point. Vlain's speed was impossible; his endurance inhuman and his skill with weapons unparalleled. As fearless and ferocious as the woodlanders were, Caladin would much rather fight them than Vlain.

"Captain Caladin!" his scout whispered as he drew closer.

"What is it?" Caladin snapped.

"There's a tree blocking the road just beyond the curve there. Do you want to chop it apart or go around it?" the young man asked.

"Endlin's beard!" Caladin snarled. He hadn't thought the day could get any worse. "Let me take a look." The big man urged his horse into a canter and soon rounded the corner to gaze at the redwood that blocked the road. He shook his head and frowned. "This feels wrong," he said.

"That was my thought as well, sir," the scout replied.

"Look at the base of the tree," he ordered the man. "Let me know if it fell with its roots intact or if it was cut down."

"Aye, aye, sir," the scout replied. He got down from his horse then walked into the dense underbrush that lined the side of the road. By now, the column of legionnaires had caught up with Caladin.

Danorus, Caladin's second in command, shook his head in dismay as he looked at the giant tree. He let out a low whistle and brought his horse up alongside Caladin's. "Feels like an..." but he was caught off by a piercing scream.

Caladin looked wildly about as he tried to pinpoint the source of the scream. "Scout! Scout! Was that you? Report!" he bellowed. An ominous silence filled the air. Caladin scowled and was about to yell out to his scout again when a hail of arrows and spears shot out from the underbrush. Two arrows thudded into Caladin's chestplate. He instantly raised his shield to block the next volley. Since he was expecting more arrows, he was surprised when a wooden spear slammed into his shield. A reddish-amber glob of what looked like tree sap splattered off its tip and into one of his eyes. Before he could react to the hellish, burning sensation, an arrow grazed his cheek, and another one grazed his forearm. A fiery pain soon radiated throughout his face and arm.

"Ambush!" He screamed. "Raise your shields! They put poison on the arrows!" He didn't know if his men heard him or not due to all the commotion around him. Horses whinnied in fear, and men shouted and cursed as the arrows and spears thudded into bodies. Pandemonium reigned.

Caladin hunkered down behind his broad, curved shield as the third volley of projectiles shot out from the bushes not far from where the scout had disappeared. Suddenly, a large rock slammed into his shield with such force that he was pushed back in his saddle. Caladin gritted his teeth in anger, but he couldn't risk reaching for his crossbow until the lethal barrage ended. Finally, it stopped. The huge man snatched his crossbow from its place on his saddle. He was about to return fire when another barrage erupted from the bushes. Unfortunately for the legionnaires, this one came from the opposite side of the road and thus caught them all off guard. An arrow sank into Caladin's meaty calf as well as his shoulder. The fiery sap on the arrowheads made him swoon in agony.

"Swetch soides!" he screamed, only to realize the poison was affecting his speech. Most of his men were caught off guard by the sudden change in the direction of attack. He watched as over a score of them fell to the ground. Panic seized him. He knew forward movement was impossible due to the downed tree, and the dense foliage prevented him from seeing any of their attackers. He blindly fired several bolts into the bushes, hoping to hit some of their assailants by chance.

"Retrit! Retrit!" he screamed at the top of his lungs. He knew a hopeless situation when he saw one. The fiery poison was already interfering with his motor skills, making it increasingly difficult for him to think or move. It was only a question of time before they were all killed.

Caladin turned his horse around and dug his spurred heels into its sides, causing the draft horse to bolt straight into his men. The legionnaires who could still function followed him. His horse's hooves thundered on the road as it reached a full gallop. Caladin was glad to see the men in the middle of the column had yet to be attacked.

"Go! Fell bek! Retrit!" he croaked as the poison continued to paralyze his vocal cords.

Thankfully, most of the men understood him despite his rough speech. They turned their mounts around and followed him back toward camp, back towards safety, towards life itself.

No sooner had the retreat begun than a score of towering wood golems exploded out from the underbrush on either side of the road. Each one was twice as tall as a man, had glowing green eyes, and their huge, clawed hands dripped with the same fiery sap that coated the woodlanders' arrowheads and spear-tips. Caladin looked back to watch as they carved a bloody path of carnage through his legionnaires and their mounts. The dying men screamed in agony as they were ripped to shreds. Some of them called for their mothers in their final moments. Caladin looked away from the horrific scene to focus on what was before him. He careened wildly off of several of his legionnaires who were too slow to move out of his way. Eventually, he shot past them to gain the open road. A feeling of relief flooded through him, but it vied with the poison that burned in his veins and threatened to immobilize him. Caladin tried to call for a retreat again, but his vocal cords no longer worked.

He risked another look back and was glad to see most of his legionnaires were following him. He could see the look of defeat on their faces. They knew they had lost the battle. Thanks to Vlain, the woodlanders had known they were coming and had set the perfect ambush. In fact, Caladin had felt a sense of impending doom before he had even left camp, but Prydus's fury had compelled him to chase after Vlain. Caladin didn't care what Prydus did to him when he got back. He could demote, jail, or whip him, but at least he'd be alive. He urged his horse on faster and faster until the gloomy, rain-drenched landscape was nothing more than a vague blur.

***

Vlain stood beside Caernos on top of a grassy knoll. Man, and centaur looked out at a large gathering of Findalorans. The village of Orrn was primarily occupied by centaurs, but there was a smattering of other races present as well. There were even scattered pockets of humans here and there, but none were former legionnaires. Vlain was the only non-Findaloran present. He had thought it wise for his men to remain on the outskirts of the village until the inhabitants of Orrn grew accustomed to them. His men were being supervised by Oudeteros in the construction of several lodges where they'd live while they fought the 9th Legion.

Caernos cleared his throat then began speaking to the crowd in his booming baritone voice. "Good people of Orrn, I have gathered you here today to share the good news. As you have no doubt heard, the village of Algos was destroyed by Man. It was attacked and burned by an army sent by a human emperor from a capital city called Elamara far to the south. Due to the ongoing conflict between the Faldinites and us, Man has decided to wage war on us. They seek to remove us from Findalora, our ancient home, but we shall prevail!" The crowd went wild. Deafening, angry outbursts filled the air as the Findalorans pumped their fists, shouted, and howled in defiance. After a moment, Caernos raised his hands to appeal to them to quiet down. They eventually heeded his request. The centaur placed a hand on Vlain's shoulder. "Thankfully, the White Stag changed the heart of the man you see here. His name is Vlain, and he's one of the fiercest warriors you'll ever meet. However, despite his talent for war, Amani appeared above him when we spoke in the forest. As you all know, the dove is an emissary of the White Stag, and she only appears to those who serve peace." Caernos patted Vlain's shoulder as he scanned the hundreds of faces in the audience. Most of the Findalorans stared at Vlain suspiciously, and some mumbled curses. "I know what you're thinking: how can a warrior sent to kill us serve Amani? I don't know the answer to that question. I can only tell you the dove appeared above Vlain, and that her presence has ALWAYS revealed an agent of peace. Vlain and I spoke about negotiating a peace treaty, and he went back to his commander to convince him to meet with me. Unfortunately, Commander Orilius isn't interested in peace. After he learned that, Vlain could no longer serve him with a clear conscience. He defected from the 9th Legion and brought over five hundred legionnaires with him. So, you can already see Amani's plan unfolding. She was wise to choose him as her servant." Caernos paused to raise one of Vlain's arms high, prompting some of those in the audience to grudgingly clap in approval.

Caernos lowered his arm then resumed speaking. "Here's what I ask of you, treat Vlain and his men with respect and honor. He'll demand the same from his former legionnaires whenever they interact with us. I must caution you, however. If anyone kills one of Vlain's men, then the transgressor shall be put to death. Should anyone harm his men, they shall be severely punished and banished forever. I wish to be clear when I say Vlain and his men are under my FULL protection. Should any problems arise between you and them, you will go to Oshur or one of my royal guards. If I need to get involved, I will do so, but I'll remain impartial at all times. You must understand this because Vlain and his men will be fighting for us in the coming days, and they bring with them much experience and wisdom. They need us, and we need them if we're to win the war. That is all. I bid you a good day," Caernos concluded.

Vlain was pleased with everything Caernos had said during his speech. Of course, they had already agreed on how Vlain's men would live and function in Findalora, but it was still good to hear it publicly stated. He had hoped for a warmer reception from the crowd, but he knew in his heart that was unrealistic considering how recent the battle of Algos had been. Hopefully, in time, they'd come to realize he could be trusted and relied upon. He'd just have to be patient.

As Vlain watched the crowd disperse, he noticed a limping centaur bearing fresh wounds. He realized he was one of those brave souls who had volunteered to ambush the 9th Legion if Prydus tried to retrieve Vlain and his men. Vlain figured he would, and he had been right. He had volunteered himself and all the former legionnaires to assist with the ambush, but Caernos had said it wasn't necessary. The king had sent his best archers, spearmen, dozens of druids, and many golems to repel Caladin and the one thousand men under his command. Thankfully, only a handful of Findaloran fighters had died, and only a dozen or so had been injured by random bolts fired by Caladin's men. The dense foliage and the element of surprise had greatly assisted the Findalorans during the brief skirmish. However, the casualty rate for the 9th Legion had been very high. Caladin had lost over one hundred men even though the ambush had only lasted a few minutes.

Although Vlain didn't like it when others did the fighting for him, part of him had been glad he hadn't had to kill men he had grown to know and like. Perhaps Caernos had anticipated the psychological toll it would take on Vlain and his renouncers and had factored that into his decision to exclude them from the fighting. Vlain was thankful to him whether the thought had crossed his mind or not.

The fighter smiled and nodded appreciatively at the centaur as he limped past him. "Thank you for fighting on our behalf," Vlain said. Since Vlain wore a necklace of understanding, the centaur had no trouble comprehending him.

"We are all one people now," the Findaloran replied as he ambled away.

Vlain turned to face the king. "And thank you for taking us in and protecting us," he said.

"I always honor my promises, and I have no doubt you'll earn your keep in the coming days."

Vlain was about to respond when Maiva, Ganymay, and a horde of younglings suddenly entered the clearing. Maiva broke into a run and opened her arms wide when she saw Caernos. She had almost reached him when she saw Vlain standing beside him. The fawn skidded to a stop and instinctively pulled her slingshot from her pocket. She was just about to reach into a pouch to pull a spiked venom ball out when the king's voice stopped her.

"Hold, dear Maiva!" he boomed. "Vlain's no danger to anyone. He and his men have joined us in the war against Man. Put your weapon away and be at ease." Maiva did as he asked, although her expression remained wary. "Come here," he gently said as he spread his arms. The two of them embraced, then the king stepped back to look at her. "You look hale and hearty, as do the younglings. Thank you for faithfully following my orders."

"You're welcome, my king," Maiva replied. "We spent all day in Algos looking for my father, but we couldn't find him. Tell me, is he here?"

"No, but he soon will be," Caernos said. "I sent a small force through Orrn's green gate to the one in the Cave of Sanctuary two days ago. Although Haephius was injured during the battle, he's recovering nicely. The gnome healers have greatly helped him. Your father, Zenda, and the elderlings will soon return. They're just waiting for their wounded to finish healing before they travel through the green gate."

"Thank the White Stag!" Maiva exclaimed. "May I use the gate to see him now?"

"So long as you go alone. We don't want to deplete it with too much traffic right before a large group passes through it," Caernos explained.

"Thank you, my king! I'll go right now."

Maiva turned to leave, but Vlain spoke to her before she got far. "Maiva!"

"Yes?" She said, twirling around to gaze at him with a mixture of emotions.

"I'm sorry for all the harm I've caused you and your people. Your father was likely injured because of one of my orders. Had I known then what I know now, I never would have..."

"It's all right. Knowing my father, he probably gave as good as he got."

"You speak the truth," Vlain said with a rueful chuckle. Maiva smiled, then turned and walked toward Orrn's green gate. "I'll take my leave as well," Vlain said with a slight bow as he addressed Caernos. "I'm sure my men could use my help with the construction of the lodges."

"Not so fast," the king said. He had been holding a black leather bag during his speech, which he now offered to Vlain. "There are nine more understandings in here. Give them to all of your officers so they can translate for the others."

"I will do so," Vlain said with a grateful smile as he took the bag. Caernos watched the fighter walk away. He shook his head in wonder at the strange twist of fate that had transformed a fearsome enemy into an ally. The White Stag was undoubtedly full of surprises.

***

Caladin stood tall and at full attention in front of Prydus. He had a bandage over one eye, and bandages were wrapped around his calf, deltoid, arm, and cheek as well. Although he had spent a whole day in the tent of healing, his body was still recovering from the effects of the poisonous sap. As was his habit, Prydus began pacing back and forth as he berated the huge man. Whenever he posed a question, he'd pause and glare icily at Caladin while he answered. No answer, however, was ever good enough for Prydus. No matter what Caladin said, his replies only served to further enrage his superior.

"Tell me again. How in Taloria did you manage to lose one hundred and twenty legionnaires in just ten minutes?!" Prydus shouted.

"It was a well-planned ambush," Caladin said for the third time. "There was a giant tree blocking the road. I sent a scout to see if it had been cut down, then arrows and spears..."

"Yes! I know all that," Prydus hissed. "What I want to know is, why didn't you take the battle to them?! Why didn't you wade into the forest and devastate them with your two cohorts?"

"We couldn't see our attackers," Caladin replied. "We were firing blindly into the bushes, hoping to hit the beasties by sheer..."

"It didn't occur to you to enter the forest so you could see them?"

"The wooden monsters appeared before we could mount a counter-attack..."

"Oh, yes, the wooden monsters," Prydus said mockingly. "Oudeteros had remarkable success defeating them with cooking oil and burning arrows. Why didn't you employ the same tactics?"

"It all happened too fast," Caladin said in a tired voice. "My men were dying by the score; they started to panic..."

"Or was it you who panicked?" Prydus pressed. "If the men see their leader panic, then they'll soon follow suit."

"I'll admit, I was startled by the first volley, but I kept my head," Caladin replied. "I've turned it over in my mind a thousand times. Nothing we could have done would have worked. We were in a kill box, and they were..."

"I'm demoting you to lieutenant," Prydus snapped. "And you'll spend a week in the brig with nothing but bread and water. That'll give you plenty of time to brush up on your battle tactics. Guards!" Two burly legionnaires who had been standing off to the side snapped to attention. "Take him to the brig," Prydus commanded as he gave Caladin a withering look. As soon as the guards had removed Caladin from Prydus's tent, he flopped down in his throne-like chair and began sulking.

Snill, who had been quietly watching the drama unfold, finally broke his silence. "Had Caladin not given the order to retreat, we would have lost even more legionnaires," he said. Prydus gave him a stern look but remained silent. "Still, all may not be lost," he said in his high-pitched, nasally voice.

"We just lost over six hundred legionnaires, if you count those who deserted with Vlain," Prydus shot back. "How can we salvage that?"

"True enough," Snill continued. "But we can gain that back and more if we roll our dice right."

"How so?" Prydus asked.

"Do you remember the fight Vlain had with the barbarians in the tavern?"

"Of course, what does that have to do with our troop strength?"

"The barbarian lands aren't all that far away, and they have a deep hatred for Vlain. We can capitalize on that," Snill said with a sly smile.

"Go on."

"The emperor gave you a considerable war chest. Why not use some of it to hire a barbarian army? They already loathe Vlain and have frequently clashed with the woodlanders over the years. You'd be paying them to do something they already want to do."

Prydus stroked his chin as he listened. "Your idea has merit."

"Since we lost over six hundred legionnaires, and since Caernos's army may greatly outnumber our own, let's hire a thousand barbarians to fight for us. We'll be ahead by four hundred."

"That's why I keep you around, Snill. Your counsel is second to none," Prydus admitted.

"Excellent. Then it's settled," Snill said with a satisfied smile.

"Not so fast. The barbarians may turn our offer down."

"I highly doubt that. Offer their chieftain ten bricks of silver. He'll bulk at that and likely double it, which is still a bargain. They'll play right into our hands."

"Not a bad strategy," Prydus replied. "And as you said, they hate Vlain. But I don't think they'll mix well with the legionnaires. Barbarians are messy and undisciplined."

"There's no reason to bring them together," Snill advised. "Since their lands lie west of the Last Wild, have them attack Caernos's forces from the western flank while we attack from the south."

"Yes, they'll be forced to fight on two fronts," Prydus said. "But I don't know if we'll be able to lure the beasties out of their forest anymore. Vlain will undoubtedly tell them about our plan to draw them down into the plains where your catapults can make short work of them."

"But there are other ways to lure them out. For example, we could set the trees on fire by using my catapults to hurl balls of flaming pitch into the forest. They'll get so tired of putting out fires they'll emerge from the woods to fight us on open ground."

"I like what I'm hearing, Snill," Prydus said. "We can start the war as soon as the barbarians have agreed to our terms."

Snill shook his head in disagreement. "I wouldn't advise fighting through the winter this far north. Blizzards and snowstorms will quickly put our fires out. Not to mention the threats of frostbite, hypothermia, and low morale to our legionnaires. Winter is often a deadlier adversary than the one you fight on the battlefield."

"True," Prydus conceded. "Unless the beasties force our hand, we'll wait for spring to come, and then," a low cackle issued from Prydus's throat. "Then we'll unleash hell on them."

***

The ceremony began right after the former legionnaires finished eating breakfast. Vlain had them assemble in a field behind the grass huts, which served as their temporary living quarters. They stood at rigid attention while Caernos, fifty druids, and over one

310

hundred artists entered the field. The king walked around the rectangular formation of men, admiring their motionless discipline, precise arrangement, and the bravery they exhibited in the face of the unknown. The druids formed a line facing the men and separated themselves by ten feet. The artists, specializing in tattoos, piercings, brandings, and other forms of body art, formed a line perpendicular to the druids. They each carried a wooden stool and a bag filled with tools and supplies. The artists set their stools down, sat on them, and began pulling various tools out of their leather bags.

"The day has finally arrived," Caernos said to Vlain as he completed his walk around the formation. "Your men look ready."

"As ready as they'll ever be," Vlain responded.

Caernos nodded, then turned to address them. "The blood oath ceremony will soon begin. If any of you wish to leave, now's the time." None of the men moved so much as a muscle. "The artists will use a sharp needle to push hundreds of copper pellets under your skin. They'll form a multi-layered band around your left upper arm. The druids will then cast a spell of binding onto the copper bands, which will ensure your loyalty to the people of Findalora. Should any of you disobey one of my commands, or violate one of our sacred laws, then the bands will set your blood on fire. You shall burn from the inside out. The ceremony you're about to undergo is called the blood oath because your blood will burn should you break your oath of fealty to me. You shall recite this oath right before the band is enchanted. They will then become visual reminders of your oath and provide the ultimate incentive to honor it. The spell will last for one year. Hopefully, we'll have won the war by then. If not, the spell will be recast. Unless you choose to remove them after you've fulfilled your oath, the bands will remain in your skin as a permanent reminder of your service to Findalora's people. I require all of my soldiers and servants to wear one. In fact, I bear the band of loyalty myself," Caernos said as he pointed to his arm. A band formed from ten, tightly spaced rings of tiny, raised bumps encircled his muscular limb. "There are no exceptions to this requirement if you wish to serve our kingdom. In return for pledging your loyalty to me today, I promise to never issue an immoral, corrupt, or unlawful command. I swear this upon my soul and the souls of my forefathers!" Caernos boomed. He turned his attention to the long line of skin artists. "You may proceed."

"You heard him, men," Vlain bellowed. "The man to the far left in each row will go first, followed by the next in line, and so on until you've all received the band." The men did as he ordered. Vlain watched as they kneeled in front of the artists, who each held a sharp-edged, metal tube with one hand, and a thin metal pole with the other. He soon realized the hollow tubes were filled with copper pellets. The artists used slender iron rods inside them to repeatedly shove the pellets under the men's skin. Every now and then, the artists pulled the rods out of the tubes to add more pellets into them. The artists would occasionally tell the men to lift and rotate their arms so they could connect and complete the bands. The men's arms soon looked red, bloody, and swollen. The first men in line left the artists and walked over to the druids after an hour had elapsed.

Vlain listened intently as they began repeating an oath, which the druids, who all wore understandings, recited to them in Emblin: "From this day forth, I will abide by the laws governing all Findalorans. I promise to conduct myself with honor and integrity at all times. I will obey the king's commands whether they come from him or have been passed down to his subjects. All this, I swear, on this day, before the White Stag and his people. Should I fail to honor this binding oath, then may flames of wrath boil my blood!"

As soon as the men finished repeating the oath, the druids wrapped both hands around their arms. They closed their eyes and began silently mouthing the words of a spell. A bright, orange flash of light briefly appeared around the bands, which always startled the men. They looked groggy and disorientated afterward. The druids then guided them to a vacant section of the field and had the men sit down so they could recover from the dizzying effects of the spell.

Vlain's eyes scanned the line of druids, searching for one in particular. He found Iolee just as she laid her hands on Meris's arm. He watched as his friend of over twelve years shivered from the force of the loyalty spell as it seeped into the copper pellets embedded in his skin. Meris pitched forward and would have fallen if Iolee hadn't steadied him. The druidess guided him to the recovery area and helped him sit down. Vlain watched as he clapped Oudeteros reassuringly on the shoulder, and began speaking to him, then he looked away.

One by one, all of Vlain's renouncers went through the process. The men recovered for a time in the field, then walked back to their grass huts when they felt better. The ceremony repeated itself until they had all gone through it, and the morning became evening.

"You were saved for last, Vlain, just as you requested," Caernos boomed in his baritone voice.

Vlain blinked several times, then nodded in understanding. He was nervous, even afraid. The foreign emotion caught him off guard because he hadn't felt it in years. He wasn't scared for himself; he was worried about the druid who would cast a spell on him after he had received the loyalty band. He kept stoically silent as the only remaining artist shoved pellet after pellet into his brown skin. The pain was minor but relentless, and it lasted for over an hour. Finally, the artist pushed the last pellet into his arm just as the field was growing dark.

Caernos walked beside Vlain as they made their way to Iolee. She was the only druid left now. "The time for the truth is at hand," Vlain began. "There's a powerful enchantment on me. It protects me, allows me to beat any opponent, surmount any obstacle, win any contest. I'm afraid of what it might do to Iolee when she casts the loyalty spell on me," he confided.

"It all makes sense now!" Caernos exclaimed. "How did you acquire such potent magic? Was it bestowed upon you by the Goddess you call...?"

"I'll tell you later. Right now, I'm worried about Iolee."

"We could always use another druid," Caernos suggested.

"Whoever takes her place will be in the same danger," Vlain explained.

"Then what should we do?" Caernos asked.

"It just came to me," Vlain replied as he stopped in front of Iolee. He bowed his head in greeting. "Good evening," he said softly to her.

"Good evening," she said as her lips formed an affectionate smile. "Are you ready?"

"No," he replied, causing Iolee and Caernos to stare at him in confusion. "Not until you place a protective ward around yourself." Iolee looked at Caernos, who appeared to be equally befuddled. "I wear a powerful enchantment that protects me from all manner of things. I don't know what will happen when you cast your spell. I'm hoping a defensive ward will keep you safe if the results are...unpredictable."

"What type of enchantment do you speak of?" She asked.

"One fulfilled by a wish," he said.

Iolee's eyes grew wide. "Did you find a...?"

"It's a long answer, so I'll tell you another time," Vlain cut in. Iolee looked at him doubtfully. "I promise, Iolee. You can hold me to it, as can you, my king," Vlain said as he looked at Caernos. The king nodded in acceptance of his terms. Vlain looked expectantly at Iolee.

"Very well," the druidess replied. Vlain and Caernos watched as she raised her hands above her head and began an incantation. Nothing happened at first, then she dropped her hands, and as she did so, her fingers left behind tracers of flickering red light. Iolee crossed her hands back and forth several times in front of her chest. A honeycomb lattice of red light formed around her, then it was gone in an instant. It happened so fast, Vlain almost doubted he had seen it. "It's in place," she said. "Are you ready to proceed?"

"I am," Vlain said reluctantly. Iolee was startled to see fear lurking in his amber eyes. She took a deep breath then recited the blood oath for Vlain, and he repeated it line-for-line. The druidess then raised her hands again and began chanting the loyalty spell. Vlain shut his eyes, held his breath, and looked away. Iolee lowered her hands then wrapped them around Vlain's muscular arm. A bright, orange explosion of light and heat sprang off of the fighter's skin, knocking Iolee flat on her back. The blast even shoved Caernos back several feet. Vlain cringed in anticipation as he opened his eyes and looked around. Caernos was startled, to say the least, but he didn't appear injured. Vlain then saw Iolee lying on the ground. He sprinted forward, dropped to his knees, and skidded to a stop beside her. He tried to lower his ear to her mouth, but his head was repelled by her red-tinged ward. Vlain shoved his hands under her back to prop her up. The pressure from Vlain's hands revealed a hexagon pattern formed by a shimmering, red light that subtly resisted his touch.

"Iolee! Talk to me! Are you alright?" the words rushed from Vlain's mouth.

The druidess didn't move for a moment, then her mouth twitched, and her eyelids fluttered open. She muttered something unintelligible, then gazed up at Vlain. Iolee raised a hand to gently touch his plain, rugged face.

"Thank you for the warning, outlander, but could you stress the danger more next time?" Her smile remained, but her brow was furrowed.

Vlain nodded in agreement. "I tend to understate things," he said with a sigh. "Are you hurt?"

Iolee slowly stood up. "I don't think so," she answered. "No, I don't think I am," she said with more certainty. "Do you feel differently? Does your blood burn as if you have a fever? Are you dizzy?" she asked.

"I feel the same as always," Vlain answered. Iolee and Caernos both stared at him in cool amazement. They had never met anyone immune to the loyalty spell. It was a spell of binding, after all, and was meant to force a powerful enchantment on a person. Vlain, however, had clearly been unaffected by it.

"I think the magic in you deflected it," the druidess said. Vlain and Caernos nodded as her words sank in. Vlain knew she understood the workings of magic on a deep level since all druids were required to study it during their long years of training.

"I thought something like that might happen," Vlain said.

"What do we do now?" Iolee asked Caernos. The king shook his head in uncertainty, obviously at a loss.

"We become blood brothers," Vlain said without missing a beat. "We cut our palms open with my knife and shake hands. We let our blood commingle and thus unite us in a bond of blood and friendship. That'll bind me to your people and our mutual cause more than any spell could."

Caernos smiled, although the shadow covering his face prevented Vlain and Iolee from seeing it. "Pull forth your dagger and make your cut," the king said. Vlain did so, then handed him the bloody knife. Caernos slashed the sharp blade across his gray-skinned palm. Blood oozed from the deep wound. Vlain raised his palm to Caernos's. They clasped their wounded hands together, forcing their blood to mix.

"United in blood," Vlain solemnly stated.

"United in blood," Caernos repeated. Centaur and man dropped their bloody hands to their sides. "Iolee, would you mind?" the king asked her. Iolee crossed her hands in front of her chest, prompting a bright red flash of light to briefly appear around her body. She could touch them now that she had dispensed with the ward. The druidess took each of their hands in hers and imagined that their deep cuts were healing. A faint green light radiated out from her palms as she did so. Vlain and Caernos grimaced in discomfort as their flesh rapidly knitted itself back together again.

"Good as new," Vlain said as he ran a finger across his smooth palm.

"You really have to work on your warnings," Iolee playfully reminded Vlain.

"She's right, you know," Caernos added.

"I'm never going to hear the end of this, am I?" Vlain asked while shrugging his shoulders.

His expression looked both resigned and amused.

"Never," Iolee and Caernos said in unison, causing Vlain to start chuckling.

***

Maiva stared at her father from across the room as he laughed and joked with Zenda. She thanked the White Stag for the thousandth time since she had found him alive and well in the Cave

317

of Sanctuary. The arrow wound in Haephius's back had scared her, to say the least, but the gnomes had done an excellent job of healing him. One of their healers had told Maiva that Haephius was expected to regain the full use of his legs, and she had been right. Maiva knew it could have played out very differently had the arrow hit a different spot. So, she had prayed all night to the Stag to show her appreciation for sparing him from a graver injury.

After Haephius and the injured elderlings had recovered, they had all filed through the shimmering green gate in the cave only to step out into the village of Orrn. King Caernos had warmly welcomed them and had then taken Haephius to Orrn's best forge. Haephius, much to the chagrin of the previous blacksmith, had taken over the forge. Today had been his first chance to thoroughly inspect it, and Maiva could tell Haephius was dissatisfied with it. Although it had all the essentials for metalworking, the bellows were smaller than he was used to, and the ventilation wasn't up to his standards. He had shared his findings with the king, and Caernos had said he would send workmen over tomorrow morning to begin renovations.

Maiva knew why the king was rolling over sideways to accommodate Haephius. He was placing the formidable responsibility of forging thousands of weapons and armor for the Findalorans in the upcoming war on her father's shoulders. Of course, Haephius wouldn't meet the challenge alone. He'd delegate most of the work to the small army of blacksmiths and journeymen who had volunteered to work for him while forging only the most elite weaponry himself. Part of Maiva wished her father could rest and relax for once in his life, but his own success had been his undoing. Not only was he an incredibly talented blacksmith, but he was a findoree with the natural ability to imbue his creations with magical properties. Such a unique and exquisite talent set made rest an impossibility. Maiva, like her mother before her, would have to step in now and then to make sure Haephius was getting enough food and sleep. She didn't look forward to the arguments those actions would kick-off.

"Where are you right now, my dear?" Haephius asked.

"Busy worrying about you," Maiva admitted. "I inherited that job now that mom's gone."

"You can count on me to help," Zenda said.

"What's this?!" Haephius exclaimed. "You're both ganging up on me?"

"Uh oh," Maiva said with a giggle as she played along. "Don't tell the king, or we'll both be banished forever."

"I don't need the king to banish you," Haephius said in a playfully ominous tone. "The requirements of supper can do that all on their own."

"Supper already?" Maiva asked.

"Why yes," Haephius replied. "We've been inspecting this Stag forsaken forge for the better part of the day. The shadows grow long, and my stomach's rumbling, which means it's time to eat. Maiva, gather some food from the garden. Zenda, fetch water from the well. While you both do that, I'll gather firewood with which to cook our dinner and push back the autumn chill."

"Aye, aye, Master Haephius!" Maiva snarkily replied. She turned to leave, but then she spun back around. "Am I to presume we'll have no meat with dinner?"

"Oh, I'll take care of that," Haephius said with a knowing smile as he vigorously rubbed his hands together.

Zenda went one way, while Maiva went the other. The young fawn felt a strange, prickly sensation crawl across her forehead as she stepped outside. She had become accustomed to it by now and knew exactly what it meant. The sun had set, which activated the star mark that lay dormant and unseen on her forehead during the daylight hours. Maiva had also learned she was more prone to dreams and visions at nighttime, which, of course, was when she had received the star.

Maiva grabbed a discarded potato sack as she neared the garden. She stooped down to dig up several potatoes, onions, and squash from the garden, then dropped them all into the sack. She was about to head back into the forge when she felt dizzy. Maiva quickly sat down lest she lose her balance and fall. It was then that it happened. Maiva was staring at a green rose in the garden when its form began to warp and shimmer. She watched in awe as the green petals morphed into a beating heart formed from vibrant green energy. The living light shimmered and pulsed each time the "heart" beat. A wave of green light shot out into the valley with each beat. The rhythmic, steady beats sent visible shockwaves into the surrounding garden, which had now ceased to be a garden. Maiva was now staring down into a section of Findalora that was unknown to her. A dark shadow lay across the expansive valley into which she gazed, and there, in the center of the vale, lay the beating green Heart. Maiva suddenly felt the desire to possess it. She reached out her hand to grab it, but as soon as she touched the rosebud, the vision disappeared altogether. Maiva felt a pang of loss at its abrupt disappearance.

"What have I just seen?" she asked herself as she stood up. She shook her head in hopes of clearing the bizarre vision from her mind, but it was no use.

It was there to stay. Maiva walked back into the forge. Zenda had since returned, bearing a bucket of well water, and her father was busy lighting a fire in the stove. She lifted the bag and dumped the vegetables onto the only table.

Maiva remained silent while they all prepared supper. Haephius had somehow acquired a duck during his search for firewood. No doubt, an admiring apprentice or a generous resident of Orrn had seen him wandering about and had offered him the bird. Maiva chopped the vegetables while he prepared the duck. Zenda laid out plates, utensils, and cups. Haephius placed the duck on a steel pan then shoved it into the woodstove along with the vegetables.

"Shouldn't take long, now," Haephius said. He was just about to sit at the table with them when his eyes suddenly grew big. "How could I forget!" he exclaimed before shooting off into the dark hallway beyond the forge. He returned a minute later, bearing a large bottle of blue-tinted wine. "Word has it; this vintage was made by none other than Oisin Corcra himself. Bottled in his famous Purple Vale, it was!" Haephius said.

Maiva looked intently at him. She had told him about her chance meeting with the wild Lillen when she had roamed the lands around Barum Field in search of game for the younglings. "I thought he was known for his potent weed," she shot back.

"Undoubtedly," Haephius conceded. "But he also makes wine, and this is supposed to be some of his best. Would you like to taste test it while we wait for supper?" Maiva and Zenda nodded "yes," prompting Haephius to pour each of them a cup. The three of them took a drink. Haephius and Zenda smiled dreamily, but Maiva resisted the powerful effects of the wine. She had words to share.

"Oisin told me you made his skipping staff and carved his purple diamond pendant. Is that true?" she asked.

Haephius enthusiastically nodded up and down. "It is. I was young back then, and eager to make a name for myself as a findoree blacksmith. Crazy Oisin was one of my first customers. Thankfully, he was pleased with my work, and his praise brought me so much business I had to hire..."

"I had a vision while I was in the garden," Maiva suddenly cut in.

"Just...just now?" Haephius asked with a trace of discomfort. He was adjusting to his daughter's new powers of foresight, which still made him uneasy.

"I was picking vegetables from the garden when I saw a rosebud turn into a green, beating heart. It looked like it was made of solid light, and I could sense as well as see that it was hidden in a dark valley..."

"Please," Haephius interjected as he placed a hand over hers. "It's bad luck to mention that place."

"What place do you speak of?" Maiva pressed.

Haephius took a deep breath then looked away. He would have remained silent had Maiva not grabbed his forearm. "It's called the Dark Vale," he said softly. "It's a valley where we send our outcasts, our criminals, our lost souls."

"Have you ever heard of this place?" Maiva asked Zenda.

Zenda hesitantly nodded "yes." "Once, when I was very young, but never again after that."

"Why didn't you ever tell me about it, poppa?"

"I was going to when you got older," Haephius replied. "But they took you from me, and then all of this began," he said with a wave of his hand.

"The Dark Vale," Maiva repeated. "Is a prison where we send our undesirables?"

"It's more than that," Zenda said before Haephius could reply. "It's filled with monsters, and evil, and darkness. It's ruled by the Black Bea..."

"That's enough," Haephius snapped. "Don't speak its name!"

Maiva looked at her father in alarm. She was shocked to hear such fear in his voice. "Who are you talking...?"

"No!" Haephius said with finality. "I won't discuss it anymore."

"Very well," Maiva calmly replied. "What do you make of the Green Heart?"

"I have no idea," Zenda admitted.

"Of course not," Haephius said. "You're both too young to catch the reference." Both fawns leaned in, hoping to hear more, but Haephius grew silent.

"Father, please..."

"It's too painful," Haephius sadly replied. "Ask a druid if you want to know more."

"A druid?" Maiva asked. "Why would they know?"

"Because it's part of their lore," he stated. "Now, who's ready for more wine?" he asked. Both fawns had been so entranced by the strange conversation they had only taken one drink from their cups. Before they could answer, Haephius refilled their cups then checked on the duck.

Maiva raised her eyebrows as she looked at her friend from across the table. Zenda did the same. Maiva mouthed the words: "We'll talk to the druids later." Zenda nodded in agreement.

WARMASTER

Chapter 12

Danorus sighed and rolled his eyes in exasperation as he listened to the barbarian chieftain named Vashi make what must have been the eighth toast for the night. The messenger for the legionnaires, and the contingent of nine men tasked with protecting Danorus, had been sitting quietly and patiently in the corner of the drinking hall for hours. Vashi's advisor had listened to Danorus when he shared Prydus's proposal with him earlier and had relayed it to the chieftain. He had then told Danorus he'd get to talk to the chieftain directly at some point during the fall celebration that night, but the opportunity never seemed to arrive. Vashi, or one of the various clan leaders, always had another toast to make or a long-winded story or joke to share. The only thing that made the night bearable was the endless supply of ale, mead, and food the servants brought to the legionnaire's table. Unfortunately, the ubiquitous food and drink were starting to make some of the men in Danorus's party lethargic. Danorus contemplated whether he should interrupt the proceedings or simply leave when Vashi finally finished drinking from his horned cup and fixed him with his gaze.

"I've yammered enough tonight, my brothers and sisters," the old, bearded, and potbellied barbarian exclaimed. "I'll turn the floor over to a messenger sent from the 9th Legion now." The crowd began to boo and hiss at the mention of one of Elamara's legions, which highlighted the long-running feud that simmered between the empire and the barbarians. "I know, I know. Our southern neighbors have been a thorn in our side and have coveted our lands for decades, but you may be interested in what the man has to say." With that said, Vashi sat down then waved at Danorus, indicating he should come forward.

The legionnaire stood up and walked into the center of the great hall. Although he was pleased that his moment to speak had finally arrived, Danorus suddenly felt uneasy and self-conscious as hundreds of unfriendly eyes focused on him. He had thought he would speak privately to Vashi, but the chieftain apparently wanted him to address the entire crowd.

"Greetings, good people of the north!" Danorus bellowed. His only response was a deafening silence. He proceeded as if he had just received a warm response. "I'm Danorus, the messenger of the 9th Legion. Tonight, I speak on behalf of my leader, Commander Orilius, who has the full support of the emperor." The frosty silence continued to fill the hall. "By now, most of you have probably heard we're at war with the woodlanders. I know you've also fought them for many years." Several men in the back of the hall shouted curses to show their disdain for the woodlanders. "Yes. I can assure you; we feel the same way about them. For too long now, they've intimidated our hunters, stole our lands, attacked our caravans, and terrorized the good citizens of Faldin. Well, no longer! We just won our first battle in the war. In fact, we defeated them in their own forest! The 9th Legion clashed with them in a village called Algos, which we burned to the ground." Danorus paused to let his words sink in. Scores of men nodded in approval, and some of them even raised their eyebrows to show they were impressed with his words. "Although we're winning, it never hurts to have more allies in our corner. That's why Commander Orilius is offering you a chance to join the fight." Danorus paused to turn his full attention to Vashi. "Chief Vashi, we're prepared to shower you with silver marks should you commit your clans to our cause. What say you?"

Vashi frowned and stared intently at Danorus before speaking. "Although we've clashed with the beastmen many times, we currently have no quarrel with them. You should also know we never wage war during the winter unless we're forced to do so."

"I can assure you we won't engage the enemy until spring," Danorus replied. "And although you may not have any qualms with the beasties right now, it's probably just a question of time before the next feud arises between you and them. Isn't that always the case with border disputes and unruly neighbors?" Vashi's frown diminished somewhat, but he remained silent. "Let me further sweeten the pot," Danorus said with a sly smile. "The champion known as Vlain turned traitor and now fights for the woodlanders. If you agree to fight for us, then you'll get a chance to make him pay for what he did to you years ago." Murmurs of approval filled the hall as the crowd digested Danorus's words. Vashi's frown disappeared at the mere mention of Vlain's name, and Danorus saw the keen desire for vengeance appear in his eyes. "Who among you wouldn't like to see his head mounted on a pike?"

A tall barbarian with long black hair and smoldering blue eyes suddenly leaped to his feet. "Vlain beat my father and brother senseless in Faldin!" he shouted for all to hear. "Then he had us thrown into the stockade! And what was our crime? My father tried to tip a tavern wench!"

Danorus was thrilled to see the swift effect his words had had. "What's your name, good sir?" he asked the glowering barbarian.

"Kovan, this is my father, Brenor, and my brother, Wrothgar. We're the head of the Battleaxe Clan," the brawny man proudly stated as he pointed to each of his relatives. Brenor was a middle-aged man with red hair, a red beard, and gray eyes. He wore a steel helmet that sprouted one broken horn and one whole. Wrothgar was a giant of a man with long blond hair and a shortly cropped beard. An intricately designed war hammer was strapped to his broad back.

"Wouldn't you like the chance to make him pay for what he did to your family?" Danorus asked.

"Aye! I told Vlain I'd kill him if he ever came near our lands, but I'll gladly travel to the Last Wild and kill him there! Truth be told, I'd do it for free, but if you're willing to pay me, then it's all the better," Kovan answered.

"Excellent!" Danorus said as a satisfied smile formed on his broad face. "You should be able to make short work of that traitorous scum, judging by the looks of you. Is there anyone else who longs for revenge and a chance to earn some coin?" The crowd erupted into a chorus of whooping shouts and war cries. Some men began to rhythmically stomp their feet on the hardwood floor. The sound grew in intensity until Danorus's ears began to buzz.

Vashi waved his hands back and forth to quell the crowd. After they finally quieted down, he gave Danorus a look of approval. "There's your answer, legionnaire. Come, let's work out the specifics of payment while my people resume their feast."

Danorus flashed a victorious smile at his fellow legionnaires, then turned and followed Vashi out of the noisy hall. Things were working out better than he had anticipated.

***

Caernos wore his dragon bone crown once more. Even from a hundred feet away, Vlain could feel his regal presence and a sense of authority so strong it had the consistency of gravity. He smiled because he knew the secret of Caernos's power: dragon glamour courtesy of the long-dead worm known as Raisszann. Caernos had also reclaimed Svartur, his nearly indestructible ebonite sword, from the cold currents of the Rendel river. The centaur gently placed the flat side of the blade against Prince Vulkas's forehead. The mighty minotaur knelt before him as thousands of onlookers watched the coronation ceremony unfold.

"With the sword of my forefathers and the crown of your father, I name you king of the minotaurs." King Caernos received King Hez's iron, spiked crown from Oshur's outstretched hands, then placed it atop the bull's head. "Now rise, for you are a prince no longer. From this day on, you shall guide your people with the noble

327

spirit and kind heart of a king!"

An explosion of excited shouts and thunderous applause filled the air. King Vulkas rose to his full height of over eight feet, then leaned forward to press his forehead against King Caernos's. King Vulkas smiled, and the crowd went wild. Some threw orange rose petals, while others threw autumn leaves high into the air. It was official. Findalora had a new monarch.

"How exactly does the Last Wild have more than one king?" Meris had to shout the question into Vlain's ear due to all the noise.

"All of the other kings and queens acknowledge King Caernos as their supreme ruler because he hails from the oldest dynasty and thus speaks for all of Findalora. Or, to put it another way, each of them has a voice, but his is the loudest," Vlain explained.

"Sort of like our emperor?"

"A bit more flexible than that," Vlain said with a wry grin.

Meris gave him a thoughtful look, then shook his head in understanding. "I think I get it. Some kings are kinglier than others. I have one more question, and it's crucial."

"Go on."

"Do we get booze now?"

A hardy laugh erupted from Vlain. "Yes, my friend."

No sooner had Vlain answered than dozens of brawny minotaurs and centaurs emerged from the forest with barrels of ale, mead, and wine tucked under their arms. Meris's eyes grew wide, prompting Vlain to laugh again. The former legionnaires made their way to the royal table at the front of the field. The large, circular table was laden with wooden plates, cups, and eating utensils. Before they sat down, an elderly satyr and a young fawn appeared to set rolls of freshly baked bread and thick blocks of cheese down onto the table.

The men sat down just as Caernos, Oshur, Haephius, and Vulkas arrived. Oshur and Vulkas seated themselves, but Caernos remained standing as was his way. More waiters arrived, bearing pitchers full of ale and trays laden with an assortment of delectable meats and vegetables. Meris poured Vlain and himself a cup of ale just as Oudeteros and Iolee arrived. Vlain jumped up to pull Iolee's chair back from the table. The druidess gave him a strange look.

"Is this some sort of Elamaran custom?" she asked as she sat down.

"Yes, it's called being chivalrous," Vlain said.

"And what does that word mean?"

"It's when men do nice things for women."

"Because they feel obligated, or because they expect something in return?" Iolee asked with an arched eyebrow.

Vlain was deciding how best to respond when Caernos suddenly cleared his throat and raised a glass of wine. Everyone at the table soon followed suit.

"A toast to the new King of Valaren!" Caernos boomed in his baritone voice. "May your wit sharpen with age while your ax grows dull from disuse."

"Neither is likely to happen, but I'll drink to it anyway," Vulkas replied, drawing a laugh from all those at the table.

They made toast after toast and worked their way through plate after plate as the afternoon gradually wore into evening. At first, they spoke about the coronation, but the talk inevitably shifted to the coming war. Caernos asked Haephius if he was pleased with how the workmen had upgraded his forge. The blacksmith said he was but complained about not having enough apprentices to train and how he needed more iron to arm the Findaloran army. Caernos said he'd get him more of each.

The king was about to address Vlain when Vulkas approached him then guided him away from the table to speak privately. The fighter watched them intently. A nearby tiki torch illuminated them, making it plain to see how heated their conversation was. Vulkas gesticulated with his hands as he drove home a point. Caernos listened patiently, then sternly shook his head from side to side. Eventually, Vulkas stormed off then disappeared into the milling crowd of revelers.

Caernos trotted back to the royal table. Vlain couldn't read the monarch's expression due to the plane of shadow on his face, but he saw that his tail violently jerked to and fro, and his glowing white eyes had narrowed to thin slits. Caernos lifted a horn full of mead to his lips, then gulped it down within a few seconds. He wiped his mouth with the back of his hand, and took several deep breaths to calm his nerves. After a few moments, he walked over to Vlain and placed his hand on his shoulder.

"I would like to speak to you in private," his deep voice rumbled.

"Certainly," Vlain replied as he stood up. Man and centaur made their way to the edge of the field where they could talk without being overheard.

"Vulkas is as brave and honorable as they come, but he's also stubborn," Caernos began. "His father, King Hez, was the warmaster of my army, and now that Vulkas is king, he's inherited the title."

"Warmaster. I'm assuming that's the equivalent of general?" Vlain asked.

"Yes. I rule Findalora, but the warmaster guides and directs the actions of our army."

"I see," Vlain said. "So, what's the problem?"

"Given your inside knowledge of the 9th Legion's tactics and strategies, I want you to be the new warmaster. It makes the most sense and should reduce our casualties while expediting our victory. I have faith in your leadership."

"But..." Vlain prompted.

"King Vulkas acknowledged your high value as a fighter and wants you to act as his chief war advisor, but he refuses to relinquish the title of warmaster."

Vlain sighed in frustration. "As king of Findalora, can't you make him step down and appoint me despite his wishes to the contrary?"

"I could," Caernos admitted. "But King Vulkas would perceive it as a slight and would thus lose face. The minotaurs might then decide to fight Man on their own, separate terms. I don't want such an outcome. If we're to win, then we must fight as a unified force, coordinating our efforts in the most efficient and complementary manner."

"So, what's the alternative?" Vlain asked.

"There's an ancient rule when it comes to the position of warmaster," Caernos began. "The current one can be challenged by anyone who wishes to take the title. The challenge consists of ritual, unarmed combat. Normally, I'd suggest this, but..."

"I'm merely a man and half his size," Vlain finished for him.

"Less than half, I'd say," Caernos said. "Tell me honestly, can even your enchantment guarantee victory against such an opponent?"

"I'm not the one you should be worried about," Vlain confidently replied. "I was beating you before we both fell off the cliff, remember?"

"How can I forget?" Caernos asked with a gruff laugh. "But you had your fabled swords with you. This combat will be unarmed."

"It makes no difference," Vlain answered. "The enchantment will hold."

"I hope so. Vulkas is strong even for a minotaur, and he's also a highly skilled warrior. You need to know what you're getting into."

"I appreciate your concern," Vlain said.

Caernos studied him for a moment. "Your confidence carries the same weight as my authority when I wear this dragon crown. I believe you when you say you'll win."

"As you should. I never lie about such matters."

"Then I suppose the fight will be easy for you."

"No, not easy," Vlain replied. "I can still get hurt. In fact, I often do. Fighting Vulkas will probably be a painful affair, but it's worth it. I'm tired of being restrained. I want to lead, and as you said earlier, none of your people know the 9th Legion like I do."

"Then it's decided," Caernos said with a relieved sigh. "I'll inform him of your challenge. The fight will occur within the next few days."

"Very well," Vlain said. "Now, let's get back to the party. There are spirits to be imbibed and games to win."

"I hardly think it fair for you to play against the others," Caernos said.

"I'll keep your secrets if you keep mine," Vlain replied with a sly smile.

***

It was the first day of winter when King Caernos's shield-maidens finally returned from their mission in the northernmost reach of Findalora. Maiva and Zenda were walking across the town square when the green gate suddenly flared to life. The two young fawns paused and waited to see who would exit from the shimmering green portal. They didn't have to wait long. Boudika, the leader of the shield-maidens, was the first to emerge. The proud centaur warrior tossed her long, auburn tresses from side to side as she surveyed the village of Orrn. Her suit of armor was a deep crimson, and a dark blue cape billowed out behind her. Boudika's face was smudged with dirt, and her form-fitting, steelwood armor bore numerous scrapes and gouges. However, she still looked beautiful, even radiant, as she walked down the ramp from the green gate.

Dozens of female centaur warriors emerged from the green gate to follow Boudika down the ramp. They all looked war-torn and weary. Next, came a score of horse-mounted female fawns and satyrs. Then, over a score of female minotaurs, followed by a dozen green-cloaked druidesses. Maiva gasped as she saw the last figure emerge from the swirling green gate. The warrior would have looked just like a brown-skinned human if not for her gigantic proportions. The dark-haired giantess stood over sixteen feet tall and was covered in dark green steelwood armor. She carried a wooden shield with one arm and a spiked steel mace, the size of a man, with the other. A faint quiver shot through the ground each time she took a step. Maiva and Zenda stared at her in awe. They had heard legends about the fierce giantess known as Gaerna the Great but had never laid eyes on her until now.

"Maiva Delinor! Is that you? How you've changed!" Boudika

said as she trotted toward her. Maiva smiled, which revealed the dimples on her cheeks. Fawn and centaur embraced. Zenda pushed a strand of hair out of her face as she watched the happy reunion unfold. "Did you escape from Vorsord's manor, or did he finally come to his senses and release you?" Boudika asked.

"Neither. Another man let me go," Maiva explained.

"Who?! One of the Faldinites?"

"No, his name's Vlain. He used to serve the southern empire known as Elamara." Boudika stared at her incredulously, which prompted Maiva to speak further. "I know it's a lot to take in, but so much has happened since you left. I'll fill you in on all of it later," she said.

"I'll hold you to that, little one," Boudika said. "And who is this?" she asked, nodding at Zenda.

"This is my dear friend, Zenda," Maiva said.

"It's an honor to meet you again, Dame Boudika," Zenda said with a bow.

Boudika studied Zenda's pretty face for a moment. "We've met before?"

"I was a tender youngling back then, so I'm not surprised you don't recognize me. You were leading a parade through Algos when I gave you a laurel wreath to celebrate your victory over Ursis, the giant bear."

The light of recognition dawned in Boudika's brown eyes. "Ah, yes! I remember you now. You were such a sweet little sapling," the captain of the shield-maidens said with a warm smile.

"How did things go with the dragons?" Maiva asked Boudika.

The centaur let out a weary sigh. "The Get of Raisszann put up quite a fight. We slew three of them, but the others flew off over the ocean where we couldn't follow them. I have no doubt they'll return in the spring to wreak more havoc."

"We have plenty of havoc here for you in the meantime," Maiva said.

"So, I've heard," Boudika replied. "I can't believe Algos is gone. I can only imagine the pain you both must feel."

"It hasn't been easy," Zenda said.

"Where are you all off to now?" Maiva asked.

"To the armory, then the stables, then the bathhouse," Boudika replied. "After that, we'll dine with the Grey King. You should both join us at his lodge tonight. It'll be quite a feast."

"We'd love to Dame Boudika..."

"Just call me Boudika," the centaur said. "No need to stand on formality."

"Very well, Boudika. We'd love to."

"Good. I'll see you there." Boudika patted them both on their shoulders, then galloped off to catch up with her entourage.

"She's still breathtaking," Zenda said as she watched her go.

"As strong as steelwood and as beautiful as the sunrise. At least that's what my father used to say," Maiva said.

"Sounds like he had a crush on her," Zenda said with a smile.

"Who hasn't?" Maiva replied, prompting them to both laugh.

***

Prydus and Snill stared intently at the war model, which covered a large table inside the commander's tent. The Faldinite craftsmen had done an exemplary job of mimicking and miniaturizing the terrain just south of the Last Wild, including the plains around Fort Faldin. Snill set several tiny models of catapults and ballistae onto the landscape just north of the fort, then carefully arranged them into a wide semi-circle. Prydus then placed a dozen models of legionnaires north of the war engines. He thoughtfully stroked his chin, then stepped back to analyze the scene.

"How many barbarians did Vashi promise us?" Snill asked in his creaky voice.

"One thousand," Prydus replied with a smile.

"Well, that's good news," Snill said as he placed several tiny wooden models of barbarians on the terrain to the west of the legionnaires.

"Put them farther to the west," Prydus instructed him. Snill did as he said. "Good. I want Vlain and his beastie friends to fight on two fronts. We'll attack from the south while the barbarian rabble assaults their western flank."

"A pity we don't have another force that could attack their eastern flank. Perhaps we should split our legionnaires into two parts, so we can do just that," Snill said.

"No," Prydus decisively answered. "We'll keep the legion together since we'll most likely be outnumbered by the beastmen. Don't worry, though; I'm assembling a small but potent force that'll wreak havoc among the woodlanders and Vlain's traitorous force."

"Do tell," Snill prodded.

"When the time's right," Prydus said as a predatory smile formed on his handsome face. To drive home his point, he yanked a dagger out of his boot then slammed the blade down into the southern edge of the "Last Wild."

Snill's eyes hadn't been able to catch Prydus's movement on account of his incredible speed. He had simply blurred from one position into the next. Snill stared at the quivering dagger for a moment, then finally asked the question that had been on his mind for some time now.

"What happened to you, commander?" he asked.

Prydus gave him a sly smile. "What exactly do you mean, captain?" he coyly replied.

"I asked you once before, and you were about to answer, but we got interrupted. Anyway, don't think I haven't noticed you're faster than before, and you have more energy than any man should. What's more, your eyes shine with a strange light, and your skin has a golden glow to it. What's your secret? I promise not to tell a soul."

Prydus's smile broadened as his eyes narrowed to thin slits. "I told Brinhilda I was blessed with extra life by Jaina, after praying to Her every night for three years. That's my official explanation for the change you see in me."

"And the real reason?" Snill asked. "I've known you for most of my life, and you've never struck me as a religious or pious man."

Prydus's smile suddenly vanished, only to be replaced by a crafty, alert expression. " I'll share a kernel of truth with you, but you must swear not to reveal it to anyone."

"I swear on my life, commander."

Prydus yanked the dagger out of the model then sat down on his throne-like chair. "I'll say this much, there's an animal of a rare and precious sort, that roams the Last Wild. Legend has it; if a man consumes part of its body, his life will be extended. But that's not all. He'll become greater in all ways than he was before."

It was Snill's turn to smile. "Let me guess, you've consumed this animal?"

"I have."

"But how? I've seen no hunters returning from the Wild with exotic animals. How did you come by this creature?"

"Come now, Snill," Prydus said in a chiding voice. He tossed his dagger into the air and caught it several times in a row. "We both know hunters have been trapping and selling animals from the Last Wild for decades now. Elamara's black market is rife with cures, potions, and all manner of elixirs made from the bodies of rare and magical beasts. It's difficult, but not impossible, to acquire such elixirs in the back alleys of our fair capital."

"Ah, I see now," Snill said. "You got a hold of something back home. Something potent enough to enhance you. But why start taking it now?" he asked.

"Isn't it obvious? If I'm to defeat Vlain, then I must become more than a man."

"He's a gifted warrior, to be sure, perhaps the best I've ever seen, but more than a man?"

Prydus rolled his eyes. "Did you not see his eyes glow when he fought Caladin? That was most unnatural. And did you not sense his magic when he won the game of Six?"

"No on both counts," Snill admitted. "I wasn't looking at his eyes when he defeated Caladin, nor did I feel any magic during the game. Are you a sevlin, commander?"

"Yes, but that must also remain between us."

"Undoubtedly," Snill said. "Can you cast spells like a mage?"

"No, I can only sense magic, not control it, and I'm telling you,

Vlain reeks of it! There's a powerful enchantment on him, and I suspect it gives him an unfair advantage over the rest of us. I had to level the playing field somehow, or I'd stand no chance of defeating him when we finally meet on the battlefield."

"I see," Snill said, somewhat taken aback by the information. "I hope whatever you're taking isn't dangerous. I'd hate to lose you when the war starts. The morale of the entire legion would fall."

"Fear not for my safety, Snill," Prydus said in a consoling tone. "As long as I don't take too much, I'll be fine."

"Glad to hear it, sir."

"Now, since I shared my secret with you, I want you to do two things for me."

"You have only to ask."

"Repeat my official explanation whenever the men wonder aloud at my transformation. Secondly, help me spread the rumor that Vlain acquired his hidden power by consorting with Thania and other evil beings. Tell all who will listen that he traded his soul for invincibility and that he exists solely to do Thania's will."

"Consider it done, commander."

"Good. You're free to go."

Captain Snill snapped his heels together, saluted Prydus, and exited the regal tent.

"I'm coming for you, Vlain," Prydus said as he spun the dagger about in his hand.

***

"Are you sure you really want to do this?" Oudeteros asked.

"You asked me the same thing right before I fought Caladin,"

339

Vlain responded with an amused expression. "And we both know how that turned out."

"True, but that monster over there makes Caladin look like a little boy," Oudeteros said as he stared at King Vulkas, who stood on the far end of the indoor stable yard as he talked to Charolais.

"The bigger they are…" Vlain began.

"The harder they hit," Meris finished.

"Thanks for the support," Vlain replied with a sour look as he went through his stretching routine. "Truth be told, my only regret is that King Caernos won't let us bet on the fight."

"Why is that?" Meris asked.

"He felt it would make a mockery of the tradition," Oudeteros answered.

"King Caernos is old-fashioned," Vlain elaborated. "He thinks wagering on a time-honored tradition would pervert it. I see his point."

"Well, that's a shame. I could do with more coin in my pocket," Meris quipped.

"And what exactly would you spend it on?" Vlain asked. "We're living in the Last Wild, for Jaina's sake."

"A man with a wife and children can never have enough coin," Meris said in a sagely voice.

"Your words ring true," Vlain replied.

"Hear me!" King Caernos's deep baritone voice suddenly boomed from above. The king stood on the second floor of the building. He rested his veiny hands on the balcony as he looked out over the indoor stable yard below. "We are gathered here to preside over a duel in which the title of warmaster hangs in the balance. King Vulkas of Valaren will defend the title from the man known as Vlain Verous. Fighters are you ready?" the king asked.

"Aye, my king!" King Vulkas bellowed.

"Aye, King Caernos," Vlain casually replied.

"Let the fight begin!" Caernos said as he slammed his fist down onto the wooden balcony.

Iolee, the druidess, stood to the king's right. A concerned expression formed on her beautiful face as she gazed down at Vlain, who looked so small and fragile compared to the massive minotaur. Maiva Starmark stood to Caernos's left. She shook her head in disbelief as she stared at the seemingly insane human as he raced toward Vulkas. Given his fearsome reputation, Maiva didn't know whether she should worry about him or Vulkas. Haephius stood next to her, Zenda stood beside him, and Oshur stood to her right. A dozen other Findalorans stood around them, and Gaerna crouched down behind them all. The ten-foot-tall ceiling was far too short to allow the giantess to stand upright, and the floorboards creaked and groaned in protest beneath her ponderous weight.

"Good luck," Oudeteros said to Vlain as he scrambled to get out of the stable yard.

"Go easy on him, buddy," Meris said as he jumped over the gate to stand in the hallway.

"No promises," Vlain said as he started sprinting toward the hulking minotaur.

"I'll make this as quick and painless as possible," Vulkas said as they neared each other.

"That's funny. I was gonna say the same thing," Vlain replied.

Vulkas blasted steam out of his nostrils, then lowered his sharp horns. Vlain would have been impaled had he not leaped up to slam his knee into the minotaur's nose. Their combined momentum multiplied the force of the already considerable blow. A painful shock coursed through Vulkas as Vlain's kneecap broke his nose. Vulkas's momentum pushed Vlain forward, but the crafty fighter grabbed the minotaur's horns and jumped over him to land nimbly on the straw-covered ground.

Vulkas skidded to a stop before he collided with the wooden gate that separated the stable yard from the hallway. Oudeteros and Meris fell back in fear, thinking the minotaur would blast through the gate to collide with them, but by then, Vulkas had already stopped. The monstrous minotaur whipped around, only to receive a kick from Vlain in the solar plexus. Vulkas gasped as the air was forced out of his lungs, but to his credit, he swung at Vlain's face. The fighter ducked beneath his fist, grabbed Vulkas's wrist, twisted to the side, and used his momentum to flip the minotaur's six-hundred-pound body over his shoulder. Vulkas's eyes widened in alarm as he sailed through the air to land heavily on the ground.

"By the White Stag!" Maiva exclaimed as she watched Vulkas land in a heap. She wouldn't have believed it if she hadn't just seen it. "How is that possible?" she asked Caernos, who watched the fight with his glowing white eyes. The king shook his head from side to side to indicate he was at a loss. However, a knowing smile formed on his face, but Maiva couldn't see it due to the perpetual shadow on his face.

"You'll pay for that, outlander!" Vulkas roared as he charged Vlain.

Vlain, who had been closing in on Vulkas so he could wrap his arms around his thick neck, was caught off guard as one of the minotaur's horns sliced into his side. Vlain cursed in pain, and his eyes blazed to life. They glowed with a light like that of the setting sun. Vlain snarled then dropped down to kick at Vulkas's kneecap from the side. The minotaur's kneecap was violently shoved to the outside of his leg, causing him to lose his balance. He crashed to his knees, thereby causing further injury to the wound.

"Stay down," Vlain said in a low voice. "There's no way you can win, and I don't want to hurt you any more than I have to."

Vulkas looked at him in disbelief. He blasted steam out of his nose, then roared as he stood up and limped toward Vlain. The fighter held his bleeding side with one arm as the minotaur hobbled toward him. Vulkas attempted to backhand Vlain, but the wily fighter ducked, then jumped into the air and slammed his elbow down into Vulkas's throat. The minotaur coughed and gagged as he fell back. Vulkas punched Vlain again, but the fighter rolled with it, grabbed the minotaur's wrist, and sharply jerked it to the side. A loud crack filled the air then Vlain brutally flung Vulkas to the ground. He pulled the minotaur's arm behind his back then drove his knee down into the arch of his back.

"Yield, King of Valaren, or I'll break your arm as well as your wrist," Vlain said in an ominous tone. His volume was so low only Vulkas could hear him.

"I'll rip you to pieces, you hairless ape..." Vulkas said while gasping in pain. The minotaur tensed his good arm and legs, indicating he was about to leap up off the ground.

Vlain gritted his teeth as he wrenched Vulkas's arm back at an unnatural angle, thereby breaking it at the elbow. The minotaur bellowed in agony, causing Vlain to release his arm. The minotaur writhed in pain on the ground. Vlain kept his knee in the small of his back as he leaned down to whisper in his ear.

"Are we done, or should I proceed?" he asked.

The king tried to rise again, but Vlain shoved his knee deeper into his back while simultaneously grabbing his wounded wrist and elbow. The minotaur gasped then slapped the ground several times with his good arm, indicating he wished to surrender. Vlain withdrew his knee from his back and raised his hands into the air while ignoring the pain from the bloody wound in his side.

"King Vulkas has surrendered!" he shouted.

King Caernos nodded in understanding. Although he had expected this outcome, he had still been surprised at how abruptly the fight had ended. "As you can all see, Vlain is the victor and thus the first man to become warmaster," he boomed. "Well done, outlander."

Vlain knelt beside Vulkas. "Give me your good hand. I'll help you get to the druids and shamans so they can heal you," he told him.

Vulkas gave him a scathing look. "You may have defeated me, but I'll never ask for your help," he bitterly replied. "Go enjoy your praise. My people will tend to me." Even as he spoke, Charolais appeared beside him. She draped Vulkas's good arm over her neck, then helped him stand up.

Vlain was trying to think of a reply when Iolee walked up to him. She draped his arm over her shoulder then gave him a concerned look. Her sparkling hazel eyes rendered him speechless. "Let me support some of your weight," she said gently. "Your ribs look broken, and that gash in your side is losing a lot of blood."

Vlain nodded his consent. Charolais and Iolee guided their charges out of the stable yard and into the hall. The druidess took Vlain into a small, empty stable across the hall while Charolais took her king into the stable next door.

"Enchantment or not, you're going to get yourself killed one day!" Iolee said as she placed both hands on his broken ribs.

"Not if Jaina has anything to say about it," Vlain replied while coughing up blood.

Iolee rolled her eyes in exasperation, then focused on initiating a healing spell. A soothing, green light soon radiated out from her hands. It didn't take long before Oudeteros and Meris rushed into the stable to kneel beside their wounded leader.

"Are you gonna be alright, boss?" Meris asked as he gazed down at him.

"I'll muddle through as I always do," he replied with a bloody smile.

"Good," Oudeteros said. "Because we'll have plenty of new coins to share with you later," he whispered into his ear.

"What are you talking about?" Vlain asked.

"We bet on you in advance and surprise, you came through," Meris said with a wink and a nod.

"But the king said no betting. You'll get us all…"

"Relax, boss," Meris cut in. "The bets were made by our renouncers who remained back at the lodges. We kept it all hush-hush."

"You mean, they bet against me?!" Vlain exclaimed. "My own men?"

"I'm afraid most of them did. I mean, it was you versus a blaeting minotaur! But it worked out in our favor," Oudeteros said. Vlain grimaced in pain as he tried to laugh.

"That's enough!" Iolee shouted. "I'm trying to concentrate! Get out of here, both of you!" The druidess slapped at Oudeteros and Meris as they scrambled to get away from her.

"You get used to their antics after a while," Vlain said apologetically. Iolee placed a hand over his mouth and put the other one on his ribs. She smiled despite herself as she met his mirthful gaze.

A DARING RAID
Chapter 13

All eyes were on Vlain as he completed a complicated attack routine. He had just deflected a minotaur's incoming scimitar, then slipped past his guard to rest the edge of his blade against the pulsing artery in his neck. Vlain's faintest movement would quickly end his opponent's life if he so chose it. The bull blasted steam out of his nostrils, signifying his frustration and shame at being bested by a human. More than anything else, Vlain was teaching the Findaloran army lessons in humility, lessons they were painfully taking to heart.

"Does everyone understand what I just did there?" Vlain asked the gathering of minotaurs, centaurs, fawns, and satyrs. "Always remember, you can redefine the battle at any time. You're never stuck with what you're given," Vlain finished.

Percheron, a veteran warrior and one of Vlain's captains, snorted derisively, then turned and trotted away from the demonstration. Vlain scowled as he watched the centaur's retreating form. Percheron had expressed his dislike of Vlain's tactics, strategies, and combat drills all week long, and some of the troops were starting to notice. The fighter had had enough of his belligerent attitude. He couldn't risk losing face in front of the Findalorans, especially with war looming.

Vlain jumped onto his unremarkable horse then urged it to a full gallop. He envisioned the upcoming fight as he approached Percheron, but Ardennais suddenly appeared in front of him. Vlain dug his heels into his steed's sides to stop it before he collided with the brown-skinned centaur. Anger welled up in Vlain's chest as he stared him down.

"You better have a good reason for this!" Vlain shouted.

A calm smile dominated Ardennais' face as he looked at the fighter. "It just so happens, I do," he replied. "Let's talk for a moment. The troops will be fine. I asked Oudeteros to cover for you so the training will proceed according to plan."

Vlain reluctantly followed Ardennais as he led him out to a snow-clad field. Gusts of wind grabbed loose snowflakes that rested on the deep drifts and scattered them into a fine, white flurry. Vlain shielded his eyes as he came up alongside Ardennais.

"Explain yourself, lieutenant," Vlain demanded.

"You meant to fight Percheron just now?" Ardennais asked.

"If it came to that."

"You don't have to," Ardennais explained. "I can tell you why he's angry."

"Very well. Speak."

The centaur grabbed his hood and pulled the fabric down to block the cold drafts of air from flowing down his neck. Vlain stoically ignored the icy tendrils of the wind as they stung his scarred, weathered face.

"Percheron lost a son during the battle of Algos," Ardennais said.

Just like that, Vlain's anger was extinguished by the chilling touch of loss. "Did I kill him?" he asked, fearing the response.

"No, warmaster. He was captured by the 9th Legion. We can only wonder at his fate."

"What's his son's name?"

"Ferox," came the reply.

"Ferox is most likely being kept in the dungeons beneath Fort Faldin," Vlain explained. "I had no blaeting idea, but it all makes sense now. Percheron can't focus on the training because he's too worried about his son, and he holds me responsible for his capture."

"In part, at least," Ardennais said.

"Why didn't he come to me with this?" Vlain asked.

"For the same reason, I didn't tell you my brother, Curajos, was also taken captive. We're still learning to trust and forgive you. It takes time..."

"Time we don't have," Vlain said as a gust of wind sprayed, tinkling, jagged shards of ice at his face. "For what it's worth, I'm sorry about your brother."

"Thank you. I hope this revelation changes how you see Percheron and myself."

"It does indeed," Vlain said as he turned his steed around and rode away.

***

"How may I help you, Warmaster Vlain?" Oshur asked as the fighter closed the door behind him, then wiped his snowy boots off on a bristled mat.

"I need to speak to the king," he sternly replied.

"He's wrapping up a meeting but will be done shorty. Please, have a seat..."

"I'll remain standing, thank you," Vlain said, trying his best to keep the edge out of his voice. None of this was Oshur's fault after all.

The fighter began pacing back and forth in front of the roaring fire in the hearth as the bespectacled satyr watched him. Vlain also watched the scribe when he thought he wasn't looking. The diminutive goatman was using a sharpened feathered quill to write a letter to someone in an elegant, cursive script. Somehow, the repetitive, scraping sound of the quill moving against the parchment calmed Vlain's nerves. Perhaps it was because he could predict the sounds and movements or because it was a civilized action in an otherwise wild and rugged place.

Suddenly, the door to Caernos's office opened. Maiva Starmark walked out into the hallway. She bowed before Vlain then walked out of the lodge. A curious expression formed on Vlain's face as he bowed back. He watched her disappear into the snowstorm outside. Vlain wondered what their meeting had consisted of, but he knew better than to ask.

"Warmaster!" Caernos boomed. "This is an unexpected surprise. Do come in," the centaur said as he held the door open for him. "What brings you here?" he asked as he shut the door.

"I just need a moment of your time," Vlain replied in a clipped tone.

"You can have more than that," Caernos replied as he waved at the three padded, plush chairs in front of his tall desk. Vlain sat down in the one in the center.

"I'll cut straight to the heart of the matter," Vlain began. "Percheron is mourning the loss of his son, Ferox, and he holds me partly responsible for his capture. Ardennais told me his brother was also taken by the legionnaires, but he seems to be handling it better."

"I was aware of these unfortunate events," Caernos replied with a heavy sigh. "But have no fear. I'll talk to Percheron..."

"Please don't," Vlain interjected. "He has good cause to be angry with me. I still represent the 9th Legion in Percheron's mind.

I deserve his anger due to my past actions.”

“All Findalorans know you and your men have renounced the ways of the empire to which you belonged. You even took our blood oath. The events that transpired during the battle of Algos, no matter how disturbing, must be forgotten in light...”

“Maybe they shouldn’t be forgotten,” Vlain cut in. “Maybe they should retain our attention.”

“What good would come of that?” Caernos asked.

“If we address the giant in the room, perhaps we can subdue him.”

“So you mean to speak with Percheron about his lost son? Clear the air...”

“I intend to do more than that, with your permission, of course.”

“Go on,” Caernos prodded.

“How many Findalorans do you think were captured at Algos?” Vlain asked.

“At least twenty.”

“And we still hold ten legionnaires captive from the same battle. Legionnaires who refused to renounce the 9th Legion and the Elamaran Empire.”

“What are you proposing?” Caernos rumbled.

“We conduct a prisoner exchange.”

“I would have already done so had your comments about Commander Orilius’s mindset not discouraged me.”

“Prydus would definitely shoot an exchange down. He’d much

rather torture your people for information than exchange them for his own men. Which is why we shouldn't give him a choice in the matter," Vlain said with a sly smile.

"A forced exchange?" Caernos asked.

"We drop the legionnaire prisoners off at Fort Faldin, head down to the dungeons beneath the tower, and free the Findaloran captives. Once Ferox and Curajos are back among us, Percheron and Ardennais will be able to fully focus on war preparations and training. And it wouldn't hurt to have twenty more warriors fighting for us either."

Caernos thoughtfully rubbed his chin as he considered Vlain's proposal. "A daring raid, to be sure," the king rumbled. "But our casualty rate would be too high."

"Not if we strike in the dead of night during a blizzard," Vlain responded. "Don't forget, I know the timing and strength of the guards that patrol the fort, and a snowstorm would mask our approach until we're right on top of them."

"But Prydus would send reinforcements from the camp you lived in."

"I doubt they'll arrive before we reenter the Wild. Prydus won't risk sending more men into the forest after the ambush that cost Caladin and his force so many lives."

"We could lose many people in the attempt. It's too risky..."

"I'll minimize the risk as much as possible," Vlain countered. "Let me have twenty of your best warriors, and I'll bring ten of my renouncers. I'll lead them to the fort and guide them with my knowledge of the enemy's..."

"I only need to know one thing, Vlain," Caernos rumbled.

"Yes, my king."

"Can you do it with little to no loss of life?"

"I can have us in and out of there before Prydus knows what hit him," Vlain answered.

Caernos stared at him for a long moment before he shook his head in agreement. "Very well, warmaster. You shall have your raid. Gather your warriors before I come to my senses," he said with a gruff laugh.

"Thank you, your excellency," Vlain said as he bowed, then turned and strode out of the room.

***

"I can't believe we're headed to Fort Faldin of all places," Oudeteros said, shaking his head in disbelief. The southerner rode his steed to Vlain's left.

"And during a snowstorm, no less," Meris said, who rode to Vlain's right.

"It's the last thing Prydus would expect, and the blizzard will prevent the legionnaires from seeing us until it's too late," Vlain said.

"True enough, but if any of us are captured, Prydus will torture us then hang us in Faldin's town square," Oudeteros replied.

"Then don't get captured," Vlain said with a grin before urging his steed into a gallop.

The other renouncers, Belor, Paetro, Hildin, Denin, Rivers, and two other men, followed along behind Vlain and his two captains. They were all clad in dark brown, steelwood armor, the chest-plates of which bore the image of the White Stag. A Findaloran artist had painted the head and antlers of the benevolent animal god in white paint on their armor. The men wore insulated leather suits beneath their armor to protect themselves from frostbite and, as a last-ditch, protection from bladed weapons. Each of them also wore a helmet carved from a solid piece of steelwood. Since he was warmaster, Vlain was the only one who had a green cape clasped to his backplate. It twisted and curled gracefully in the wind as he rode his steed through the swirling snowflakes.

Vlain reined his horse in as soon as he saw a long, rectangular-shaped wagon. Visibility was so poor on account of the cloud-covered sky, the dark hour, and the blizzard that his horse nearly ran into the back of the wagon. Vlain waved and nodded at the quartet of shamans climbing into the back of the fully enclosed, armored wagon. A thick bed of straw and heavy, woolen blankets had been laid down on the floor. They'd provide padding and bedding to the wounded prisoners they'd rescue from the dungeons of Fort Faldin. Vlain saw that each of the shamans carried packs filled with herbal medicine, bandages, and water. He was glad they were coming along. Although druids were talented healers, shamans specialized in repairing the body and could heal a wound or reverse an illness faster and more thoroughly than most druids could. Iolee was an exception since she had trained as a shaman before joining the Green Order.

The ten legionnaires who had refused to renounce the 9th Legion had been bound, gagged, blindfolded, and placed at the front of the wagon. Vlain had personally seen to it that they were kept in good health, despite their refusal to side with the woodlander army. He doubted Prydus was extending the same courtesy to the Findaloran captives who had languished in Fort Faldin's dungeons for the past few months. Still, his conscience wouldn't have had it any other way. Vlain figured the legionnaires should be respected even though they were prisoners. He had told the shamans to guide the men out of the wagon and into the courtyard when they arrived at Fort Faldin.

Vlain guided his nondescript horse to the front of the wagon so he could see Iolee. She sat beside Bollis, the driver of the team of eight horses that would haul the battle wagon to Fort Faldin and back. A satyr archer sat next to Iolee on the wide driver's seat.

"Evening, boss!" Bollis shouted. "Fine weather we're having, eh?" the round, jolly man asked as Vlain stopped his steed beside the wagon.

"Couldn't ask for better, given what we're about to do," Vlain agreed. Iolee got down from the wagon seat and walked over to Vlain. "Are you sure you want to come?" Vlain asked as she held her hands out a few inches away from his chest. "I could assign other druids to this detail."

Iolee looked hurt. "Why would you want someone other than me?"

"You're the one I want," Vlain said. "I'm just protective of you."

"The warmaster of Findalora's army shouldn't have favorites," Iolee said teasingly.

"I shouldn't, but I do," Vlain replied. He watched as a bright red flash briefly highlighted a curved, hexagonal web of shimmering energy that now covered his body. The fighter grabbed Iolee's slender hand. Although their mutual wards prevented their fingers from touching, Vlain knew she would still get the meaning behind the gesture. "Be careful tonight," he said softly.

"I'll muddle through like I always do," she replied with a grin. Vlain smiled because she was using the exact words he had spoken when they had first met in Algos. Iolee walked back to the wagon and resumed her seat behind the restless team of horses.

Vlain assumed Iolee had already put protective wards on Bollis and the satyr archer. Since it was too draining and dangerous for a druid to summon more than a few wards at a time, Vlain wondered where the other druids were. Vlain's renouncers would require protection as well. Five horse-mounted druids suddenly rode up to the wagon as if in answer to his thought. The group consisted of Dinn, Xerlith, Ibin, Batutta, and Rowan. Vlain watched as eight hulking wood golems lumbered up behind the druids and their steeds. The golems remained in place as the druids placed wards on all of Vlain's men.

No sooner had the last ward been summoned than a large group of woodlanders, led by King Vulkas, arrived. It was strange to see the proud monarch without the sharp-edged iron crown on his head. It was equally strange to see him and the minotaurs behind him, mounted on horses since the beastmen preferred to walk. The requirement for speed tonight, however, had forced everyone to ride. King Caernos had disapproved of Vulkas participating in the raid, but he hadn't forbidden him from doing so. Vulkas knew it was risky for a king to come along, but he hoped to encounter Caladin so he could exact revenge on him for killing his father, King Hez. Vlain doubted the big man would be at Fort Faldin since he usually stuck to the campground south of the fort. He had told Vulkas as much, but the minotaur hadn't been dissuaded. Caernos insisted that Vulkas not reveal his kingly status by wearing his crown. The king had also loaned him his strength-amplifying armband to improve his odds of survival. Runes of power glowed with a bewitching blue light on the steel band. Haephius had improved on the original spell after Vlain had broken it so that it now increased the wearer's strength four-fold instead of three. Vlain wondered what Vulkas could do with all that power since he was already considered strong even by minotaur standards.

Vlain wasn't surprised to see Charolais, the shieldmaiden, beside King Vulkas since they were close, but he was pleasantly surprised to see Boudika, the captain of the shield-maidens, standing next to Charolais. The veteran of a thousand battles looked beautiful and deadly in her red, form-fitting steelwood armor. Vlain figured she had pulled her hair back into a ponytail to make it easier to don her helmet. The fighter nodded in greeting as he looked at Boudika. The battle-hardened centaur nodded back at him.

Gaerna, the giantess, had also wanted to come along, but Vlain had told her no. Although he valued the considerable power she would have brought to the fray, she was too large to enter the narrow corridors that led to the dungeons beneath Faldin tower. She would have to remain in the courtyard outside, where her huge size would make her an easy target for archers and spearmen. Vlain didn't want to risk losing such a great warrior. It was better to reserve the giantess for the upcoming war.

"Do you require wards, my king?" Iolee asked Vulkas.

"My druids attended to us before we set out," he replied in his gravelly voice.

"Very well," she replied. "We are ready, warmaster."

All eyes fell on Vlain. "Thank you for volunteering to be part of this raid," Vlain began. "I won't bring up the plan since we've gone over it a hundred times in the last few days. Each of you know your role and what's expected of you if we're to bring our woodlanders back tonight. So, there's only one thing left to say: cut down anyone who gets in your way!"

Percheron led the Findaloran war cry. "Uukhai!" he shouted at the top of his lungs. The rest of the Findalorans joined in. "Uukhai!" went the ancient battle cry. Vlain smiled at the aggression and determination he saw in their eyes.

"And what do you have to add to that?" he asked his renouncers.

"Oorah!" Vlain's former legionnaires shouted as one.

"Good!" Vlain said with a predatory smile. "Now that you've gotten that out of your system, we'll need to be silent until the fighting begins. We wouldn't want to let the enemy know we're coming. Move out!" he bellowed.

As the horses plowed through the rising drifts of snow, Vlain noticed how animated and alive Percheron and Ardennais looked. He had never seen such fire in their eyes. Apparently, his instincts had been right. They needed this raid to properly lead the legions of Findalorans under their command. Even though he was the warmaster, Vlain couldn't be everywhere at once. He needed confident and focused leaders to weld the army of woodlanders into a fearsome, fighting force.

Vlain shifted his gaze from the centaur captains to a young fawn named Yezrial, who rode beside him. He knew little about "Yez," as he liked to be called, other than three things: he was Haephius's nephew, he used to be a shepherd of a flock of sheep, and he had an incredible throwing arm. Haephius had told Vlain that Yez could hit a fly with a stone from a hundred yards away. Vlain had asked Yez to demonstrate his talent. The young fawn had picked up a stone then used it to knock a brass pitcher off a fence post from over a hundred yards away. Vlain had laughed and clapped him on the back.

King Caernos had forbidden Haephius from participating in the raid since his skills as a magic-using blacksmith were too valuable to risk in the event of his death. So, Haephius had loaned his enchanted lightning gloves to Yez. Vlain and the others would soon get a chance to see what the young, curly-haired fawn could accomplish with those devastating weapons, weapons that had almost laid Vlain low.

The hours ticked by even as the leagues did. The blizzard intensified as they rode south, preventing Vlain from seeing more than a few yards ahead. Thankfully, Iolee, and the other druids, had cast spells on their eyes, which enabled them to see better than cats in the dark and farther than eagles. Even with these magical enhancements, however, they had to pause the wagon every so often to get their bearings. Vlain, who had a great sense of direction, knew he would have gotten hopelessly lost if not for the druids.

After another hour had passed, Iolee asked Bollis to halt the horses. She then softly called to Vlain. The fighter rode over to the wagon. "The gate is only a few paces away," she informed him.

The fighter squinted as he gazed straight ahead, but he couldn't see the guardhouse he knew was behind the gate. He shook his head in amazement at her unnaturally keen vision. "Well then, let's get to work," he replied.

Vlain raised his crossbow up to waist level. Yez and Iolee jumped down from the wagon seat as Belor got down from his horse with his crossbow in hand. The four of them soon encountered the barred steel gate. Iolee placed both hands on the lock in the gate's center. She closed her eyes and quietly mouthed the words of a spell. A few seconds later, the tumblers in the lock moved about until it snapped open. Iolee shoved both halves of the gate open, then reached into the folds of her thick, green cloak to pull out a short, thin blowgun from one of her pockets. She raised it to her mouth as Belor and Yezrial surged forward.

"Hey! Who goes there?!" came a startled voice from out of the gloom.

Vlain watched as Yezrial hurled lightning bolts at two men, who then fell face-first into the snow. Belor fired steel bolts into two other legionnaires who were about to pull their swords from their sheaths. The last sentry turned and ran back into the small guard shack. He reached for a steel horn that rested on a desk as Iolee blew a dart at him. The tiny projectile lodged itself in the man's neck. He yanked it out of his skin as he glared at Iolee's cloaked and hooded form.

"What did you..?" he asked before he collapsed onto the

shack's floor.

Vlain led the war party into the courtyard. Thankfully, the snow, which was nearly a foot deep now, muffled the sound of the wagon wheels. The eight wood golems passed Vlain as they took the lead and fanned out in front of the procession. King Vulkas, Boudika, Charolais, and a mixture of other Findalorans and renouncers soon caught up to Vlain. Try as he might, he couldn't see the faintest traces of Faldin tower or the fort beneath it. He had been navigating by memory alone when Iolee ran up beside his horse.

"Use those magic eyes of yours to guide us to the first door you see," Vlain told her. The druidess nodded obediently, then moved ahead. Vlain and the others followed her. Within less than a minute, Iolee had located one of the iron doors that lead down into the bowels of Fort Faldin. They all dismounted as Iolee approached the door. She pressed both of her gloved hands against it, then summoned a spell to unlock it. Click. The door swung open. Vlain waited for the war wagon to pull up beside them, then wrapped his knuckles against its stout door. It soon opened to reveal the goatish face of a satyr shaman.

"Have the golems take our captives to the side of the drawbridge over there," Vlain pointed to the right. "That way, they'll be safe when the fighting starts, and the legionnaires should discover them after they drop the door down."

"Aye, warmaster," the shaman replied.

Vlain turned his attention back to the war party and nodded toward the door Iolee had just opened. "King Vulkas, take some druids and ten of your warriors to the left while my renouncers and I go right. Get as many prisoners as you can back to the wagon. We won't have long before the alarm is sounded." Without waiting for a reply, Vlain ran down the stairwell into the inky darkness.

The faint firelight of a torch soon became discernible in the distance. Vlain pulled both of his orichalcum swords from their sheaths as he approached a shadowy corridor that ran from left to right. He paused to let Iolee and his renouncers catch up, then took the passage to the right. Fortunately, there were barred, rectangular openings in the upper part of the doors. However, the first cell was so dark that Vlain motioned for Iolee to peer inside with her cat-like eyes. She nodded from side to side, indicating the occupant wasn't a Findaloran. They went on to the next cell and the one after that before the druidess finally nodded up and down.

"There's a minotaur inside," she said.

"Open her up," Vlain replied. Iolee put her hand on the lock. The door soon popped open. The torchlight from the hallway illuminated the dank, squalid cell. The massive bull inside sat up as Vlain and Iolee walked in.

"We're here to free you," Vlain informed him in perfect Findaloran, thanks to the understanding he wore. "Are you hurt? Can you move?"

"They broke me arm a while back," the bull rumbled in the gloom. "But I can manage."

Vlain noticed he cradled one arm with his other. "Paetro!" he called out as he turned his head toward the corridor.

"Yes, sir?" the young man called back.

"I'm sending a minotaur out. Guide him back to the wagon, then return to me."

"Aye, aye," came the response. Vlain and Iolee helped the minotaur stand up from the scattered hay that constituted his bedding. The fighter scowled when he saw how thin the prisoner was. He also noticed how cold the cell was. Prydus was clearly doing everything he could to break his captives. They helped the minotaur get out to the hall. The bull leaned heavily on Paetro as they made their way down the hall toward the wagon that waited in the courtyard.

Vlain was pleased to see Meris and Dinn had just freed a captive from the cell to the right of the one he and Rowan had emerged from. They went to the next cell and released an emaciated centaur. The poor creature was so weak from starvation and thirst that it took both Denin and Rivers to support him as he hobbled down the corridor. Once again, Meris and Dinn had already moved onto the next cell down the hall. They led a pale fawn out of the darkness then Vlain and Iolee went to the next cell. The cycle repeated itself until they had released nine Findaloran captives.

While they were checking the last few cells in the corridor, a legionnaire sentry suddenly rounded the corner to come face-to-face with Vlain. The fighter slit his throat open before he could make a move or call for help. Regret and sadness swept through Vlain as he caught the man and guided him to the ground. Even though he hadn't known this particular legionnaire, it was the first time he had killed one. Vlain shoved his feelings away since he needed to focus on the current mission. Lives depended on his leadership.

Unfortunately, another sentry had seen Vlain kill his partner. "We're under attack! We're under attack!" he repeatedly shouted as he turned and ran back the way he had come. Vlain contemplated shooting him with his crossbow, but it wouldn't have made any difference. The alarm had been sounded. It was only a question of time before the corridor was swarming with legionnaires.

"Back to the courtyard!" Vlain shouted. Iolee took off in front of him, which was good because they hadn't gone far when a group of legionnaires rounded the corner behind them and started firing their crossbows. Vlain whirled around to face them while sheathing one of his swords and raising his crossbow to chest level. He ran backwards as several bolts thudded into the magical ward around him. Vlain returned fire, bringing two of the six men down. The remaining four ducked back behind the corner. By now, Iolee had outpaced Vlain since he was running backwards.

"Vlain, you traitor! We'll see you hang for this!" one of the men bellowed.

"I doubt that, cur!" Vlain shouted back. "But come and get me if you're feeling man enough!"

He continued running backwards down the hall. Although the men didn't appear again, they occasionally stuck their crossbows out from behind the corner to blindly fire bolts at him. None of them hit his ward, however. As Vlain closed in on the stairwell that led out of the dungeons, he saw Iolee race up the stairs while King Vulkas and some of his minotaurs waited in the corridor for him.

"Making friends, I see," Vulkas boomed bemusedly.

"Everywhere I go," Vlain replied with a grin. "How many captives did you free?" he asked as they ran up the stairs.

"Eight. Three died in their cells." "I'll avenge them when I meet Commander Orilius on the battlefield." Vlain could hear the hate in his voice.

"What about Caladin?" Vlain asked.

"Oh, I'll kill him first," Vulkas answered. Vlain chuckled darkly. He was about to ask Vulkas to leave some enemies for him to fight when they emerged from the fort and into a storm of steel bolts and steel-headed arrows. The deadly projectiles rained down from a nearby parapet.

"That would be the welcoming committee," Vlain shouted over the din.

"You Elamarans have strange customs," Vulkas rumbled.

Vlain watched as Iolee and Meris helped the last of the former captives, an emaciated centaur, get into the back of the wagon. Iolee held the centaur's arm with one hand and grasped the wagon's door frame with her other one for support. Suddenly, a javelin blasted through the torso of one of the horses that pulled the wagon. The javelin had been launched from a ballista mounted on the parapet overlooking the courtyard. The horse's sudden collapse spooked the others in the team, causing them to bolt forward, which in turn caused the wagon to lurch forward. Iolee lost her grip on the door frame, then fell, and would have smacked her head against the rear edge of the wagon if not for her ward. She then tumbled out into the courtyard. Vlain surged forward, but before he could reach her, a javelin careened off the ward that covered her back. A bright red explosion of light filled the air as the ward abruptly disappeared. Vlain looked up to see another ballista swivel on its mount so it could fire a finishing shot at Iolee. The fighter leaped into the air then landed on top of her just as a javelin slammed into his ward. A red flash of light indicated his protective barrier had also met its demise. Vlain jumped up and pulled Iolee to her feet. He half dragged half ran with her to the back of the wagon, then threw her inside. Iolee cried out in surprise as she landed on the soft hay lining the floor.

"Vlain! What are you doing..?" Iolee asked.

"You're too vulnerable out here without a ward," he explained.

"But you lost yours too..."

"I'll muddle through. Stay in the wagon and help the shamans heal those we rescued." Iolee nodded. Vlain slammed the wagon door shut, pulled his steelwood shield off his back, and turned toward the parapet. He had just planted his feet in a wide stance when a javelin hit his shield with such force that he slid backward over six feet through the snow. The javelin bounced off his shield to smack into the ward that covered Vulkas's face. The minotaur grunted in surprise and took a step back. The javelin went spinning out into the courtyard. Vlain saw that a small crack had formed in the center of his shield, but it still remained whole.

"Shields up!" Vlain bellowed. "Those javelins can destroy a ward with one hit, so don't depend on them anymore," he shouted out to his war party. The fighter dodged an incoming javelin by a hair's breadth, then raced to the front of the wagon to see what had spooked the horses. He soon saw one of them bleeding and dying in the snow. Vlain wildly looked about as his mind sought a solution. Ardennais came galloping up just as Vlain slit the suffering horse's throat.

"If we cut off its harness, then the other horses can still..." Ardennais began.

"No, losing a horse will slow the wagon down," Vlain responded. Man and centaur jumped as a javelin slammed into the ground less than a foot away from them. "I need you to take its place," Vlain told Ardennais. Vlain knew it was considered an insult for a centaur to haul loads or pull wagons and carriages, but no replacement horses were available. Fortunately, Ardennais nodded in agreement. Vlain unclasped the dead horse from the harness then clasped it onto Ardennais's body. All the while, steel bolts and arrows rained down around them from the tall wall surrounding the fort. The lethal projectiles bounced harmlessly off Ardennais's ward and ricocheted off Vlain's steelwood armor. The fighter finished clasping the harness onto the centaur, then stepped back. He looked up at Bollis, who sat in the driver's seat, holding the reins.

"Get out of here!" he ordered the big man.

"You got it, boss," Bollis replied. "Hiya, hiya!" he yelled, giving the horses and Ardennais the cue to start running. The war wagon lurched forward.

"Belor!" Vlain called out.

"I know. Get on the roof," the archer replied.

Vlain mounted his horse as the archer grabbed his crossbow and a bag filled with loaded magazines from his saddle, then jumped off his horse to land on the wagon's side. The fighter watched as he hauled himself up onto the wagon's roof. Belor would shoot at any legionnaires that might be foolish enough to pursue the wagon. Vlain ordered several Findalorans and renouncers to go protect the wagon as it lumbered out of the courtyard. He then ordered his war party to form a wedge-shaped formation facing the drawbridge door. Vlain knew it was only a question of time before it dropped to emit a wave of legionnaires, and he wanted to buy the wagon time to get away.

Suddenly, powerful light beams shined down on them from the parapet and tower. Vlain figured the lights must have been magical in nature because they didn't have the reddish hue of torches and were unnaturally intense. The fighter squinted as he looked up at them. He raised his shield with one arm and his crossbow with the other.

"Well, well, well. If it isn't the traitorous Vlain," a high-pitched, creaky voice shouted. It seemed to come from a dark figure standing behind one of the ballistae that lined the parapet.

Vlain instantly recognized the owner of the voice. "Snill, you shrew-faced bastard! Come down here so we can work this out, man-to-man," he replied.

"You'd like that, wouldn't you?" Snill shot back. "I like my chances up here better, though."

"You would, being the coward you are," Vlain replied.

"Any last words before I lay you low?" Snill asked.

"Thania take you," Vlain said as he fired his crossbow. It was an impossible shot, but the bolt grazed Snill's helmet nonetheless.

The legionnaire cursed in alarm and instinctively jumped back even though it had already bounced off the wall behind him.

"You'll pay for that, you stupid brute," Snill yelled. "Fire!" he ordered the legionnaires who manned the three other ballistae and the twenty legionnaires who stood by with crossbows in hand.

"DINN! Get those blaeting golems out in front of us. We need cover, damn it!" Vlain bellowed at the druid.

"Why don't we leave, warmaster?" the druid asked. "We've already rescued the prisoners, and we're sitting squirrels down here."

"Because we need to buy the wagon more time to get away. Now, do as I say," Vlain replied.

Dinn nodded in understanding, then closed his eyes as he concentrated. Soon, all eight hulking golems had arranged themselves in front of the war party. They casually absorbed the steel bolts and arrows that rained down from the high wall, but the javelins sank deep into their wooden bodies. Now and then, one streaked past a golem to hit a Findaloran or renouncer behind them. Whenever that happened, a bright red flash filled the air, indicating another member of the war party had lost their ward. The ballistae stopped firing for a moment. Vlain ordered everyone to raise their shields during the brief pause. The ballistae then began firing again, but this time they launched steel balls the size of grapefruit at the golems. Even their tough, wooden bodies soon withered beneath the relentless assault. Vlain watched in dismay as an occasional arm or leg was blasted off a golem's body.

"Return fire!" Vlain shouted. He took a knee then aimed carefully at a legionnaire who stood on the wall, holding a crossbow. He steadied his hand, held his breath, and pulled the trigger. The bolt sped forth to bury itself in the man's throat. Vlain watched as his lifeless body pitched forward then fell into the courtyard. The fighter trained his sights on another legionnaire and also brought him down. Vlain went on to fatally shoot two more men after that.

Emboldened by Vlain's success, Boudika stooped down to pick up a discarded javelin. She galloped forward as crossbow bolts and arrows rattled harmlessly off of her ward, then hurled the javelin at a legionnaire that manned a ballista. Although it fell short of hitting him, it broke the ballista's strings. Boudika smiled in victory as she watched the legionnaire inspect it. Nothing he did worked, however, because it didn't fire again. A steel ball bounced off Boudika's ward, causing it to blink out of existence. After that, the centaur raised her shield and grew more careful.

Following Boudika's lead, Vulkas ripped a javelin out of a golem's side, then launched it at a ballista-firing legionnaire. The missile blasted through the man's chest and back plate and pinned him to the wall behind him. A chorus of cheers erupted from the war party.

Next, it was Meris's turn. He fired a bolt from his crossbow, injuring a legionnaire manning a ballista. Unfortunately, another legionnaire quickly stepped in to resume firing it. Then another legionnaire started using the ballista, which had belonged to the man Vulkas had just pinned to the wall.

Vlain heard Snill's cackling laughter as he fired a javelin from his ballista at Meris. A red flash signaled the abrupt demise of his ward. The renouncer raised his shield and stepped closer to a golem he was using for cover. Vlain swore in anger. He knew if he didn't do something soon, his people would start dying. The fighter carefully set his sights on Snill and pulled the trigger. His aim was true, for the bolt shot forth to bury itself in the legionnaire's eye. Snill fell back with a cry, prompting several of his subordinates to run over to check on him. Vlain laughed darkly as the men carried him off the parapet and through a door that led into the tower. Once again, however, another legionnaire rushed in to use the unmanned ballista.

"Get me up there!" Vlain said to Vulkas.

The minotaur gave him a surprised look then shrugged his mighty shoulders. "You're one crazy son of a bitch. You know that?" he said as he grabbed Vlain by the back of his belt and backplate.

"Just do it," Vlain replied as Vulkas prepared to throw him.

The next thing Vlain knew, he was airborne. His eyes watered, and the wind roared in his ears as he shot face-first through the cold, snowy air. Vulkas had gauged the throw perfectly. Vlain landed nimbly on the ballista Snill had manned, much to the shock of the legionnaire who had just taken control of it. Vlain kicked him so hard that his nose flattened against his face with a burst of blood. The back of the legionnaire's head slammed against the wall behind him then he lost consciousness. Vlain pulled his swords from their sheathes then leaped at the legionnaires who fired crossbows at him point blank. He swatted their bolts out of the air, and the remaining ones bounced off of his armor.

Boudika swore in awe as she watched Vlain carve through the legionnaires like a bloody hurricane. The fighter cut off limbs, heads and disemboweled a man all within a few seconds. The men fell back from him in terror as his eyes began glowing like red-hot coals. Vlain mercilessly pursued them up and down the parapet.

Boudika and the others tore their eyes away from the carnage Vlain was causing when they heard the drawbridge door chains get released. The door slammed down, and out streamed over sixty horse-mounted legionnaires. The men threw hollow, glass spheres full of oil at the golems then others fired flaming arrows at them. Soon, the golems were reduced to walking bonfires.

Vulkas roared out a primal challenge, then stooped down, grabbed a javelin, and threw it. The missile blasted straight through a legionnaire and the man who rode behind him. The minotaur then pulled his massive, double-headed ax off his back and fearlessly waded into the men.

Meris watched as Boudika pulled a white sword from its sheath that looked like it had been carved out of ivory or white marble. The centaur then raced forward to meet the oncoming legionnaires. The renouncer shook his head in amazement as she cut through the enemy's shields, armor, and swords as if they were all made of soft wax. It was like watching Caernos's black blade in action back when they had fought in Algos. Meris wondered what strange type of stone the weapon had been carved from. He looked on as Boudika rapidly killed several more legionnaires, then urged his horse into the press of men. Everything became a blur for Meris after that. Now and then, he saw his fellow renouncers, Oudeteros, Hildin, Paetro, Denin, and Rivers, ferociously fighting against the legionnaire cavalry. Then he was forced to focus on his own survival as they came at him.

"Traitor! Betrayer! Deserter!" The legionnaires spat insult after insult at him, but all it did was make Meris angry, which made him fight harder. Meris ran a man through with his sword and smashed his shield against another legionnaire's face. He then looked up quickly to see how Vlain was faring on the parapet. The fighter looked like a rampaging lion surrounded by snapping jackals. Every time the legionnaires tried to corner or overwhelm him, Vlain would do something unpredictable or nearly impossible. Meris watched as he ran straight up a wall, then back-flipped and landed on the parapet behind his attackers. He kicked a crossbow out of a man's hands, caught it, and emptied the entire magazine into the startled legionnaires. Vlain dropped the crossbow when it clicked empty, then resumed carving through the men with his flashing, blurring blades.

"Kill the traitors!" a legionnaire roared in the distance, but it sounded to Meris like the man's voice came from the direction of the dungeons beneath the fort. Sure enough, a glance that way showed him that over thirty legionnaires were emerging from those doors. If he didn't do something soon, the war party would be surrounded.

"Yez!" Meris shouted. The young fawn turned away from a legionnaire he had just electrocuted. "They're attacking from the dungeon doors. Bring 'em down!" Meris ordered. The fawn nodded, then unleashed a brutal barrage of crackling lightning bolts at the oncoming wave of men. Meris pulled his crossbow out then assisted Yez by rapidly firing at the men. The two of them felled over a dozen legionnaires in a few seconds.

Meris had just run out of ammunition and was reloading his crossbow when a legionnaire kicked him in the chest, causing him to fall back into the snow. The man raised his sword and was about to bury it in Meris's face when Percheron suddenly appeared. He hurled a discarded javelin through the legionnaire's shoulder, then decapitated him with his bastard sword. The centaur caught the man's falling sword with his free hand, then galloped straight into a group of legionnaires to hack at them with both blades.

Meris kissed his fingertips then held them up to the snowy sky. "Thank you, Lady Jaina," he said reverently. He then got back up on his horse, pulled out his sword, and urged his steed forward so he could defend Percheron's back.

Vulkas lumbered past Boudika as she swiftly executed four men with her spinning, slashing white sword. Although her ward had long since disappeared, she fought as if she were invulnerable. Vulkas smiled grimly as he watched her work. The minotaur didn't stop until he reached the drawbridge. He then planted his hooves wide apart, raised his massive battle-ax with both hands, and brought the curved blade down onto one of the lengths of chain that connected the thick wooden door to the wall. Sparks flew as the ax blasted through the metal links. Vulkas ran to the other side of the door and cut that length of chain apart as well. He then dropped his ax, reached down and gathered both lengths of chain in his hands, and wrenched them free of their fastenings at the top of the door. Just then, a group of legionnaires closed in to attack him. Vulkas whipped the thick chains out in front of him as if they were only light pieces of rope. He lashed the legionnaires again and again until they were reduced to a mass of bloody, broken bodies. Only then did he drop the chains, pick up his ax and chop off an outer piece of the door. Vulkas then picked up the heavy wooden barrier and jammed it into the door frame. Although it didn't seal the door shut, it made it impossible for any more mounted legionnaires to enter the courtyard. Now the men could only squirm past the tilted, wedged door one at a time. However, those few who did found Vulkas's gleaming ax waiting for them.

Oudeteros marveled as he watched Vulkas, Boudika, and Yezrial fight. Of course, Meris and the other renouncers were impressive in their own rights, but the southerner had never seen the likes of the Findaloran warriors before. Unless, of course, he included Vlain in his appraisal, but that was hardly a fair comparison. No one could match Vlain's lethality. Oudeteros looked up at the warmaster as he finished off the last legionnaire on the parapet.

A legionnaire suddenly fired a volley of bolts at Oudeteros. The southerner raised his shield to block them since his ward had evaporated a few minutes ago. What Oudeteros didn't see, however, was that another legionnaire was simultaneously closing in on him from behind. The man pulled out his sword and was about to run him through when Vlain launched off the parapet to tackle the rider. The fighter's momentum ripped the legionnaire out of his saddle, and both men went tumbling out into the courtyard. Vlain felt a rib break as he landed heavily on his side. If not for the cushioning effect of the snow, the impact might have killed him. The legionnaire rose first and ran straight at Vlain. The fighter pulled a knife from his belt and hurled it straight into the man's throat. The legionnaire died gasping on top of him.

Oudeteros, who had taken care of the legionnaire in front of him, turned his steed around then guided it to Vlain, who was slowly and painfully rising up from the bloody snow. "You alright, warmaster?" Oudeteros asked.

Vlain nodded as he struggled to catch his breath. The sharp pain in his side was distracting, but he still smiled that crazy smile. "Hell of a night, isn't it?" he asked.

Oudeteros couldn't help but laugh. "Hell of a night," he agreed. Vlain and Oudeteros paused as they looked out across the courtyard. All was still and quiet. They had killed every legionnaire that had been sent to stop them. Oudeteros shook his head in disbelief. "We did it," he said to Vlain.

The fighter smiled grimly. "Let's catch up to the wagon," he shouted out to the war party. "They'll send another wave soon, and we'll need to be long gone by then."

Boudika led Vlain's horse over to him. "You fought like a god. I'm honored to call you my warmaster," she said with a bow.

"You were quite a sight yourself," Vlain replied as he bowed back. "I'm assuming that's an ivorite sword?" he asked.

"Yes, her name's Hvitur," Boudika answered.

"You made her sing tonight," Vlain replied. "Now, let's get out of here!" he shouted out.

Vlain and his war party caught up to the wagon about an hour later. The fighter had been worried that legionnaires from the camp south of the fort might have sent a force to attack it, but thankfully they hadn't done so. The war wagon made good time as it plowed through the deep snow. Bollis waived happily at Vlain and the others as they pulled up beside him. "Was wondering where you were, boss," the round man shouted. "Did you give 'em hell?"

"Thania's greeting them in her dark hall as we speak," the fighter answered.

"We wiped out at least three platoons, and Vlain killed Snill," Oudeteros added.

"Jaina's living light! Wish I could have seen that," Bollis said with a sigh.

"You'll get to see plenty of action in the days to come," Vlain reminded him.

"True enough," Bollis replied. "I'm just glad that little weasel got what was coming to him."

The blizzard had abated by now, and a half-moon peaked out from behind roiling clouds as the war party rode along in tactical silence. Vlain continuously scanned the glistening, snow-covered plain behind them, but there were no signs of pursuit. He was glad of that because there had been enough blood-shed already and because the thought of killing more legionnaires sickened him. Although he had acted tough and unfazed during the battle, he had known and even liked some of those he had slain. He shook his head at the cruelty of the situation.

NEW ALLIANCES

Chapter 14

Vlain pulled the crisp, early morning spring air deep into his lungs as he walked along the trail with Iolee. A dense fog obscured anything more than a stone's throw away, and patches of snow covered the forest floor wherever shadows lingered during the day. They took a sudden turn in the trail, which brought them into what Vlain assumed was a wide, flat meadow. However, he couldn't be sure how big the meadow was due to the poor visibility. The druidess pointed at a log to the right of the trail, indicating she wished to sit. Vlain nodded as they veered toward it. Iolee sat down then pulled her hood back to reveal her face. The fighter repositioned the swords on his belt then sat down beside her. Silence reigned as they soaked in the peaceful stillness of the meadow.

"I can tell this is a special place," Vlain's deep voice punctured the quietude. "A strange magic fills the air...and something else."

"What do you think that *something else* is?" Iolee teasingly asked.

"Not sure yet," Vlain replied as a thoughtful expression formed on his weathered face.

"You'll find out eventually," Iolee said.

"You like keeping me in the dark, don't you?" Vlain said with a chuckle as he reached out to hold her hand. The druidess gripped his hand tightly in return.

"I do," she admitted. "But only because you keep so many secrets yourself."

"Trust me. It's for everyone's good."

"How can we know if you won't tell us?"

"You'll find out eventually," Vlain replied with a grin.

Iolee rolled her eyes in exasperation. "You can throw my words back at me all you want, but you know I made a good point." Vlain pulled his gaze away from hers but continued to smile his crooked smile. "We've been...well...I don't know what you'd call what we have, but it's been going on for weeks now, yet I barely know anything about your past," Iolee pressed.

"You have only to ask, my lady," Vlain replied while trying to prevent the discomfort he felt from creeping into his voice. He wanted to be honest with Iolee. He trusted her and cared for her greatly, but his past was such a tricky, unpredictable thing. Some people gazed at him in wonder when he shared it, while others were filled with dangerous envy.

"Very well," Iolee said. "Tell me about your family."

A frown replaced Vlain's smile. "There's not much to tell, really..."

"Let *me* be the judge of that," Iolee interrupted.

"My father serves in Elamara's sixth legion," Vlain began. "He's stationed in one of the empire's southern provinces. My mother works as a maid for the only wealthy family in the village where I was born and raised."

"What's the name of it?"

"You wouldn't know..."

"I want to hear the name."

"Vaya," Vlain answered.

"Now we're getting somewhere," Iolee said as she squeezed

his hand.

"My brother and sister live there as well..."

"Are they older or younger than you?"

"I'll answer all your questions if you let me," Vlain grumbled.

"Please, go on," Iolee said apologetically.

Vlain picked up a twig from the frost-covered ground then began twirling it in his free hand. Iolee was wondering if he'd continue when he finally started speaking again. "My sister is eldest, and my brother is the youngest."

"Ah, you're the middle child. That would explain some things," Iolee said as she pushed her long bangs out of her eyes.

"Such as?" Vlain inquired.

"I'm sorry. Please go on," she prompted.

"My sister's a baker. She's married with two children. My brother's a stonemason. He and his wife have one child."

"Are you close to your siblings?"

"Might be if I saw them more often."

"I see," Iolee said. "Do you have children?"

"Thirteen, an unlucky number," Vlain replied with a gruff laugh.

"You have thirteen children?!" Iolee asked as she snatched her hand away from his and stood up. She placed her hands on her hips as she stared down at him. A look of incredulity formed on her pretty face. "Why so many?"

"Why not?" he asked, shrugging his shoulders.

Iolee shook her head in disbelief. "What are their names?"

Vlain scrunched up his face as he scrolled through his memories. "I came up with a jingle to help me remember. There's Riffir, Donbur, Tolli, Koin, Gadif, Tinber, Iver, Sadiff, and Roin, but Zedif, Vellin, Rombis, and Jaimz would never forgive me if I forgot their names," Vlain said in a sing-song voice.

"I don't know what's more impressive," the druidess began. "That you sired thirteen children or that you remember all their names. Their mother deserves an award for bringing so many people into the world."

"Then four awards would be needed since they have four different mothers," Vlain stated.

"Four! How many times have you been married?"

"Four times," Vlain grudgingly admitted.

"You've had four weddings?!" Iolee all but shouted. "By the White Stag! Are you married now?" she asked anxiously.

"Don't fret," Vlain said with a wink. "I got divorced from number four last year. I wouldn't be with you otherwise."

"Why so many wives, Vlain?!"

"I blame it on the blaeting road," he said in a weary voice. "I'm rarely in one place for long. But I want to hear about you. Have you ever been married? Do you have any children?"

Iolee looked out across the fog-enshrouded meadow before answering. "I've never been married, but I've been in a few relationships. I don't have any children."

"Do you want them?" Vlain asked.

"Maybe one day."

"Brothers, sisters?"

"I'm an only child."

"That would explain some things," Vlain said with a wry smile.

"Like what?"

"Never mind. Tell me about your parents." A look of discomfort bordering on panic formed on Iolee's face, which made Vlain immediately regret asking the question. "You don't have to answer if it makes you..."

"No, it's alright," Iolee lied. "My mother was a shaman. She died when I was young. I was raised by her sister, a well-respected herbalist. My aunt lives in a little village far from here. My duties as a druid keep me so busy that I don't get to see her often."

"I see, and what of your father?" Vlain asked.

"I don't talk about him," Iolee quickly replied.

Before Vlain could respond, his eyes caught movement in the distance. Two figures suddenly emerged from the icy fog surrounding a cluster of aspen trees. One of the figures had a womanly shape and wore a dark green, hooded cloak, signifying she was a druid. The other figure had a man's build and wore the turquoise-colored cloak of a shaman. Iolee followed Vlain's gaze until she, too, saw the figures.

"Ah, there they are," she said as they drew closer. Iolee had invited Vlain to go for a walk through the forest so they could eventually meet up with her druid friend Rowan and her shaman husband. Vlain wasn't sure if Iolee saw it as a double date or merely a chance for him to get to know some of her friends. He was open to either possibility and relished the opportunity to speak with Rowan about matters regarding her father, Vorsord.

"Iolee! Vlain! I hope you haven't been waiting long," Rowan

exclaimed.

"Rowan! Tanvir! Don't worry. We've only been here a short while," Iolee said as she walked over to Rowan. Iolee hugged her, and Tanvir then turned to look back at Vlain. "Warmaster Vlain, this is Tanvir, the shaman."

"Nice to meet you," Vlain said as he extended his hand.

Rowan whispered into Tanvir's ear. The shaman blushed, then shook Vlain's hard, calloused hand. "Sorry to hesitate," the young man replied. "Rowan is still teaching me your customs."

"Then we're both in the same carriage," Vlain replied, using an old Elamaran saying. Vlain quickly sized up the man in front of him. Tanvir was slender, of average height, and appeared to be in his mid-twenties, just as Rowan was. The shaman had turquoise-colored eyes, long brown hair, and a short, well-trimmed beard covered his handsome face. His earlobes had thick ivory gauges in the center, and a long braid descended from the left side of his head down to his chest. Vlain could see a fierce intelligence burning in his eyes. The fighter instantly liked him, which was rare for him to do.

Tanvir was taking stock of Vlain as well. He seemed to be impressed by Vlain's muscular build, battle-scarred face and piercing, amber eyes. Vlain doubted he had ever seen his like before since he had probably never left the Wild.

"Congratulations on becoming our new warmaster," Tanvir said. "You're the first and only outlander to have ever earned the title."

"I had to best a minotaur in unarmed combat to get it," Vlain replied.

Tanvir shook his head in amazement. "Rowan told me about your fight with King Vulkas. I wish I'd seen it with my own eyes! She also told me you fought alone against a platoon of legionnaires at Fort Faldin and emerged victorious. Incredible, to say the least." There was admiration in the shaman's eyes, but also something else. Disbelief? Suspicion? Vlain couldn't be sure, but he wondered if Tanvir suspected there was something unnatural about him. Since Tanvir was a findoree, Vlain figured the shaman might be able to sense his powerful enchantment.

The fighter decided to change the subject to prevent Tanvir from asking him any revealing questions. "I've been a soldier since I was sixteen, so fighting's as natural to me as breathing. Still, I thank you for the compliment. Come sit with us," Vlain said as he sat back down on the log. "Tell me, what exactly are we waiting for?" he asked after everyone had gotten comfortable.

"You'll see soon enough," Iolee said with a mischievous smile.

"Ah, more surprises," Vlain replied.

"It'll be worth it," Rowan said. "While we wait, tell us how you and the other renouncers like living in Findalora. What do you and your men think of us?"

"We think highly of you. As for the forest, it's stunningly beautiful, vast, and mysterious. I wish I could spend the rest of my life traveling within it so I could see all the different regions. Only then could I get to know its many inhabitants."

"Spoken like a true lover of the White Stag's green halls," Rowan replied. "However, it would take you several lifetimes to see all of the forest and get to know each race that calls it home. I've lived in the Wild for a few years now, and I've barely scratched its surface."

"And yet, you became a full-fledged druid in that time. What made you do that?" Vlain asked.

Rowan gave Iolee a loving look. "This woman here inspired me to undertake that journey because she saw my potential and my longing for a purpose," she said as she squeezed Iolee's arm. "And this man here encouraged me every step of the way," Rowan said right before she kissed Tanvir on the cheek.

"I see," Vlain said. "But why didn't you ever return to your father's home to tell him you had found love and a new purpose in the Wild? Why not set his mind at ease, and help repair the rift between the Findalorans and Faldinites?"

A frown formed on Rowan's pretty face. "I miss my mother and my brothers and sisters. My father, however, did something unforgivable, and because of that, I'll never willingly lay eyes on him again. But it's alright because I have a new family now," she said as she wrapped an arm around Iolee and Tanvir.

"What did Vorsord do that was so unforgivable?" Vlain asked. "Was it his slaying of the minotaur?"

"That's part of it," Rowan replied. "But it's also because of the hunts he led into Findalora."

"The loss of an animal's life is no small thing," Vlain agreed. "I lost my horse, Viscol, not long ago, and I'll mourn him forever, but it seems to me you could forgive your father for sneaking into the Wild to bring down game. Perhaps he was simply trying to feed your family?" Vlain knew he was pressing Rowan hard, but he felt he had to learn why she had stayed away from her family.

"Must you ask so many questions?" Iolee asked him. "You don't have to answer that, Rowan."

Tanvir gave him a stern look. Rowan remained silent.

"As your warmaster, I could order you to answer the question because that incident is partly responsible for the war we're about to wage. I won't use my rank in that way, however. Instead, I ask as your friend."

"A friend wouldn't ask such a..." Iolee began.

"It's alright," Rowan said, holding up her hands. "He has a right to know what my father and Lord Bevel were up to." Vlain leaned closer as the young, red-haired woman paused to take a breath. "Vorsord wasn't just hunting any old game in the forest. He was hunting one of Findalora's most sacred and magical animals. We call them kylan, but you call them unicorns."

"Your dad was hunting unicorns?!" Vlain exclaimed. He jumped up off the log and stared at Rowan with an amazed expression. "I thought they were just legends..."

"They're as real as you and me," Tanvir said.

"And how was Lord Bevel involved?" Vlain asked.

"Vorsord sold the horns to Bevel, who had his servants take them to the capital city of your old empire, where they were sold on the black market," Iolee answered. She was standing now too. "Both men profited greatly, judging by the houses and other things they bought soon after."

"Did the minotaur die defending the unicorns?" Vlain asked.

"Yes," Iolee answered. "He was a distant cousin of King Vulkas and a friend of mine. Xalin was his name. He happened to be traveling through the forest when Vorsord, and one of his hunting parties, cornered a unicorn. If not for Xalin's brave sacrifice, it may not have gotten away."

"And *that* is why I'll *never* forgive my father!" Rowan all but snarled. "His actions by themselves are despicable, but he didn't only endanger his family that day; he helped push Findalora into a state of war. Now, we'll all pay for his moral failings." Her voice was saturated with bitterness and resentment.

"It all makes sense now," Vlain said.

"No," Iolee said. "It can't because you haven't seen everything yet."

"There's more to the story?" Vlain asked.

"Turn around and look over there," Iolee said as she pointed at the copse of aspen trees.

As Vlain turned around, a ray of sunlight shone through the gray clouds onto a group of unicorns threading their way through the aspen trees. The fighter shook his head in wonder as he gazed at the majestic beasts that steadily approached them. They were all lean, muscular, and their eyes glowed with purity and vitality. There was also a faint white glow emanating from the long horns that jutted out from their foreheads. All twelve of them were different colors, though some differed by only the palest of hues. They ranged from white, pink, brown, gray, light blue, and purple to black. The male in the lead had a gorgeous, glossy black coat with a long mane of hair that fell down his neck. He trotted proudly and purposefully toward Vlain.

"You brought me here to see unicorns," Vlain said.

"I brought you here to meet them," Iolee replied as she grabbed his hand.

"I hate to bring up a painful fact," Vlain began. "But neither of us are pure of body, and I, for one, am not always pure of heart."

"Your admission is hardly surprising," Iolee said with a faint smile. "But I sense more good in you than bad, and that's enough for them to trust you too."

"I thought you have to be a virtuous virgin, or something like that, to be accepted by a unicorn."

"Don't worry about all that. Just enjoy the moment," Iolee responded. The druidess reached into one of the pockets within her voluminous green cloak, then pulled out a juicy red apple. "Of course, a little bribery never hurt either," she laughed.

The quartet slowly approached the blessing of unicorns. As Vlain grew closer, he saw the ebony stallion had a short, curly beard that sprouted from his chin. He also noticed he was the only one with a curved horn. The tip of the horn looked wickedly sharp, and his was the longest among the blessing. The magnificent creature blasted steam out of his nostrils as he trotted forward, then stopped when he was a short distance away. Iolee nudged Vlain, causing him to look back at her. She waved the apple around, indicating he should take it. He was about to reach for it when he changed his mind and shook his head "no." Vlain didn't want to bribe the proud stallion into letting him get close. He wanted their meeting to be authentic and pure.

The fighter held his hands up to show he meant no harm. "Easy there," Vlain said as he neared the beautiful beast. "I come in the name of peace." He used his gentlest voice, yet he still expected the unicorn to bolt away at any moment. He, of all people, knew how impure he was in both body and mind. Undoubtedly, the stallion would sense it as well, and then he'd run back into the forest with the rest of the blessing in tow. Only, it didn't happen. Vlain's heart began racing as he got closer to the unicorn. Some instinct told him to kneel and reach out his hand, so he did. The stallion snorted nervously, tossed his black mane about, then lowered his head. Vlain's fingertips brushed against the softly glowing horn. A surge of energy shot through him, and a vision sprang into his mind. He saw himself riding the black unicorn as a dark, spectral forest loomed in the distance. He could see skeletal trees from afar, and a fell black mist filled the air. Next came a scene in which a sea of men marched toward Vlain and the unicorn as they proudly stood on an outcropping of white stone. Lastly, he saw himself and the unicorn as they galloped fearlessly toward a host of legionnaires. Vlain saw it all in a flash. The emotions it raised left him with a sense of awe. He shook his head to bring himself back to the present, then softly ran his hand over the animal's snout.

"Not sure what's happening here," Vlain admitted. "But it feels right, doesn't it?" The unicorn whinnied, reared back, and kicked at the air with his front legs. He then dropped back down onto all fours and began pawing at the ground with one of his front hooves. Vlain suddenly knew what he was supposed to do. He stood up, walked to the unicorn's side, grabbed his mane with one hand and his back with the other, then pulled himself up. Vlain half expected to be bucked off, but it didn't happen.

The unicorn whinnied softly, then turned around to look back at his colorful blessing. Although Vlain couldn't hear or see anything, he suspected that the ebony unicorn was secretly communicating with the others. Slowly, one by one, they turned and trotted back into the aspen forest. The black beast then turned to face the druids and the shaman, who watched the scene with wide eyes and mouths agape. A soft, joyful laugh escaped from Vlain's lips, and a delicious sense of peace enveloped him. Suddenly, he knew the unicorn's name.

"In all my years, I've never seen a kylan let someone ride it," Iolee said as she gazed up at Vlain. "Does your luck have no bounds?"

"It's not luck. It's fate," Vlain explained. "I can't tell you how I know, I just do, and I can tell you something else."

"What's that?" Iolee asked.

"His name's Ombra, and he has volunteered to serve as my steed until the war's over," he answered. Without a word, Iolee, Rowan, and Tanvir each dropped to a knee and began praying to the White Stag. Iolee led the prayer in which they thanked their god for his generosity and benevolence in their time of need. Vlain closed his eyes and savored the happiness and gratitude he felt. Part of him felt like he had just found a long, lost friend, while the other part felt like he had finally come home.

***

Maiva smiled as she watched Yezrial give Zenda a purple wildflower he had just plucked from the ground. Zenda blushed when she saw the flower in his hand. She gave him a quick, embarrassed smile, then mumbled an awkward "thank you." The young fawn had been flirting with her all day. Maiva couldn't tell if Zenda felt the same way about Yez or if she was just being polite and tolerant of his advances. Yez had been picking flowers and serenading Zenda for hours. Maiva thought it was sweet that he was willing to go to such lengths to win Zenda's affection, even if his love for her proved unrequited. There had been so much violence, tension, and stress lately that it was nice to witness young love for a change.

Yezrial bowed after Zenda thanked him, then raced off ahead of them. He had volunteered to be their scout while they scoured the countryside for ingredients required to make Haephius's latest creation. Maiva had filled a pouch full of brimstone and another full of sulfur, and Zenda's bags were filled with red fire stones, which were native to Findalora. Thankfully, Haephius had already obtained the rare and precious rubies he required for his spell. As usual, her father had been ridiculously secretive about what he was crafting. After Maiva had pressed him for answers, he had revealed it was another mighty weapon they could use in the war against Man, but that was all he would say. Maiva knew better than to question him further.

Zenda suddenly dropped back on the trail until she was side-by-side with Maiva. "Do you think we have enough ingredients yet?" she asked. "My pouches are full to bursting. Perhaps we should head back now?"

387

"Is that your way of saying you're tired of Yez hitting on you?" Maiva playfully asked while gently elbowing Zenda in the side.

Maiva's words caused Zenda to blush. "He's sweet, and I like him...I just don't know if I like him like that," she replied. "I need time to..."

"You don't have to explain yourself," Maiva interjected. "I just like giving you a hard time."

"Or maybe you're jealous that he isn't hitting on you?" Zenda said with a sly smile.

"That must be it," Maiva replied as she rolled her eyes.

"I knew it," Zenda said with a laugh. "But seriously, when are we heading back?"

"Soon," Maiva answered. "I figured we could take a break somewhere up ahead, then go back. Sound good?"

Zenda nodded up and down. The two of them walked on in silence for a moment. They rounded a curve in the trail then came upon a small clearing. The sound of rushing water caused Maiva to search for the source of the sound. She soon spotted a wide, shallow river to their right. Yezrial was busily picking berries from a bush to the left of the trail.

He gave them a broad smile as they approached. "My stomach was rumbling, so I figured you both might be hungry as well," he explained.

"You figured right," Maiva said. "We haven't eaten since breakfast, and all this walking and searching for stones has gotten me hungry. How about you, Zen?"

"I could do with some berries," she admitted.

"Then rest beside the river while I finish gathering them," Yez said. "I won't be much longer." The two fawns walked down the gentle slope that led to the river's edge then sat down in the tall, soft grass. Maiva leaned forward and shoved her cupped hands into the cold, rushing water. She lifted them to her mouth several times and drank deeply. Zenda followed suit. No sooner had they settled back down in the grass than Yez appeared with a heaping assortment of wild berries. He poured some into Zenda's hands and then Maiva's.

"Aren't you going to have some too?" Maiva asked.

A guilty smile formed on Yez's face. "I stuffed my face while I waited for you to catch up," he admitted. "So eat to your heart's content."

While they devoured the sweet fruit, Yez fished a panpipe flute out from his satchel. He soon began playing a light, whimsical tune currently popular in Findalora. Both Maiva and Zenda began tapping their hooves in time to the song without realizing it. Zenda waited for Maiva to finish eating, then jumped up from the grass and extended her hand to Maiva.

"Come dance with me," she prodded.

"Oh, alright," Maiva said with a grin.

Both fawns were soon twirling each other about in the little meadow as Yez danced beside them and played the merry tune. Maiva and Zenda laughed wildly as they danced around in an ever-widening circle, arm-in-arm. The fawns became so absorbed in the music and merry-making, as fawns are prone to do, that they failed to see a group of renouncers when they rode up to the edge of the clearing.

Paetro, who was in the lead, signaled for the men behind him to stop their horses. He smiled as he watched the fawns dance and frolic in the tall grass. Although his eyes took in all three figures, he mainly focused on Maiva. Something about her laugh and the fluid grace-fullness of her movements captivated him. She looked so exotic and otherworldly, yet innocent, playful, and approachable as well. Paetro didn't know what to make of her or his feelings about her. All he knew was that her beauty enchanted him.

"Are you just gonna stare at them all day?" Hildin, his twin brother, asked. Paetro blinked several times, as if he was waking from a trance, then looked back at him. "The men are tired, and we need to get the game back to camp so it can be prepared for dinner."

They had been hunting all day and had brought down pheasants, deer, and an elk, the bodies of which were draped across their horses. Paetro knew Hildin was right. It was hard to keep the nearly six hundred renouncers fed even with the help of the woodlanders, who supplied them with whatever food they could spare. They should be getting back to camp, not loitering in the forest to watch fawns dance and frolic. Paetro knew all this, but he didn't want to leave. The female fawn with the brown hair had a hold on him, and what's more, he missed hearing music.

"You go on ahead. I'll meet you back at camp in a while," he heard himself saying.

Hildin looked at him as if he was crazy. "You're gonna stay here with those woodlanders? What if they don't want your company? Ever think of that?"

"Then I'll leave," Paetro said as he urged his horse forward into the clearing. Hildin shook his head in bewilderment, then ordered the men to follow him back to camp. Paetro rode over to the dancing fawns then stopped his steed when it was a stone's throw away from them. Yezrial was the first to notice him. He immediately stopped playing his panpipe, which caused Maiva and Zenda to stop dancing. They looked in the direction where Yez was staring, then gazed in uncertainty at Paetro.

"I'm sorry to interrupt, but I heard you playing, and I was

drawn to the music," Paetro said with a friendly smile.

"You're a fan of music?" Yez asked.

Since Paetro was an officer, he wore an understanding which enabled him to comprehend the Findaloran language. The enchanted necklace also helped him form the words required for a reply, though speaking was trickier than listening. "I am," Paetro admitted. "In fact, I play the lute."

"Aha!" Yez exclaimed. "A fellow musician! Do you have it with you?"

"I do."

"Then break it out so we can play together." Paetro got down from his horse then pulled the small lute out from a saddlebag. Maiva watched him intently. She remembered running into Paetro during the attack on Algos. She had been leading a group of younglings toward the green gate in the Meadow of Knowing, and Paetro had been fighting a wood golem when they had suddenly come face to face. Although Maiva had forgiven the former legionnaires, now known as renouncers, they still made her nervous. She forced herself to smile at Paetro as he walked by out of politeness, but she remained wary.

"Good afternoon, ladies," Paetro said with a nod as he passed the female fawns.

"Good afternoon to you as well, renouncer," Zenda replied.

"You may call me Paetro," he said in response to Zenda's greeting, but his eyes were focused on Maiva. Maiva smiled but said nothing. "Why don't you resume playing that tune, and I'll jump in when I feel ready," he said to Yezrial.

Yez nodded in agreement, then lifted the panpipe to his lips and resumed playing. Paetro tapped his foot to keep time, then started strumming his fingers across the lute's strings. Maiva and Zenda began dancing again, but they did so self-consciously now that Paetro was there. Their movements were more restrained, and their pace more measured and refined than before.

Paetro began to sing. His voice startled the fawns at first, but they soon began to enjoy his smooth tenor. Paetro improvised as best he could on the spot. He sang of what he had seen in the Last Wild, of an endless wilderness, rolling rivers, misty meadows, and the wildlife that inhabited them. The subject and focus of Paetro's song soon shifted to that of a beautiful female fawn who danced and twirled beneath a giant tree as the wind blew leaves off its branches. The leaves from the tree spiraled down all around the fawn as she leaped about in the tall grass. A curious expression formed on Maiva's pretty face as she gazed at Paetro. She didn't know if he was singing about her or about a fawn out of some legend, but she enjoyed the lyrics just the same.

Suddenly, a blue jay landed on the ground a few feet away from Maiva. The little bird cocked its head to the side as it gazed up at her. Maiva locked eyes with it. Nothing happened at first, but Maiva soon felt the power within her awaken. Instead of seeing a blue-jay, Maiva now saw a purplish-blue bird with two long, prominent feathers that sprouted up on either side of its head. Its body was similar to that of a large hawk. Maiva blinked her eyes several times, but the image of the strange-looking bird remained there on the ground instead of the blue-jay.

"Do you see that bird there?" Maiva asked Zenda.

Zenda looked down at it. "The blue-jay? I guess it wants to watch us dance," she replied with a laugh.

Maiva's eyes narrowed as she stared at the oddly shaped bird. She stopped dancing and then walked over to it. She knelt down and was about to touch it when it suddenly flew away. After it landed on the ground again, the image of the strange bird was replaced by that of a blue jay. Maiva shook her head in confusion and was about to resume dancing when something told her to follow the bird. She did just that, and as she drew closer, she noticed it was staring intently at her. Its body language implied that it was impatiently waiting for her to catch up. Maiva walked toward it, and once again, it flew away right before she could reach it. Zenda stopped dancing to stare at Maiva.

"Are you tired of dancing?" she asked.

"I don't know why, but I need to follow this bird," Maiva distractedly replied. "It's leading me somewhere, and I want to know why."

Zenda waved her hands at Yez and Paetro, indicating they should stop playing their instruments. Yez eventually saw her and dropped the panpipe from his mouth. He then signaled to Paetro. The renouncer had a faraway look as he sang and strummed the lute, but he soon became aware of Yez and stopped playing.

A sheepish expression formed on his face. "Did my lyrics not please you?" he asked Zenda.

"Your lyrics were fine, outlander," she replied. "But Maiva has decided to follow that blue-jay. She thinks it's leading her to something, and I don't want her to go off alone."

"Then let's accompany her," Paetro good-naturedly replied.

"She gets like this when she's having a vision or seeing into the future," Zenda explained as she turned to follow her friend out of the clearing.

"Oh, that's right. I heard about how Maiva received a symbol from the White Stag on her forehead," Paetro said. "What's it called again?"

"The starmark," Yez answered.

"And it made her psychic?" Paetro asked as he climbed up onto his horse.

"Yes. It was Maiva who warned us that Man would attack Algos. She is the only reason we were prepared for you," Zenda said.

Her words stung Paetro's heart. "I'm sorry for all of that. I would go back and change it if..."

"What's done is done," Zenda replied. "And I, for one, forgive you, but I didn't bring it up to make you feel bad. I just wanted you to understand how powerful and accurate her visions are. She received a mighty gift that night, and we are all thankful for it."

"I understand," Paetro said.

They all grew silent as they followed Maiva out of the clearing and into the forest. Maiva followed a narrow trail that wound through dense clusters of bushes filled with thorns and brambles. Zenda, who followed behind her, was thankful for the path. Without it, they would have all been torn and bleeding by now. Yezrial came after Zenda. Although he was a fun-loving fawn, he also had a cautious side, and it was that side that caused him to pull out the lightning gloves. Paetro, who brought up the rear, watched as Yez put on the deadly, magical gloves. The renouncer figured he was donning them in case they ran into predators. However, he still shivered when he remembered how many legionnaires had been felled by those brutal weapons during the battle in Algos.

The trail soon led out into a barren, wind-swept plain. The quartet had to be careful where they stepped due to the numerous sharp stones in the ground. Paetro's horse stumbled several times and nearly fell once. The renouncer soothed his horse with reassuring words while fondly petting the side of his neck.

Eventually, the trail led down into a shallow valley, and that was when they all saw it. A purplish-blue bird, the size of a dragon, lay stomach down with wings outstretched in the center of the valley. It looked like an exotically plumed hawk but a thousand times larger. Maiva figured it had recently crash-landed there, for several trees had been uprooted and had fallen onto its enormous back. She watched as the blue jay continued to fly toward the gigantic bird below.

"By the White Stag! Look at the size of that thing?" Zenda said when she caught up to Maiva.

"My father once told me about birds that grow bigger than houses," Maiva replied. "I think he called them roks."

"I guess that was what you were meant to find," Zenda said.

"I guess so." Maiva was about to descend into the valley when Yez came running up.

"Let me take the lead, Maiva. It could be dangerous if it's still alive," he said in a rush.

"I'll go with him," Paetro said as he brought his horse to a stop behind them. The renouncer pulled his shield off his back, then removed his spear from its holder.

"Very well," Maiva agreed. "But don't hurt it unless it gets aggressive. I mean that."

"You have my word," Paetro replied.

"Mine as well," Yez said. The quartet resumed its march down the hill. Maiva watched as the blue-jay flitted ahead of them, always staying out of Yez's reach. She wondered if the little bird was friends with the rok or if it had been sent by the White Stag to guide her to it. There was no way to know, but both prospects intrigued her.

They reached the bottom of the valley a few minutes later. Yez escorted Maiva as she walked to the rok's head. The titanic bird's eyes were half-open, and its tongue was protruding out of its monstrously large beak. It looked as if it were either dead or deep in sleep. Maiva leaned closer to its nostrils to listen for its breath. Her eyes lit up in excitement.

"It's breathing! It's alive," she exclaimed.

"It must have been a brutal landing. It's a miracle it survived," Paetro said.

"It has so many wounds on its body. I wish one of us was a shaman or a druid so we could heal them," Maiva sadly stated.

"I have a plan," Paetro began. "Me and Yez will work together to get the trees off of its back while you and Zenda go to Orrn to fetch healers."

"You go, Zenda," Maiva replied. "I'll gather healing herbs, then start treating its wounds."

Paetro got down from his horse, then beckoned Zenda to him. "Do you know how to ride?

"I'm not that good, but I can manage," she admitted.

"Don't worry. Gabler's a good horse. He's quick and smart. He'll get you there in no time." Paetro pulled a food bag, water-skin, and an ax out of the saddlebags, then helped Zenda get onto the horse. "Hold on tight," he instructed her. "Hyaahhh!" he shouted as he slapped Gabler's rump. The horse bolted back up the hill that they had all just descended.

"We'll help your friend as best we can," Maiva said to the blue-jay that was now perched on the rok's gigantic beak. She then walked off in search of herbs.

Paetro was about to hack away at a thick pine tree that had

fallen onto the rok's back when Yez grabbed him by the arm. "That'll take too long," the fawn told him. "I did an experiment a while back. Figured I'd try cutting a log into smaller pieces with my gloves, and it worked beautifully."

"Alright, let's see what you can do," Paetro replied.

"Genlin!" Yez said, causing a blueish-white bolt of lightning to form in his right, gloved hand. The young fawn gripped the other end of the shimmering, humming bolt with his left hand, then pressed it down onto the tree trunk. Tiny flames erupted from the point of contact, and small pieces of wood exploded outward. Paetro watched with wide eyes as the lightning bolt quickly cut through the wood. Wisps of smoke curled upward from where the lightning had scorched the tree trunk. Yez gave Paetro a triumphant smile.

"Jaina! You weren't joking. Wish I had a pair of gloves like that."

"I'm afraid they're one of a kind," Yez said before turning his attention back to their task. The man and the fawn fell into a pattern after that. Yez would use the lightning bolt to cut the log shorter, then Paetro would heave the piece of wood off to the side. Yez would then move further up the tree, and they would repeat the process. Things got tricky when they had to stand on the rok's back and work. Yez had to be careful not to cut through the wood for fear of electrocuting the gigantic bird. Paetro told him to stop when he got close to the feathers, then he lightly chopped at the wood with his ax until it fell apart. In this manner, they cleared off all of the trees from the rok's back in a short time.

Paetro clasped Yez by the shoulder. "Good job," he said with a smile.

"Haephius deserves the compliment," the fawn humbly replied.

"Can you both give me a hand?" Maiva asked. The fawn had

returned from gathering herbs. She had stuffed one of Paetro's saddlebags full of various plants known for their restorative properties. Maiva dumped the bag's contents onto a wide, smooth, flat stone, then snatched up a rock from the ground.

"What do you need us to do?" Paetro asked.

"Grab a stone and mulch these herbs into a paste," she said as she tossed a rock at Paetro and Yez. "After that, we'll massage it into all the wounds we can find."

It took the three of them less than twenty minutes before they completed the task. After that, they pushed the paste onto flat rocks, walked around the rok, and applied it to all of the cuts and scrapes they could find. Maiva put the last mound of paste on her rock then gently smeared it into a gaping wound above the rok's beak.

The rok's eyes suddenly snapped open wide in alarm, and the animal lunged forward and snapped at her with its gigantic beak. Maiva instinctively launched backward, thereby avoiding what would have been a lethal bite. Yez and Paetro raced over to check on her. The renouncer raised his spear, and Yez prepared to hurl a lightning bolt at the rok, but Maiva's words caused them to stop.

"Don't!" She yelled while slowly backing away from the advancing bird. "She's just scared. Give me a minute. I'll calm her down." Paetro and Yez nodded in agreement but kept their weapons poised and ready. "It's alright," Maiva said in a soothing voice. "I mean you no harm."

That was when it happened. Maiva's mind reached out to link with the rok's. The fawn could "see" the rok battling a black dragon in the frigid sky of the far north where the towering trees of the Last Wild yielded to the barren, wind-swept tundra. Boudika, Gaerna, and the other shield-maidens anxiously watched the struggle raging above them. The dragon raked its claws across the rok's chest and side, then reared back its head. However, before it could blast fire from its mouth, the rok clamped its gigantic talons around the dragon's snout, thereby clamping its jaw shut. It then drove the dragon to the ground head first. A thunderous crash filled the air. The titanic animals thrashed about as they each fought to subdue each other. The ground shook and quivered as if an earthquake was underway. Every time the dragon tried to blast the rok with fire, the bird either used its beak or talons to throw it off balance. Eventually, the dragon slammed its tail against the rok's chest, which sent it flying back. Before it could close in on the injured bird, Boudika ordered the shield-maidens to attack the roaring dragon. The injured rok flew away at that moment. Maiva assumed the bird had flown south after its vicious battle with the dragon and had crash-landed in this lonely valley when its injuries finally overcame it. The vision matched what Boudika had told Maiva when she had dined with the shield-maidens at King Caernos's lodge after they had returned from their dangerous mission. Boudika had told her that a rok had intervened right before a dragon was about to attack them.

"You must have been the rok that saved them," Maiva said with a trace of awe. "Thank you for helping my friends. Please let us help you now." Either the rok understood Maiva, or it could sense her kindness, for it soon resumed a sitting position. "That's it. We're all friends here."

"I think you're getting through," Yez said.

"How do you know it's a her?" Paetro asked.

"I...I don't know," Maiva answered. Maiva slowly started walking toward the rok while reaching out toward it. The colossal bird began making a low, throbbing sound with its throat, which reminded Maiva of a cat purring, then it extended its neck so that its head was within her reach. Maiva gently petted the giant lavender feathers that lined its face. The fawn knelt down then leaned against its massive head as she stroked it. Paetro and Yez watched in amazement as the rok closed its eyes and rested its head at Maiva's feet.

"Will you look at that!" Paetro said with a smile.

"You're one of a kind, Maiva," Yez said with a sigh.

Just then, the sound of horse hooves on stone was heard, causing all three of them to look up at the hill from which they had previously descended. Zenda was mounted on Paetro's horse, and she led a small party consisting of two druids and two shamans. Paetro recognized the druids who rode behind Zenda as the satyr named Dinn and the fawn named Xerlith. However, he didn't recognize the two shamans who rode behind them.

"Looks like you made a friend, Maiva!" Zenda shouted out excitedly. The rok looked up at the newcomers, and for a second, it looked as if it would get agitated again, but Maiva quickly soothed it with kind words while she stroked its feathers.

"This is the rok that helped Boudika and her shield-maidens when they fought the dragons up north. We have a hero here," she told Zenda as the fawn approached. "Better stop the horses there though. I don't know if she'll see them as prey or not," she advised.

"How could you possibly know this was the rok that helped the shield-maidens?" Zenda asked. Maiva pointed at her forehead. "Oh, that's right. How could I forget?"

"Move slowly and speak softly," Maiva said. "She's still skittish." Zenda nodded then relayed her advice to those behind her.

"By the White Stag," Dinn said as he got down from his horse. "Do you know how rare roks are these days?" The satyr asked as he cautiously approached Maiva.

"Quite rare, I'd imagine," Maiva replied.

"I don't think one's been spotted in over ten years."

"What a magnificent animal!" Xerlith said as she drew closer. "It's as big as a dragon."

"Which would explain why it felt confident enough to fight one," Maiva said.

"And that would explain the size of the wounds," Dinn said.

"What do you want me and Yez to do?" Paetro asked.

"Please gather more herbs," Maiva replied.

"Are you sure you'll be safe?" Yez asked.

"Yes. I think she trusts us now," Maiva replied.

"I'll go with you," Zenda said as she walked toward Yez and Paetro.

"I don't think you met these shamans before," Dinn said to Maiva. "Allow me to introduce Leighis," he said as he pointed to a diminutive young woman. "And this is Sanador," he said, pointing at the tall, older man behind Leighis.

"Pleased to make your acquaintances," Maiva said as she nodded at each of them.

"Not as pleased as we are to meet *the* starmark," Sanador said with a bow.

"It is truly an honor to meet one who has been blessed by the White Stag," Leighis said as she, too, bowed before Maiva.

"May His light shine upon you," Maiva replied.

"And also on you," Sanador said, completing the saying.

"Given the size of this animal, it'll take all four of us working in concert to effectively heal it," Dinn began. "Xerlith and Leighis, since you're the lightest, please climb onto its back to work on the wounds there." The druidess and shaman nodded in agreement, then carefully began climbing up onto the rok. "Sanador, you and I will work on its sides, back, and front."

"Very well," Sanador replied.

"You're sure the bird won't feel threatened by us?" Dinn asked Maiva.

"Yes. I can sense her pain, but she's no longer afraid," Maiva answered.

"Very good," he said.

A smile formed on Maiva's pretty face as she watched the blue-jay flit all about the rok in a protective manner. "It's alright, little one," she said. "We're here to help your friend, not hurt her." She then closed her eyes and projected a mental image of the druids and shamans healing the rok's wounds. When Maiva opened her eyes, she noticed the blue jay had settled on the rok's beak again and seemed to be regarding her with trusting eyes.

The druids and shamans all closed their eyes then summoned the considerable energy required to heal the colossal bird. They all laid their hands on the rok simultaneously as if they were one being. Maiva passed the time by petting the bird's face while softly singing a song to her. She wasn't sure why she felt so protective of the massive bird. It was in Maiva's nature to help animals when she saw they were injured or starving, but this time there was an urgency in her desire to lend aid. Maiva wondered if it was a result of the psychic abilities the White Stag had granted her.

Before Maiva knew it, Dinn walked up to her. "It is done," he said. "The herbs you pressed into her wounds earlier helped speed up the healing process. Xerlith! Leighis! Come on down!" Dinn called to the druidess and shaman.

No sooner had the woman and fawn descended to the ground

than the rok stood up. The druids and shamans cautiously backed away, but Maiva stood her ground. The giant bird locked eyes with Maiva for several seconds. Dinn had a feeling they were silently communicating. Maiva stepped to the side after a moment, then the rok spread its massive wings and began flapping them as it hopped forward. The tips of its wings scraped against both sides of the valley, and the tremendous wind they generated pushed Maiva and the others down as if a hurricane was battering them to the ground. Suddenly, it was airborne. Maiva stood back up as it gained altitude. She smiled when she saw the little blue jay flying alongside it. The rok grew smaller and smaller as it ascended. Eventually, it disappeared into a vast puffy cloud that glowed pink and orange due to the light cast by the setting sun.

"I wonder if we'll ever see her again," Dinn said as he stood up.

"Oh, we will," Maiva replied with a secretive smile.

DARK VALE

Chapter 15

A cool, invigorating breeze washed over Vlain as he walked along the firing line. It was mid-spring in Findalora. Nature was returning to life all around him. Flowers were blooming, trees were budding, and the woodland animals frolicked in the green, misty meadows. However, the woodlander army largely ignored the forest's quickening pulse, for there was a war to prepare for. Vlain watched as archers fired volleys of arrows into distant targets. Now and then, the warmaster paused to adjust an archer's elbow or stance to improve their accuracy.

Eventually, he left the archers to walk over to the marksmen who fired the newly made repeating crossbows. Haephius, the master blacksmith, had successfully replicated the ingenious design, and his assistants were now manufacturing them by the hundreds. Vlain had helped him here and there with suggestions. The familiarity of the crossbow design had haunted Vlain until he finally made a connection. One night, while he and Haephius had been adjusting the tiller, he finally remembered where he had seen it before. Years ago, when Vlain had visited the famous philosopher and inventor known as Phaelos, he had seen the design on the master's workshop table. Vlain dimly recalled seeing a much younger Snill lurking in the background while he had discussed the new crossbow with Phaelos. Snill had been one of Phaelos's pupils back then. Vlain learned later that Snill had been kicked out of his school for stealing the other students' ideas. Apparently, Snill had stolen Phaelos's plans for the repeating crossbow before leaving the engineering school in disgrace. Vlain figured Snill had also pilfered Phaelos's designs for the catapults and ballistae he was always bragging about. Phaelos had later told Vlain that he had scrapped his plans for the crossbow, catapults, and ballistae because they had all worked too well. He didn't want to be responsible for bringing so much death and destruction into the world. Snill, however, had had no such reservations and although he was intelligent, he lacked originality and imagination and had thus stolen Phaelos's ideas. Vlain had chuckled to himself when the revelation hit him.

The warmaster offered several tips to the woodlanders who fired the crossbows. He helped them with their breathing and trigger control to boost their accuracy. Then he drifted over to the spear throwers. Haephius had forged a new type of spear out of black iron that was lightweight, tough, and extremely sharp. He combined it with an atlatl, a short wooden stick that added extra velocity and range to the spear. Although Haephius hadn't invented it, he had refined the handle and the spur from which the spear was launched. Some of their best spearmen, such as Paetro, could hurl the new spears over one hundred and twenty yards with the atlatl's help. Vlain had practiced with it intensively in the last few weeks and had learned to flip his wrist in such a way as to make the spear shoot forward with deadly speed. He gave the spear-men tips on how to use the atlatl so they, too, could throw their spears with the same lethal results.

Vlain was about to check on a large group of woodlander swordsmen who were training in a field when he was suddenly intercepted by the king's scribe Oshur. As usual, the prim and proper satyr was dressed like a dandy gentleman from the Elamaran capital. Oshur's style of dress and mannerisms always made Vlain chuckle.

"Warmaster, the king, has called for an emergency meeting and requires your immediate attendance," Oshur informed him.

"Right now? I'm in the middle of training the troops," Vlain grumbled.

"It's a matter of grave import and cannot wait," Oshur replied.

"Very well," Vlain called Meris over and told him to put the woodlanders and renouncers through various drills, culminating in a mock battle at the end of the day. He knew his capable second in command would take care of everything during his absence. Vlain then walked with Oshur to the king's lodge. "So, what's all this about?" Vlain asked the little goatman.

"You'll know soon enough," was all he got in reply.

Oshur guided Vlain into the sprawling lodge, which the king had commandeered for his stay in Orrn. They passed the king's royal guard, composed of burly centaurs, in the spacious foyer then entered a dimly lit room. Oshur closed the heavy, wooden door as Vlain took stock of the woodlanders who sat in a circle, facing each other. Of course, Caernos was there, who, as usual, chose to stand rather than sit. Next, there was Vulkas, who looked massive in the medium-sized study. Then there was Boudika, Maiva, Haephius, Iolee, and lastly, a tiny little man dressed in a garish purple outfit. Vlain would have mistaken him for a small child if not for the black, curling mustache and sharply-pointed goatee on his pale face. Vlain raised his eyebrows at the strange sight, then smiled and nodded at Iolee. The druidess nodded in reply but failed to return his smile. She looked tense, worried, and on edge. Her expression alarmed Vlain. He wondered what was amiss as he and Oshur took the last two available seats within the circle.

"Greetings, warmaster," Caernos rumbled. "I'm sorry to pull you away from training, but I've just received news from our esteemed Portal Master, Oisin Corcra," the king said. He swept his hand toward the little man in purple. "His news is so important I deemed it necessary to assemble all of you. We'll now commence the meeting. Oshur, start recording the minutes." The scribe opened a leather-bound book filled with blank, white pages, then rested his other hand, which held a feathered quill, on top of the first page.

"Before I share what Oisin told me, I must first inform our

outlander, Warmaster Vlain, what the Heart of the Forest is," Caernos boomed. Vlain noticed the king's words caused Iolee to shut her eyes and bow her head. "Thirty years ago, a druid by the name of Cyndriss saw fit to create a reservoir of great magical power. This reservoir is commonly referred to as the Heart of the Forest, but it has also been called the Green Heart or Forest Heart. Cyndriss's reason for making it was thus: since druids, and all other findoree, quickly run out of energy to use magic due to natural limitations, why not store excess energy in a large crystal during peaceful times so it can be used later in a crisis? In this manner, a druid, or any other magic user, could siphon energy from it without endangering themselves. Cyndriss quickly put his plan into motion. Every day, druids and shamans deposited small quantities of their personal power into the crystal. Eventually, the Green Heart held a vast amount of energy. In time, a crisis came along in the form of a wildfire that threatened a village. Cyndriss single-handedly saved the town from destruction by drawing on the power from the crystal, which he used to put out the fire. He was hailed as a hero and visionary for having the foresight to create the Green Heart. After that, all magic users were encouraged to contribute a portion of their power to the crystal. For years, all went according to plan. Disasters and threats arose from time to time, but Cyndriss, and other druids, used the Heart of the Forest to stop them. Over time, the crystal became sentient and could communicate with the druids and assist them whenever they used it.

However, things took a turn for the worse when Cyndriss made a secretive alliance with a great evil in his quest for more power. The evil I speak of is called the Dark Hunger, and it is the White Stag's antithesis. It takes the form of a giant black boar and has always been a bane to the people of Findalora. The Black Beast, as it is also called, greatly desired the Green Heart. It slowly seduced Cyndriss with promises of godhood. He fell under its spell and took the crystal to a cursed place in the forest. From that day on, the Heart of the Forest has been lost to us. That is until Oisin learned of its possible whereabouts," Caernos finished.

"With all due respect, me king, there's nae 'possible' 'bout it." Oisin chimed. "I saw the crystal when I was in the Dark Vale rescuin' me nephew, Tynan. It was blazin' like a green star in the gloom!"

"Oisin, please," Caernos calmly stated. "You'll get your turn to talk, but I first need to tell Warmaster Vlain what the Dark Vale is. Your story won't make sense to him if he doesn't have that piece of information first."

"Sorry, me king," Oisin said as he gave the king a seated bow. "Please go on." Vlain smiled in amusement as he stared at the little man.

"As I said, Cyndriss took the crystal to the Black Beast, which resides in a cursed valley we call the Dark Vale. The curse and how it came about is a different tale. Suffice it to say, it's an evil place, and we avoided it at all costs up until Cyndriss absconded with the Green Heart. After that heinous act, however, the druids and shamans grew fearful that either Cyndriss or the black boar would one day emerge from the Dark Vale, wielding the power of the crystal. Prompted by this fear, thousands of findoree traveled to the cursed valley to form a magical barrier around it. One of the druids, named Ellia, decided to make it a one-way barrier that was only accessible from the outside. Thus, the Dark Vale became a prison into which we now cast Findalorans who commit evil acts. Anyone can enter, but none may leave. Now, Oisin, you may share your recent tale with the assembly."

"Thank you, me king," Oisin began. "A few days ago, I went ta see me Lillin relatives that live in a village called Bollibrook, which is only a few leagues away from the Dark Vale. While I was there, me nephew Tynan was playin' a game with his friends. They did somethin' dumb, as wee ones are known ta do. They challenged each other ta see who could get closest to the barrier 'round the cursed valley without fallin' in. Bein' the genius he is, Tynan got closest and fell in. Course, he couldn't get out after that. Me sister begged me ta enter the Dark Vale so I could get 'im out. Since he's kin, I agreed right 'o way. I walked through the barrier and searched for 'im. I gave all o' the dark druids, evil folk, and monsters quite a scare!" he exclaimed. "You should have seen their faces while I skip-walked 'round their valley like I owned it! It was downright beau..."

"Oisin, stay on topic," Caernos rumbled.

"Yes, me king," the Lillen said as his expression grew stern again. "There I was, desperately searchin' fer..."

"What do you mean by skip walking?" Vlain asked.

Oisin held up a cylindrical walking stick made of smooth black iron. A purple, multi-faceted gem, the size of a small apple, rested on top. "I use me walkin' stick ta skip space durin' a journey so I can travel faster. I take a step, then it skips me ahead a hundred paces, and so on."

"Fascinating," Vlain replied. "And how did you manage to get past the magic barrier?"

"I'll tell ya if ya let me finish," Oisin replied. "Durin' me search o' the Dark Vale, I came upon an evil lookin' altar. Cyndriss and his foul druids were 'bout ta sacrifice me nephew ta the Dark Hunger! Can you believe that?!" he shouted at the top of his lungs. "Well, I put a stop ta that right quick, let me tell you! I killed some monsters and druids, then cut Tynan free o' his bonds. Course, Cyndriss and the others tried ta stop me, but ya can't hit what ya can't see..."

"What do you mean by that?" Vlain asked.

"I can turn invisible," Oisin snapped impatiently. "Now, let me finish me tale. They were runnin' 'round like lunatics tryin' ta catch us, but it was nae use. We were too fast for 'em, and me skippin' staff was beyond their reckonin'. At one point, we passed a cave that was guarded by chatterlings. I got a quick look inside, and what do you think I saw?" he asked the assembly.

"The Heart of the Forest?" Vlain asked after several seconds had passed.

"Yes!" Oisin exclaimed. "It was glowin' like a green beacon! I didn't have time ta grab it, but I know where it's kept naow. Anyway, we ran on til we got ta the boundary line, then I skipped us past the barrier. *That's* how I got out, laddie," Oisin said as he winked at Vlain. "And that's me story," he said as he crossed his arms over his chest.

"You're suggesting we retrieve the Green Heart," Iolee stated. She still had a pained expression on her face, but she seemed determined to master her inner struggle. "The problem with that is, the inhabitants of the Dark Vale are probably furious that you penetrated their domain and thus will be on high alert."

"And Cyndriss may have moved the crystal somewhere else after he learned that you ran past the cave where it was held," Boudika added.

"Maybe he did, and maybe he didn't," Oisin replied defiantly. "It's still worth a shot."

"I'm assuming we'd gain a tactical advantage if we possessed the Heart?" Vlain inquired.

"Ya bet yer ass we would!" Oisin chirped.

"Yes," Iolee seconded. "A single druid could stand against many legionnaires on her own, or a group of druids could all pull from it as one to win a battle. It would definitely put the odds in our favor. It's pointless to discuss the Heart, though, since the Dark Hunger may have drained it by now."

"Even if it hasn't, I assume Cyndriss placed extra security around it, and it could be a while before he relaxes his guard," Boudika said.

"Then again, he might not expect us to reenter his domain so soon," Vlain countered.

"If we do so, we face a serious challenge," Haephius said. "The only way to defeat the barrier from within is by assembling thousands of findoree to open it, which is impractical, or by using Oisin's skipping staff, which I made, by the way," the blacksmith said with a proud smile. "Since Oisin can only skip with one other person, he and that individual would have to fight their way through scores of dark druids, monsters, and criminals to win the Heart and fight back through them to get out. It's a suicide mission," he concluded.

"I made it in and out, and I can do it again," Oisin proudly stated as he puffed out his chest.

"That's only because you had the element of surprise," Boudika replied.

"And who would be brave enough or foolish enough to volunteer for such a mission, aside from yourself, Oisin?" Iolee asked.

"Hey, lassie! That's not very nice..." Oisin objected.

"I'll go," Vlain said with a reckless grin. "It sounds like my kind of mission."

"I like this one! He's got fire in his guts," Oisin exclaimed.

"After you penetrate the barrier, you'll be completely on your own," Caernos's rumbled.

"I know that, but I also know how much the Green Heart could help us."

"You're too valuable to risk losing, warmaster," Boudika said. "We need you to lead our army to victory. Please don't throw your life away in..."

"He's meant to go," Maiva interjected. "I saw it in a dream last night. I saw Vlain and Oisin running through the Dark Vale, searching for the Green Heart." A hush fell over the assembly as all eyes turned to her. Iolee frowned but said nothing. Caernos stared at Vlain in silence.

"Did you see them acquire it and make it back out?" Iolee asked.

"No," Maiva admitted. "I woke before the dream ended."

"I believe Oisin and I can complete the mission. We should leave at first light, but I have one condition," Vlain said with a sly smile as he looked at Caernos.

***

Vlain leaned against a pillar that supported the grand lodge as he watched his renouncers eat and drink. Their laughter and mirth made his heart feel light and at ease. It was dinner time, and the men were busily devouring stewed venison and baked potatoes. They had brought down the deer themselves, but the woodlanders had donated the potatoes. Vlain was happily surprised to see a few woodlanders sitting amongst the renouncers. His men were starting to befriend them and thus had invited their friends to dinner. Vlain was proud of them for being open-minded and willing to accept a foreign culture.

"Have you eaten yet?" Meris asked as he approached Vlain.

"No, I was just getting a bead on morale. I have to say, it looks good."

"It does. Thanks for taking the lead, by the way."

"How so?"

"By dating a druidess, you taught the men to fully embrace the woodlanders," Meris slyly stated.

Vlain grinned, then lightly punched Meris in the shoulder. "Blaet off," he replied.

"Let's go eat, boss."

Both men sauntered over to a table reserved for Vlain's officers. His core group was there, shoveling spoonfuls of steaming venison into their mouths while engaging in what sounded like an entertaining discussion. The only one who wasn't eating was Bollis. His bowl was empty, and he had already eaten several potatoes, as evidenced by the discarded skins in front of him. Whenever he looked at the other men, they protectively covered their bowls and potatoes with their arms.

"Of all the stupid stereotypes!" Bollis exclaimed. "Just because I'm fat doesn't mean I'm going to steal your food!"

"We can't take the risk, dear Bollis," Belor said in a mockingly serious tone. "We already watched you inhale three helpings of venison, so excuse us for being wary."

"Bunch of idiots," Bollis muttered.

"What's all this about?" Vlain asked the group.

"The round one here has been eyeing our food ever since we sat down," Belor explained.

"He's biding his time. Waiting for us to let our guards down so he can make his move," Hildin said in a conspiratorial tone.

Meris chuckled, and Vlain rolled his eyes. "It's good to see you're all in high spirits after everything we've been through," Vlain commented.

"You lot can keep your damn food for all I care," Bollis grumbled.

A renouncer, bearing a tray, walked up to their table to set a bowl of venison and a baked potato down in front of Vlain and Meris. He placed a cup of ale beside the bowls, handed both men a wooden spoon, then walked away. Vlain sipped on his ale while Meris stirred the hot venison to cool it off.

"Word is, you're about to embark on a mission, warmaster," Paetro said.

"And a dangerous one at that," Hildin added.

"It is indeed," Vlain replied.

"You'll have none of us to watch your back," Oudeteros said glumly.

"That's true, but at least I'll have a Lillen at me side," Vlain said.

"What in Taloria is a Lillen?" Belor asked.

"They're a race of pint-sized people," Vlain explained. "Think of a man about a third of your height, and you'll get the idea."

"And how in Jaina's name is someone that small supposed to help you in a fight?" Bollis asked.

"His name's Oisin Corcra, and what he lacks in size, he makes up for in spirit. The little fella seems downright fearless. What's more, he can turn invisible and skip space," Vlain explained.

"What do you mean by that last part?" Meris asked.

"I think it's like teleporting through most of a journey."

"Why doesn't he just teleport the whole way?" Bollis asked.

"How should I know?" Vlain replied. "You'd have to ask Haephius; he's the one who made his skipping staff."

"I need to befriend Haephius. I want some magic trinkets of my own," Bollis said.

"Let me guess, you'd ask for a bag that could hold an endless feast," Belor said with a grin.

"Blaet off!" Bollis said as he tossed a potato skin at the archer. "That's not a bad idea, though," he admitted.

"When do you and the Lillen leave, boss?" Oudeteros asked.

"First thing, tomorrow morning."

"And what exactly is the mission?" Belor asked.

"We're going into a hostile territory to retrieve a magical item that'll help us defeat the 9th Legion."

Some of the men looked like they were about to ask Vlain more questions, but just then, a renouncer arrived at the table and whispered something into the warmaster's ear. Vlain nodded, then stood up. His expression was one of happy surprise. "Excuse me, boys, I have something to attend to," Vlain said before walking away. The men were silent as they watched him leave.

"Meris," Bollis whispered. "If Vlain's not gonna eat his meal, could you pass it this way?"

Meris shook his head and tossed a potato at Bollis's head. "Eat that," he said.

Vlain pulled the cool, fresh air into his lungs as he stepped out into the chilly night. His eyes immediately found Iolee's cloaked, shapely form. The druidess was leaning against a short, circular stone wall that ringed a well. Her arms were crossed over her chest, and her shoulders were raised, which revealed her inner tension.

Vlain had learned to read her body language by now.

"Iolee! Come to see me off?" Vlain asked. "I looked for you after the meeting ended, but you had already..."

"I came to warn you about the great evil you'll face in the Dark Vale," Iolee said as she pushed off against the stone wall. "There are things in there that will..."

"Don't trouble yourself with all that," Vlain said. "King Caernos took Oisin and me aside and told us what to expect. He listed all the monsters and creatures we're likely to..."

"Oh, really? Did he tell you about Zersis the...?"

"Big blue guy? Has the head of a horse and the body of a man? Yes. Caernos said he likes to cut out the hearts of his...

"Did he also tell you Zersis is a disgraced warmaster?" Iolee asked.

Her statement caught Vlain off guard. His eyes narrowed as he studied her troubled face. "He neglected to mention that part," Vlain admitted.

"I bet he did," Iolee went on. "I bet he also neglected to tell you what crime Warmaster Zersis committed before he slunk off to the Dark Vale."

"Tell me," Vlain prodded.

"He slaughtered a large force of barbarians who had already surrendered to us. All he had to do was escort them out of Findalora, but since he chose to mercilessly end their lives, we've had nothing but trouble with them ever since."

"Of course. People never forget such wrongs, but why are you telling me...?"

"And I trust the king told you that the dark druids twisted the keti into what we call the takers, unseen beings that only live to stalk and kill. The chatterlings are another one of their hideous creations, monsters that look like a cross between trolls and insects. They cry like newborns to lure the unwary into a trap. It's said the monsters devour every part of their victims. The dark druids also warped and twisted wood golems into perverse forms."

"The Grey King told me about all these things, though he didn't go into such...detail. Iolee, why are you...?"

"And woe unto you should you encounter the Black Beast," the druidess whispered fiercely "It's a dark god, nearly equal to the White Stag in power. Thanks to the devotion of the evil druids and the monsters who worship it, it's grown strong. If it finds you and Oisin, you'll both know terror like you can't..."

"What are you hoping to accomplish?" Vlain asked Iolee as he gently took her by the arms. "Are you trying to scare me out of going on the mission?"

"Why must you go?" Iolee shouted as she ripped herself free of his grasp. "Even one such as you can be scarred by what lies in the Dark Vale. I wouldn't wish such a mission on my worst enemies, whether they were invincible or not!"

"I'll tell Caernos I changed my mind," Vlain said with a heavy sigh. "I didn't know it would bother you so much, or I would never have..."

Iolee took a deep breath to steady her nerves. "No, I'm being selfish," she said softly. "Of course, I want you to stay at my side, but that's not what's best for Findalora. If we can retrieve the Green Heart...if it hasn't been drained dry by the Dark Hunger...then it's worth trying to reclaim."

"Then why did you just share all of that...?"

"Because I'm afraid of losing you," she admitted. "I know you'll physically prevail, but I'm afraid of what the Dark Vale might do to your soul."

"I feel your fear," Vlain said as he cupped her beautiful face in his hands. "And I'm touched by your concern, but there's something else at work here, isn't there? Not once have you mentioned Cyndriss, yet I've seen how his name affects you. Why is that? What does he mean...?"

"He's my father!" Iolee shouted. "He's my father," she said again, but her voice was soft and brittle this time. She buried her face in his chest, and her shoulders shook from the force of her sobs.

Vlain held her for a long moment, then kissed her forehead. "I understand now," he said in a soothing tone. "And I can only imagine the shame you must feel whenever someone mentions him."

"It's dreadful," Iolee admitted as she pulled away. "I can never outrun his memory, no matter how hard I try. Sometimes, I'm free of him for years, then someone says his name, and he's back again. The worst thing, though, is the look of pity people give you when they know your father's a monster, and I wonder if they think I'll become like him."

"Never!" Vlain exclaimed. "You're selfless, kind, compassionate, all the things he isn't. No one worth their salt would ever doubt you."

"Thank you," Iolee said as she used her sleeve to dry her eyes. "Now you know why I won't be one of the druids who accompanies you and Oisin to the Dark Vale. I won't be among the healers that will mend your wounds after you emerge from that dreadful place."

"I wondered why Caernos hadn't chosen you," Vlain said.

"Well, wonder no longer. He knows what being there would do

to me, and he's far too kind to put me in that position."

"That he is," Vlain agreed. "Still, I wish I'd known about all of this before; I would have run the mission past you ahead of time, so you..."

"It's alright. You know now," Iolee replied. Vlain tried to take her hand, but she stepped back beyond his reach. "I'll pray for the White Stag to protect you and Oisin, and one more thing."

"Yes?"

"If you must choose between keeping your lives and retrieving the Green Heart, leave it there, and come back to us. Too many lives have already been lost over it."

"I promise, should the situation arise," Vlain solemnly replied. Iolee gave him a thankful, teary-eyed smile, then turned and ran away before he could say another word. He watched with a heavy heart as her cloaked form disappeared into the shadows.

***

There was something wrong with this section of the forest. It resisted the vibrant green blush of spring, which had already rejuvenated the rest of the Wild. The bushes and ferns were an ashen gray, and the rare leaves that sprouted from the twisted trees were a pale, sickly green. A faint smell of decay rode high on the air. It was similar to rotting leaves but was more acrid and bitter. It was plain to see that there was a blight upon the land.

Vlain scowled as he led the party of six toward the Dark Vale. The fighter was repulsed by the foul-smelling air and decrepit vegetation. Even the lively and chipper Oisin had grown sullen after they had passed through the green gate to emerge into the Lillen village known as Bollibrook. Although Oisin's relatives had initially welcomed him and the others, they grew reticent and frightened when they learned the reason for their visit. In fact, the small,

419

brightly dressed people had quickly withdrawn to the safety of their stone houses in case the mission went afoul.

Oisin sat silently behind Vlain as Ombra bore them through the withered wilderness toward the cursed valley. Behind them came the druidesses Rowan and Xerlith, followed by the shamans Tanvir and Sanador. None of them spoke, for they were all filled with a sense of dread. The smothering silence was unwholesome, and the unsightly undergrowth combined with the noxious fumes in the air dismayed them all.

Vlain suddenly felt Oisin tap him on the back. "This be the place, laddie," he said in his high-pitched voice.

Vlain nodded, then reigned in the unicorn. "We stop here," he informed the others. He then patted his ebony steed on the neck. "I wish you could come with us," he said before sliding down from the saddle. The unicorn whinnied in reply. Vlain lifted Oisin out of the saddle then set him on the ground. The proud Lillen gave him a reproving look but accepted the help nonetheless.

"We shall wait here for you to return to us, warmaster," Rowan said.

"May the White Stag guide you and protect you both," Xerlith added.

"I'm hoping Jaina does as well," Vlain replied as he untied a leather backpack that would hold the Green Heart from Ombra's saddle, then slipped it down over his brawny arms.

Vlain adjusted the straps then looked out across the fog-enshrouded valley. The foreboding landscape made the fighter feel vulnerable and apprehensive. He reminded himself that several druids had placed four wards on Oisin and himself before leaving Orrn. Rowan had explained that each ward was slightly smaller than the previous one, thereby granting them multiple layers of protection.

In addition to the wards, Vlain had borrowed Caernos's enchanted armband, which increased his strength four-fold. Borrowing it from Caernos for the mission had been his one condition. He wore the steel band on his left arm. The runes on its surface gave off a faint, bewitching blue light. Vlain had felt as strong as he imagined a giant would after he had put it on. In fact, he felt like he was almost weightless, and he had to restrain his movements for fear of accidentally hurting those around him. Vlain noticed other differences as well. For instance, he needed to breathe more often and deeper than before. He also required more water and food. Apparently, the price for pushing his body beyond its natural limits was the need for more fuel. However, as helpful as the armband was, it also came with certain dangers. Caernos had warned Vlain that wearing it longer than a few hours would cause him to pass out, at which point he would have seizures that could eventually kill him. Vlain hoped he wouldn't need to wear it for longer than an hour at most.

Vlain looked down at the fearless Lillen beside him. Oisin wore his purple diamond flower pendant, which would turn him invisible whenever he tapped it. Of course, he also had his famous skipping staff, upon which the success of the entire mission rested. Lastly, Haephius had custom-carved a suit of steelwood armor for him in case he burned through all of his wards during the mission. True to form, Oisin had painted it purple.

"You ready?" Vlain asked as he looked down at him.

"Let's get it over with," Oisin replied.

Man and Lillen walked forward until they encountered a faint but persistent resistance. Vlain pressed forward as Oisin had instructed him and suddenly felt himself push through the one-way membrane that surrounded the valley. He tried not to gag as he inhaled the stagnant air inside.

Oisin held his small hand out to Vlain. The fighter grabbed it just as the amythos gem on top of the walking stick gave off an eerie purple light. Oisin and Vlain began running as a swirling, translucent tunnel surrounded them. It reminded Vlain of a whirlpool as they raced through it. They emerged from it a second later. The ground beneath them looked blackened and scorched, yet it didn't give off any heat. Vlain saw the skeletal remains of trees in the distance, and a foul, cloying fog filled the air. Before Vlain could take in more details, they plunged back into the bizarre spatial tunnel. They soon emerged and nearly collided with a group of ragged, wild-eyed woodlanders who raised their weapons in alarm. Vlain pulled one of his swords from its sheath in a flash, but they were sucked back into the tunnel before he could strike. The fighter closed his eyes to prevent himself from getting vertigo. Oisin had warned him about such effects, but they hadn't had time to acclimate Vlain to tunnel travel before the mission.

They raced along for a few minutes before emerging from the strange tunnel to stand in front of the narrow entrance to a cave. Two massive, gray chatterling guards eagerly clacked their mandibles together and snapped their lobster-like claws as they surged toward them. Their multi-faceted, insect-like eyes glowed with a malevolent, yellow light. Vlain sprang into action. He decapitated the guard on his left, then cut the one to the right in half at the waist. The monsters' milky white blood shot out of their ghastly wounds as they tumbled to the rocky, barren ground.

"Damn, but you're quick, lad!" Oisin remarked as they ran into the cave.

"Let's hold off on skipping until we get a feel for the cave," Vlain replied.

Oisin nodded in agreement. "I'm goin' dark naow," he told

Vlain, which was his way of saying he was about to become invisible. Vlain watched as the Lillen flickered out of sight.

The fighter stealthily crept along the long, low tunnel until it emerged into an oval-shaped cave. Several red crystals had been placed on the walls and ceiling, which gave off a wan light. Vlain's eyes, however, were drawn to the big green crystal that occupied the center of the room. It was roughly the size of a pillow and radiated a fierce, green light. He had found the Heart of the Forest! It was resting on a granite slab, just waiting to be taken. Vlain's eyes then focused on four figures that stood protectively around the great, green crystal. They were hooded and cloaked just like the druids he had come to know, but their cloaks were black instead of green. Suddenly, one of the ominous-looking men turned his hooded head to stare at Vlain.

"Savor the view, outsider, for this will be the first and last time you see it," the man's harsh voice broke the silence.

"The Heart's coming with me," Vlain evenly replied.

Moving in unison, all four druids raised the blowguns to their mouths then blew darts at Vlain as he sprinted toward them. He battered two of the projectiles to the ground even as the other two ricocheted off of his outer ward. The two druids closest to Vlain fell back. One of them pulled a dagger out of his cloak, but Vlain sliced his throat open before he could use it. Another one tried to tackle Vlain, but the fighter ran him through then yanked his bloody sword out of the man's mangled chest. He was about to engage the two remaining druids, but before he could, a puncture wound formed in one man's neck; then, a split second later, the last druid fell to the ground with two bloody wounds where his eyes had been. He groaned in agony but was silenced when his throat was cut open by an unseen assailant.

"Nice work," Vlain said to his invisible ally.

"Can't let ya have all the fun," Oisin said with a laugh. Vlain bent down to touch the Green Heart. "Careful lad, could be booby-trapped," the disembodied voice warned.

"Thought of that, but I can sense magic, and there's only a feeble amount in here," he said in a disappointed tone as he patted the crystal.

"Think they drained it dry?" Oisin asked.

"No," Vlain replied. "I think it's a decoy. Give me a minute. I'm gonna use a little trick, I know." He closed his eyes and gradually let his awareness expand outward until it encompassed the room.

Vlain was searching for a hidden source of magical power, something that met King Caernos's description of the great Heart. Suddenly, he heard footsteps coming from the tunnel that led to the cave.

"Sounds like reinforcements are comin'," Oisin chirped.

"Buy me some time," Vlain said. No sooner had he spoken than his mind encountered what felt like an ocean's worth of magical energy. He had never sensed such a high concentration of power in one spot before.

The sound of a scuffle suddenly erupted in the cave. Vlain heard the pain-wracked cries of woodlanders and Oisin's grim, cackling laughter as it echoed chaotically off the walls. He was tempted to open his eyes to see what was happening, but he kept them closed and forced himself to concentrate on locating the source of magic. As Vlain's perception narrowed, he felt a faint vibration emanating up through the soles of his feet. He jumped down from the granite slab then opened his eyes to inspect it. After a hasty search, he saw vague distortions hovering in the air in front of the center portion of the slab. A screech suddenly filled the air. Vlain figured Oisin had just skewered someone. He tried to push the blood-curdling scream out of his thoughts as he ran his hands down the front of the granite slab. Vlain felt a quiver of energy run through his palm. He pressed inward on that spot, then despaired when nothing happened. Vlain was just about to turn around to help Oisin when a shelf popped out from the slab's surface by a couple inches. He pulled the shelf toward him, and his breath caught in his throat when he saw a hexagonal, multi-faceted, green crystal lying in the center of the shelf. Vlain pulled the leather backpack off his back, lifted the heavy crystal with both hands, then shoved it down into the backpack. He lifted the pack and pushed his arms up through the straps until it slid down onto his back. The fighter tied the straps around his chest and waist, then smiled triumphantly.

"I have the crystal. The real one," he told Oisin, wherever he was.

"Never doubted ya, lad. Now how 'bout givin' me a hand?" Came the disembodied response.

Vlain shot forward to bury his blade in a dark druid's chest even as he sliced the arm off another one. He then went to work on a group of ragged-looking woodlanders. Vlain figured they were criminals who had been thrown into the Dark Vale for heinous crimes. He tore through them like a wolf among sheep. Their blood and cries filled the air as they fell to the ground. Vlain didn't stop moving until they were all dead.

"Yer eyes got a strange glow about 'em," he heard Oisin say. "What are ye, laddie?"

"Unique," Vlain replied with a grin. "Let's get out of here."

They got halfway through the stone tunnel when they encountered another horde of woodlanders. Several satyrs and fawns fitted arrows to their bows and pulled back the strings even as others prepared to hurl spears at them. Vlain knew the wards surrounding himself and Oisin would hold, but he wanted to conserve them if they were needed later. "Sheath one of yer swords so I can take yer hand!" Oisin shouted. Vlain did as he asked, then involuntarily shut his eyes as arrows and spears shot toward them. Fortunately, they blinked out of sight a split second before any projectiles could reach them. The onrushing group of woodlanders skidded to a stop and looked about in bewilderment.

Vlain and Oisin emerged from the magical tunnel a second later. They were now a good twenty yards from the mouth of the cave. Unfortunately, they had materialized in the center of a horde of chatterlings. One of the burly, gray, insect-like brutes raised a claw in the air. It would have smashed it down onto Vlain, and Oisin's hands had Vlain not reflexively jerked his hand out of Oisin's grasp. The claw passed through the empty air then thudded into the ground. Vlain's sword blurred as he decapitated the monster.

"Oisin! Where are you?" Vlain called out.

"Comin', laddie!" Oisin answered as he ran between the tree trunk-like legs of a chatterling. He had almost reached Vlain when something unseen slammed into him from the side and sent him flying off course. He cursed in confusion as he tumbled across the jagged terrain. His wards had prevented him from getting hurt, but he couldn't figure out what had hit him. Oisin jumped to his feet and was closing in on Vlain when he abruptly bounced off an invisible barrier again.

"Be on guard, Vlain!" the Lillen called out. "I'm not the only invisible one here."

A chatterling eagerly clacked its mandibles together as it lumbered toward Vlain. The warrior was about to cut it in half at the waist when someone unseen grabbed him by the wrist. Vlain instinctively slammed his head backward and encountered the same resistance he would have expected if he had just struck someone in the head. He heard something snarl and growl in pain behind him, but the looming chatterling swung at him before he could strike at his unseen assailant again. Vlain ducked beneath the grasping claw, then cut the monster's legs out from under it. He then turned to face his invisible foe. Something grabbed his ankles even as something else pushed him backward. Vlain cursed in surprise as he fell to the ground. His eyes grew wide in alarm as he saw the straps on his backpack start to unravel. Someone was trying to take the Heart of the Forest from him!

Vlain jumped to his feet then skewered the air. He felt resistance as the sword pierced what felt like flesh. The fighter yanked the blade free of his unseen enemy then watched in fascination as a tall, white-furred creature, resembling a horned ape with a long tail, fell dead at his feet. Its teeth were long and wickedly sharp, as were the claws on its hands and feet. Vlain smiled victoriously and was just about to call out to Oisin when something slammed into his back. He cursed as he stumbled forward. He stabbed wildly at the air, but he didn't encounter any resistance this time.

"You're right, Oisin," Vlain shouted. "I just stabbed a big, white thing that looks like an ape with horns. they become visible after you kill them."

"Aha!" Oisin exclaimed. "We call 'em takers because they sneak up on folks and kidnap 'cm." Something struck the Lillen hard in the chest, causing him to stumble backward. A red flash filled the air, signaling the demise of one of Oisin's wards. However, he had been in a wide stance and was thus prepared to take the hit. The Lillen wildly slashed at the air all around him, then struck the bottom of his skipping staff on the ground. The purple gem on top began to glow. Oisin continued to stab the air until he stepped into the warping tunnel.

Vlain stabbed and slashed at the air in every direction. He felt resistance now and then but mostly hit empty air. Even with

Caernos's armband lending him extra strength, he knew he couldn't keep up that pace forever.

"Quit yer slashin'! I'm right beside ye," he heard Oisin's voice.

Vlain sheathed a sword then held his hand out. He felt Oisin grasp it. They were about to skip away when a taker slashed at Vlain's throat with its long claws. A bright red light flickered around Vlain's body, letting him know that one of his wards had evaporated. However, before the fighter could retaliate, he and Oisin were sucked into the magic tunnel. A chatterling swung its claws through the space they had just occupied, even as dozens of clawed footprints formed in the dusty ground where Vlain and Oisin had just stood.

Man and Lillen skip-warped across the cursed valley with incredible speed. Vlain appeared in mid-stride every few seconds, only to blink out of sight and reappear a hundred paces away. He smiled when he realized they were only a couple of leagues away from the barrier that separated the Dark Vale from the outside forest. They were almost free!

"We're nearly there, laddie!" Oisin happily exclaimed.

Vlain nodded and smiled as he ran. They skipped space again then emerged from the magic tunnel. However, the instant they did so, something that looked like a giant, malformed wolf clamped its jaws on Oisin's skipping staff. The Lillen tried to hold onto it, but the beast flung him away as it wrenched the staff from his grasp. Oisin soared through the air then landed heavily on a jagged boulder. A brief explosion of red light revealed he had just lost another protective ward.

"I've had enough of your infernal skipping to last a lifetime, Master Corcra." The raspy voice belonged to a black-robed druid that sat on the giant wolf. Most of the man's face was obscured by shadows cast by his hood, but Vlain could see that black tears had been tattooed down his sunken cheeks. The man's eyes were solid black. The hatred and evil in them pierced Vlain to his core. The fighter pulled his other sword from its sheath as he scowled at him.

Vlain soon realized the dark druid's steed wasn't a living wolf. Instead, it was a wood golem made to resemble one. In fact, whoever carved it had twisted its form to look like a walking weapon. Sharp thorns, barbs, and clusters of spikes sprouted from its wooden skin, and black iron blades formed its teeth and claws. Two yellow crystals had been placed in its eye sockets, and they gave off a harsh, wicked light.

"Well, if it isn't Cyndriss, the black pig's puppet," Vlain heard Oisin say.

Cyndriss turned his hooded head in the direction of Oisin's voice. "The Dark Hunger will devour your soul for such insolence!" he shouted.

"I ain't afraid of it!" Oisin shouted defiantly.

Cyndriss chuckled softly. "Tell it that when it arrives."

"Me and me friend will be long gone by then."

"You're not going anywhere, Oisin, and neither is your big friend with the strange eyes," Cyndriss hissed. "Not as long as I have your staff."

"Then I guess we'll have to beat you and your wooden mutt to a pulp, then take it back," Oisin angrily retorted. "Come on, Vlain, let's stomp 'im!"

Cyndriss's head fell back as he laughed. "And how are you going to do that when I can plainly see you?" the dark druid asked.

"Visible or not, I'll stomp ya, then take me, staff!"

Vlain watched as the wolf golem snapped at what must have

been Oisin's invisible form. However, it missed him, for Vlain soon saw a black, protective ward materialize around Cyndriss's body in response to Oisin's sudden attack. The dark druid had shoved Oisin's skipping staff between his waist and wide belt. He also held his own staff, which was made from a gnarled piece of wood. It grasped a yellow crystal at the top with several short segments of wood that resembled skeletal, human fingers. Cyndriss suddenly raised his staff. The crystal at the top began to glow, and as it did, Vlain felt a warmth radiate out from the Green Heart on his back. A yellow bolt of energy shot out from the crystal to slam into Oisin's ward. Vlain heard the Lillen cry out in surprise as a cloud of dust billowed up from the ground where he had landed.

"Oisin! Are you alright?" Vlain called out.

"He knocked the wind outa me, is all" Oisin said groggily.

"I think his staff draws its power from the Heart of the Forest," Vlain said. "Hang back for a moment while I soften him up."

"So, you're smart and fierce with the blade," Cyndriss mused as he coolly regarded Vlain. "You'll still die in the end, though."

"If I had a coppermark for every time some damaged soul like you has threatened me, I'd be even richer than I already am," Vlain replied.

The fighter sheathed one of his swords, then picked up a jagged stone from the ground and hurled it at Cyndriss face. Due to the strength-enhancing armband, the projectile hit Cyndriss's black ward with incredible force. The dark druid cackled as the stone harmlessly shattered into tiny fragments.

"A paltry attempt at best. If that's the best you can do..." Cyndriss derisively began.

Vlain had started running as soon as he threw the stone and quickly covered the short distance between Cyndriss and himself.

The wood golem reared up to maul him, but the fighter slashed his sword through both of the creature's crystalline eyes. He then pulled his second sword from its sheath and decapitated the golem in one blurring movement. The headless golem began running chaotically about in every direction as Cyndriss fought to remain in the saddle.

"Having trouble?" Vlain asked with an amused smile. The dark druid pointed the crystal in his staff at him in response. A yellow bolt of energy shot out from it. Vlain casually sidestepped it. "A paltry attempt at best," the fighter said. "If that's the best you can do..."

"You dare mock the Black Beast's high priest?" A deep voice bellowed from behind Vlain. The fighter whirled around, then ducked just in time as a dark blue creature slashed at him with a black iron saber. Vlain's eyes narrowed as he backed away to study his new adversary. The woodlander had the head and neck of a horse, the muscular torso of a man, and a horse's lower legs. His eyes were solid black, just like Cyndriss's, and he, too, had black tears tattooed on his cheeks, but the horseman's were solid streams rather than individual teardrops. The sorrowful-looking tattoos made the blue woodlander look even more ominous and intimidating.

"And who might you be?" Vlain asked.

"I am Cyndriss's left hand, the Dark Hunger's champion, but you may call me Warmaster Zersis," the woodlander snarled as he swung his saber at Vlain's neck.

The fighter deflected the blow, and as he did so, he realized Zersis held an identical sword in his other hand. He also noticed that a thick, cloying, black smoke stubbornly clung to both blades. Either that or the smoke poured forth from the metal itself. Vlain couldn't be sure which was the case, but he had a feeling that the black smoke was poisonous.

"Warmaster, you say?" Vlain asked as he parried a thrust and countered accordingly. "I happen to be Findalora's current warmaster. You may call me Warmaster Vlain."

Zersis snorted in derision. "Your title, lofty as it may be, won't save you, outsider," he growled as he thrust both swords at Vlain's chest. The fighter whirled to the side then launched his own attack sequence on Zersis's unguarded left side. "I'll place your head on a pike before the day is through." The horseman said as he expertly blocked both of Vlain's swords.

"Are all you prisoners so ill-mannered? If so, I'll have to teach you how to behave," Vlain said as he crossed his blades and launched a scissor attack at his adversary's thick, equine neck. Zersis let his head fall back as he retreated. Vlain's blades passed harmlessly through the air. The disgraced warmaster tensed his muscular legs, then leaped forward. He aimed one saber at Vlain's neck and the other at his chest as he descended. Rather than retreat, Vlain stepped forward and deflected both blades off to the side. However, the bold attack had been a setup, and Zersis kicked Vlain so soundly with his hoof that a red flash of light shimmered across his body. The fighter's eyes narrowed in anger.

"That's one ward down," Zersis said with a smirk. "If you wear any more, I'll peel them off one by one, just like I'll peel off your skin..."

"Shut up and fight," Vlain snapped as he rapidly slashed and stabbed at his opponent.

Both warriors locked blades. Zersis strained with all his might against Vlain, and had the fighter not worn Caernos's enchanted armband, he would have been hard-pressed to repel the horseman. With his amplified strength, however, it was no contest. Vlain began pushing his stubborn opponent back foot by foot towards the cliff behind him. He didn't know how deep the drop was, but he hoped it would be enough to at least stun Zersis. However, the horseman twisted to the side at the last second, causing Vlain to surge forward. The fighter reeled as he stopped at the cliff's edge, then he whipped around to face Zersis. The horseman kicked at him again. Vlain did the unexpected by dropping one of his swords and grabbing Zersis by the ankle. He yanked him toward the ledge with all of his enhanced strength. Zersis would have been thrown out into the air above a gulch far below had he not driven a saber into the rocky ground to anchor himself. Vlain dove to the ground to retrieve his sword, then repeatedly hacked at the horseman's head, but Zersis deflected the fighter's blows as he stood back up.

"I'm pleased to face a worthy adversary," Zersis said as he charged at Vlain. "It will make my victory all the sweeter."

***

"So, you've taken to hiding in the shadows like the little rodent you are," Cyndriss shouted as he walked through a narrow, maze-like canyon, the floor of which was littered with boulders and shale. He stopped moving while he waited for a reply, but none came. Even the fiery-tempered Lillen was apparently too wily to give his location away so easily.

Cyndriss was angry because he had been forced to remove the enchantment from his golem steed, which had left it lifeless. However, it had been necessary because after being decapitated, the creature had gone into a frenzy, making it dangerous and unusable. Cyndriss now suffered the indignity of walking rather than riding, and it galled him. He intended to take out his wrath on Oisin when he finally cornered him in one of the many dead ends.

Already, a ring of woodlanders and hulking chatterlings had formed around the rim of the small canyon. Their eyes shined with blood lust as they scanned the canyon for any traces of the Lillen. Cyndriss had only to signal them to come down to help him hunt for Oisin, but he wouldn't give it. This was his hunt, and he refused to share his prey with his underlings.

The sound of falling stones caught Cyndriss's attention. He ran between the twisting walls of the canyon until he came to a dusty corner. Several small rocks and pebbles were falling down a small mound of dirt in the corner. Cyndriss kneeled to study the soil. Sure enough, the Lillen had left behind a small boot print.

"You're only prolonging the inevitable, Oisin," Cyndriss shouted. "Why drag it out? If you reveal yourself; I promise to make your death quick and painless."

Silence was his only answer. Cyndriss had lied earlier when he had claimed to be able to see the Lillen. Oisin's invisibility spell was too potent for even a druid's trained eye to pierce. However, the same could not be said for the purple pendant that held the enchantment. Although Cyndriss couldn't see Oisin, he could see a faint, rippling distortion in the air in front of him, which gave away the pendant's location. Thus, he could track Oisin by following the trail of magical energy it gave off. Unfortunately for Cyndriss, it was much harder to detect a slight distortion than an unconcealed Oisin. On top of that, Oisin moved with a stealthy silence, which was a trait all Lillens possessed.

"Have at thee, bastard!" Oisin hollered as he launched off the canyon wall and drove his rapier and dagger straight down at Cyndriss's neck. Once again, a dark smokey cloud appeared between Oisin's blades and the druid's skin, indicating his ward was still effective. Undaunted, the Lillen hacked, slashed, and stabbed at Cyndriss over and over. "I'll tear through yer blasted ward eventually!" Oisin shouted defiantly.

"You still don't get it do you?" Cyndriss asked. "My staff is linked to the Heart of the Forest, which teems with power. You couldn't penetrate my ward if I stood here for a year and let you slash away. I thought you were smarter than that," Cyndriss said disappointedly.

"I know yer staff and the Heart are linked, ya daft idjit!" Oisin countered. "I heard Vlain say as much, but I'll be damned if I don't go down without a fight."

"A noble but useless sacrifice," Cyndriss said as he raised his staff.

The yellow crystal at the top began to glow. Suddenly, Oisin felt airborne. He slammed into the canyon wall so hard that faint cracks appeared where the ward surrounding his head had collided with it. Oisin grunted as he landed on his feet. He didn't know how long his two remaining wards would last, but he intended to make the most of that time.

"For the White Stag and the glory of Findalora!" Oisin screamed as he raised his rapier and dagger, then charged straight at Cyndriss.

A wicked smile formed on the dark druid's pale face. "How amusing," he said as he raised his gnarled, wooden staff. The yellow crystal pulsed again. Even the two wards surrounding Oisin couldn't prevent him from getting whiplash as Cyndriss slammed him against the canyon walls like a battered marble in a child's twisted game.

Vlain's heart sank as he heard Oisin's pained cries in the distance. He wanted to help him, but he had his hands full with Warmaster Zersis. In fact, their fighting styles were so similar that Vlain felt like he was fighting his own shadow. By now, they were both panting from exertion and covered in sweat. Vlain gritted his teeth then launched another attack against his adversary. Sparks flew as the two combatants repeatedly blocked and parried each other's blades. Part of Vlain had to admit he liked fighting him. It wasn't often that he fought someone of this caliber. Zersis always seemed to anticipate what Vlain would do next, and thus had a suitable counterattack ready.

Vlain smiled grimly when he noticed how badly he had damaged one of Zersis's black smoking sabers. His orichalcum blades, enhanced by the philosopher's stone, were chewing up his rival's inferior weapons. It was only a question of time before he hacked his way through them.

"What are you smiling about, you hairless ape?" Zersis snarled.

"You'll find out soon enough, you ugly bastard," Vlain spat back.

Vlain's comment must have enraged the horseman, for he redoubled his efforts to land a killing blow. Vlain blocked the assault while patiently waiting for the battered metal to give way. The minutes slowly ticked by. Zersis pressed him harder than ever. Vlain wondered how much more punishment the blade could take when he finally sliced through it. His sword would have cut into Zersis's face if not for the black, protective ward that surrounded him. Even so, the horseman was startled and dismayed as he watched his shorn blade fall to the ground. "One blade down," Vlain said.

"I only need one to kill you," Zersis replied. The horseman threw the grip of his broken sword at Vlain's face, but the fighter batted it away. Zersis had meant to distract Vlain by throwing it at him while he thrust his other blade into his abdomen, but Vlain saw the attack coming and countered accordingly. "If you drop...the Heart of the Forest... and leave the Dark Vale...I'll let you live," Zersis told him through gritted teeth after they had locked blades again.

Vlain raised his eyebrows in surprise. "I thought you were gonna peel my skin off," he said with a smirk. "What happened to all that tough talk?"

"It's plain to see...we're too...evenly matched...to end this fight any time soon," Zersis replied right before he broke away from Vlain.

"I don't care how long it takes," Vlain replied.

"Oh, but you do," Zersis sneered as he slashed at Vlain's legs. "I can tell you're worried about your little friend."

Vlain leaped over Zersis's slashing blade. "Oisin's as tough as they come. He'll be fine," he said after he landed.

"Why then did I hear him cry out in pain a minute ago?" The horseman asked as he thrust his sword at Vlain's crotch.

"Those were just the sounds of combat," Vlain replied as he hammered Zersis's blade down with his own, then slashed at Zersis's black iron chestplate. He smiled when he saw the horseman's black, smoky ward dissolve. His last blow had finally removed his enemy's magical protection.

"You just lost your ward, and you're down to one sword now," Vlain announced. "Is that why you want to end the fight?"

Zersis warily circled Vlain. "I have an ax strapped to my back, so I'm hardly beaten," he said as he charged him while holding his saber straight out before him.

Vlain side-stepped the attack. Sparks flew as Vlain hacked at the horseman's chewed-up saber. Zersis grunted as he desperately parried him. Suddenly, Vlain hacked through his second saber. The horseman rapidly retreated as he reached for the double-headed ax strapped to his back, but Vlain leaped forward and kicked him soundly in his chestplate. The runes on the enchanted armband blazed with a bright blue light as they amplified his strength. A deep dent, in the shape of Vlain's boot print, formed in the black iron even as a loud crunch was heard. A bloody sigh escaped from Zersis's mouth as his sternum cracked, then he went flying backward. Vlain had patiently waited to deliver the killing blow until he had positioned Zersis in front of the cliff once more. The fighter watched as the horseman flew out into the air then dropped out of sight beneath the cliff ledge.

"Well fought," he said before he turned and ran in the direction in which he had last heard Oisin's cries.

A bright red flash filled the air as Cyndriss used the enchanted crystal in his staff to pin Oisin against the canyon wall. The Lillen struggled and squirmed but was unable to get free. If not for his one remaining ward, he would have already been dead from the crushing force.

"You still have one ward left, I see," Cyndriss commented as he inspected the air in front of Oisin. "Good. I want you to suffer a bit longer before I end your miserable life." Suddenly, Oisin laughed despite his pain. Cyndriss stared at him in confusion. "What's so funny?" he asked.

"Here I am...beaten and... pinned ta a wall... but yer the one...who's about to die. Who says...the Stag doesn't have...a sense of humor?!"

"What are you prattling on about?" Cyndriss asked.

"Take a look...behind ya...and find out," Oisin said.

"I'm not falling for..." Cyndriss was shoved forward as Vlain slammed both swords into the black ward that covered his back. The dark druid whirled around to confront him.

"YOU!" He bellowed in disbelief. "But Zersis has never lost a fight. He..."

"Wasn't up to the task," Vlain said with a grin.

He raised both swords for another strike, prompting Cyndriss to raise his staff. Vlain sliced the wooden staff in half while simultaneously cutting through the yellow crystal. A bright, yellow flash of light erupted from the broken crystal, and a deafening boom was heard as Vlain was knocked off his feet. The blast hurled Cyndriss against the canyon wall even as Oisin's invisible form fell to the ground.

Vlain was the first to stand up. He sheathed a sword, then raced over to Cyndriss, who was on all fours and still reeling from the explosion. The fighter yanked Oisin's skipping staff out from behind the dark druid's leather belt.

"I'll take that, thank you," Vlain said as he scanned the narrow canyon. "Where are you, Oisin?" he asked.

"Right here, laddie." The Lillen's weak voice came from a spot a few feet away from Cyndriss.

Vlain sheathed his sword then strode over to where he saw the faint imprint of Oisin's back in the dusty ground. "Take my hand," Vlain said to the air. Oisin groaned in pain as Vlain hauled him to his feet. "Are you hurt?" he asked.

"A bit roughed up, but I can still run," Oisin answered.

"Good..." but Vlain was interrupted when Cyndriss suddenly stood up and pulled a long, black whip and a curved dagger out from the inner folds of his cloak.

"You won't be going anywhere..." he began.

"I can see why Iolee hates you," Vlain said. The words had an immediate effect on Cyndriss. A look of despair formed on his face, and his arms fell slackly at his sides. Vlain exploited his unguarded position by kicking him hard in the stomach. Cyndriss's back slammed into the fragile canyon wall. Vlain and Oisin backed away as it crumbled down on top of the dark druid. Cyndriss's cries filled the air as sharp pieces of shale sliced into his skin, and heavy stones crashed onto him. A dust plume rose up as the small avalanche covered the druid. Cyndriss was now buried beneath hundreds of pounds of rocks and dirt.

"I could kiss ya for that," Oisin said.

"I'd rather you didn't," Vlain said.

Vlain and Oisin's moods turned somber once again when they saw scores of chatterlings and woodlanders leap down into the canyon in a mad rush to get to them. Vlain figured there were many unseen takers among them as well.

"It's time to go," Vlain said as the horde raced toward them.

"I'll let ya do the skippin' this time," Oisin told him.

"Don't mind if I do," Vlain replied.

The Lillen had shared the magic word that activated the staff with Vlain back in Orrn in case he needed to use it during the mission. Vlain had only to repeat the word: "Gimrin," which meant "activate," three times in his mind to cause the staff to form the spatial tunnel. Vlain did just that, then he and Oisin raced into the churning tunnel which appeared before them. Man and Lillen blinked out of sight, a second before a dozen chatterlings lumbered around a sharp corner in the canyon. The huge beasts looked about in vain, for their quarry was gone.

***

Vlain sprinted across the bleak, steaming hellscape as fast as he could. The skipping staff pulsed with violet light each time it formed a tunnel. Oisin ran beside him at first, but he soon succumbed to his injuries. Although a protective ward still surrounded him, his head and neck ached from whiplash, and Vlain suspected he was also concussed. What's more, Oisin's little legs couldn't keep up with Vlain's inhuman pace, so he eventually picked the Lillen up and slung him over his shoulder.

A feeling of relief washed over the fighter when he saw the distant forms of the woodlander druids and mages who had accompanied them there. They looked like they were less than a league away! With the help of the skipping staff, they could make it there in...

Vlain and Oisin had just entered the warping tunnel. They were in a fluid, energetic state when a pair of massive jaws punctured the translucent membrane. The fighter shouted in alarm and confusion as the jaws ripped him and Oisin out of the tunnel in mid-skip, then threw them high into the air. Man and Lillen were separated as they each flew off in different directions. A red flash of light shimmered around Vlain's body as he skidded to a stop on the rough, stony ground, indicating he had just lost another ward. His hand slammed against a stone, causing him to lose his grip on the skipping staff. It tumbled across a patch of gravel, then shot under the lip of a boulder and was lost from view. Vlain's heart sank as he watched it disappear.

The fighter leaped to his feet. As much as he wanted to retrieve the staff, he resisted the urge and waited to see where Oisin's body would land on the dusty ground. He had to pinpoint his location to have any hope of finding his invisible companion later. Unfortunately, his search was interrupted when a gigantic, black boar materialized out of the gloom and charged straight at him. It was bigger than a house, had long curling horns on its head, and multiple razor-sharp tusks jutted out of its fetid mouth. Its eyes were deep, dark wells filled with hatred, and it exhaled a black mist. The boar's growl was louder than thunder. Vlain felt the reverberations deep in his chest. He had just enough time to pull his swords from their sheaths before it was on him. Man and god collided with a fearsome sound. Vlain gritted his teeth as he shoved his orichalcum blades against tusks that were longer than his swords. He strained against the Dark Hunger, but he was steadily pushed back even with the armband's help. Part of him felt that the struggle was pointless and doomed, but he rejected those thoughts because he knew they didn't come from him.

You will NOT take that which is mine! A harsh, strident voice invaded Vlain's mind like a stabbing knife. He was so stunned by the seething hatred and aggression in the voice that he almost faltered. Almost. The wiser part of him knew he must fight like never before if he was to survive.

The Heart of the Forest was never yours, Vlain mentally snapped back. *Cyndriss made it, then betrayed the people of Findalora when he brought it to you. You're just a thief!*

Speak reverently when you address a god, for you are nothing more than a fragile, fleeting thing! I will live on when you are naught but dust on the air! The beast blasted back.

The boar reared back then bared its tusks as it shot forward. Vlain rolled with the hit to reduce the damage to his last ward, then dropped to his knees and shoved a blade up through the boar's lower jaw. The Dark Hunger growled in pain as the sword sliced through its flesh. It jerked away so violently that it almost ripped Vlain's sword from his hand. The fighter fell back as he yanked the blade free. The boar was about to launch at him again when it snarled in pain and suddenly whipped around to bite at the air.

"Leave me friend alone, or I'll make bacon outa ya!" Vlain heard Oisin yell.

"Oisin! You live!" Vlain shouted. The fighter felt a surge of relief.

"Of course, lad! I won't let you take all the glory for yer..." but Oisin's was cut off when the Great Beast raked its huge tusks across him. A flickering red light filled the air, letting Vlain and Oisin know that the Lillen's last ward was now gone.

Oisin fell back a step as he sheathed his dagger and pulled a circular shield off his back. He then ran under the boar's lower jaw and thrust his rapier up into its throat. Oisin cackled maniacally as he raced beneath the Dark Hunger, lengthening the wound in its supernatural flesh with every stride.

"Nicely done!" Vlain shouted. Although he couldn't see Oisin, he could see the damage that the Lillen's blade was doing, and he could hear the boar's pained growls. "I'll hit him high while you hit him low," Vlain yelled as he leaped onto the boar's back. He thrust both orichalcum blades down into the boar's strange flesh, then raced along its spine. Vlain ripped his swords free, then shoved them down until they were both hilt deep in its head. The Dark Hunger nearly bucked him off when it reared back and roared in pain.

"That's how it's done, boyo!" Oisin exclaimed. The Lillen shot out from beneath the boar and was about to turn around to slash at its hindquarters when it kicked him in the back. Fortunately, the Lillen's steelwood armor absorbed most of the blow, but the kick sent him flying into a boulder. Vlain heard Oisin cry out in pain, then he heard nothing but silence.

"Oisin, are you alright?!" Vlain yelled as he clung to his sword grips while the giant boar violently bucked beneath him.

Your little rat friend is dead! The Dark Hunger's voice intruded into Vlain's mind. *He lies there, broken on the ground.*

You lie! Vlain responded. *You can't see him, so there's no way you could know that.*

Fool! I'm a god! I don't need to see his body when I can see his spirit. There's no hiding from me in my own realm.

The Dark Hunger raced toward one of the few remaining trees that filled the valley. Vlain was forced to leap off of its back to prevent himself from getting crushed between the boar and the pine tree. He hit the stony ground so hard that his last ward dissipated after absorbing the jarring impact.

Vlain began running toward the boulder beneath which the skipping staff had disappeared. However, as fast as he was, the Dark Hunger was faster still. It soon blocked his path then lowered its tusks as it pawed at the hard ground.

No! Came the hateful voice. *You won't be leaving my realm, little man,* the boar thought as it charged him.

We'll see about that, pig, Vlain replied as he veered to the right. He didn't know where he was going. He only knew that he had to keep a safe distance between himself and the Dark Hunger until he could think of a winning strategy. The boar should have been grievously wounded from all the damage Vlain and Oisin had inflicted upon it, but it appeared to be strangely unharmed.

I hate fighting gods, Vlain thought as he sprinted through the desolate landscape. His eyes searched for anything that could aid him in his struggle against his supernatural foe. Suddenly, he saw a long, thin log lying on the ground, the tip of which terminated in a sharp point. It looked like a gigantic spear. Vlain's eyes narrowed in anticipation as he raced toward it.

Where are you going, fool? The beast's hateful voice burrowed into Vlain's mind.

Come along and find out, Vlain thought back.

The Great Beast did just that. It was only a short distance behind him and gaining fast when Vlain sheathed his swords, skidded to a stop, and reached down to grab the log. The runes on the enchanted armband glowed brightly as it increased his strength. Even so, Vlain struggled to raise the heavy log. He then planted the back end of the log in front of a boulder. The Dark Hunger realized what Vlain was doing at the last second. It tried to stop, but its momentum carried it forward until the tip of the fallen tree punctured its throat then punched out between its shoulder blades. The giant boar groaned in agony as it stared balefully down at Vlain. The fighter expected to see blood and viscera flow down the log, but a black mist flowed out of the ghastly wound instead. Vlain pulled a hatchet out from behind his belt then hurled it at one of the boar's eyes as it struggled to free itself from the log. The curved blade sank deep into the huge, dark eye. Vlain yanked a second hatchet out from his belt and was about to throw it at the boar's other eye when it suddenly flung the fallen tree out from its neck. The Dark Hunger reared back and roared, and as it did, Vlain realized that its recent wounds were nearly healed.

Do you have any other tricks you'd like to try, little gnat?! The great boar spat into his mind.

Just one, Vlain thought as he threw his second hatchet into the boar's other eye. The curved blade cut neatly through the tough, black membrane, but the beast ignored it as it bore down on Vlain. The fighter pulled both swords from their sheathes, and his eyes blazed like the setting sun. *If this is how I'm meant to die, then so be it,* he thought as he prepared to collide with his adversary.

"Quick! Take me hand, laddie!" The words came from Vlain's left. Vlain sheathed a sword then reached out for the Lillen's invisible hand even as the Dark Hunger closed in. Vlain felt Oisin's little fingers as they grasped his calloused palm, then both of them turned and ran toward the barrier that surrounded the Dark Vale. The Great Beast roared as it raced toward them and spread its monstrous jaws wide. Vlain grimaced as he felt the boar's black breath wash over his back. His skin blistered and boiled even as his steelwood armor began smoking and disintegrating. He gritted his teeth in pain as he poured all of his energy into running.

Vlain thought Oisin had come to him so that they could die fighting together, but when the skipping tunnel formed in front of them, he realized Oisin must have retrieved his staff while Vlain had fought the boar alone. His heart soared as hope returned to him. Man and Lillen ran into the tunnel as the Dark Hunger's black, poisonous breath assaulted them. The boar was just one step behind them. Its mammoth jaws edged closer and closer to the Green Heart that was strapped to Vlain's back. The boar was about to bite down on the crystal when Vlain and Oisin blinked out of sight. The Great Beast roared in fury.

"I can nae...keep it up...anymore," Oisin said as he pitched forward in mid-stride. Vlain figured his injuries had caught up to him again, along with exhaustion from fighting for so long.

Vlain caught the Lillen and once more slung him over his shoulder as he ran. Oisin had sense enough to hand the skipping staff to Vlain. The fighter took the staff and mentally activated it. The Dark Hunger was rapidly closing in as the magic tunnel formed in front of them. They suddenly appeared a hundred paces away and repeated the pattern several more times until they drew close to the magical barrier that separated the Dark Vale from the rest of Findalora.

Vlain risked a quick look back after they had emerged from a skip. Sure enough, the Great Beast was hot on their trail. Vlain mentally activated the skipping staff one final time as the giant boar leaped forward. Man and Lillen slipped into the warping tunnel as the Dark Hunger landed in the spot they had just occupied. It snapped its mammoth jaws on nothing but air.

"Warmaster Vlain is drawing close!" Rowan shouted as she peered into the gloomy valley.

"Thank the White Stag," Xerlith whispered as she watched Vlain run towards them.

Suddenly, the fighter appeared right in their midst. He was panting and covered in sweat. Vlain skidded to a stop, then set

Oisin's invisible body down in the tall grass beside him.

Tanvir and Sanador were about to rush over to him when a booming sound suddenly filled the air. The druids and shamans turned as one to look in the direction of the Dark Vale just as the Dark Hunger collided with the invisible membrane that surrounded its cursed domain. The giant boar strained against it, and as it did, the space in front of it began to bulge forward.

Rowan gasped in astonishment and fear as a rainbow sheen flickered across the bulging barrier that struggled to contain the furious, rampaging god. Fearing the barrier would break, the druids and shamans backed away. Rowan raised her hands and began whispering the words of a defensive spell, but the stubborn barrier suddenly shoved the Great Beast back. The bulge flattened, and the rainbow sheen surrounding it abruptly disappeared.

Enjoy your victory while you can. The Dark Hunger's booming, telepathic voice spat into their minds as it angrily paced back and forth behind the barrier. *But know this; I will have vengeance upon you!* Before anyone could respond, the beast's huge body began to disperse like smoke on the wind.

THE DREAM

Chapter 16

"What's wrong with him?" Caernos asked as he looked down at Vlain, who was naked from the waist up. The fighter was lying on his back in a large bed, the sheets of which were damp from his sweat.

Iolee sat on the edge of the bed as she tended to him. "He's flush with fever and has terrible nightmares," she responded. The druidess dipped a rag in a pail filled with cold water, wrung the water out, then placed it on Vlain's hot forehead. Iolee placed her other hand on his muscular chest and marveled at the heat that poured off him. She lowered her lips to his ear. "Come back to me, Vlain," she whispered.

"I thought he was invincible," Caernos rumbled.

"I think he still is," Iolee replied. "Whatever his body's fighting appears to be quite deadly, but he won't give in to it. It's a stalemate."

"But you and Tanvir thoroughly healed him, so why is he sick?" Caernos asked.

"I wish I knew," Iolee said, shaking her head in frustration. "We have no idea what he was exposed to in the Dark Vale. It could have been poison or an evil spell of some..."

"But his wards should have protected him from all that," Caernos objected.

"He told me he lost his last ward while fighting the Dark Hunger. Perhaps it cursed him before he could leave the valley," Iolee thought aloud. "I was afraid something like this might happen, and I said as much."

"You did indeed, but Vlain knew what he was getting into..."

"Did he really?" Iolee sharply asked. "Even most Findalorans don't know what lurks in the Dark Vale, nor do they comprehend the powers of the Black Beast. How could we expect an outlander to fully understand these things?"

"Vlain knew he would be in grave danger during the mission, yet he volunteered for it anyway," Caernos countered.

"That's because he's too brave for his own good and too willing to sacrifice himself for the betterment of others. Perhaps we took advantage of his noble nature and enchantment for our own selfish gain," Iolee bitterly responded.

"You raise valid points," the king admitted. "But what's done is done." Caernos began pacing back and forth. "It's been three days since Vlain and Oisin returned from the Dark Vale, and Vlain took ill as soon as he got back. How much longer do you think he can last like this?"

"I don't know," Iolee answered. "Perhaps far longer than nature would normally allow. His enchantment could drag this out indefinitely, turning a blessing into a curse."

"So, we have gained the Green Heart, but we may have lost our warmaster and a dear friend. One step forward, one step back," Caernos said with a frustrated sigh.

"Nothing comes without a price," Iolee sadly agreed.

"How fairs, Oisin?" Caernos inquired.

"Lillens are remarkably resilient," Iolee answered with a faint smile. "And Oisin seems doubly so. His wounds are healing nicely, and he's as feisty as ever. He wants to return to his home in the Purple Vale, but we insisted on another few days of bed rest."

"Strange that he didn't acquire the same illness that plaques

Vlain," Caernos rumbled.

"Yes and no," Iolee replied. "Vlain was the one who carried the Heart of the Forest, so it was he who bore the full wrath of the Dark Hunger. Also, he fought it longer than Oisin did, and he fought it alone while Oisin retrieved his skipping staff."

The thick plane of perpetual shadow on Caernos's face prevented Iolee from seeing the expressions that played out on his bestial face. "Many songs will be sung of Vlain's valor," he promised Iolee.

"He deserves them all, but he deserves his health and life even more."

"I couldn't agree more," Caernos said as he gently laid a hand on her shoulder. "I know how much you both mean to each other." Iolee fought back her tears as she placed her hand over the king's. "I must take my leave now. Matters of state demand my attention. I leave Vlain in your capable hands. Let me know if his condition changes for better or worse." With that said, the centaur king walked out of the room.

Vlain suddenly cried out and swung at the air, causing Iolee to back away from him in alarm. He was clearly caught in the grips of some nightmare-fueled delirium. All she could do was stand there and watch it play out for what felt like the hundredth time. Iolee cursed under her breath. Despite all of her considerable talents and abilities as a healer, she was powerless to help the man she loved.

"Fight hard, Vlain," Iolee whispered fiercely. "Fight hard, and return to me."

***

The dream began as it always did. Vlain ran through the hellish Dark Vale alone. He figured Oisin must have abandoned him, or perhaps he had been killed by the cursed valley's monstrous denizens. In the end, all that mattered was that he was alone. At least for now. Vlain knew that the Dark Hunger was never far off. Although he had just finished killing it a short while ago, he knew it would regenerate and find him once more. They would fight again, and if Vlain was lucky, he'd win, thereby buying himself more time. No matter how hard he fought, however, he could never kill the evil that was the Dark Hunger. How could he, when he was merely a man and his foe was an aspect of existence? No, the best he could hope for was temporary victories so that he might live a little longer. Vlain pulled both swords from their sheaths as he entered a maze-like canyon. Although it was too narrow and confined to contain the black boar's vast bulk, he figured a chatterling or taker might be lurking behind one of the boulders or blind curves. The minutes ticked by as Vlain cautiously made his way through the canyon. Surprisingly, nothing and no one attacked him. He rounded the next corner only to come face-to-face with evil, but not the evil he had expected.

Vlain tightened his grip on his swords as he met the hulking man's gaze. His hair was pitch black, as was his shortly cropped beard, which contrasted with his alabaster skin. His piercing blue eyes gleamed with cunning and cruelty as they bore into Vlain's. Most men would have flinched and looked away, but Vlain narrowed his amber eyes as he took stock of his age-old adversary. Nothing had changed about him. Nothing ever did. The centuries were powerless to alter him after Jaina had cursed him with unending life for killing his own brother at the dawn of mankind. In fact, he often tormented Vlain by mentioning his timeless nature. He had promised Vlain, that one day he would be too old and frail to stop him.

"I knew I felt the presence of evil," Vlain said as he raised his swords.

"It's not me you have to worry about this time," his nemesis said with a sardonic smile.

"Evil is evil," Vlain replied with a shrug. He hated the fact that he was the one man who could elicit fear from him. Fortunately, Vlain had always been able to channel it into aggression.

"Perhaps I could help you defeat it?" the man asked. "You know that nothing could stop us if we teamed up. All of Taloria would tremble before..."

"It's never going to happen," Vlain answered decisively. "How many times must I tell you?"

"In that case..." The man's deep voice suddenly became a long, low-pitched growl as black smoke billowed out of him. A black cloud rapidly engulfed him and expanded outward, forcing Vlain to back away. A savage roar erupted into the air, which caused the hair on the back of Vlain's neck to bristle. He knew that roar and who it belonged to. The Dark Hunger exploded out of the black cloud as it charged straight at Vlain.

"You're getting more creative. I'll give you that," Vlain said as he raced forward to collide with his opponent.

Man and god battled without mercy, without restraint. It was ugly and vicious, and barbaric.

The Black Beast's huge, sharp tusks scored several hits on Vlain, leaving him with deep cuts that bled freely, but the fighter stubbornly ignored his gruesome wounds as he pressed his own attack. He repeatedly clove through the black boar's strange body until it was little more than trembling scraps of black smoke. Only then did he relent; only then did he back away to watch as the smoke dispersed.

"And now you'll reform to attack me anew..." Vlain said wearily.

Until all the stars have dimmed and died, and time itself is swallowed by oblivion! Came the boar's harsh, strident voice into his mind. *There's no escaping from me, little man. Not while there's a part of me in you!*

The black smoke soon coalesced back into the form of a gigantic, rampaging boar. Vlain was stunned at how rapidly it had regenerated this time. It was all happening much faster. The Dark Hunger roared as it bolted toward him. The fighter shouted out in defiance, then leaped forward to meet its charge. If he was going to die, he would make it pay dearly first.

***

Iolee kept her distance until Vlain ceased thrashing about. She sat back down to soothe him after she was sure that his feverish nightmare had concluded. The druidess dipped a washrag into a bucket, wrung the cold water from it, then pressed it against Vlain's forehead. Iolee thought about enacting a healing spell, but she instantly dismissed the idea. She had learned the hard way that such spells often backfired by fueling his next delirium with fresh energy. So, she kissed his lips instead, then stood and straightened out the folds in her cloak.

"I must take my leave for a while, my love, but I promise to return soon," she said right before she walked out of the cabin.

She hadn't gone far before she encountered Vlain's core group of renouncers. The men looked anxious and worried as they approached her. Some bore carved wooden likenesses of Jaina or the White Stag in their hands, while others held bowls of soup seasoned with healing herbs.

Meris was the first to break the silence. "Me and the men...well...we just wanted to thank you for all you've done for Vlain in the past few days," he said.

"You don't have to thank me," Iolee said. "He's our warmaster, our friend, and it's my duty as a druid to care for him."

"I know you love him, as do the rest of us," Meris said softly as he placed a hand on her shoulder. "May we sit with him for a while?" he asked.

"Of course," Iolee replied. "But keep your distance," she warned. "His nightmares make him violent and unpredictable. He might mistake you for whatever hounds him in his dreams."

"We'll take your words to heart," Meris said.

"Tell me, are there more fires in the forest?" she asked, dreading the answer.

"Yes," Meris reluctantly replied. "A few more in the south, and a stubborn one started burning in the east last night."

A pained expression formed on Iolee's careworn face as she digested the dire news. Meris gave her a slight bow then he and the rest of Vlain's entourage walked past her and entered the cabin. The druidess smiled sadly as she watched them walk inside. She knew it was hard for them to see their normally invincible leader laid low by anything. It didn't make sense to them that a fever should threaten his life after he had survived a brutal encounter with a dark god. He had emerged victorious from the Dark Vale, bearing the Heart of the Forest of all things! Iolee was still struggling to come to terms with the strange outcome the hands of fate had fashioned.

This isn't supposed to be happening, she thought to herself. *No lasting harm should ever come to Vlain. We need him now! It's not fair!*

Iolee walked with purposeful strides toward the tallest tree she could find. As she did so, the evening breeze brought the smell of ash and soot to her nose. A cold fury rose within her as she thought about what the 9th Legion was doing to her home. Eventually, the druidess stopped in front of a pine tree that seemed to stretch to the upper limits of the sky. She closed her eyes then expanded her awareness until she encountered the giant tree's subtle yet persistent life force. Adjusting to the alien nature of its thoughts was jarring at first, but Iolee had become adept at it after a lifetime of training. After establishing a bond with the tree, she envisioned its branches reaching down to her. Upon opening her eyes, she was pleased to see that the branches had formed a radial staircase, which she could now quickly ascend. She climbed to the uppermost branch within a matter of minutes. A strong wind pushed the hood off her head and buffeted her shoulder-length hair. A sense of vertigo and a fear of heights suddenly gripped her. Iolee grabbed hold of the tree trunk, and the feel of the solid, rough bark in her hand steadied her nerves and resolve.

From her lofty vantage point, Iolee could see for many leagues in all directions. Smoke billowed up from the forest in several areas, indicating the presence of surging wildfires. However, the thickest column of smoke came from the east, which validated what Meris had told her earlier. Iolee scowled in anger when her eyes fell upon the distant catapults that continuously launched balls of flaming pitch, bales of burning hay, and other combustibles far out into the forest. The 9th Legion had begun its relentless assault on Findalora several days ago. Teams of men must have been manning the catapults both day and night, for there had been no break in the carnage.

"How I hate you!" Iolee hissed through clenched teeth as she gazed at the engines of destruction, which looked like tiny toys from so far away. She had asked King Caernos if she could lead an assault force of druids and warriors against the legionnaires, but he had told her no. When she had asked why he had told her that that was precisely the response Commander Prydus wanted to elicit from them.

"He wants to draw us out into the open, so he can slaughter us with his war machines," Caernos had rumbled.

"But if we don't defend our forest, we'll lose our homes and be forced to flee deeper into Findalora. Please, let me do something, my king!" She had pressed.

"You are doing something by helping Vlain," Caernos had replied. "We need our warmaster now more than ever, and you are one of our most gifted healers. If you can't bring him out of this fugue, I doubt anyone else can. And would you really want to be away, fighting the legion if Vlain were to die, or would you rather be there at his side when it happens?"

"You know the answer," Iolee had replied. "I just wish there was something more I could do."

"Be patient," Caernos had told her. "Should Vlain recover, I'll send you to bolster the teams of druids and shamans that are fighting the fires. They've already done much to contain the damage and have even extinguished several fires."

Iolee had wanted to respond that it didn't matter because new fires were constantly popping up to take their place, but she had remained silent. She knew the king was right. She would never have forgiven herself if she had been gone when or if Vlain succumbed to his fever.

Iolee was about to descend from the giant tree when the tower on Fort Faldin caught her attention. Prompted by a hunch, the druidess cast a spell of far-sight on her eyes, which allowed her to see farther and with greater clarity than an eagle. After the magic had taken effect, she looked at Fort Faldin's solitary tower again. Sure enough, someone was standing on top of it. The distance was too great for even her enhanced eyes to gather defining details about the person. Still, Iolee had a feeling she was gazing at none other than Commander Prydus Orilius. A fit of fiery anger smoldered within her as she stared hard at the tiny figure.

"Would that I had the power to end your life this instant!" she shouted into the wind.

***

A predatory smile bloomed on Prydus's handsome face as a gust of wind bore the smell of smoke and ash to his nostrils. He raised a spyglass to his eye and then surveyed the burning Wild. Everything was going according to plan. Almost everything. Vlain still hadn't taken the bait. Prydus had expected the brash fighter to lead a force of wild-eyed woodlanders hell-bent on revenge for setting the forest alight, but it hadn't happened. Why? There was no way Prydus could know, and he hated that. What was Vlain waiting for?

Prydus would have settled for a retaliatory force of woodlanders even if Vlain wasn't among them, but even that hadn't happened. The commander had struggled to keep his rising anger and frustration to himself. He wanted, no, needed revenge on Vlain for attacking Fort Faldin and freeing the prisoners of war that had been kept there. Prydus needed to show his men that he was the more capable leader, that he possessed the finer military mind, but Vlain was denying him the opportunity.

The commander took a deep breath to steady his nerves. He knew he'd eventually get the chance to prove his mettle to his father and all of the high-ranking officers back in Elamara when the war finally began. Prydus would show them all that he was worthy of the rank of grand general. He'd prove to everyone that he had risen to the peak of military power, not due to his father's protective interventions, but by his own merit. Moreover, Prydus needed to show the spirit of his dead mother that he was a worthy heir to her legacy. Although she had died when he was only twelve summers old, she had instilled in him a powerful; some might say, ruthless ambition. In fact, she had told him on her deathbed that she would watch him rise to power from Jaina's shining halls. Prydus had no intention of disappointing her or his father even if he had to burn the whole, blaeting Wild down!

The commander savored the sight of the burning wildfires that his men had ignited in the forest. He was about to leave the lookout when the distant image of a person standing at the top of a giant pine tree in the woods caught his attention. An amused smile formed on his golden-hued face as he focused the lens on his spyglass. He could see that whoever it was, wore the green robes of a druid, but that was the only detail he could discern from so far away. Prydus wondered if the person was looking back at him at that very moment.

"I see you, cretin. If you were within archery range, I'd kill you on the spot," he growled right before he snapped the spyglass shut and turned away. He was on the verge of descending the steep, spiral stairwell that led down into the tower and the fort beneath it when he paused to look back at the Wild. "Make your move, Vlain. I'll be waiting," he said in a low, threatening voice before he disappeared into the dark stairwell.

The End

EPILOGUE

Prydus crossed his arms over his gold-plated chestplate, and his brow furrowed as he scrutinized the assortment of weapons that lined the wall of the forge. There were swords, axes, spears, shields, knives, and a few other tools of war that he had never seen before. The craftsmanship on all of them was superb. Every weapon's design combined deadly efficiency with an artistic sensibility.

"Feel free to test any of them, my lord," Evel Kenzi said. He was a tall, broad-shouldered man who had a shaggy, black beard and the muscular build of a blacksmith.

Prydus pulled an arming sword down from the narrow shelf where it had rested. The commander studied the bronze-colored blade for signs of impurity. Try as he might, he couldn't find any. He then inspected the hilt, pommel, and sword grip, which had been wrapped in black leather. Prydus had to admit it was a thing of great beauty.

"Strike it as hard as you can," a tall, thin, clean-shaven man with long black hair pointed at a thick slab of granite that rested on a worktable. His name was Rezin Kenzi, the blacksmith's younger brother. He was a mage who specialized in enhancing the attributes of metals. The blacksmith and mage had labored for years to forge a reputation for themselves as makers of elite, enchanted weapons.

Prydus walked over to the stone slab, gripped the sword with both hands and swung it down with a fraction of his inhuman strength. The bronze-colored blade cut neatly through the granite and the table below it as if they were both made of soft snow. The commander smiled as he gazed down at the sword in admiration.

"I'm sorry about your table," Prydus said. "I'll pay for a replacement."

"Think nothing of it, my lord," Rezin replied. "You're stronger than most, but that sword will cut through solid granite even if it's wielded by a weakling."

"And the blade won't be damaged," Evel added.

"Most impressive," Prydus replied.

"So, would you like to buy it or any others?" Rezin asked.

"No," Prydus said. Both of the Kenzi Brothers frowned in response to his answer. Rezin was about to speak when Prydus held up a hand to silence him. "I want you to make a sword for me."

"Unfortunately, the upcoming war has made us too busy. We've been working through the night to arm our Faldinite patrons, and even the barbarians have asked us to..."

"Will this be enough to put me at the top of the list?" Prydus tossed a bulging, red velvet pouch at Rezin.

A startled look formed on the mage's face as he caught the pouch. He opened it up and peered down into the interior. His eyes grew large when he saw how many gold marks were inside. A smile formed on his lean face. "It would indeed! Tell me, what do you have in mind?" he inquired as he placed the pouch on a tabletop.

Prydus pulled a small rolled-up, tan-colored parchment out from a leather satchel connected to his belt, then handed it to the mage. "It's all there. The dimensions, the weight, the specific alloys, and, of course, the desired enchantments."

Rezin unrolled the parchment, then studied the designs. He let out a low whistle. "It will be a sword like no other," he said.

"You sure you can pull it off?" Prydus asked.

Rezin looked hurt for a second. "It will be a challenge, but yes. We can."

"I'll need it in one month."

Rezin raised his eyebrows in surprise. "Normally, such a project requires at least a few months, but we'll work faster since you're being so generous."

"And since there's a war coming, that we must win," Prydus added.

"Absolutely," Rezin agreed. "I have no doubt your sword will inspire great confidence in your men while striking much fear into your enemies."

Prydus gave him a tight, controlled smile. "See that it does," he said before walking out of the forge.